THE WILD CHILD

THE WILD CHILD

1961, Liverpool. Flora Wilcox's fatherless daughters couldn't be more different – Hilary is serious, hardworking and bespectacled, while Isobel is an attractive blonde who seeks fun and excitement. When Isobel's boyfriend drops her to take up with Hilary, a rift develops between the girls, and even their mother can't build bridges. While Hilary settles into wedded bliss and motherhood, Isobel escapes to London and a passionate affair with a much older married man. As Isobel worries whether her secrets will find her out, Hilary's twin sons are struggling with dyslexia. Can the sisters support each other when they need it most?

THE WILD CHILD

by

Anne Baker

Magna Large Print Books
Long Preston, North Yorkshire,
BD23 4ND, England.

British Library Cataloguing in Publication Data.

Baker, Anne
    The wild child.

    A catalogue record of this book is
    available from the British Library

    ISBN   978-0-7505-2839-9

First published in Great Britain in 2007
by Headline Publishing Group

Published in Large Print 2007 by arrangement with
Headline Publishing Group Ltd.

Magna Large Print is an imprint of Library Magna Books Ltd.

Printed and bound in Great Britain by
T.J. (International) Ltd., Cornwall, PL28 8RW

To Emma, my new daughter-in-law.

CHAPTER ONE

1961

Flora Wilcox got off the bus in Claughton to hurry home. It was her younger daughter Isobel's nineteenth birthday and she'd been persuaded to leave while the girls had a party. She'd been reluctant to do so.

'For heaven's sake, Mum, we won't wreck the place, I promise. It's just that a parent can cast a bit of a damper on the fun.'

Since Harold, Flora's husband, had been killed in the war, she'd lived for her daughters. Now they were grown up she didn't want to be excluded. It had made her lay down firm rules for the party: just a few friends to be invited, it must be over by midnight and no noise to annoy the neighbours. She'd tried to say no alcohol, but Isobel had been cross.

'Mother, we've got to have a bowl of punch and a few beers in, it wouldn't be a party otherwise. Everybody does at least that. I suppose you'd like me to ask my friends to a birthday tea with jelly and balloons?'

Flora had set a limit on the alcohol supply and was hoping for the best. She'd been to the Ritz in Birkenhead to see an indifferent film with her sister Mavis Caldwell. Most of the time, her mind had been on what Isobel might be getting up to.

When she'd been about to leave the house, Isobel had said, 'Why don't you go back with Aunt Mavis for a cup of tea before coming home?'

But Flora had not. Mavis wouldn't want her there at this time of night, and she was worried about what all those teenagers might do to her house. She didn't altogether trust Isobel, who could be wild at times, but her other daughter Hilary was four years older and much more sensible. She'd promised to keep order and make sure nothing was damaged.

Isobel wanted to have dancing. Flora had stood by and watched the girls roll up the living room carpet and bring down their record player. She'd set out the best buffet supper she could achieve on the kitchen table, and stayed around long enough to be introduced to those guests she didn't know. Hilary had put on a record to warm things up, and the party had started well.

Isobel had invited Ben Snow, her boyfriend. Flora had seen his almost new Ford Cortina in front of the house many times, either picking Isobel up or dropping her off, though she'd met Ben only briefly before. She'd been thinking about him in the cinema. He'd grasped Flora's hand warmly and she had been quite taken by his tousled hair and friendly outgoing nature. She approved of his fawn corduroys, his collar and tie and scarlet V-necked sweater. She could almost see her face in the shine on his brown brogues. She'd thought him quite a serious young man, but his smile was that of a toothpaste ad and lit up his face.

They'd met at some party before Isobel had even started her teacher training, and he'd been

12

her boyfriend for over a year. A little older than Isobel, he was a salesman for a firm of seed merchants based in Chester and wore a suit and a tie to work. Flora had been given to understand he was the most important boyfriend Isobel had ever had, and that things were serious.

Tonight, he'd put his arm round her daughter in a proprietorial gesture which had made Flora think he might well become her husband. Isobel, her cheeks flushed with excitement, had looked very pretty in her yellow party dress, as she'd introduced him to Hilary.

Isobel was the beauty of the family, with corn-coloured hair and blue eyes. Flora had felt a pang for her elder daughter, who was more like her in every way: Hilary had inherited her rather ordinary brown hair and the need to wear glasses. She was not exactly plain; no girl of twenty-three could be. Now she was over fifty, Flora understood that youth was attractive in itself. Hilary could be relied upon to be responsible and do what was needed.

As she walked along Woodsorrel Road, Flora could see her living-room light shining through the curtains. It was in a group of roads that all had flower names, where the houses were mostly terraced but not the more frequently found Victorian type. These, she thought, had been built about 1920 and provided generous-sized rooms. She was proud of her home: despite the odds she'd come up in the world. There were sounds of merriment within but they were not unduly loud. She slid her key in the front door and let herself in.

The hallstand was overloaded with coats. Flora adjusted her rimless spectacles and peered into the half-obscured mirror. Hilary said the specs looked so good on her that she'd chosen the same style for herself, but tonight Flora looked tired and more wrinkled than she'd supposed. She'd made her paisley-patterned dress herself but it wasn't a great success. It didn't hang right.

In the living room the couples were gyrating round with great vigour to a jazz record Isobel played a thousand times a week. Dancing had certainly changed since her day. Flora was surprised to see Hilary throwing her arms about and kicking up her heels with Ben, Isobel's boyfriend, jigging about opposite her. They were laughing together and obviously having a good time, as was everybody else. She looked round for Isobel, but she wasn't there.

In the kitchen, the food she'd laid out had been demolished and the plates more or less emptied. She picked up a ham roll and bit into it, then went upstairs to find Isobel.

The door to the big back bedroom the girls shared was firmly shut. Flora opened it and put on the light. Isobel was lying in her party finery on her bed, her face the picture of misery. Flora thought she might have been crying.

'What's the matter?'

Isobel was angry. 'She's taken over everything. She's spoiled my party.'

'Who?'

'Hilary, of course! It's my birthday, my party, and I can't get a look in.'

'Well, you won't if you hide up here. Why don't

you come down and dance?'

'He wants to dance with her.'

'Ben, you mean?'

'Who else could I possibly mean? He's my boyfriend, not hers.'

It took Flora the best part of half an hour to put the guests out politely, and another hour to clear up after them. She had to press the girls to help. They were putting more energy into bickering than tidying up.

It happened virtually overnight. Ben Snow stopped squiring Isobel round and attached himself to Hilary. Flora couldn't understand why. Isobel was pretty; she was sociable and bubbly, always out having a good time, boyfriends flocking round her. Flora had thought it likely she'd marry young. Hilary had always been more reserved. She was a staff nurse at the Birkenhead General now, and content to have a quieter time.

Flora didn't need to ask if Isobel minded. She could feel the tension between the girls mounting. She'd heard ever more frequent and violent spats from the bedroom they shared.

One night, she'd been watching television with Isobel, who'd come in ten minutes earlier, when Hilary arrived towing Ben behind her. She announced, 'Ben has asked me to marry him, and I've said I will.'

Flora got up and switched the television off. Isobel's mouth had sagged open.

'You're engaged?' Everyone could hear the shock in Isobel's voice. She turned on Ben. 'You've asked Hilly to marry you?'

Flora was surprised too. It seemed to have come about in no time at all. Even so, Isobel had another boyfriend now, called Eric, so she shouldn't have taken it so much to heart.

Flora thought it was because Ben had proposed to Hilary and not to her. Once her daughters had been close friends, but this blew the relationship wide open. She found it very upsetting that the two people she loved most in all the world couldn't get on.

Things became worse when Hilary asked if Ben could move in with them after they were married. 'Just for a few months, Mum, to give us time to get a home of our own together.' Flora hadn't been able to say no.

Isobel really resented being asked to take her bed into the third bedroom, which was of box-room size and was used as a dumping ground for everything they didn't need regularly. It wanted redecorating and there was nothing but worn lino on the floor.

'I'll get some paint,' Flora told her, 'and I could make new curtains for you.'

'I'll help you do it up,' Hilary added anxiously.

But over the dinner table that night, Isobel exploded. 'I'm sick of this. All you two talk about is wedding cakes and double beds. I don't want to think of Ben in bed with Hilly.'

She'd moved to the boxroom with ill grace. Flora was left in no doubt that Isobel felt she was being pushed out.

Flora counted the day her husband Harold had been killed as the worst in her life. Widowhood had been her lot ever since, and nothing worse could befall any happily married woman. She'd been left grieving at the age of twenty-eight, with a toddler of almost four and a new baby expected in four months' time. They'd both wanted a family, but she'd been left to bring it up on her own.

She was determined her children would have a better life than she'd had. Flora had left school at fourteen to start as a mother's help to a family called Fraser. For her, work never finished; she'd hardly had a moment to herself.

Flora came from working-class stock. Her father had been a docker and her mother had cleaned offices and looked after other women's children. The Frasers had not been rich – their house was only marginally bigger than the one she had now – but it was in a middle-class area, much smarter, and fitted out with every comfort.

Mr Fraser had been a manager at the gas works and he'd insisted that all four of his children stay on at school and get some qualification they could use to earn a living.

Flora had taken that message to heart. She knew that with a qualification she could earn more. During the war, she worked part time in a munitions factory and went to night school to get her School Certificate. She was aiming at office work, but a course in shorthand and typing cost more than she could afford.

She counted herself very fortunate that at the end of the war there'd been such a shortage of schoolteachers that the government had brought in a shorter one-year training scheme and offered grants to anybody willing to train. Flora had jumped at the chance and had pulled herself and her family up by her boot straps, by working as a primary school teacher. She'd coached her girls for the eleven plus exam and both had got grammar school places. She'd insisted both her girls train for a career too.

Hilary had been dreamily romantic and said she wanted to write books. Since neither of them had the slightest idea how to go about that, Flora had told her to choose a less hazardous way of earning a living. She'd decided on being a nurse, which pleased Flora since the training cost nothing. Isobel had had a lot of daft ideas like going on the stage, and had wanted to leave home to give the latter a try. Flora had refused to help further that ambition, and tried to press her into following in her sister's footsteps.

'Absolutely not. Nothing would make me be a nurse,' Isobel said through clenched teeth. 'I'd hate it. I couldn't. And I'm only staying here with you because I can't find anywhere else as cheap.'

After a great deal of argument and indecision, she opted reluctantly to try teacher training.

Isobel burned with hostility every time she thought of Ben Snow. He was doing his best to stay out of her way now, so she couldn't give him a piece of her mind. Instead she vented her wrath on her sister, although she knew it upset her mother even more than it did Hilary.

'I wish you'd stop fighting,' Flora told Isobel. 'You've got another boyfriend, so what's the problem?'

'Oh, Eric! He's just someone to go out with.'

'He's a nice lad. Very helpful. I like him.'

'You would.'

Eric had served his apprenticeship as a plumber and, because Isobel had asked him, he'd fixed their leaking lavatory and refused to accept payment for his work. Isobel didn't like his old banger of a car and his none too clean finger-nails. Though he was more generous with drinks at the pub than Ben, he was not somebody she'd ever get serious with. She was aiming higher.

'I'm not hanging around here for the likes of Eric Eliot. Once I'm qualified I'll be off.'

'Where to?'

'London perhaps, somewhere where I can have a bit of fun.'

'Mum doesn't want you to leave home,' Hilary said one day when they were washing up. 'She wants us all to stay together.'

Isobel thought Ben and Hilary were getting married with indecent haste. The date set was only eight months after she'd introduced them. Not that the wedding was going to be anything posh. It was to be at the register office and Mum was planning to follow it with another buffet at home.

'It doesn't sound very exciting,' she told them when they were all sitting round the table one evening.

Ben said, 'We want to save up for a place of our own.'

'It's the state of marriage we want,' Hilary explained, 'not a big party.'

'I wouldn't settle for a wedding like that,' Isobel

19

told her. 'It'll look positively mean.'

'No it won't, Izzy,' her mother said. 'They're saving for more important things. It'll be a quiet wedding; that's what they both want.'

'I suppose it means there won't be many guests either?' she asked.

Hilary invited only the two families and one or two friends. Her mother was sewing outfits for both herself and Hilary. Isobel didn't think either turned out well, although Mum's stone-coloured suit wasn't too bad. The bride wore a fairly ordinary green dress with a hat from C&A Modes that didn't quite match the colour. Isobel insisted on buying her own dress of a paler green and felt she looked smarter than the bride.

The wedding party gathered in the register office in Birkenhead Town Hall, and after the short ceremony they came back home to eat the buffet lunch they'd all helped to prepare and set out in readiness. Mum had even made the wedding cake. Isobel thought it tasted fine but looked amateurish, with a sea of homemade icing decorated with wedding bells bought in Woolworths.

She thought it a joyless wedding as well as a quiet one. Aunt Mavis turned up looking like a crow in the black hat and black dress that she wore summer and winter. There was a button missing on the bodice and Isobel could see dire-looking greyish pink underwear beneath. It was hard to believe she was Mum's sister, because Mum always tried to look well groomed, and if only she'd get over her obsession with the sewing machine she might look quite reasonable.

Ben's family was no better. Isobel had already

faced them, having been invited to Sunday tea as Ben's girlfriend. His mother Ethel, stout and almost two decades older than Mum, had married late at thirty-six, and had been widowed five years later. Ben's father had been killed in the war too. She had a dissatisfied droop to her mouth that made her look miserable. Her hard gaze had swept Isobel from head to toe and shown immediate disapproval. Isobel hoped for Hilary's sake that her mother-in-law liked her better, and was glad she didn't have to pretend to be nice to Mrs Snow as Hilary was doing now.

Ben had twin aunts, Primrose and Prudence, spinsters in their fifties, who'd worked all their lives as ward sisters at Birkenhead Children's Hospital. Although they didn't dress exactly alike they chose such similar clothes – high-necked, long-sleeved dresses in nondescript shades – that they seemed as alike as two peas.

At the wedding reception they sat side by side on Mum's settee, each with the left ankle neatly crossed over the right and her arms folded across her very ample chest. They had grey hair permed to look as much like the Queen Mother's as possible, and their heads turned in unison to listen to whoever was talking. All three sisters lived in a large old house on Borough Road, which Mrs Snow thought vastly superior to the Wilcoxes'.

Isobel had heard that Primrose and Prudence both played the mandolin and together they could belt out very jolly tunes.

'They do rousing stuff,' Ben had told her. 'You should hear them play "The Campdown Races".'

Looking at them, Isobel thought it didn't seem

likely, though anything would be better than this desultory chatter. But Ethel hadn't thought Ben's wedding a suitable occasion for their party piece so the twin aunts hadn't brought their instruments.

The happy couple left in the late afternoon for a three-day honeymoon in Llandudno. Both Hilly and her mother prided themselves on managing their money well, but Isobel thought that for Hilly's wedding they'd taken thrift a bit too far.

Flora watched Hilary take her marriage vows and thought she'd never looked happier, while her younger daughter looked tense and miserable. The groom was a nice enough lad, but she blamed him for the change in Isobel. She felt she'd loved her daughters equally when they were small, and she'd certainly devoted herself to their welfare and upbringing. They'd turned out to be very different. Isobel was the dizzy blonde, who always wanted to be centre stage and made a fuss of. Hilary was a home-loving body who looked after everybody else.

Flora's sister Mavis was sitting quietly in the corner eating steadily from a plate heaped high with party food. With her stringy hair and black dress she was like a spectre at the wedding. Flora felt responsible for her sister in much the same way as she did for her daughters, which was odd because Mavis was nearly sixteen years older. It wasn't love that bound her to her sister it was pity. Mavis had never married and life seemed to have passed her by.

She'd only ever had one job, having worked as an accounts clerk in the investment department of a big insurance company. She'd sat at the same desk in the same back room all her working life. In her early years she'd had the same ideas as Flora, and had gone to night school to improve her qualifications. She'd wanted to have letters after her name.

Although she'd achieved that, promotion had never come. Her ambition had been to work with the stockbroking team, but, though she'd asked to join it, it had never happened. Flora knew she'd become resentful and angry at being passed over. She'd tried to persuade Mavis to look for another job but she never had, and eventually she'd stopped expecting anything to change.

She'd retired at sixty years of age with a small pension, together with a lump sum of three thousand pounds. Flora was afraid she was finding it impossible to change the habits of a lifetime and was still spending her days poring over the *Financial Times* and similar periodicals, becoming a bit of a recluse.

Mavis said she didn't need other people, but Flora thought that was nonsense and had tried to provide her with something of a social life. If only the two brothers who'd come between them in age had lived, she might have had more help. They'd both joined the Merchant Navy and first one and then the other had gone down with his ship during the Battle of the Atlantic.

Mavis had always lived in the house in which they'd all been born. The Caldwell family home was a rented two up two down terraced property in Birkenhead's North End. It had been built to house the labour force in the middle of the nineteenth century when the docks along the Mersey were being constructed, and it still had the same furniture and even some of the rugs and curtains it had had in her childhood.

Flora remembered that as children they had been told not to bring their friends home, because their father had disliked having other people in the house. He'd been very introverted and in his old age had rarely gone out. Mavis took after him and Flora felt fortunate to have inherited her mother's more outgoing personality.

She went over to have a chat, taking her own drink and a bottle of white wine to refill Mavis's glass. Flora had long had in mind that she should invite Mavis to move in with her once her girls were off her hands. She mentioned it now while the house was looking its best with all the flowers Ben had brought from his garden at home.

'I'd rather stay where I am,' Mavis said ungratefully. Then, after a large gulp at her wine: 'You could come back home and live with me if this place will be too much for you.'

That was the last thing Flora wanted. It would be a slide down the social ladder and there was no comfort to be had in Mavis's house. She was quite pleased to be able to say, 'I didn't mean right away, of course. With Ben moving in we need all the space we've got, and Isobel won't be off my hands for another few years.'

During the months that followed, Flora didn't find her own house all that comfortable. The girls hardly spoke, Ben felt trapped between them and the atmosphere became even more strained.

Hilary was working shifts and was often not home for the evening meal. Isobel stayed out more and more to avoid coming face to face with Ben. Flora was relieved when the young couple eventually managed to buy a small Victorian cottage in Bebington, one of the outer suburbs. Within a year they were gone.

'Thank goodness,' Isobel said, and moved her bed back into the larger bedroom.

Now there were just the two of them at home, Flora expected them to draw closer. When her daughters were growing up she'd felt they were a tightly bonded family. She wanted to see more of Isobel in the evenings and at weekends, but however hard she tried Isobel seemed set on going out and about with her own friends.

CHAPTER TWO

1963

For Isobel the years were passing quickly. She didn't have to work too hard in class and what she sought in her leisure hours was a good time. She had a succession of boyfriends, a ready supply of partners to take her out to parties and dances, and they all wanted to enjoy themselves. Once or twice she imagined she'd found the right one to make her happy, but they soon wanted to move on. Isobel thought of her college years as her youth and that adult life would only start when she was qualified and able to earn her living.

Ever since she'd left school, she'd earned a little pocket money during the summer holidays by working at the Walker Art Gallery in Liverpool. This was her fourth summer here and she felt like an old hand. They put together special programmes on art for children in which she was involved and also had occasional exhibitions when pictures were sent from other galleries.

It was a hot day and the group she was taking round was smaller than usual. One man stood out from the others because he'd asked a lot of questions; with his head of thick silver hair and pencil-thin moustache, she thought him a distinguished old gentleman.

They were holding a special exhibition of paintings by Monet and Renoir, the French Impressionists. He'd stood for a long time in front of the blue umbrellas of *Les Parapluies* and the colourful theatre scene *La Loge*. She had to hurry him to keep her group together.

He was so interested that he stayed on at the end of the tour, wanting to know more. She told him all she could and he complimented her on the extent of her knowledge.

Isobel laughed. 'It's part of the job. I'm given great tracts about the exhibits and told to commit them to memory. I don't forget because people like you grill me about them several times a day.'

'But you are interested, I can see.'

'Yes, I am. Are the French Impressionists your favourites?'

'Well, I'm particularly keen on British nineteenth-century painters like Sir John Everett Millais.'

'So am I. Have you seen *Bubbles?* The picture he painted which was used to advertise Pears Soap? That's one of my favourites.'

'I know it. Is it here?'

'No, it's at the Lady Lever Art Gallery over on the Birkenhead side. But we have several of his other pictures here.' Isobel directed him to another gallery where he would find them.

He thanked her and turned to go. Isobel was thinking of getting herself a cup of tea before she had to show the next group round when she was alarmed to hear a skid followed by a heavy thud and turned to find he'd fallen. She hurried to help him up.

'No, I'm too heavy for you,' he told her. 'I'll manage by myself.' But a security guard had come to help too and together they lifted him back on his feet and took him to sit on the bench that ran down the centre of the gallery.

'Are you hurt?' Isobel asked.

'No, no. I'm all right.'

'Shakes you up, a fall like that.'

'I feel such a fool... I must have slipped.'

'There's nothing on the floor to cause it.' The security man had gone back to look.

'Too much polishing,' Isobel said. The wooden flooring had a well-cared-for shine.

'Probably my new shoes.' He lifted one foot up. Isobel looked at the sole of pale new leather.

'Perhaps you're right. I'm afraid you've hurt your hand.' There was a graze on the heel of his palm. 'Let me take you to the staffroom,' she said. 'There's a first aid box there and I can get you a cup of tea.'

'I'll be all right...'

'Come on. It'll make you feel better.' She took him to wash his hand and then anointed the graze liberally with antiseptic and stuck a plaster on it. She poured him a cup of tea from the staffroom pot and sat down to drink hers with him.

'You've been very kind,' he told her when she said it was time for her to take another group round.

When the art gallery closed that evening, she was rushing towards Lime Street Station to get the train home when she saw him wandering around with a map and a guide book in front of St George's Hall. She stopped to ask how he was.

'A magnificent building,' he told her, when the greetings were over. 'I'm very impressed with your city.'

'I live here, so I suppose I take it for granted. Where d'you come from?'

'London.'

'That's a big place.'

'I spend most of my time in Brixton.'

She could see he was trying to make up his mind about something. He blurted out, 'Would you take pity on a lonely visitor and have a drink with me?'

Isobel didn't hesitate. He seemed a lovely old man and she was always looking for something different. 'I'd like that.'

'Good. Well, you're bound to know the best place to go?'

'Yes. This way. I come to this pub for my lunch

28

on pay day with the staff from the gallery. The older ones say it's noisy but I like it.'

He told her over a glass of wine that his name was Rupert Broadbent and he was in Liverpool on business. 'I'm killing an odd hour or two by looking round. It's an interesting place.'

'Rupert.' She giggled, thinking of Rupert Bear. 'I shall call you Rupes.'

'You can call me what you like.' He smiled.

'What sort of business?'

'I have a small factory making furniture.'

'Smashing. Luxury sofas and all that?'

'No, desks mostly, school and office furniture. I'm looking for work, hoping to fill my order books.'

'There's a big office block being built just up the road.'

'Yes, there are several not far from here; a couple of new schools too. I'm staying for a few days because councillors and education committees don't make decisions in a hurry, and being in a strange place away from home is lonely.'

'I'd love to get away from home. My family get me down.'

'Tell me about them,' he said.

'There's just my mother and me at home now. My sister is married but she's in and out of the house more often than I am.'

Isobel saw him as a father figure. He was old enough to be that, if not her grandfather. 'My father was killed before I was born. I'm twenty-one now. How old are you?'

He laughed. 'You're a very direct young lady. I'm sixty-three, and to save you asking, I have a twenty-three-year-old son called Sebastian, and a twenty-five-year-old-daughter called Charlotte. She works in my business.'

Isobel told him about her rather strained family relations and was surprised to hear that he thought his were, if anything, worse.

'Why?' she wanted to know.

'It's a long story.' She could hear the pain in his voice. 'I've never got on well with Sebastian. As an adolescent, he was rebellious. I wanted him to come into the business and eventually take it over from me, but he dug in his heels and said he wanted nothing to do with it. He didn't want a life like mine and he was going to do his own thing.'

'And has he?'

'Yes. He doesn't come near these days.'

'So he earns his living some other way?'

'Yes. He's a primary school teacher and apparently wants no help from me.'

Isobel giggled again. 'I've just completed a teacher training course.'

He smiled ruefully. 'There must be some attraction in teaching children. What made you decide on that?'

'My mother's a teacher. She nagged me to choose a career, but I couldn't think of anything I really wanted to do. There's a big teacher training college at Chester. Some of my friends were going and teaching seemed as good as anything.'

He looked shocked. 'That doesn't sound the best reason for choosing a lifetime career.'

Isobel shrugged. 'Think of the long holidays we'll get. Anyway, it seems your son likes it.'

'Perhaps. I don't think he realises even now what an asset I was trying to give him. I've spent my working life building up this business for my family. I wanted Sebastian to have a good life working for himself and he's tossed it back in my face.' Rupert sighed. 'Tell me about teaching.'

'I can't tell you very much yet. This year I've been going into different schools for practical training. I'll be starting my first job in September.'

'Do you have one lined up?'

'Yes. I've been offered one in Birkenhead – that's where I live – but I'd love to get a job somewhere else and leave home at the same time.'

'Then why don't you?'

Isobel sighed. 'For me, it always boils down to lack of money. It's cheaper to live at home, isn't it? And it's not easy to find a place for oneself.'

After a short pause, he asked, 'Are you hungry?'

'Starving.' She looked at her watch. Usually by this time she'd have eaten.

He was smiling. 'We're getting on rather well, aren't we? Would you have dinner with me?'

Isobel laughed aloud. 'Wow, yes. That would be great.'

'Good. I was hoping to go home tonight, but I'm having to stay over for more talks tomorrow.'

Isobel liked him. To have dinner at a restaurant with him sounded more exciting than going home to a meal her mother would have cooked.

He asked, 'Do you want to ring home to let your mother know you'll be late?'

There was no telephone at home and already it was an hour and a half later than Isobel normally returned. No doubt Mum would have been trying to keep her dinner warm ever since. It would be dried up and horrible now and Mum would be cross.

'No, there won't be anyone there. Mum said she was going out tonight,' she lied.

'Come along then. We might as well go back to my hotel for dinner. I'm staying at the Adelphi.'

'That'll be great! It's reputed to be the most expensive hotel in the city but I've never been inside.'

'Quite old-fashioned now,' he said. 'But very comfortable. Is it too far for us to walk?'

'No. It's only a couple of hundred yards from here.'

As soon as they were swept through the entrance by the uniformed doorman, Isobel paused to feast her eyes. 'It's like being transported back to Queen Victoria's day.'

He took her to the bar, sat her down at a table and ordered drinks, then told her he wanted to go up to his room for a few minutes. Isobel was left admiring the formal elegance of her surroundings and thinking he couldn't be short of money.

Over the meal of many courses that followed, she heard a lot more about his family troubles.

'Sebastian moved out of the house when he was eighteen and that soured things. There hasn't been much harmony at home since,' he said sadly. 'My wife took his side. She blames me for splitting up the family. My daughter too, I suppose.'

'Your son put himself through college?' Isobel asked. She knew to a penny how much it had cost her mother to support her. 'That shows grit – it would take some doing.'

'No, my daughter pleaded on behalf of her little brother. He has no money sense, lets it pour through his pockets like water. I gave her money to meet his living costs and fees while he trained and told her to dole it out in small amounts.'

'That was generous of you.'

'Without some sort of training he'd have ended up as a labourer, wouldn't he?'

'That's what my mother said about me, that I'd end up on the tills at Woolworths.'

He smiled. 'I couldn't let him starve, but he cut himself off from me. I've seen him only once since then and that was at his grandmother's funeral. He was quite belligerent, though he did thank me for his allowance.'

'But you have a daughter who works for you?'

'Yes, I see a lot of Charlotte. She's efficient and I hope she'll learn to run the business, but I don't think she's that interested. She tells me she doesn't want to work all her life. Probably feels she wants the sort of life her mother's had, looking after a home and babies.'

They sat over coffee until it was quite late. Isobel found him fascinating and put off going home for as long as she could. She stood up at last, quite prepared to run across the road to Central Station to catch a train home.

'It's getting late now,' he said. 'I don't like to think of you walking about alone in the dark. I'll ask them to call a taxi for you.'

'It costs a fortune to take a taxi through the tunnel.' She was aghast. 'And I've got my return

33

ticket for the train.'

'What about the other end?'

'It's not far. I can get a bus. I do every day, honest.'

'I insist,' he said, and slipped out to ask the hall porter to call one. When the man came in to say the taxi was at the door, Rupert took her out, saw her into it and paid the driver.

When Isobel tried to thank him, he kissed her cheek and said, 'Thank you for your company. I was expecting a long lonely evening on my own but it's been very pleasant.'

Isobel wished he'd been her father. She would have been more than willing to work in his business and thought his son was a fool to turn down a chance like that.

The following evening at locking up time, Isobel was showing the last visitors out of the Walker Art Gallery when she found Rupert Broadbent waiting for her. The late sun was glinting on his thick silver hair. She thought he looked very handsome. She said, 'I thought you were going home today?'

He was smiling. 'I could go now, but I don't feel like driving down to London. I've been in talks all day. It's been a long hard slog and I'm exhausted. But I've got three big orders.'

'That's good, isn't it?'

'Excellent. How about having dinner again and helping me celebrate?'

Isobel couldn't believe her luck. 'That sounds smashing. Nothing I'd like better.' Mum had been angry with her last night and still frosty at breakfast, but there was no way of letting her know she'd be late again tonight.

He took her to a restaurant in Lord Street which was much less formal than the Adelphi. He was relaxed and she felt at ease with him. Tonight, he didn't seem old at all; he could have been any age. He had deep green eyes that smiled in a flirtatious way into hers across the starched white cloth. She felt suddenly charged with emotion though she carried on talking about her family, telling him how much she wanted to leave home to get away from them.

'If you're really serious about it,' he said slowly, 'I could help you find somewhere to live. Have you ever been to London?'

'No, but I'd love to.'

'It's full of life and seems like the centre of the universe. But I don't know whether you'd be able to find a teacher's post. Would you like to try?'

Isobel felt lifted on a wave of exultation. 'Would I like to...? That's the pinnacle of my ambition.'

He was shaking his head. 'What am I thinking of? I shouldn't be persuading you to leave home like this.'

'But it's what I've always wanted.'

He patted her arm. 'You must think it over carefully, take your time. Don't jump into something that later you find you don't want.'

Isobel felt the years coming between them, pushing them apart. 'You're acting as though you're my father. You're spoiling things.'

He smiled. 'I don't want you to come to any harm. You're very young...'

'I told you, I'm twenty-one. That's the truth.'

35

'Well, if you're sure, I'll give you my address, but you must talk to your mother about it. Make certain it's what you really want first. I'll do nothing till I hear from you.'

That night, as he hailed a cab to take her home, he said, 'I might as well come with you for the ride. The driver will have to come back to this side of the river, won't he?'

As they were driven through the Mersey Tunnel, Rupert kissed her, but not in the way a father would. His breath was warm against her cheek, and his moustache tickled. It filled Isobel with desire; she felt drawn towards him like metal to a magnet. She felt hope, too, so strong as to be almost a conviction, that she would see him again.

When the taxi was pulling up in front of her house, Rupert moved away from her. She wondered if he expected her to invite him in and introduce him to her mother, but she couldn't face it. Mum would have worked herself up into a rage by now and wouldn't understand.

She searched his face in the half light and thought he was gripped by the same rampaging emotion. It cut her to the quick to get out without letting him know how she felt. Her heart lurched when she turned on the doorstep to see the cab drive away. Her cheeks were burning as she let herself into the house.

As she'd expected, Mum was furious and full of questions about where she'd been on the last two evenings, and even more inquisitive about whom she'd been with. Isobel didn't want to talk about Rupert. She wanted to go straight up to bed and relive the wonderful evening she'd had.

She'd felt a little in love with him from the moment he'd fallen in the gallery and she'd tried to help him. Tonight when he'd shown her the bruise and healing graze on his palm she'd felt a surge of affection. He was a very handsome man with an aura about him of one who lived expensively.

She thought her love must have shown on her face as clearly as she'd seen it on his. She was almost sure he'd been as full of pain at their parting as she was, and torn between hope and despair for the future. She made up her mind to do all she could to get a job in London so that she could find him again. By the end of a week, when he'd been rarely out of her mind, Isobel knew she was head over heels in love with Rupert Broadbent. She longed to join him in London and get to know him better.

She knew teaching jobs were advertised in the professional journals and went to the central library in Birkenhead to see if there were any vacancies in Brixton for which she was likely to be considered. No, but there were two vacancies in Clapham and one in Clerkenwell.

She had to consult a London street map to find out if they were near Brixton. She decided Clapham was, and scribbled down the names and addresses of the schools. She applied for both. Then she took out the business address Rupert had given her. Mark the envelope Personal and Private, he'd directed. She wrote and told him what she'd done.

A week later, she received a letter inviting her to come for an interview. Her heart was pounding as she rang Rupert from a public phone box. To hear his voice sent ripples down her spine; he told her he'd meet her train.

Isobel took great pains with her appearance, buying a new suit in grey flannel and a scarlet silk blouse. When she saw him waiting at the ticket barrier, his dark green eyes smiling at her over the crowding passengers, she was glad she'd come.

It was lunch time. 'We'd better have a bite to eat first,' Rupert said. He was dressed with great formality: a good quality wool suit and a silk tie, highly polished shoes. He looked conservative in his tastes, an elderly middle-class gentleman who would never stray from his wife. Not at all the sort of man to have a girlfriend like her. Isobel had her first misgivings. Was she expecting more from him than he was prepared to give?

'Lovely to see you again,' he said. 'I do hope you get this job.' He drove her to the education office, getting her there in good time. She felt reassured as she went up the steps into the building.

Isobel was keen to get the job and let her enthusiasm shine through at the interview. She was told immediately that they would welcome her services. It seemed one vacancy had already been filled, and she was allotted a teaching post at a primary school in Clapham South.

When she came out, feeling victorious, Rupert was waiting in his car, reading a newspaper that he'd spread across the steering wheel. He beamed at her news. 'Not far from my office.'

'What about your works?'

'The same place,' he said. 'I'll take you to see the school.' It was the summer holidays and the place was closed, but at least Isobel could see where it was. Then he took her to see two flats that were available to rent.

'You can walk across the common to the school from this one,' he said. 'It shouldn't take you more than ten to fifteen minutes.'

Isobel was thrilled. It was a top floor two bedroom apartment with magnificent tree-filled views across the common. She hardly seemed to be in a big city at all. The furnishings were new and luxurious. She knew her mother and sister would be very impressed.

'But what is it going to cost? I don't think I'll be able to afford this.'

He was serious. 'You don't have to. I'll pick up the tab.'

'Rupes, I can't let you do that...'

He took her into his arms and kissed her full on the mouth. It made her cling to him and return his kisses. He whispered, 'Yes you can, if you let me come and see you sometimes.' He gave her another hug. 'I have to tell you... I've been in love with you since that day in the Walker Art Gallery when you talked about the Renoir paintings.' His eyes were gazing into hers. 'And then I went and slipped like a silly old man.'

'You don't seem old to me.'

'I thought I was past feeling like this.'

Isobel reached up and kissed him. 'I'm thrilled. It's what I've hoped for.'

'You don't mean...?'

'I love you too. I want you to come and see me

as often as you can.'

She thought he needed a bit of encouragement. She was undoing the buttons on his well-cut wool jacket and sliding it off his shoulders, unknotting his silk tie.

He caught her hands in his and said, 'There's one other thing... I want you to be discreet. Don't mention it to anybody. You must understand that I can never marry you.'

She smiled. 'You told me. You're already married.'

'Yes, for almost thirty years.'

'Poor old Rupes. You're very old-fashioned. Queen Victoria is no longer on the throne, you know. Times have changed.'

He sighed. 'It would be embarrassing for my family if our arrangement became public knowledge. For me too, and it might affect my business. Charlotte would be very cross with me. She'd think I was a very foolish old man.'

'You really do need cheering up. You need to enjoy yourself more. Let yourself live.'

'I'm too old for you,' he said. 'Ridiculously old.'

'Rupes, age doesn't enter into it. I don't think about it at all, and neither should you.'

'But you look even younger than you are. You must have boyfriends of your own age?'

'Not at the moment. I have had, but nothing long term.' She thought of Ben Snow and said defiantly, 'I've never found anyone I've fancied as much as you.' She was taking off her own jacket, hanging it neatly on the back of a chair. 'It's my best suit.'

'You do understand what you'd be getting

yourself into?'

'Oh, yes. If you pay my bills it makes me your mistress. Officially your mistress.'

'Isobel!' He seemed shocked but couldn't help laughing. 'A mistress? You're quite a girl. I've never had a mistress before.'

'Well, you've got one now.' She giggled. 'And I love the idea.'

'You do?'

She nodded. 'I think about you all the time. Dream about you.'

He was suddenly serious. 'You're very young. I don't want to take advantage of you.'

She grinned at him. He knew how to give her a good time and he had plenty of money. 'I feel it's more a matter of me taking advantage of an unhappy man.'

That made him smile. 'In that case...'

'Let's just enjoy each other. Have fun.'

Rupert Broadbent was not the first man to make love to her – the sixties were heralding a more relaxed era and Isobel wanted to experience all there was – but no man had thrilled her as Rupes did. Sex with him was wonderful, but there was more to their relationship than that. He was a companion she never tired of.

Isobel accepted the conditions he put on their liaison and was very happy as Rupert's mistress. He bought her clothes and took her out to dinner and to theatres. At least once a week, she cooked a meal in the flat for him. She saw him regularly and occasionally he stayed overnight.

After a settling down period in her job, Isobel found she could cope with it, though the children were not the easiest to teach. For some, English was not their first language.

She knew her colleagues at school thought she had money of her own because she lived on the more expensive side of the common and always had new smart clothes. Her life revolved round Rupert. As time went on, he took her away for an occasional weekend in the country and once they went to France. He showered gifts on her: flowers, chocolates, perfume, records and books. Isobel felt she couldn't have a better time. She was in love with him and he with her, and it added sparkle to everything. Isobel wondered how long it would last.

She knew her mother would be up in arms if she knew what Isobel was doing. She would say an alliance like theirs could have no future and she was probably right. For Isobel, it was enough to have Rupert's love now. She was happy with that and thought he was too. The future would have to take care of itself.

Occasionally she went out with a group of her younger colleagues. They discussed their boy-friends all the time but she didn't talk about Rupes. They even teased her about her lack of boyfriends, but she laughed it off easily.

Almost every week she received a rather anxious letter from her mother, asking how she was getting on and whether she liked living away from home. She sent her parcels of homemade jam and large fruit cakes. Isobel replied with brief notes and postcards and was careful never to mention Rupert's name.

Flora kept inviting her to come home during

the next school holidays, so that when they came round Isobel felt obliged to go.

As the date came closer she felt more reluctant. Rupert said she should go and bought her train ticket for her. He even drove her with her small suitcase to the station, where he kissed her with such tenderness she could have been leaving him for years.

CHAPTER THREE

'Going down to London was the best thing Isobel could do,' Ben maintained. 'She'll be loving it down there.'

'I hope so.' Hilary felt guilty because she'd taken Isobel's boyfriend from her.

'I couldn't help myself,' he told her. 'Not once I'd got to know you. Isobel and I weren't serious. I think she was going off me anyway. Don't you worry about her.'

Ben was a lovely person. Hilary counted herself blissfully happy as his wife. She'd been drawn into his family, but wasn't sure whether his mother really welcomed her. She was invited to tea every Sunday she wasn't working. If she was, Ben went alone.

'I wish I didn't have to,' he confided, 'but Mum expects it.'

Mrs Snow usually greeted Hilary with, 'Your poor mother had a hard life bringing up you and your sister. I understand only too well; I know what it's like to bring up a child on one's own. I've done my share of it.'

'My mum's fine,' was all Hilary could say.

Another regular question was, 'When will Isobel be coming back?' Hilary had no idea. 'I'm sure it's upsetting for your mother. She must miss her.'

Ben's twin aunts often worked on Sundays too. Hilary always enjoyed it more if one or both were there, though they both kept asking when she and Ben were going to start a family.

'Not just yet,' she always replied. 'We want a family, but we need a year or two on our own first. We want other things as well.'

'You've got a home of your own,' Aunt Prue said. 'Isn't it better to have your family while you're young?'

'All in good time,' Ben told them.

Hilary was happy with their cottage, which they'd furnished with pieces bought from auction sales and second-hand dealers, but they did not intend to live there for ever.

She and Ben had the same goals. Although he enjoyed working as a salesman, they both knew it wasn't a job that would bring much in the way of luxuries. Ben was convinced he would eventually earn enough to bring them the higher standard of living they wanted by running his own garden centre.

He was ambitious and had drawn up what he called their life plan. He believed in hard work, self-help and thrift. He'd said, 'Everything in its time. If we both work hard and stick at it, things will work out just as we want them to.'

Hilary wanted the things he wanted and was content to do all she could to further Ben's ambitions. But she had ambitions of her own too. For as long as she could remember she'd wanted to write the sort of romantic fiction she enjoyed reading. Full-length novels pleased her most, but she read anything she could get her hands on.

Since she was about fourteen she'd been trying to get her ideas down on paper. She'd started half a dozen books but they'd all petered out before the end. She felt she needed to know more about the techniques of writing fiction, but scanning the library shelves for advice didn't seem to help.

Mum told her she needed to live a bit first and that there was no hurry to get started. Hilary thought otherwise. She knew that to write a book would take a huge amount of time and felt it would be wiser to try short stories first. The format must surely be easier than the full-length novel. She started reading all the short stories she could get her hands on, but the ideas wouldn't come. If only she could get something published, she'd feel she was on her way.

After the schools broke up for the Easter holidays, Flora heard that Isobel would come home for a few days. Not for Easter itself, but afterwards. She hadn't even come for Christmas.

Flora had worried about her being alone in a big city and the rather guarded notes and cards she'd received did nothing to dispel her anxiety.

Unfortunately, Isobel hadn't given them much notice of her visit and Hilary would be at work when she was due to arrive at Lime Street. Ben

45

should have been too, but said he could spare an hour or so to pick her up.

'After all, it's quite an occasion, Izzy coming back to see us.'

His firm had withdrawn the Ford Cortina and supplied him with a later model. The paintwork sparkled and it smelled new inside. Ben looked smart in his salesman's suit. He managed to park and he and Flora walked to the ticket barrier together. They were a little early and had five minutes to wait before the train came in. Flora could feel her anticipation growing.

Soon the passengers were streaming through the barriers. She tried to look at each face but they were coming too fast. Was Isobel here? The crowd was beginning to thin and she couldn't see her.

'Has she missed the train?' she asked Ben.

'Hello, Mum.' It was Isobel's voice. She planted a brisk kiss on Flora's cheek. Heavens, she hadn't recognised her own daughter! 'Hello, Ben. Good of you to come and meet me.'

London had put a gloss on Isobel. She'd always been pretty but now she looked like a model from the cover of *Vogue*. Her cashmere coat in muted blue and grey check was fabulous, and as for her hair! She'd had the corn colour nature had given her brightened to a true golden blonde. It was cut to enhance her face, too.

'You look very well,' Ben told her.

'So do you.'

He picked up her suitcase and led the way back to the car. 'I hardly recognised you.'

Flora took her arm. 'Lovely to see you again,

Izzy. I have missed you.'

Flora had worked amongst schoolteachers for much of her life but Isobel didn't look in the least like one. She looked sophisticated now. Silly to think she couldn't stand on her own feet: clearly she was very much in control of her life. This was what she'd wanted.

'How's Hilly?' she asked Ben.

'Fine. On top of the world really. She's been promoted to ward sister.'

'Good for her. She's working at Clatterbridge Hospital now?'

'Yes, and enjoying it. I'm very proud of her.' He had a bemused smile on his face.

Flora said to her, 'And like me, you've settled down in teaching. I'm proud of my two girls.'

She made a great fuss of Isobel with tea in bed every morning, and tried to draw her out about her life in London. She finally asked her outright if she had a boyfriend. 'No, Mum,' Isobel said.

Once inside her old home, Isobel felt her old life close about her. Time had stood still here. Mum fussed round her like a mother hen. Every meal was planned and half prepared well ahead. Flora was always suggesting they go somewhere or do something, but Isobel no longer wanted to go round the Liverpool shops or the market. If she saw something she liked and bought it, Mum would be upset by what she paid and she'd get a lecture on being extravagant. Anyway, there were much better shops in London. Biba was her favourite.

Hilary and Ben had invited her and Flora round for supper the following evening.

'Ben's mother and the twin aunts are coming too, so the family can see something of you,' Hilary said. 'They want to hear all your news.'

When Isobel and Flora arrived, the three sisters were already there, Mrs Snow sniffing with a head cold.

'I'm sure your poor mother would like to keep you here longer than two or three days,' she said. 'When are you coming back for good?'

'I've no plans for that,' Isobel said briskly. 'Enjoying myself too much down there.'

'I'm glad my child doesn't desert me like that.'

'Poor Ben,' Isobel said to him behind her hand. Since he'd latched on to Hilary, he'd never seemed comfortable in her presence and she saw no reason to put him at ease.

Seeing him again made her wonder what had attracted her to him in the first place. Yes, he was good-looking, with tousled fair hair that fell forward over his face. She noticed now that his fingernails were bitten down and his movements were quick and nervous. What did he have to be nervous about if he and Hilary were as happy as Mum said?

They were still living in the same cottage. Flora had smartened it up recently by re-covering the settee and making new curtains and cushions from remnants. It was quite a tight fit with five guests. To Isobel, it looked cramped and down-market after her own apartment.

Both Hilary and Ben were making an effort to be as welcoming as possible, but in some ways they hadn't moved on. They were still talking of starting a family, as they had from the time they got married. They were still giving everybody to understand they were saving up for a better future first. At least Ben was now talking of starting a business of his own.

Isobel couldn't see that as an advantage. 'But if you gave up your job, you'd lose your car, wouldn't you?' she asked.

She saw the car as just about the only benefit marriage to him was bestowing on her sister. It was right in character that he was putting off his business plans until they'd saved up a bit more. Isobel told herself it was all talk.

For Hilary, it might or might not be jam tomorrow, but Isobel was well content with the jam she had today and thought she might have had a lucky escape from Ben. She'd have liked to go back to London straight away, but Mum had invited Aunt Mavis to tea the next day.

'She'll be cross if she misses you,' she'd said.

Isobel didn't think she'd care one iota but decided she'd stay only one more night. It would be a relief to go back to London and Rupert.

It was Isobel's second year at the school, and on the first day of term she was in the staffroom when the headmistress ushered in two newly appointed teachers. She announced in strident tones that drowned out the buzz of holiday chatter, 'I want to introduce Naomi Griffiths who will be teaching year two, and Sebastian Broadbent, our new remedial teacher.'

Isobel was startled. To hear the name Broadbent gave her a jolt that made her heart bounce like a ball in her chest. She couldn't quieten it for five minutes nor trust herself to talk to him.

To look at, Sebastian was a younger edition of his father. He had rich brown hair but the same high-bridged nose and green eyes. He didn't have Rupert's broad shoulders and confident manner, or his air of prosperity, and he was showing all the uncertainties of youth.

She told herself not to be a fool; curiosity was making her hover closer. Rupert would want to know about his son.

She asked him where he'd been teaching before and it seemed he'd taught in several schools in and around London. He said he'd even tried a sales job for a while as a change. He told everybody he was divorced and living in rooms.

When she told Rupert this, he said, 'He hasn't settled into teaching then. Probably too proud to come home and confess he's made a mistake. I bet if I were to offer him a job in the business now, he'd jump at it.'

'Are you going to?'

He was shaking his head in indecision. 'Do you think I should?'

Isobel shrugged. 'If it's what you want, why not?'

'It's what I once wanted,' he said slowly. 'Relationships are funny things. Once they've gone sour it's very difficult to turn them round. I'm like him: I don't know what I want now.'

'Then there's no need to do anything.'

'I don't want him to know about you and me,' Rupert warned. 'Say nothing. Don't even mention my name.'

'Do you want me to look for another job?'

Isobel had thought he might.

'Do you want to? You like it at that school.'

'I'd rather stay where I am. I've never felt so satisfied with my lot before.'

'Then stay. It won't occur to Sebastian that there could be a connection between us. No reason why it should.'

Sebastian was the only man on the staff and all the women were interested in him. The older ones wanted to mother him and the younger ones were sizing him up as a boyfriend. Isobel didn't tell his father that whenever she went into the staffroom, Sebastian's gaze seemed to find her and follow her round.

In 1964 Hilary applied for the vacant post of theatre sister and got it. She'd always loved theatre work: it kept her on her toes and was never boring. She saw it as a step forward in her nursing career, but she'd let her writing lapse.

Now she was twenty-six, she realised if she was ever to produce anything it was time she made a start. It occurred to her that articles might be easier than short stories, and perhaps she ought to begin with those. Suddenly she found the energy to write again, but it wasn't easy to find the time.

Ben was pleased with the way his life plan was working out. Their savings were growing and he said they should begin to look round for a plot of land suitable for setting up his garden centre. It wasn't easy; very little land came on the market. After six months of searching, he was becoming disheartened.

Then, one evening, as soon as Hilary walked in

from work she could see Ben was alight with excitement. His eyes were sparkling as he pushed an estate agent's brochure in front of her. 'Look at this. It's just what I've been waiting for.'

She read: *Farm for sale. Oak Tree Farm comprising house, farm buildings and one hundred and fifty-four acres of prime land is to be sold at auction in ten lots.*

Hilary protested, 'Ben, we don't want a hundred and fifty acres even if we could afford it.'

'Read on. Just lot number nine. Twenty acres with main road frontage and mains water. That sounds ideal – exactly what I've been looking for.'

She frowned. 'You said ten or twelve acres would be ideal.'

'Twenty would be better. I know I'll need less to start with but I can always expand.'

'Lot eight is ten acres. That will surely go cheaper?'

'We need main road frontage if we want to sell, don't we? It could make all the difference. I want to take you to see it.'

'You've seen it yourself?'

'Yes. I passed it today. The auction was advertised on a hoarding. I went to the agent to get the details. Let me take you now – it doesn't matter if supper's late tonight.'

Hilary agreed to be driven out to see the land. She knew Ben had been planning this ever since they were married. She felt a frisson run up her spine, half excitement half unease: it now seemed he was ready to take the next step. In the car, he couldn't stop talking about it.

'The soil's not too heavy – it's brown medium

loam, and has been down to permanent pasture for some years, grazing land for sheep and cows. It's well drained and slopes gently towards the south, exactly what I need. Best of all, hundreds of people drive past it every day.'

Hilary hadn't been able to picture how much twenty acres would be. When he stopped at the gate, she looked across a huge field.

He said, 'Come on. There's another field behind this one.'

She tried to imagine having a house built here. It was an absolutely marvellous position. Of course, Ben would have to have his glasshouses and shop buildings here too, but even so...

'See that little spinney over there?' he said. 'I shall keep that if I can. Our house will go on that side, and I'll group the buildings I need for the nursery here.'

'Can we afford it?'

'We've saved enough to act as a cushion and a down payment. Land like this doesn't often come up.'

It was on the busy thoroughfare wending its way upriver from Birkenhead through the homes of some of Merseyside's major industries, soap at Port Sunlight and margarine at Bromborough, and onwards to Chester through several of the Wirral's pretty villages.

'The land is part of Oak Tree Farm. If I get it, I'll call it the Oak Tree Garden Centre.'

It was near what had once been a small village just beyond Eastham, but hardly rural. Every year, the urban sprawl reached further and further into the countryside. The heart of the village remained

53

– the church, the pub, the school and a few cottages – but in recent years new estates of small houses had been built round it, one after another. Each new house had gardens to the front and the rear and would need bedding plants, shrubs and seeds. It was not quite a suburb; people still thought of it as a village and it was considered a desirable place to live.

'What d'you think?' Ben asked her. 'Shall we go for it?'

'I think you'll have to try.' She knew there'd be no talking him out of it and she too was eager to get on with their life plan. She'd love to have a baby and a bigger house. Aunts Prudence and Primrose were forever talking about the delights of bringing up children.

'We spend our working lives caring for them but our one big regret is that we haven't had children of our own. We can't wait for you and Ben to start a family.'

Ben never tired of explaining why they must get the business started first, and now he could talk of nothing else. There were three weeks to wait before the auction. He busied himself making sure he could borrow any extra money he might need to finance his dream. He took his own family out to see it and then told Flora about it. She was teaching during the week, but he took her to see it on Sunday. Hilary went along for a second look.

She could see her mother frowning as she strode over the grass. 'It's a risk,' she said. 'With a job like yours you'll always earn enough to keep the wolf from the door.'

'I want more than that,' Ben told her. 'I want to provide Hilary with some of the good things of life.' He explained where he thought the house would go and where the business buildings.

'This is farmland, Ben. Is there planning permission for what you want?'

'No. I'll apply for that when I know I have the land.'

'Ben! You scare me. That doubles the risk. It could take ages before you hear anything.'

'I shall rent it out as grazing for six months.'

'What if planning permission is refused? I understand quite a lot of applications are.'

'Then I'll have to sell it again.'

'But you could lose money.'

'Not necessarily – I might *make* money on it. Prices do go up. And if I get permission, it'll mean whatever I pay will look very reasonable.'

'The risk terrifies me,' she said to Hilary.

'Ben is strong and it's what he wants.' Hilary knew nothing would dissuade him now: he was really keen to get it. She didn't think she could stand the stress of the auction and elected to go to work as usual. Ben took a day off in order to attend.

He bought the lot for slightly less than the price at which it had been valued, and was in a triumphant mood for days.

Isobel thought she had everything to make her happy. Being Rupert's mistress suited her. He told her he loved her and, more important, he showed that he did. He visited her apartment often, paid all her bills without question. At weekends, he took her for trips on the river in his motor boat and to restaurants, generally driving some distance to avoid meeting anyone who might recognise them.

The years were passing very comfortably. Isobel continued to go home to see her family when the school broke up for a holiday, mainly because her mother expected it. She felt sorry for Flora. Mum had had a terrible life and now she was getting old.

She thought Ben was doing better. He and Hilary thought themselves very lucky and had been crowing with triumph during her Easter visit. They'd been granted a change of use on the farmland they'd bought and been given outline planning permission not only for the garden centre buildings but for a house too. It was a huge hurdle out of the way and it meant they could go ahead.

Hilary showed her the detailed plans Ben had had an architect draw up for him. Isobel had to hand it to them: the garden centre would be a place they could be proud of when it was finished. Ben was setting up his business and planting things, but had not yet given up his job. He planned to open his shop when summer came. Hilary was working all the hours God sent now in order to pay for it all, and Mum was talking of selling her house and moving out Eastham way to be near them. Isobel never stayed more than a few nights. She liked London and Rupert's company better.

Rupert rarely spoke of his family but he was upset one weekend when he came to see her.

He'd talked of retiring in the next few years.

'It's Charlotte,' he said. 'She wants to get married and her husband will be taking her out to Hong Kong.'

'That means she won't be taking over the business from you when you retire?' Isobel knew how disappointed he'd feel.

He was indignant. 'D'you know what she said? That school furniture was boring and really a man's thing and she's had enough of it. And if only my business were dress designing or cake making she'd be more interested. I mean, dress designing! I wouldn't know where to begin.'

'What are you going to do?'

'I'm worried about the business. My second in command could run it but I'd have to go in once or twice a week to keep an eye on things. I'd never be really free of it.' Rupert sighed. 'The sensible thing would be to sell it, if I can find a buyer. I think I'll try.'

'If you could, you'd be able to relax.'

'Yes. I'd be able to go away more.'

'But I wouldn't be able to come with you, except during the holidays.'

Isobel was happy with the way things were. She was enjoying the company of the other teachers. She gave no hint to them that she was anybody's girlfriend, but she understood that her colleagues felt that wives held all the cards and mistresses were to be pitied. She thought them wrong. The wife had to keep house and look after the children. She preferred to be wined and dined and taken out. But all the same, she was beginning to feel she was on the edge of Rupert's life when she wanted to be everything to him. She didn't like to think of him going home to a wife and daughter. She wanted the attention he gave them for herself.

The weather was growing colder and the nights longer in the early winter of 1965. It was Saturday. Hilary and Ben had spent most of the day indoors as blustery winds hurled rain at their windows.

'I'd love to go somewhere warm for a real holiday,' Hilary said. They'd had breaks at regular intervals, but the need to save had kept them at home.

'We've both got holidays due.' She held up a magazine that was advertising Nile cruises. 'Doesn't this look great?'

Ben took it from her and she knew he was tempted. 'It isn't very expensive,' she urged. 'Not at this time of year.'

'Perhaps it's time we indulged ourselves,' he allowed.

'We could both do with getting right away and forgetting the life plan.'

'Only for a little while. Egypt would be marvellous; there's so much to see.'

'It would still be warm there.'

'Let's go,' he said. 'Let's see if we can go before Christmas. We'll reward ourselves.'

'It'll do us good.' Hilary smiled. 'It'll be fun.'

That they hadn't had a proper holiday since they were married made it all the more enjoyable.

'Absolute heaven,' Hilary said, stretching out

on a steamer chair in the sun and watching the banks of the Nile unroll slowly before her.

It turned out to be a fantastic holiday until she caught a tummy bug. She wasn't the only passenger to do so, and two or three days later she'd forgotten about it. She came home looking suntanned and feeling set up for the winter. Back at work she recommended the Nile cruise to her colleagues.

It came as something of a shock to Hilary when, a few weeks later, she began to suspect she could be pregnant. Ben was even more shocked. According to his life plan, they were to wait another three years before starting their family.

When the New Year came in, they had to accept the pregnancy as fact, she told him. 'I'm thrilled about it really. Glad there'll be no more waiting.'

'But if we'd waited, you'd have been able to give up work to look after the baby. Now I don't think we could afford that.' Ben had put himself in charge of contraception when they were first married and had used sheaths, but the early sixties had brought the pill. They'd both been keen for Hilary to take it, and it had worked perfectly until now. 'I don't know how it happened.'

'I think it must have been that attack of vomiting and diarrhoea on the boat. Didn't I say at the time?'

'You were feeling better by then. Anyway, nothing's guaranteed, is it?'

'Never mind the life plan.' Hilary laughed. 'What does a few years matter? I really want this baby.'

All the family, her side and Ben's, were thrilled

at the news.

Hilary had another shock a few months later, when she went to the antenatal clinic and was told that two foetal hearts could be heard and she was carrying twins. She went home feeling subdued; the thought of coping with two babies was daunting. She said ruefully to Ben, 'Right now, one would have been enough.'

Ben kissed her gently. 'Beyond our powers to control, I'm afraid. Never mind, love. We always planned two so we'll have our family complete without you having to go through the discomforts of pregnancy and childbirth again.'

Hilary saw the logic of what he said and was comforted.

CHAPTER FOUR

Rupert had paid for Isobel to have driving lessons, and when she passed her test he bought her a car. She loved her scarlet Mini.

When, in the New Year, her mother wrote to tell her that Hilary was pregnant, she was surprised her sister had done more than talk about starting a family. She wrote Hilary a letter of hearty congratulation, but felt somewhat sorry for her. She hoped she knew what she was letting herself in for.

From that moment all Mum's letters were about Hilary's pregnancy and how much they were all looking forward to the new baby. Then

60

Mum wrote again. *Such a lovely surprise. Hilary has been told she's having twins. We're all very excited though she seemed a little hysterical when she telephoned to tell me.*

Isobel felt she'd be more than a little hysterical if it happened to her and couldn't understand why Mum was surprised. She was a non-identical twin herself – her brother had not survived infancy – and Ben had identical twin aunts, so there were twins on both sides of the family.

Rupert planned his sales trips for the school holidays so Isobel could go with him. She'd been to Birmingham, Newcastle and Glasgow and enjoyed them all, even though she'd had to spend some time on her own while Rupert worked.

In May he promised to take her on a real holiday in the summer. Years ago he'd been to Florence and he fancied seeing it again. He told her about the beautiful sculptures and buildings, brought her books and brochures and tried to share his passion for it with her.

'It sounds a fabulous city,' Isobel said and was really looking forward to it, but before they were due to go she began to suspect she might be pregnant too. The very thought made her curl up inside with horror.

She'd seen this as the worst possible scenario from the moment she'd taken up with Rupert, but knew it was a hazard of having regular sex. She'd been sensible and gone to the family planning clinic to get the pill, so why hadn't it prevented this? She was certain she'd taken it every night – well, almost certain.

Isobel knew the news of her pregnancy would

61

have the very opposite effect to Hilary's. Her mother would be shocked to the core if she had a child out of wedlock. Not that she saw much of the family any more. The time she spent on Merseyside added up to only three or four weekends each year.

She worked out that her baby would be only a few months younger than Hilary's twins. That was frightening and brought reality home to her. What was she going to do?

She had more than enough of children at school; the last thing she wanted was one of her own. She saw a good deal of Rupert at weekends but generally on only one night during the week. She was on tenterhooks until he came and she could share her worries with him. Her first thought was to have an abortion. She wanted her pleasant way of life to continue.

There was much discussion in the press about making abortion legal in the UK but at the moment it was not, though she'd heard it was possible to travel to Sweden and have an abortion there. She was expecting Rupert's sympathy and perhaps his help to terminate the pregnancy. Instead, Isobel saw a slow smile spread across his face.

'How amazing! Fancy fathering a child at my age! I'm quite excited. I might still have a son to follow me in the business. It could even be twins, couldn't it? They run in your family, after all.'

Isobel was shocked. One baby was bad enough; two would be absolute purgatory.

'It'll complicate everything. Anyway, it'll be many years before he'll be any help to you, even supposing it is a son. You'd...' She'd been about to say *be working until you're ninety*, but he wouldn't like that. 'You'd have to work for ever.'

He put his arms round her. 'You mustn't worry, Izzy. I'll take care of you, I promise. I won't let you down. I love you very much. We can be happy, the three of us. You can stop working whenever you feel it's getting too much for you. I could find you a little house if you don't think this flat is suitable for bringing up a child.'

Isobel didn't doubt he'd do all the things he promised, but she liked her life the way it was. She didn't want to bring up a baby. That night she went to bed early, hoping and praying she'd made a mistake and the pregnancy was all in her mind.

When she got up the next morning, she felt so sick she had to rush to the bathroom and retch, but she brought up nothing. It drove home to her that her suspicions were well founded: she must certainly be pregnant. The same thing happened the following morning and Isobel began to wonder if it was possible for her to procure an abortion without Rupert's help. If she told him she'd lost the baby, he wouldn't know whether she'd done anything to cause it or not.

She tried to think. There had to be some way to get an abortion; there were always snippets in the newspapers about girls who did. The only person she could think of who might know was her sister. Hilary was a nurse – she'd even done the midwifery training. They'd surely teach midwives what could be taken to cause a miscarriage, wouldn't they? She could write and ask her.

But no. Isobel shivered. Hilary would never do anything against the law. She was too righteous, and anyway she was besotted with the thought of babies. Her advice would be to keep it and enjoy bringing it up. It was all right for Hilary: she was married to Ben who according to Mum worshipped her. They'd wanted babies. No, even if Hilary knew how to get rid of it, she probably wouldn't tell her. All it would do was let the cat out of the bag at home.

The following Saturday morning, Rupes came to see her as usual. He unwrapped a bottle of champagne and said, 'Put this in the fridge for later. I'm hoping we'll have a future we'll want to celebrate.'

Although Isobel was fond of champagne and it conjured up a world of luxury which she much enjoyed, celebrating the coming of this baby was not what she wanted. Rupert threw himself down on the large settee, looking stressed and in need of sleep.

'I've been thinking about what we must do. It's been going round in my head since I last saw you. Have you been able to sleep?'

Isobel shook her head. 'It's giving me nightmares.'

'Me too. We've got to get it sorted.'

That cheered her up, and she went to sit next to him. At least he wasn't going to leave it all to her.

'First, I want you to make an appointment to see your doctor, just to make sure.'

She shook her head impatiently. 'I am sure. I went to the library and got out a book on pregnancy.' She took it from behind the cushion and showed it to him. 'I've got all the signs and symptoms, morning sickness and sore breasts. There's no doubt about it.'

He put an arm round her. 'Look, I've been thinking about it and I've finally made up my mind. I think the right answer would be for us to get married.' She could hardly believe her ears. 'What d'you think? Would you be happy about doing that?'

Isobel felt a surge of joy. 'Marry you? Could we? That would be absolutely heaven. I never dreamed you'd want to. It would make all the difference in the world. I could be with you all the time.'

'We'd be a real family. I'll have a second chance. I won't make the same mistakes with this child. I'll give it more time, show it more affection. I'm older and wiser now.'

'I'm thrilled,' Isobel said. 'But you're already married.'

'Yes, and it's Charlotte's wedding next Saturday. Once that's out of the way I'll ask Margaret for a divorce. I'm not making her happy any more.'

'You'd rather be with me?' Until now, Isobel hadn't been able to imagine saying that to him.

'You know I would.'

She sighed with relief. This was an outcome beyond all her expectations.

He said, 'We probably won't be able to do it right away. I'm sorry – it'll mean waiting...'

'It'll be worth waiting for.' Isobel smiled.

'I've some more news for you.'

'Good news?'

65

'Yes. I think I might have a buyer for my business. It'll bring enough money to provide for Margaret as well as us and the baby, and we'll none of us want for anything. It'll get rid of my worries and give us all an entirely new life.'

'That's marvellous.' Isobel felt her high spirits bubbling out. There was nothing she wanted more than to be married to Rupes.

He looked downcast. 'When I think of telling Margaret about you and the baby, I come out in a cold sweat. She's a Catholic and doesn't believe in divorce.'

'Will she say no?'

'She might. It'll certainly come as a shock. She's thought of nothing but Charlotte's wedding for weeks. We've hardly spoken of anything else.' He shivered. 'I'm not looking forward to this, but once the wedding is over I'll hype myself up and do it.' He took out his pen. 'Have you got any paper? I still have to write my speech as father of the bride.'

'I'll help you with that,' Isobel said. She could see he felt fraught.

'I want you to help me with the other thing too. How can I ask Margaret for a divorce without hurting her too much?'

For Isobel, it seemed odd to be alone on a Saturday. Rupert usually spent the day in her apartment but she knew he wouldn't be able to come today because it was Charlotte's wedding day.

'I'll come down on Sunday morning,' he'd said. 'As soon as I've done the deed. I want to get that over and done with.'

Isobel knew now that Rupert lived in Putney. On Saturday afternoon, feeling at a loose end, Isobel decided to drive over to the church where the wedding was being held. She was curious about Rupert's wife, whom she'd never seen, though there had been a photograph of her in a newspaper when she'd won first prize for her floribunda roses in a flower show. Margaret had looked stout and matronly.

She parked her car a short distance away, afraid it might embarrass Rupert to know she'd come to watch. When she reached the church she found the service was in progress and a small crowd had gathered at the gates. Isobel hung back.

The bride came out with her veil thrown back and her cheeks flushed. Isobel thought she looked very happy. There were oohs and aahs from the crowd when the bride half turned and they caught sight of the full glory of her oyster satin wedding gown. It had been gathered up in a bustle of lace and tiny rosebuds at the back.

Isobel watched the photographer line the wedding party up on the steps. Charlotte was attended by four bridesmaids in lavender gowns and a small pageboy held up her train. All the men were in morning dress. Isobel caught her breath when she saw Rupes looking strained but handsome. She searched the faces for Sebastian, but he was not amongst them. He'd talked to her in school yesterday and neither of them had mentioned this wedding.

She thought Margaret looked tense and rather severe, and older than her own mother. She was wearing an elegant blue two-piece with a large hat. Isobel felt sorry for her: her world was about to collapse. She was moving off when she saw Naomi Griffiths with Barbara Ward, another teacher from the school. She offered them a lift back to Clapham.

'No thanks,' Barbara said. 'We live near here.' They suggested having a cup of coffee and Isobel went with them to a café in a nearby road.

'That was Putney's wedding of the year,' Naomi said. 'You saw the bride, didn't you?'

'Yes,' Isobel said. 'Gorgeous dress.'

'She's Sebastian's sister. I heard Miss Molyneaux ask him if she was.' Miss Molyneaux was their deputy headmistress and close to retirement age. 'She'd heard the banns being read out in church. Posh wedding, isn't it?'

Isobel felt a jab of anxiety. Did they wonder why she was here? She ought to offer some reason, but couldn't think of one. 'I didn't see him there.'

'He was in the crowd watching. We've just spoken to him.'

'In the crowd?' She frowned. 'Why wasn't he in church with his family?'

'He told us his father threw him out of the house years ago and turned his mother against him. But he said he could get on with his sister, she was all right.'

Isobel said, 'Doesn't look like it, or he'd have been inside in his morning dress, doing the ushering or whatever.'

'Well, you know what Sebastian's like...'

'I quite like him,' Isobel said quickly. He was always ready to talk to her.

She did a little shopping and went home feeling

keyed up. Now she'd seen Margaret, she could picture Rupes telling her he wanted his freedom. The images stayed with her all evening. She was exultant. She loved him and soon she'd have him to herself. The last few years had been good for her, but now she felt she was looking at a golden future.

Isobel was awake early on Sunday morning, though she hadn't slept well. She couldn't get Rupert out of her mind. He could be in the throes of telling Margaret at this very moment. She knew he'd been dreading it and she was afraid he'd be finding it painful. He hated hurting anybody.

She felt too jittery to bother with breakfast and made do with a cup of tea, expecting to hear him ring her doorbell at any moment. He hadn't put a time on when he'd arrive, but he'd said he wanted to get it over and done with as early as possible. Isobel decided he'd be with her by ten o'clock at the latest. It was almost routine for him to pop in about that time, bringing the Sunday papers with him.

She went round her flat with a duster but in truth it was already clean and shining. She was careful to keep it so and living alone made it easy. When he came, she'd make a pot of the strong black coffee he liked, and she'd bought croissants yesterday in case he'd had no appetite for break-fast at home.

As time went on, she grew more on edge and couldn't keep her eyes away from her watch. Ten o'clock came and went. Perhaps the Broadbent family had overslept? They were having the reception at his home; a marquee had been set up on his back lawn. Rupes had told her that after the wedding breakfast he'd booked a band to play for dancing in the entrance hall of their house, where there was a parquet floor and plenty of space.

Eleven o'clock came and went. Isobel was growing anxious and kept going to the window to look at the road along which he must drive. The angle was too steep for her to see if his car was already in the car park. She hoped it was and he was on the way up; she waited but her doorbell didn't ring.

At midday, she made herself some coffee and ate a croissant. Perhaps Margaret was upset and he needed to reason with her before coming. He wouldn't leave her if she'd become hysterical.

By two o'clock Isobel was really worried. She couldn't imagine what was keeping him, unless Margaret had refused to allow him a divorce. But he was usually very thoughtful for others and he'd know she'd be on hot bricks waiting for news. Why didn't he ring her?

She wanted to phone him and even thumbed through the directory to find his number. He'd asked her not to ring his home, but that was before Margaret was supposed to know of her existence.

If Isobel needed to contact him, he'd asked her to do it while he was in the office and to use his private line. He'd said if his secretary should answer, it meant he wasn't there, so would she put the phone down without speaking and try again later. But today being Sunday, nobody would be in his office. Just to make sure she rang there, but as she'd expected there was no reply. Isobel decided to ring his house. It could easily be Rupes who picked up. If a woman answered, she knew what to do, but the phone rang and rang there too. She had to assume that he wasn't at home either. She'd hardly ever needed to contact him: he was punctilious about ringing her, but why didn't he ring now? This wasn't like him.

By four o'clock, Isobel was feeling desperate. It was a sunny afternoon and she'd have liked to go out for a walk to clear her head, but she didn't want to leave the flat in case he came. He had his own key and he'd no doubt wait, but... She was edgy and insecure. She longed to see him again and feel his arms round her, and decided there was nothing she could do but stay where she was until he came.

She couldn't settle to anything, afraid now that something he hadn't expected must have happened. She felt miserable, almost abandoned. Isobel couldn't remember a Sunday when he hadn't been to see her. They both looked on it as the best day in the week.

Isobel tossed and turned for most of that night, but she got up to go to school the next morning. Rupert would know she'd be there and he'd be in his office. She'd ring him in her mid-morning break and talk to him. She told herself she wouldn't worry if after all Margaret had refused him a divorce. Even if they couldn't marry, he could move in with her and it would be almost as good.

She found it reassuring to be busy at school. There was a payphone in the staffroom but she couldn't talk to Rupert while her colleagues were within hearing. There was a public phone box a little further down the road and she ran to that, but when she got through on his private line a girl's voice answered and she put the receiver down again feeling hot and tense with frustration. She'd have to try again at lunch time.

When she got back, Sebastian was in the staffroom getting himself a cup of instant coffee from the urn. She picked up a cup and saucer and went to take her turn.

'I understand your sister got married on Saturday,' she said.

'Who told you that?'

'It was the talk of the school. You know how women love a big wedding.'

'Some of them went along to see it.'

'I did. I bumped into Naomi outside the church just at the right moment, but I didn't see you there.'

'I was.' He seemed shame-faced. 'Just to see Charlotte in her finery. I wasn't invited,' he said gruffly. 'The family have disowned me.'

'A posh wedding,' Isobel said but he was off before she'd filled her own cup and when she looked round she saw Naomi had cornered him. It was plain he knew no more than she did about events at Rupert's house.

At lunch time, she went back to the phone box feeling a bit apprehensive. She'd made up her mind that this had gone on long enough and if the secretary answered again, she'd ask to speak to Rupert. She took a deep breath before dialling his number and prayed that this time he'd be there. He wasn't. It was his secretary's voice again.

'Good morning,' Isobel said as breezily as she could. 'Can I speak to Mr Broadbent, please?'

There was a momentary pause, during which Isobel realised it was now afternoon.

The girl asked, 'Who is speaking, please?'

Isobel hesitated. She managed to say, 'I'm a friend. I want a word... It's a personal matter, not business.'

'Oh!' Another awkward pause. Then the girl said, 'I'm sorry to have to tell you that Mr Broadbent suffered a heart attack yesterday morning...'

Isobel gasped out loud. The phone box seemed to be circling round her. 'Is he in hospital? How is he?'

'I'm afraid he didn't survive.'

'What?' Isobel's knees were turning to jelly. 'What happened?'

'He died before the ambulance reached him. I'm very sorry...'

With shaking hands, she slid the receiver back on its rest and bent over it, trying to get her breath. A fat woman was banging on the glass wanting to use the phone. Isobel let herself out and sank down on the grassy bank a few yards away. She felt dazed. It was a damp day and none too warm, and passers-by turned to stare at her, but she didn't care.

Tears of grief were rolling down her cheeks. Rupes had seemed so full of life last time she'd seen him. Now he was gone and she'd never see him again. She loved him – she'd never loved anyone like this before. She couldn't manage without him.

At last she pulled herself to her feet. It was one thirty and she had to be back in school for the afternoon session by one forty-five. She hadn't been at her best this morning, and the last thing she felt like doing was facing a classful of ten-year-olds now, but she'd have to do it and go on doing it.

She went to the cloakroom to wash her face and try to pull herself together. Naomi was there combing her red hair.

'Have you heard?' she said. 'Sebastian had a phone call during lessons this morning. After the wedding, his father had a heart attack and collapsed. He died just like that.'

She managed to say, 'Poor Seb.'

'He's been given compassionate leave. The head is taking his class this afternoon. His dad must have found the wedding very stressful.'

The bell sounded and Isobel was glad to get away from her. She felt sick and confused and was no better when afternoon school was over and she was free to go home. It was a relief to be on her own. She felt exhausted and went to lie on her bed.

Everything had changed. She'd lost her lover and her protector too. She needed to think, but her mind wouldn't function properly. She fell asleep and it was nearly seven when she woke up. If anything she felt worse: dopey and hung over.

She was bereft and couldn't believe she'd never see Rupert again. She wished she knew more about what had happened. Had he told Margaret he had a mistress he wanted to marry because she was pregnant? Had they had an argument, a row? It seemed more than likely that her pregnancy had helped cause his death. That made her feel sick again and icy cold inside.

No doubt Sebastian would know more when he came back to work, but his mother was hardly likely to divulge intimate details to him. It would be too painful. Isobel didn't think she need worry about Seb's knowing very much. Would he be back tomorrow? She had no means of knowing that either.

She really needed an abortion now. No girl had ever needed one more. Without Rupes she'd never be able to manage. But she had no money to pay for it and get herself to Sweden, and no way of knowing how to go about it.

It was dusk when she decided she couldn't lie on her bed any longer. She'd probably spend the whole night tossing and turning if she did. She decided to go out for a walk before she realised it was raining. She put on her mac and took her umbrella, but the rain was heavier than she'd supposed when indoors. She got into her car instead, and set off without giving any thought to where she was going. She found herself driving along the road in which Rupes had lived. She knew his address but he'd asked her never to go there and she hadn't.

She passed his house and stopped her car a little further along the road. She got out and walked back, but there wasn't much to see. The house was some way back from the road and surrounded by trees. It looked Edwardian and was very substantial. It was the sort of house she'd expected Rupert to live in. Through the double wrought-iron gates she caught a glimpse of the marquee still erected behind the house. It looked forlorn amongst the dripping trees.

Where was Rupes now? She didn't know whether he was in a hospital mortuary or in a chapel of rest somewhere. She didn't know anything. She eyed the gravelled drive on the other side of the gates. His family would know, but she couldn't ask them.

She went home and looked round her apartment. Rupes had given her many of the things here, and she had a few of his personal possessions. He'd kept some clothes here, mostly informal things he could be comfortable in. She brought them all out of her wardrobe and laid them out across her bed. They had traces of Rupes's aftershave on them. She buried her face in them and drew breath into her lungs in great gulps. The scent brought him back to life for a few moments.

It wasn't until two days later that she found his gold cigarette lighter under the little table at one end of the settee. He must have dropped it there and not noticed. She cradled it in her hand until it became warm; a small memento that she could keep. It had his initials RRB engraved on it. Isobel had never smoked, but she carried it around in her pocket for a while. She'd seen him flick the flame to life and draw on his cigarettes, and she'd treasure it always. It was like keeping a little bit of Rupes with her.

She was not only sad, but bewildered and confused too. Things were going to be very different for her from now on. She was pregnant and would have to stop working before the birth. How was she going to manage for money?

Oh, God! It could be twins! If it could happen to Hilary, it could happen to her. And without Rupes, she had nobody to turn to.

CHAPTER FIVE

Isobel got up to go to work again on the Tuesday morning although her eyes looked red and swollen. She couldn't afford to jeopardise her job; she would have to live on what she earned from now on. She put on more make-up than usual.

The school was only fifteen minutes' walk away across the common, but she always drove there because she didn't have many other opportunities to use her beloved Mini. She was passing a newsagent's when a placard outside caught her eye. *Tragic end to wedding*, she read. She couldn't stop in the traffic, but did so as soon as it was possible and ran back to buy a copy of the paper.

She looked at it in the car straight away, and found a short paragraph in the stop press. It read, *Following the wedding of his daughter on Saturday, prominent Putney businessman Rupert Broadbent was taken ill and collapsed at eight o'clock the next morning.*

Isobel's heart sank. It certainly looked as

though he had been telling his wife about her. *The bride and groom stayed overnight at the Dorchester Hotel intending to fly to Italy for their honeymoon. They returned home immediately. See page 5.*

Isobel thumbed through to page 5, and found a full account of the wedding with a picture of the bride on Rupert's arm. It made her eyes burn with tears again. She folded the paper quickly and sat blinking hard. She mustn't cry now.

When she felt more in control, she went on. She was walking into school when she saw Sebastian ahead of her. She would have liked to catch him up and ask him about his father, but didn't feel she had a firm enough hold on her tears.

She felt better by the time the mid-morning break came round. Sebastian was drinking coffee at the long staffroom table surrounded by sympathisers. Isobel pulled a chair up close to him.

'Sorry to hear about your father,' she said. 'A dreadful thing to happen.'

'He's putting on a brave face,' Barbara said.

'Well, we were estranged,' Seb added. 'He really wasn't part of my life any more.'

Miss Molyneaux said, 'He was still your father. He must have loved you. Did he have a bad heart?'

'Well, my mother says not. He was always out in his boat acting like a man half his age.'

Isobel agreed with that. He'd had loads of energy; he liked to swim and play tennis.

'Has he remembered you in his will?'

'Naomi, you nosy parker!'

'As a matter of fact, he has,' Sebastian said. 'I

78

never thought he would.'

'He had plenty, hadn't he? He must have been worth a packet.'

'He hasn't left me all that much. My sister's getting more.'

'Never look a gift horse in the mouth,' Miss Molyneaux brayed. 'I expect he was a good father to you.'

'He was very strict and autocratic,' Seb said. Isobel couldn't see Rupes being like that. 'He wanted to mould me into an image of himself. I had to do exactly what he said. I couldn't cope with that.'

'When's the funeral to be?'

'Saturday, at two o'clock. So his work force can go.'

The bell rang and the staffroom emptied rapidly. Isobel and Sebastian were the last to move. She squeezed his hand and said, 'You're all churned up inside, aren't you?'

He was drawing in his lips and his eyes glittered with unshed tears. 'If only things could have been different between us...'

She couldn't stop herself saying, 'I really am sorry.'

She went back to her classroom wondering if Rupes had left her any money. She was badly in need of it, but no, he wouldn't have done. He'd probably written his will years ago. Perhaps even before they'd met. If only...

He'd have wanted to leave her something now she was expecting his child and he'd certainly have left the child enough to cover its keep and education. Seb had been sent to some expensive boarding school, not to the local comprehensive.

But Rupes hadn't known he was going to die. He'd been thinking of exciting trips away from home: the Florence holiday in late August and a sales trip to Germany at half term so she could go with him. He'd thought he had all the time in the world.

She was blinking hard against the tears again. It was a help to focus on the children.

The following Saturday was another dark damp day. Again, Isobel felt nauseous as she got out of bed, and it added to her misery. She couldn't see the common from her windows; it was shrouded in heavy mist.

She wanted to go to Rupert's funeral but was nervous of doing so. She didn't want Seb to see her and start asking questions. She longed to be part of what was happening to Rupes, to be near him for one last time. She'd been cheated out of saying goodbye to him, and she decided that the funeral was the best she could have now. She meant to go, even though Seb would think it strange if he saw her.

She had a fawn mac with a hood that she could pull over her face, and a navy umbrella to hold in front of her. She drove part of the way but left her Mini in a wide suburban road some distance from the church; Seb would recognise the car. Soft rain was falling steadily from a leaden sky; every tree and bush dripped with moisture. Isobel felt all nature wept for Rupes.

She had almost reached the church when the hearse drove slowly by, the coffin inside decked with flowers. To think of Rupes lying there made her stomach churn. It was followed by a long line of limousines and she caught a glimpse of Margaret, Charlotte and Sebastian, all dressed in black, in the first one. He was at the far side of the car; she didn't think he could have seen her.

She was glad to find the church was packed and there were many people outside. A big turn-out for his funeral meant she'd be able to lose herself in the crowd. These would be his employees, paying their last respects. Most were dressed in black from head to foot: it was all very sombre.

She squeezed into a pew at the back and shivered as she waited for the service to start. She couldn't think of Rupes as dead. Images of him at the helm of his boat, of him enjoying a glass of wine in her flat, of him in bed, crowded her mind.

She hung back to watch the chief mourners follow the coffin on its bier to the church door. Following a little behind his mother and sister, Seb looked cold and grey-faced too. After the service, umbrellas were opened as the coffin was put back in the hearse for its final drive to the crematorium.

Isobel kept to the back of the crowd which began to thin as mourners got back into their cars. She wanted to follow, to see Rupes to his final resting place, but already tears were flooding down her face. She must not let Seb see her grief.

The rain grew heavier and drummed on her umbrella as she strode away, seeing nothing. She was worried now about the changes his death must bring.

She had no idea how she was going to manage. The rent of her apartment was beyond what she could afford from her salary. She didn't have her family's thrifty ways, and Rupert by his generosity had encouraged her to spend on luxuries. She'd come to expect to have her every whim satisfied, but what she missed most was not having Rupes to turn to for help. She would have to manage on her own, and she forced herself to think about her options.

She could throw herself on Margaret Broadbent's mercy and ask for help for Rupert's child. But even as she thought about it, Isobel knew she would never find the courage. Both his wife and his daughter had looked grey-faced and withdrawn, so different from their appearance only one week earlier at the wedding. They were immersed in their own grief and wouldn't be able to help anybody. Even if Rupes had told Margaret about the coming baby, she could deny it and say she didn't believe her.

It was plain to Isobel that to acknowledge her husband's pregnant mistress was the last thing Margaret would want to do. Rupes had always been kind and generous but Margaret didn't look that sort. It was far more likely she'd feel that Rupes had betrayed her, and be hurt and humiliated. She'd be more likely to swear vengeance on Isobel's head than show her kindness. No, it would be wiser to stay well away from her.

Once back in her apartment she looked at the rent book. It was in her name but Rupert had paid the rent quarterly, and the next four weeks were covered. She hoped that would give her time to find something cheaper. Feeling restless, she made herself something to eat and then set off round the local estate agents, hoping to get that settled.

A few hours tramping the wet streets confirmed what she'd suspected: it was an almost impossible task. The Labour government had been enforcing rent control for some years and that meant there was no incentive to build homes for rent or even repair those already rented. Sitting tenants had been given assured tenancies at low rentals for as long as they wanted them.

These days, the sole means of renting accommodation was through the council. The only other way to put a roof over her head was to buy one. Isobel knew that both these routes were impossible for her at the moment.

A recently built luxury apartment such as hers had been deliberately priced at a level that was not covered by the Rent Act. She began to think she should try to get a lodger to pay half the rent. After all, the flat had two bedrooms and two bathrooms and plenty of living space.

She'd heard the other teachers railing against their housing difficulties. One of them might want to share her flat. There was a notice board in the staffroom. Isobel wrote out her notice on a postcard ready to put up on Monday. She was there earlier than usual and Sebastian happened to be standing behind her when she pinned it up.

'Wow,' he said when he'd read it. 'You wouldn't consider me, would you?'

'No. I was thinking of a girl. Anyway, you

mightn't like it. You haven't seen it yet.'

'I'll like it, own room and en suite. I can guess what the rest of it'll be like. You wouldn't believe how hard I've tried to find somewhere decent to live. I've got two rooms at the moment in an absolute ruin and I have to share bathroom and kitchen. It's more than grotty – there's rats, mice and woodlice.'

Isobel said, 'Why don't you go home and live with your mother? She'll probably want you to go back now.'

He looked uncomfortable. 'I've been away so long. It mightn't work out.'

'I want another girl. That's the respectable thing.'

'Why have anybody? You've lived there alone for a long time, haven't you?'

That took the wind out of her sails. 'I need company,' she said. 'It's a bit lonely.'

He tried to persuade her. 'Oh, Izzy, come on. We've always got on well together.'

She sighed. She'd had her own reason for being friendly to Seb. His admiring gaze had always followed her round the staffroom. He reminded her of Rupes.

Naomi had joined them and was reading the notice. She said, 'I'd love to share your apartment. When can I see it?'

Isobel wasn't sure she could live with Naomi. She didn't like her that much.

'Hey,' Sebastian said, 'I opened negotiations first. You'll give me first refusal, won't you, Izzy? That's only fair.'

'I shouldn't really. My mother would have a fit.'

'Need she know?'

Isobel weakened. 'You'll have to do your share of cleaning.'

'I will, I promise. I can cook too.'

'I could take you to see my place this afternoon when school's over. Are you free then?'

'You bet. That suits me fine.' He pulled her notice off the board and pushed it into her hand. 'No point in leaving it there. You'll get inundated with offers.'

All through the day, another idea was growing in Isobel's mind. Seb was keen, and he made it obvious he liked her. He was in the habit of searching her out and chatting her up. He was going to inherit a little money from Rupert; he was even a bit like him. Help to pay her rent was what she'd sought, but she needed much more than that.

She needed a father for her baby. Who better than Seb? He might even want to marry her.

Later that afternoon, Sebastian was in high spirits. His eyes went round her apartment taking in the details.

'I love it. I'd count it an honour to come and live here. I'll move in straight away.'

'Don't you have to give notice on your present place?'

'Yes, but it's a rat hole. No point in staying there when I can come here. Besides, I'm afraid you'll change your mind.'

'I ought to. At school they thought it very daring of me to have you as lodger.'

'Only Miss Molyneaux. She's old, and it's the

modern thing. Are you rich, Izzy?'

'Heavens, no.' She'd never felt more skint.

'All this and a nice little car too. Will you give me a lift to work in the mornings?'

'If you're ready on time and you'll pay something towards the petrol.'

'You've got a deal. I've a lot of stuff to bring round. How about you helping me move it?'

'That's not part...'

He put a finger on her lips. 'I know that. You help me move my clobber in and I'll buy us a pub dinner tonight. How about it?'

Isobel smiled. 'That's different.'

She made three trips because the Mini wouldn't hold much. She found it, if not exactly fun, a pleasure to have something to do after the misery of the last week. She had a look round Seb's rooms and was glad she wouldn't have to live in such a place.

With his belongings strewn round her spare bedroom, he said, 'We've done enough for one night. Let's go and eat. I'm starving.'

Isobel hadn't eaten properly over recent days and found suddenly that she was hungry too. Like his father, Seb enjoyed wine with his dinner and ordered a bottle. She sipped at it and found it remarkably like the wine his father had ordered for her. They'd both had their tastes shaped by Rupes. She drank a little more than usual and Seb ordered another half bottle.

He seemed gauche compared with his father but any company was better than being on her own. It seemed odd to be taking him into her apartment, but as soon as she'd locked the door behind them he'd taken her into his arms and was kissing her.

'I've always fancied you,' he told her. He didn't turn her on as his father had, he didn't have his finesse, but he had more energy and his body was young and virile. Isobel let him make love to her, and all the time imagined it was Rupert come back. She spent the night with Seb in his bed. To have unprotected sex seemed to be a good idea. Seb went off to sleep very quickly but she lay there thinking. She came out in a lather of sweat when she remembered she had his father's clothes in her wardrobe and his cologne and a shaver in her bathroom. She must get rid of those tomorrow, before Seb saw them.

The next morning, she awoke to his kisses and he made love to her again before going to school. Isobel felt very much better but she was weighed down with guilt. She shouldn't do this to him. She shouldn't do it to any man. She shouldn't deliberately set him up to believe the coming baby was his.

But still she drove home at lunch time to clear the shelves in her bathroom and dump Rupert's toothbrush and shaver in the bin. His cologne and his brush and comb followed, but she stopped and retrieved the comb. It was nothing special, just a plain tortoiseshell comb, but Rupes had used it. That would have to be her memento from now on. Nobody would read anything into a plain comb.

She collected all Rupes's clothes into plastic bags and took them to a charity shop. It had been a dangerous thing to bring Seb home before she'd done this. But perhaps he wouldn't have recognised his father's sports jacket even though he'd often worn it. Seb hadn't seen much of his father over recent years. All the same, she couldn't afford to have any obviously male objects in her flat.

There was still Rupes's gold cigarette lighter. She wanted very much to keep that, but it would be safer if she did not. She couldn't risk Sebastian's recognising it. For heaven's sake, it had Rupes's initials engraved on it. She wrapped it in a clean handkerchief and put it in her handbag. The following day she went into town in her lunch break and sold it to a jeweller who advertised in his window for old gold. It upset her to think that what had made her value it, his engraved initials, reduced its value.

Then she went back to her apartment and had another careful look round to see if there was anything else of Rupes's that she'd missed. There wasn't, and it made her feel a little safer.

That night she let Seb cajole her into his bed again. She wanted to be with him. She'd felt so alone since Rupes had died, it was a comfort to be cuddled close to another human body.

It became routine for them to sleep together. Isobel lay beside Sebastian listening to his steady breathing and pondering whether she should tell him the truth. But he hadn't got on with his father. It might turn him off her. Her coming child would be his half sister or brother. If Seb knew that, would he be prepared to bring it up as his own? She was afraid he wouldn't. It gave her the occasional sleepless night, but teaching was hard work, and generally she was so tired she slept.

For the baby, it had to be the right thing. Not only would it have a father but it would have its rightful name. The problem was, there were two months to be accounted for.

Time and time again, she found herself going over and over the same ground. Would it be better to throw herself on his mercy? He was enough like his father to be kind and generous, but all the same...

She knew she must decide whether to be honest with him now or for ever keep her mouth closed; that it would be far worse if he found out later. She tried to summon up the nerve to tell him. She even rehearsed a few words in her mind, but they were never spoken. She and Seb were getting on well and she was afraid she'd spoil that and he'd leave her high and dry. She desperately needed his help to get her through this pregnancy; her only alternative would be to go home to her mother.

Within a fortnight of Seb's moving in, they were running out of money and were reduced to walking to school and back and having to eat at home. He was quite a good cook and for the next week they were able to buy a bottle of wine to have with their dinner.

'We aren't very good with money, are we?' She thought of the thrift shown by Hilary and her mother.

Sebastian said, 'I was brought up with plenty and I enjoy what it can buy. It's not easy to cut back.'

Isobel sighed. 'Me too.' She had to say that or Sebastian would ask how she'd managed to pay her rent before he moved in. She'd always thought of her attitude to money as relaxed: it was meant to be spent and enjoyed.

Pay day came round and they had a night out to celebrate. Mindful of the fact that this month the rent must be paid, Isobel collected Sebastian's share and paid it while she had the money. He talked of his coming inheritance, but he didn't say how much he was expecting.

'I wish it was more,' he said when she tried to find out if it would be enough to make life comfortable for them. Sebastian was keeping in touch with his mother now. 'I was at loggerheads with my family for years,' he told Isobel. 'Long enough to regret it, but I couldn't see any way to heal the breach.'

'Family relationships can be difficult,' Isobel said. She should know, she had her share of them.

'Now Dad's died I'm sorry, but it's too late,' Sebastian said sadly. 'It's changed everything. I won't let that happen with my mother. She's old and she's on her own now Charlotte's gone to Hong Kong.'

Some days he called at Margaret's for an hour's chat on his way home from school, and his Sunday afternoons were usually spent with her.

He and Isobel were going out almost every night. Sometimes locally, but it was easy to get up to the West End by bus or tube. Like his father, Sebastian was keen on seeing the latest shows and visiting good restaurants. At first,

90

Isobel found it invigorating and great fun, but when she began to feel weary and in need of more sleep her enthusiasm for nights out waned. She tried to hide this from Seb; it was part and parcel of being pregnant.

There was the other problem that twins ran in her family, but she shut her mind to that. She'd had so much bad luck, it surely couldn't get worse.

Over the following weeks Isobel tried to forget Rupert, but she couldn't. Taking up with his son seemed disloyal to Rupes when she'd really loved him, but she was growing fond of Sebastian and beginning to rely on him. The last thing she wanted to do was hurt him, yet what she was proposing to do was outrageous. He'd be horrified if he knew – almost anyone would be.

She tried to lose herself in whatever enjoyment Sebastian suggested, but she was full of doubts and misgivings. She felt confused and mixed up.

Despite their money problems, the need to hide her pregnancy and her worries about the future, Isobel felt she was able to have a good time. Seb wanted sex much more often than his father had and it took up many of their evenings.

'Shouldn't we be using something?' he asked one night. 'I mean, you don't want to get pregnant, do you?'

'I'm on the pill,' she lied and was instantly full of remorse. There were some in her bathroom cupboard but she'd stopped taking them as soon as she realised she was pregnant. She added so as to prepare him, 'I just hope I started soon enough.'

Hilary knew something about midwifery; she'd trained and qualified some years ago. In those days, the staff had been of the opinion that when fellow midwives and nurses came in to give birth things usually went wrong, and with twins problems were almost guaranteed.

Because she was expecting twins, Hilary was required to attend the antenatal clinic almost every week and told to take extra rest. She felt perfectly well except that she was enormously big. However, the theatre gowns hid that, and she stayed at work until she was thirty-one weeks.

She was looking forward to several weeks of leisure and time to do some writing. She'd had her first success with an article she'd sent to a nursing journal on the role of the theatre sister. Following an interesting discussion with Aunt Primrose, she was writing another for a popular mother and baby magazine on soothing a child's fears when it had to go into hospital.

But on her next antenatal visit her blood pressure was up and her ankles were swelling. She wasn't so well after that and began to feel some trepidation when she thought of her confinement.

When she went to the maternity block for her next antenatal check up, they admitted her straight away, saying she was showing signs of pre-eclampsia. A worried Ben brought in a bag with her nightdresses, dressing gown and something to read. For once, Hilary found she wasn't interested in books.

At the thirty-fifth week, the obstetrician told her she'd need a Caesarean section and he'd do it that day. That sounded scary; Hilary had never had an operation before. She was going to be cheated out of the birth experience and on top of that it was their fourth wedding anniversary. Ben had booked a table in a posh restaurant.

She was back on the ward but still drowsy when the sister told her she was the mother of non-identical twin boys and that they were both normal and healthy. She drifted off again feeling relieved and well satisfied.

When she recovered enough to hold the babies, they placed one in each of her arms. Both smelled of baby powder; they had little tufts of fair hair and stared wide-eyed up into her face. She felt an immediate tug of mother love and tightened her arms protectively round them. They were absolutely gorgeous.

Ben came in to see her. 'I'm thrilled with them,' she whispered. He was clearly over the moon, loosening their wrappers to see their tiny limbs, each perfect. The labels on their wrists read, *Baby Snow twin one* and *twin two*.

'We've already decided on names, haven't we?' Charles and Andrew. One weighed five and a quarter pounds and the other five and a half, which she considered good birth weights for twins of that gestation.

She took them home and Ben's family came round the next day to see them. Mrs Snow peered into their cradles. 'Lovely babies,' she said and sank down in an armchair. She was no longer feeling well.

The twin aunts wanted to hold them and couldn't tear themselves away. 'I was so hoping they'd be identical like us,' Primrose said. 'But even so, twins are very special. They'll never feel lonely. We never do unless we're apart at work.'

'And that won't be for much longer,' Prue said. 'We're due to retire in September.'

'If we miss the hospital babies, we'll be able to come and see yours, Hilary.'

CHAPTER SIX

In July, Isobel received a letter from her mother announcing that Hilary had had her twins. Their birth sent Mum into paroxysms of joy. She wrote that she was thrilled; they were beautiful non-identical baby boys, and Hilary and Ben were in raptures. Isobel wept a little knowing how different it was likely to be when she gave birth, but went into the bathroom to hide her tears from Sebastian. The next day, she pulled herself together and bought silver christening mugs to send to the twins.

It was too soon for her to announce her pregnancy, but the time would come when she'd have to tell Seb. It was now too late to be honest with him. Almost by default she was set on a course to deceive. She couldn't date conception earlier than the night he'd moved into her apartment. This would have to be a seven month baby.

Even if Seb suspected the baby wasn't his, he must never know the whole truth: that the baby was his father's. It would make things a hundred times worse.

Isobel now worried about what he would do when she told him she was pregnant. Impossible for her to guess. His father had offered marriage, but would he? She was growing attached to him even if she didn't have the passion for him that she'd had for Rupert. Seb was good company, and she was very glad to have him in her apartment. She needed somebody to lean on, somebody to help her; she wasn't the sort to fend for herself. Even if he didn't offer marriage, she'd still want him here. She prayed he'd think it was his child. But was it the best route out of an awkward situation?

Her morning sickness had passed. She'd actually lost a bit of weight over the first weeks and she put that down to Rupert's sudden death. It had been a devastating blow, but she was feeling better in herself now, and this week she'd put on a pound in weight. Another few weeks went by and it was time to break the news to Sebastian. She chose to do it one night, after they'd been in bed for an hour and were in that dreamy relaxed state that came after making love. Seb had been at his most passionate and had had a powerful climax, and now he was full of sleepy tenderness. There'd never be a better time.

'Seb, I'm worried,' she said. 'Worried sick. I think I could be pregnant.' She'd got it out at last.

'Oh my God!'

She'd jerked him back to wakefulness. 'What am I going to do? This is a disaster.'

'Are you sure?' He sounded dubious.

'Well no, not exactly sure.' She mustn't appear too certain at this stage. 'But we didn't take any precautions to start with, did we?'

Seb groaned. 'Go and see the doctor.'

'I don't want to. Perhaps I'm wrong and it's all in my mind.'

That cheered him up. 'Perhaps it is.' He lay back thinking for a moment. 'Would it be possible to have it taken away? An abortion?'

It comforted Isobel that he reacted in the same way she had, but she'd already given considerable thought to that subject, and even done some research into the possibilities. 'It's still illegal in this country.'

'Yes, but there are women who'll do it for you, aren't there?'

'There are back street abortionists, but I wouldn't know how to go about contacting one, and I don't know anybody who would. Anyway, I've heard it said that sometimes those women end up by killing the mother.'

'So have I.'

'I'd be scared stiff. They don't really know what they're doing, do they?'

'Better not then.'

'Apparently it's legal in Sweden, they do it in hospitals, but how do I find the money to go there and then pay to have it done?'

Seb was shaking his head. 'There's talk in the papers about making it legal here.'

'Yes, but it won't come in time for me.'

'I'm sorry, Izzy. Really sorry...'

It cooled his ardour for a few days, but soon things were back as they had been.

He wanted to go to the library one afternoon on the way home from school. Isobel was

96

alarmed to find him taking out the book on pregnancy that she'd had out before. He said, 'It helps to know all about it. Sets the mind at rest.'

Isobel made a show of consulting it when they got home. 'I've got all the signs and symptoms set out there,' she told him. 'I don't think there's any doubt.'

It scared her to see Sebastian reading it avidly. It wouldn't help to have him know too much.

'You must see the doctor,' he said. 'You'll need to anyway.'

This time she agreed. Sebastian went with her but waited outside in the Mini. After keeping it to herself for so long, it seemed strange to Isobel to be talking openly about her pregnancy even to a doctor. She came out and slid back into the driving seat before showing him her prescription for extra vitamins and a card telling her to go to the hospital booking clinic.

'I'm now officially pregnant,' she told him.

The colour had gone from Seb's cheeks. 'Did he tell you when it was due?'

The doctor had examined her and said in his opinion she was sixteen weeks pregnant and the baby would be due about 10 February, but she couldn't say that to Seb. She hadn't realised she'd have to build a whole edifice of lies to cover what she was doing.

'He reckons about the tenth of April,' she said.

He stared silently out of the window for a while. Then said, 'We should get married, shouldn't we?' He was biting his lip and didn't seem all that keen. 'Is that what you want?'

'Yes.' Isobel was cautious. 'We rub along pretty

well together, don't we?'

'Course we do.' He smiled. 'I love you, Izzy.' He was staring out of the window again. Isobel had to concentrate on driving but she felt a knot of ice under her ribs. He wasn't jumping for joy at the prospect.

'Sorry,' he said after a few more minutes. 'I've been married before and it didn't work out. I'm rotten with relationships, aren't I? First Dad and then Rose.'

'What went wrong? With your marriage?'

'She left me. Walked out.'

'That's awful, but it wasn't your fault.'

He was shaking his head. It took him some time to say, 'The blame was not all hers, Izzy, don't think that. But things will be different for us. I'll try harder. I promise I will.'

Isobel felt small and guilt-ridden. She was treating him no better than Rose had. Maybe a lot worse. He'd made her curious and she started asking questions. He told her his marriage had lasted only two years and Rose had left him for another man.

'Not your fault,' she said again.

'I was a spoiled and selfish brat,' he said slowly. 'I thought I'd grown up since then and had learned some sense, but I've got you pregnant. I'm sorry about that. Probably not the best catch you could have made, Izzy. But I do love you and I want to try again.'

When they got home Isobel wept on his shoulder and he didn't understand why. 'I love you,' she said, knowing she'd been cold-blooded in making him believe he'd fathered her baby. He didn't deserve this. At that moment she came near to confessing what she was doing to him. He seemed a gentle person who'd been hurt already. Instead she told him, 'I think you're a great catch.'

He kissed her. 'We'll be fine.'

Isobel dried her eyes and tried to smile. Seb was a lovely person. He was ready to marry her and it seemed a small miracle. She was being terribly selfish and thinking only of herself but she'd have him to take care of her from now on.

Isobel's relief at having her future settled did not last long. One evening, Sebastian returned from visiting his mother and said, 'I've told her I'm going to be married again, so of course she wants to meet you. We're invited to supper next Sunday.'

That pulled Isobel up so hard, she thought her heart had stopped beating. Why hadn't she thought of this? She couldn't possibly face Margaret Broadbent!

From the moment she'd heard of Rupert's heart attack, Isobel had been afraid the stress of asking for a divorce had brought it on. She had no way of knowing how much he'd told his wife about her. Possibly her name? Possibly that she was his long term mistress? Possibly that she was pregnant? Possibly that she taught in the same school as Sebastian? Would he have said enough for Margaret to know her son was proposing to marry her husband's mistress?

'Nothing to be scared about,' he said easily. 'Mother used to be thought a bit of a battleaxe, but Dad's death has upset her. She isn't at all well.'

Isobel felt for a chair and sat down. She was terrified and it was showing on her face. She made herself smile. 'Did your first wife get on with her?'

He shook his head. 'We weren't made welcome at home at that time. They hardly met. I was the cause of the hostility, Izzy, but that's all behind me now. Mother will love you. Love the idea of a grandchild too.'

'Don't tell her about that, not just yet,' Isobel choked. If by some lucky chance Margaret didn't know everything, that might provide another clue. Isobel didn't want anything to help her link up the facts.

'Right, we won't. Not till after we're married.'

Isobel said, 'Like my mother, she might not approve.'

He was smiling. 'Lots of couples do it these days.'

She made herself say, 'I shall look forward to seeing your old home.' But dread crawled up her back every time she thought of meeting his mother.

Once she'd longed to see where Rupert lived and had asked countless questions about it. Now she told herself she was going to have that chance. She must concentrate on the house and not on what Margaret might or might not know about her. But what if she confronted her?

On Sunday evening it took Isobel a long time to get ready. 'I want to look my best,' she told Sebastian, but she felt a bag of nerves and couldn't hurry.

'You look lovely,' he told her. 'Mother will be impressed.' He drove them there in her Mini.

They were let into the house by an elderly parlourmaid in a black dress with a white organdie apron and a frill on her head.

'Hello, Dora,' Sebastian greeted her as she took their coats. 'This is Isobel, my intended. I expect Mother's told you about us?'

'Yes, sir. Congratulations. She's in the drawing room. Not too well again today, I'm afraid.'

Isobel said, 'Hello, Dora,' and put out her hand. As she followed Sebastian, she made herself look round the enormous hall with its two chandeliers sparkling high above her. The drawing room seemed to eddy before her eyes. Then she was being introduced to Sebastian's mother.

She looked haggard, old, overweight and ill. Isobel felt near panic. Was she expected to kiss her? She put out a shaking hand as she had to the parlourmaid.

'Very pleased to meet you, Mrs Broadbent,' she said. Cold grey eyes were looking her over. There was no welcome in them, no friendliness. Isobel could feel herself quaking.

'Sebastian, I'll have some more sherry.' His mother held out her glass to him. 'Help yourselves to a drink.'

Isobel felt him press a glass of sherry into her hand and cast round for something to break the silence. She didn't want to talk about herself; she was terrified of giving Margaret clues that would tie up with what Rupert might have told her. In reply to a direct question she had to say she came from Merseyside, which made her feel fluttery with panic again. She took a gulp of sherry and told herself she had to stop this. It wasn't likely that Rupert would have mentioned where she came from.

'Tell me about yourself,' Margaret said and it seemed more an order than an invitation. She managed by telling anecdotes about the children she taught and the school where they both worked. But it was almost impossible to meet Margaret's icy gaze.

Sebastian had to help his mother out of her armchair and to the long mahogany table in the dining room. It was beautifully set with silver and glass. Sebastian's childhood home was very different from hers, but she'd known it would be. The food was served by the parlourmaid with great formality. It looked delicious but Isobel found herself struggling to swallow it. She felt sick. At last they were going back to the drawing room for coffee, Mrs Broadbent unsteady on her feet.

Isobel's mouth was dry but the coffee was served in tiny cups of wafer-thin china and not much help.

Margaret's eyes came back to assess her again and made Isobel feel uncomfortable. Did she know who she was? If she did, and Isobel suspected she might, then she'd surely want to put Sebastian off marrying her. She looked at the clock on the mantel, wondering how much longer they'd have to stay. Seb was lolling back on the settee looking comfortable and unlikely to move soon.

But it was still early when Mrs Broadbent announced, 'It's past my bedtime. I tire easily these days. Sebastian, ring for Dora to help me back to bed.'

Isobel was so relieved to find her ordeal almost over that she stood up rather too quickly, and said, 'I'm so glad to have met you, Mrs Broadbent. I hope you'll feel better tomorrow'

A heavy sigh. 'Unlikely. I'm afraid I'm not in good health these days.' Sebastian was hauling her to her feet.

'Such a lovely supper,' Isobel went on. 'I've enjoyed it all. Thank you so much.'

When Dora came, the older woman straightened up. 'I hope you'll make Sebastian happy,' she said in a voice that didn't seem to hold much trust that her hope would be fulfilled. Again those cold grey eyes searched into hers. Isobel shivered. Yes, there was hostility there. She knew.

Once outside she took great gulps of the cold night air. It was over. There'd been no confrontation about being Rupert's mistress as she'd dreaded. Margaret had made no accusations. Perhaps it was pride that had stopped her acknowledging her husband had loved another, perhaps she hadn't been able to find the strength. Isobel felt stronger for having faced her. She wouldn't be afraid to do so again.

'What's the matter with your mother?' she asked, when she was safely back in her Mini.

'Heart problems.'

'I don't think she liked me very much.'

'Oh, I wouldn't say that.'

Isobel thought Margaret might say something to Sebastian when she had him to herself on his next visit. After he'd been, she had to press him to tell her, but he admitted his mother wasn't in favour of his getting married again.

'It needn't make any difference to us,' he told her.

It needn't, Isobel thought, if that was all she'd said, and was able to relax on that score.

Isobel thought she must have been out of her mind to cheat Sebastian as she had. It was giving her sleepless nights. Would she be able to get away with it without his ever knowing?

She was hoping he knew little about pregnancy and it made her nervous to see him reading the book on that subject he'd taken out of the library. She did her best to deflect his attention from it and the next day invented a reason to visit the library again. She was relieved to see him hand it in. As far as she was concerned, the less he knew about childbirth the better.

Sebastian asked, 'When shall we tie the knot? Better not leave it too long, eh?'

'What about when we break up for half term? With a bit of luck, Mum's school will break up at the same time. I could take you home to meet my family and we could be married in Birkenhead.'

He was alarmed. 'You aren't thinking of a big church wedding? I'm divorced, don't forget. I was thinking of the register office here. I'd rather not have too much fuss myself.' He sighed. 'But it's your first time. I suppose it's different for you?'

'The register office is fine by me,' Isobel told him. 'But I can't get married without inviting my mother. My sister and brother-in-law too. They'll

104

be upset if I don't and probably won't believe we are married. I could break the other news at the same time.'

'Tell them that passion overcame us, and we jumped the gun.' He was smiling at her.

'I won't put it quite like that. Not to my mother.' Isobel giggled. 'I'd better write and let her know.' Suddenly she was serious. 'You didn't tell me what went wrong with your first marriage. Only that you were at fault too.'

Seb shrugged. 'Money troubles, I suppose. Rose had a firm grip on cash, worked for a bank and earned more than I did. We bought a house and she moaned that I didn't pay my share of the mortgage, that sort of thing. Eventually she found another fellow more to her liking.'

'Total rejection?'

He nodded. 'It was very painful.'

'Poor Seb.' She shot him a wide smile. 'But lucky for me.'

'We're more alike,' he said. 'Neither of us has any grip on money.'

'Then we won't fight over it, will we?'

'And we'll enjoy ourselves.'

'Until it runs out in the middle of the month,' Isobel pointed out.

'Well, I'm used to that.'

They began making their wedding plans, or rather Isobel did. Seb was leaving most of it to her.

'We'll have no money to put on a big show,' he said, 'and there's nobody much I want to ask.'

'Not your mother and sister?'

'They probably wouldn't come.'

'I'd invite them,' Isobel advised. 'They might send us a present.'

He smiled. 'That makes you sound a bit mercenary, love.'

Isobel pulled up short. She mustn't give him that impression.

He was watching her. 'Don't worry, I know you aren't.'

She said, 'No. Look, I'd better ask my family down the day before our wedding. We could give them dinner here and have a good chat, but you'd have to sleep somewhere else. Mum would be shocked to find us living together before we were married. She's a bit old-fashioned that way.'

Seb sighed. 'I suppose I could ask Vic if I can spend the night on his couch.'

'If you wouldn't mind. Then Hilary and Ben can have your room and Mum can share my bed. It'll give me the chance to tell her about the baby while we're on our own.'

'What about my stag night? I could ask Vic...'

'Not the very last night. I have to introduce you to my family – they'll want to get to know you.'

'OK. I don't suppose it matters which night.'

'We'll need witnesses. Vic could be one. He's your friend.'

'We'd better start saving.'

'Yes. We'll want a little honeymoon, even if it's only a couple of days. It will mean my family won't stay on.'

'A few days is all we'll have off, love.' Seb beamed. 'What about Paris? It'll be the end of October – could be cold by then. That would be a good place to go, wouldn't it?'

Isobel was well pleased with the current fashions. A-line dresses hanging straight from the shoulders hid her growing bump. Rupes had bought her a blue wool one with a tiny matching jacket. It had been the very latest at the time, by Mary Quant and rather formal. She'd worn it only once and would be married in that. She had shoes, gloves and a handbag to go with it. She didn't want a hat: they didn't suit her and she thought them old-fashioned. All was going to be well in the short term.

Now that things were working out, she ought to be happy, but instead she was feeling fraught. If Seb found out later that she'd not been honest with him, it would be a disaster. She now had to keep the truth hidden at all costs. She dared not think about 10 February. It set her stomach churning.

Flora picked up several letters from her doormat. As she took them to her living room she recognised Isobel's writing on one. She ripped open the envelope expecting the usual short note, but this time it was a long letter.

I expect you'll be surprised to hear I'm thinking of getting married. The words danced off the page. Flora sat down with a little bump to read on. She learned that Isobel's fiancé's name was Sebastian Broadbent, that he was two years older than Isobel and a fellow teacher at her school. Flora was curious to know more.

She'd pressed Isobel about having a boyfriend last time she'd come up and she had at last admitted that she had one. It had seemed out of character for her not to have had one during all the years she'd been in London.

Flora had discussed it with Hilly many times. Isobel was sparse with her news, and though Flora knew exactly what teaching was like she found it impossible to get a picture of how her daughter spent her leisure time in London. She never invited them down. Flora had gone as far as to suggest she visit more than once, but there was always some reason why Isobel couldn't fit it in.

Flora wanted her to be happy, and, though she seemed to be, Hilly agreed with her that Isobel needed a husband and family of her own to be truly so. Now, it seemed, she was about to take that step and Flora was pleased for her.

It was a Saturday morning so she went straight out to telephone Isobel to say how delighted she was at the news.

'I wrote to Hilary too,' Isobel told her, 'and she's just rung me.'

'When will the wedding be? Have you set a date?'

'No, but it'll be quite soon.'

'I hope you'll come up and get married from home.'

'I don't think so, Mum. Don't set your heart on that, or a big wedding.'

Flora put the receiver down feeling disquieted. Isobel didn't seem as excited as a girl on the brink of marriage should be. To know her daughter had a husband to look after her would go some way towards easing Flora's mind.

Ten days later she received a larger and more

ornate envelope with an engraved card inside inviting her to the wedding. The date was set for the half term break. That took her breath away: half term was almost on them. Enclosed was a note asking her to travel down the day before and spend the night with them. *I've asked Hilary and Ben to do this too, so you can all come together,* Isobel had written.

Flora rushed round to see Hilary, who was still on maternity leave with her twins, to find a similar card propped on her mantelpiece inviting her and Ben.

'She's really got cracking.' Hilary smiled. 'I'm thrilled for her.'

'It seems a bit rushed.' Flora frowned. 'I do hope this Sebastian Simon Broadbent is right for her.'

'She's old enough to know. I'd love to go to her wedding, but how am I going to cope with two small babies on a journey like that?'

'It wouldn't have been too bad in the car, would it?'

At the beginning of the summer, Ben had finally given up his job to work for himself and had opened his garden centre. His smart and comfortable car had been handed back, and instead he'd bought a second-hand van which he needed to run his business.

Hilary was shaking her head. 'Then there's the wedding itself. How do I keep them quiet during the ceremony and the reception?'

'I'll help you,' Flora said. But it was Ben who sorted that.

'I'll stay home and look after the babies,' he

told Hilary.

'Are you sure?'

'Yes. The van isn't suitable. With only two seats, we couldn't fit your mother and two babies into it. You go and enjoy the wedding; you've done nothing but look after the twins since they were born. A break will do you good.'

'It's a full-time job. When would you do your work? You aren't planning to take them there?'

'I'll ask the aunts if they can help.'

It seemed Aunt Primrose would be happy to take her day off on the day they left and Aunt Prudence the following day, when they'd return. They said they were looking forward to it.

Hilary had misgivings. 'I don't want to leave them.'

'You know they'll be well looked after. It's only for one night, and you'd have to take such a lot of stuff with you and spend so much time feeding and changing them. Besides, they'd take everybody's attention away from Izzy on her big day.'

Isobel and Seb came home from school one afternoon to find a letter waiting for Sebastian.

'It's my mother's writing,' he said. 'Goody. I can guess what this is.'

'What?' Isobel busied herself putting the kettle on. He'd gone into the sitting room and didn't answer. She followed him in. 'What is it?'

'I told you my father had left me a legacy?'

'Yes.'

'Mum says she now has probate. Not before time either. She wants my bank account details and says she'll have my share paid into it.'

110

'That's wonderful.' Isobel felt a warm glow of pleasure. 'How much?' He handed the letter to her to read. 'Wow! Why didn't you say you were expecting all this? It'll pay our rent for ages.'

Seb was smiling up at her. 'We could go abroad for a decent holiday in the summer. It hurts to be given all those weeks off work and not be able to afford a holiday.'

'The baby,' she said. 'Not this year. It wouldn't be much fun with a babe in arms.'

'Sorry, no. Have you read what Mum says?'

It was a business-like letter with no family news or terms of endearment in it. There were only two paragraphs. Isobel had not read the second.

I strongly advise you to buy a small house while you have the money, she'd written. *It will stand you in good stead in future years and I'll sleep better to know you have a roof over your head.*

'It's probably good advice,' Isobel said. 'We'd be quids in if we didn't have this rent to pay.'

'It wouldn't buy anything grand.'

'If it was our own, we could make it nice.'

'Yes. Perhaps we'd better start looking round.' Sebastian's smile broadened. 'You're right.'

Thereafter they studied the property pages in the papers and couldn't pass an estate agent's window without perusing the details of every house shown there.

Flora booked two seats on the National Express coach to London and cut two packets of sandwiches for their lunch. She was looking forward to the trip. 'I'm dying to meet Isobel's husband to be. She's told us absolutely nothing about him.'

Hilary spent the journey talking about her babies. It was the first time she'd left them. 'I'm missing them already,' she confessed.

'They'll be all right with their father,' Flora told her.

'He's only going to have them at night. I hope they don't keep him awake. It's usually me that gets up to them. He's got to work in the day.'

'It'll be good for Ben. Help him bond with them.'

'He already has, Mum. He changes nappies and gives them bottles.'

Flora couldn't stop speculating about Isobel. 'I'm glad we're going to see where she's lived all this time.' When the coach drew in to Victoria, her eyes were darting round the crowd awaiting its arrival. Isobel had said she'd meet them.

'There she is.' Hilary was excited. 'It must be Sebastian with her. He looks very nice.'

'Look at her coat! It's far too short! She looks like a little girl, but this weather she'll catch her death of cold. Showing all that bare leg!'

'She's got tights on, Mum. It's fashionable. All the youngsters wear clothes like that.' Slowly the passengers were getting off and claiming their luggage.

'It's mid-thigh.'

Hilary giggled. 'Many are crotch length these days,' she whispered. 'Don't say anything to upset her.'

Flora wrapped her arms round Isobel. Her daughter was grown up now but she missed her as much as Hilary was missing her twins. It upset her to find Izzy's embrace was cool and guarded.

Sebastian shook her hand and kissed her cheek simultaneously. His green eyes were friendly; she thought she could take to him and was cheered. It surprised her to find it was Isobel who drove the smart Mini. When they arrived at the flat, she was lost for words.

Hilary gasped. 'Izzy, this is a marvellous flat – out of this world. I'd love to live here. Just look at the view, all trees. You wouldn't think you were in London. And two bedrooms, both with en-suites? Gosh, you are lucky to have a pad like this.'

'Yes,' Sebastian agreed. 'I'm going to move in with her when we're married.'

'Very sensible,' Flora assured him. 'You've managed here all along, Izzy? How much rent d'you pay?'

She saw from the expression on both her daughters' faces that she shouldn't ask questions like that. Izzy was grown up and standing on her own feet now. She'd consider her rent none of her mother's business.

'It is expensive,' Sebastian answered for her.

The table was already set for four. He plied them with sherry.

'I'm going to cook dinner here for us,' he said. 'After travelling all day you won't want to go out again?'

It was the last thing Flora wanted. She was happy to sit here and lap up the luxury of Isobel's surroundings. But she didn't understand how she'd been able to afford a flat like this ever since she'd come to London. Once Sebastian went out to the kitchen, she said, 'It's lovely here. I'm sure you're glad you don't have to start house-hunting like your sister.'

Hilary said, 'We're still in the cottage in Bebington, but it would be more convenient if we lived out Eastham way. Ben would spend less time travelling and could come home for lunch.'

'We've started house-hunting too,' Isobel said. 'Seb's father died not long ago, and we intend to buy a house with the legacy he's left him.'

'I do envy you, Izzy, not having to save up for everything like me and Ben.'

'You're doing all right,' Flora told her. 'Ben's garden shop is open now. He's got his business up and running.'

'He's having to buy in a lot of plants and things that he'll grow himself once he's properly established,' Hilary said.

Flora asked about the rest of Sebastian's family and whether they'd meet them at tomorrow's wedding.

'No, I'm afraid not.' He'd come in to put the first course of smoked salmon on the table. 'I have a sister but she's out in Hong Kong with her husband. My mother lives close but my father's sudden death has really upset her and she's not very well. We're having a very quiet wedding because of that.'

Flora said, 'Wouldn't it have been better to wait a month or two until she was over the worst of her grief?'

The moment the words were out of her mouth she knew she should never have said it. There was an awkward silence. She wondered if they'd had an argument about it, whether Seb had wanted to delay and Isobel had insisted on going ahead.

'You might as well know,' Isobel choked out. 'I'm going to have a baby, so we can't wait.' A red tide ran up her cheeks.

Flora felt stunned. She could feel her own cheeks burning too. 'I see!'

Hilary was on her feet and went to kiss her sister. 'I'm so happy for you, Izzy. Everything's happening for you without any of the waiting. When is it due?'

'April.'

'Sorry.' Sebastian looked shamefaced. 'I'm afraid I jumped the gun, didn't I?'

CHAPTER SEVEN

Flora got up the next morning full of eager anticipation to make morning tea for herself and her two daughters. She and Hilary were dressed and about to make breakfast when Sebastian came round.

He insisted on cooking eggs and bacon for them all, but it seemed wedding nerves were robbing Isobel of her appetite and she couldn't eat her share. She and Seb sat round and read the newspapers then but Flora felt restless and wanted to get on with the preparations. She and Hilary put on their wedding finery but Isobel refused any help with dressing.

A little later, she came out of her bedroom looking pale and nervous, to do a little twirl in front of them. 'What d'you think? Do I look suitably bridal?'

'You look beautiful,' Hilary said. 'Very smart.'

Flora had her reservations. 'You must have spent a small fortune on that outfit. It is smart, but not what I'd call bridal.' It was way too short. More like a medieval man's tunic and tights than a wedding outfit.

Hilary was having none of that. 'It's the height of fashion, Mum. I like it. Here, this will make you look bridal.' She pinned on Isobel's carnation spray. 'It smells lovely.'

Sebastian had gone home to change and returned at that moment with his best man, who was introduced as Victor. He drove them all to the register office and it seemed miraculous to Flora that they were right on time.

She followed behind the bride and groom as the registrar led them to a small wood-panelled room tastefully furnished with polished mahogany and fresh flowers. The ceremony seemed soon over and, after the bride and groom, Flora signed the register. She thought it the strangest wedding she'd ever attended.

On the coach going back to Merseyside later that afternoon, Hilary said, 'We had a good time, didn't we? Seb cooked us a lovely meal last night. It's not many men who would do that.'

'He said he enjoyed cooking.'

Her mother looked pensive and bothered. Hilary tried to jolly her out of her mood. 'I really enjoyed it.'

'Only us and that lad Victor at the wedding. It was all a bit strange.'

'We had a smashing champagne lunch at that restaurant afterwards.' She knew her mother hadn't got over Isobel's shock announcement.

'They probably rushed into it because Isobel's expecting. All done in far too much of a hurry.' Flora's lips twisted with disapproval. She was in one of her severe moods. 'You'd have thought his mother would have come.'

'There were lots of teachers from the school where they work and quite a few children.'

'But nobody else was invited to the champagne lunch, except us and his friend Vic.'

Hilary had thought she and Ben had busy lives when they were first married with both of them working full time. But nowadays they seemed to have even less time for themselves.

The twin babies left her little leisure. She'd had to bottle-feed them, as she'd found she hadn't enough milk to satisfy two. That meant preparing feeds which was another job but at least Ben could help, and if any other member of the family happened to be there at feeding times, they were given a baby to feed.

Hilary always rushed to pick up the first baby to grizzle for attention, in the hope that the other would doze on until she'd done what was needed for his brother. Mostly they slept between feeds, but it gave her little time to do anything else.

When Ben came home in the evening physically tired from working in the garden centre, he still had his paperwork to do. He'd spread his papers and ledgers out on the dining table as soon as she cleared away their supper dishes, and more often than not he'd ask, 'Would you mind giving me a hand? You can type so much faster than I can. I don't seem to be able to get the hang of that.'

However tired she was, Hilary would get out her typewriter. 'What d'you want me to do?'

'There's a couple of letters that need answering.' He'd lay them out beside her. 'Ask this one for a brochure and price list. And I want you to put an order in to this one.' A hand-scrawled list would be placed on top. Ben's handwriting was so awful, she usually had to ask him what he'd written. Sometimes he couldn't read it himself.

They were both exhausted by the time the paperwork was up to date, but they couldn't go to bed early, as the babies had to have their ten o'clock feed first. They each fed and changed one. The twins were beginning to sleep through until five, but even that came round long before Hilary felt ready for it.

She yawned. 'Life seems one long round of feeding and nappy-changing.'

Ben said, 'It won't last for ever, love. They'll grow up, and we'll get back to normal.'

Hilary sighed. Normal for her meant going back to work: that had been part of Ben's life plan to which she'd agreed. What she really wanted to do was write, but these days she couldn't find the energy. Her early enthusiasm for nursing was fading: it didn't mix well with family life. As theatre sister she needed her wits about her. It wasn't the sort of job she could cope with if the twins were keeping her awake half the night.

Their life plan had been blown apart by her getting pregnant three years early and then having twins. She'd laughed it off at the time and said she'd put them in a day nursery or find a childminder for them. Now she was beginning to think Ben's business plan was too ambitious. It wouldn't allow her to stay at home and look after her babies, yet to put the twins in a day nursery would wipe out most of what she earned. She and Ben discussed it endlessly He was adamant: his garden centre needed more investment.

'Mustn't spoil the ship for a ha'p'orth of tar,' he said.

Hilary felt stressed. The implication was clear: she needed to start earning again.

He said, 'What about your mother? She's talking of retiring, isn't she? Wouldn't she like to help?'

'She might want to, Ben, but talk about it is all she's done so far, and I can't ask her to take on the twins full time. It would be too much for her. Besides, we don't live close enough for her to do that.'

'We're too far away from the garden centre too. It would help if we lived closer.'

'Wouldn't it be lovely if the house we're going to build was ready? You could pop in and out all day, have your lunch with me and see much more of the twins.'

'That's years off, Hilly. We need to look for something nearby for the short term. I'll go round the estate agents tomorrow.'

'What d'you call short term?'

'Three or four years.'

'It would be even further for Mum to come and see us.'

Her mother came out to Bebington every week-end, usually arriving straight after lunch when she'd send Hilary up to her bed for an hour or two's rest. Today, Flora said, 'You look worried. Is everything all right?'

'Yes, except my maternity leave is coming to an end, and I don't think I can go back to working in the operating theatre.' She explained her diffi-culties. 'I'd never cope with the pace there as well as the twins.'

'There are plenty of nursing jobs which aren't so demanding. I suppose you'll say they aren't so interesting either?'

'They aren't, but that wouldn't worry me now. I just want to earn some money.'

'I had the same problem when you and Isobel were small. I wish I lived nearer – I could help you then.'

'Mum, you wouldn't want to be left alone with these two, day in day out. Before I get one fed, the other starts up.'

'Isobel was fairly demanding.'

'Think of having two like her to deal with. There's hardly any peace. I've been wondering if Ben's twin aunts would be willing to take them on. They've got four arms between them and they're used to babies.'

'Besotted with them, I'd say, and they're already retired.'

Hilary sighed. 'Yes, except that they don't drive and Borough Road is a long way for us to fetch them every morning and take them home at night.' She put it to Ben when he came home from work. 'We could ask them for tea, and see

120

how the land lies.'

'Perhaps even put it to them,' he said. 'They've always worked with babies; they'll be used to them. What about Saturday?'

'It depends when they can get off,' Hilary reminded him. 'You know what hospital hours are like.'

Ben rang his mother, and she told him his aunts were out shopping. He invited them all for supper on Saturday.

'You sound a bit down, Mum. Are you all right?'

'As right as I'll ever be,' she said.

'Do you good to come out,' he told her. 'I'll collect you all at six on Saturday. The babies? Yes, they're thriving, gaining weight hand over fist now.'

Hilary invited her mother too. Before the twins were born they'd frequently asked their family for meals, but this would be the first time since. As they fed one baby each, they discussed possible menus.

When the phone rang the following evening, Ben was changing Andy. He said, 'That'll be Aunt Prue to say she and Primmy can come on Saturday.'

Hilary had her hands free at that moment and picked up the phone.

'Prudence here.' Hilary hardly recognised the voice, it was so full of anguish.

'Has something happened?' She knew it must have done, and her heart began to pound.

'Ethel's ill, very ill. The ambulance has taken her to hospital.'

'Heavens! I'm so sorry.'

'She's asking for Ben. Is he there?'

'I'll put him on.'

He'd heard and had already come to the phone. She took Andy from his arms and fastened his nappy, keeping her ear attuned to what Ben was saying. Something dreadful must have happened to her mother-in-law. She sat on the settee hugging Andy to her.

At last Ben came to throw himself down beside her. 'I can't believe it!' He looked devastated. 'Apparently she found a lump in her breast about eighteen months ago and didn't say anything. Didn't breathe a word to Prue or Primmy.'

'She didn't go to the doctor?'

'No, nothing. She's been getting up every morning to make breakfast for them all, but this morning she collapsed. They're gutted that she kept it to herself, that she couldn't tell them.'

Hilary was shocked. 'That's the worst thing she could have done. You're going to see her?'

'Yes. She's been admitted to Clatterbridge. They haven't given her long.'

'Oh, Ben, how awful.' She put Andy hastily back in his crib and went to give Ben a hug. The baby bawled with fury.

'What a silly thing to do,' he railed against his mother. 'Prudence said it was as good as signing her own death warrant. I'd better go.'

'Give her my love.' Hilary's lip trembled as she picked her son up.

'Oh, by the way, none of them will be coming for supper on Saturday.'

Hilary was oppressed by the news. She'd found

her mother-in-law difficult to cope with; she was always whining about something. Nothing Hilary did pleased her, and she continually found fault with what the twin aunts did for her. Ethel Snow was quick to imply she was superior to the rest of them and didn't need to work but at the same time Hilary thought she was envious because they found satisfaction in their jobs. She was older than the twin aunts and therefore well past retirement age.

When Hilary was first married, she'd asked Ben about her. 'Did she ever work?'

'No, not after I was born.'

'Not even when you were growing up and in school?'

'No, she stayed home to look after me. She kept house for the aunts too, of course.'

'I see that as a luxury for you both. What did she do before she was married? After all, if she was thirty-six at the time she must have had a career of some sort.'

'She would never talk about that. I asked Aunt Prue and she said she worked in a shop in Grange Road.'

'Then she didn't feel superior,' Hilary said.

'No, they think that was just a front; that really she has an inferiority complex because they did so much better.'

'She seems unhappy. Rather bitter, really.'

'I don't think she can write,' Ben said. 'When I was called up for National Service, I wrote to her, but it was always the aunts who replied and sent me news of home. Sometimes they wrote down a sentence or two she'd dictated. They've always taken care of her.'

'I never realised...' Hilary tried to think. 'She can read, though. I've seen her read newspapers.'

'She pretends to read more than she does.'

'Ben! Was she ill or something when she was young, and couldn't go to school?'

'Prue says no, she just couldn't learn like the rest of us. She thinks she can write a little but her spelling's so bad she's ashamed and refuses to put pen to paper. She wouldn't do it, even to write to me.'

But Ethel adored Ben; he could do no wrong. Hilary had done her best to ignore her complaints and be as pleasant as possible to her. She'd always pitied her.

She spent a lonely evening, feeding and bathing her babies and putting them to bed. Ben rang shortly after ten, and she could tell he was very upset.

'Mum kept it to herself all these months, pretending she was well when she must have felt awful. Now, it's as though she's suddenly given up. They tell me they don't think she'll last until morning.'

'I am sorry, Ben.' No wonder she always looked unhappy.

'I'm going to run the aunts home. They're worn out, poor dears; they've been battling with this all day. Then I'll come back and sit with Mum. Is everything all right at home, Hilly?'

'Yes.'

'You go to bed then. I'll see you in the morning.'

Once in bed with the light out, Hilary wept a quiet tear for her mother-in-law. She'd had a sad life. The twins woke her just before six o'clock and she heard Ben pull up outside shortly afterwards.

'She died,' he said, 'about an hour ago. I don't think she knew I was there; she just seemed to lapse into unconsciousness. I've rung Aunt Prue.'

He was throwing his clothes off. Hilary could see tears rolling down his cheeks. She put Charlie in the middle of the bed and went to hold him.

'Oh God, Hilly. I wish she'd said something when she first found that lump. They might have saved her. She didn't have to die like this. She was only sixty-six.'

Ben was asleep before Hilary had fed the twins, and he stayed in bed all morning. She got dressed and set about her household chores thinking of her mother-in-law.

She'd always seemed depressed and a little withdrawn. Widowed after a short marriage, she'd been cared for by her sisters after that, though officially she'd kept house for them while they worked. Ethel did a little hoovering and dusting and some basic cooking. Her sisters paid the household bills, shopped, sewed, baked cakes and gardened in their off-duty time. They took her to church and to the pictures.

Ethel had never had friends except those her sisters or Ben took home. She'd never opened a book, though she'd had the wireless and recently she'd enjoyed television. Hilary thought it must have been an empty, rather dull life compared to most. She wondered why she'd found it impossible to learn to read and write like everybody else.

Flora went to the Borough Road house and

catered for the funeral tea for the family and a few friends from the hospital. Ethel's swift and untimely death cast a blight on Ben and his aunts that lasted for several months.

As the twins grew older, Hilary began taking them out and about. Ben bought her a second-hand car so she could take them to her mother's and bring them out to the garden centre occasionally. It was Hilary who put their present house on the market and found a cottage she liked in the village out beyond Eastham. It was terraced and about two hundred years old, with roses growing round the front door. Once it had had three bedrooms but at some stage the smallest one had been turned into a bathroom. Although they meant to stay there only two or three years, Ben liked it and told her she'd chosen well. Her mother loved it.

Ben was a bit switched off. It was Hilary who had to push ahead with the move but she knew it would make things easier for them all to be living close to the garden centre. She found it stimulating and enjoyed setting up her new home. She spurred Ben on to build the glasshouses he needed and to start thinking about drawing up plans for the house they'd eventually build there.

The twin aunts came round. Prudence announced, 'We're going to put the old life behind us and think of the future.'

'Very wise,' Ben said.

Primrose said, 'We've promised ourselves a really good holiday, but not this year. We need to get over Ethel first.'

'Did you ever meet Sister Mills?' Prue asked. 'We had her home to meet Ethel... No, well, she's a Canadian. Her home's in the Rockies and she's invited us to go and see her.'

'And stay a few months.'

'She says it isn't worth going all that way for a few weeks.'

Primrose said, 'And we've had enough of the Borough Road house. We were brought up there, for heaven's sake. It's time we moved.'

'It was handy for the Children's Hospital though, and Ethel liked it.'

'We'll never get over poor Ethel if we stay in that house. She's so bound up with everything that happened there.'

'Memories, you know.'

'We've decided we'd like to move further out of town and be near the garden centre too.'

Hilary helped them put their house on the market and drove them round to visit estate agents and look at what was on offer.

When she could, Flora wanted to accompany them. 'I love your cottage, Hilly. I'd like one like this myself. If you're all moving out here, I wouldn't mind coming too.'

In the meantime, Hilary put an extra bed into her second bedroom alongside the two cots, so that her mother could stay overnight.

'It's almost like living out in the country.' Flora was enthusiastic. 'I'd love to get a place here, but it would mean leaving Mavis on her own down in the North End.'

'You could ask her to live with you.'

'I already have, but she won't hear of it.'

Hilary thought it took Ben's aunts a long time to recover from their sister's death. They eventually bought an Edwardian detached house at the other end of the village. Hilary feared it would prove too large for them, but they decided to have the upstairs converted into a separate flat. As Flora was full of plans to sell her own house and move nearer as soon as she retired, they offered to rent it to her when it was ready.

'What I'd really like is your cottage,' she told Ben, 'and as you only intend to live in it for a year or two, I'll be happy to wait until it's free.'

'Excellent,' he told her. 'It'll save us putting it on the market.'

Isobel needed to go on working because they couldn't afford to pay the rent and buy essentials for the baby without her salary. She told everybody her baby was due in April.

'Could you manage to work on as far as the Christmas holidays?' Sebastian asked.

'Yes,' she told him. 'I want to go on working as long as I can.' She'd be seven and a half months gone by then, but so far it wasn't showing much. It was just too bad if she became elephantine by then.

When Sebastian visited his mother she took out the books she'd borrowed to read about pregnancy, wanting to learn as much as she could. It seemed a normal one lasted forty weeks, but it was not unusual for it to be a couple of weeks longer or shorter. She was hoping against hope that her baby would go over term. Forty-two weeks would take her into March.

Isobel had a letter from Hilary offering to send down her maternity clothes to save her having to buy her own. On the strength of Sebastian's legacy, Isobel told her not to bother. She'd never liked what Hilary wore; she thought her clothes frumpish.

They saw two or three houses every weekend. 'None are as smart as this flat,' Sebastian said.

'But far better than anything we could rent. Cheap private rented property is not only scarce but in poor repair.'

'We could put our names on the council list.'

Isobel was scornful. 'With an address like this, do you think we'd stand the faintest chance? Anyway, a flat isn't ideal with a baby. Much better if we could get a house with a small garden.'

'If we took out a mortgage, we could go upmarket a bit and get something decent while we're at it.'

Knowing how hard it was to rake up the rent for the flat, Isobel had to point out, 'We might have difficulty paying a mortgage. With the baby, it won't be so easy for me to work.'

'You'd want to though, wouldn't you? Work, I mean.'

'Ye-es.'

Isobel was longing for the security of owning their own house. Hilary had her own home and Isobel wanted her name on the deeds of one too. Eventually, they settled on a generously sized detached house in Wandsworth. It dated from the thirties and needed some refurbishing, but it had a garage and a good-sized garden. They'd have to have a mortgage.

'It's nothing we need worry about,' Seb said. 'It's a lot less than the rent we're paying here.'

It would take a few months to complete the legal formalities and though Sebastian thought they might be able to move in before the baby came, Isobel was afraid that was unlikely. She had a different timetable, and the prenatal classes she was now attending really drove that home.

They were both thrilled with the thought of having a house of their own. Isobel began to study the glossy magazines for furnishing ideas. They transferred their attention from estate agents to shops that sold furniture.

Sebastian said he knew nothing about babies. Isobel hoped he'd believe what she'd told him. Although she was heartily sick of being pregnant she wanted to stay that way for as long as possible.

Then Linda, a teacher who had worked with them for years, brought her baby to school to show round the staffroom. Naomi had made her promise to bring him. Alex was just five weeks old and they all billed and cooed over him, Seb included.

'I can't wait to be a father,' he said proudly.

'Was having him awful?' Isobel wanted to know.

'You'll forget all about that when you hold your baby in your arms,' Linda told her. Isobel had heard that many times before and was not convinced. 'My husband was allowed to stay with me when Alex was born and that helped.'

'He saw Alex being born?' Sebastian was immediately interested.

'Yes. The hospital is very go-ahead. They encourage all fathers to stay. They say it bonds them to their children.'

'I'd like that.' He was smiling. 'I'll certainly stay if I can.'

The Christmas holidays came round again. Isobel became a lady of leisure and was becoming increasingly anxious that the birth would come too soon and make Seb suspicious.

When she'd set out to ensnare him all those months ago, the important thing had been to have his financial support. Without him, she couldn't have stayed here at this stage in her pregnancy. She'd thought that to be his legal wife would banish her insecurity. It did no such thing. She was carrying a ton weight of guilt on her back, and knew she was doing her best to make things up to him.

She cooked the meals he liked and prepared as much of them as she could before he came home from school. She encouraged him to have sex when he wanted it though now she felt so fat and bloated that it was no fun for her. She even let him drive her Mini and turned a blind eye to his extravagant spending. She learned to smile when he bought her flowers she didn't want, not when the baby still needed a cot and a pram and a hundred other things. And all the time she wished she'd told him the truth in the beginning, so that she'd have nothing up ahead to fear.

Isobel was willing the days to pass, mentally ticking them off. To get past 10 February was going to be the hard part and she prayed daily that she would. She was now heavily pregnant and felt clumsy and awkward. Sebastian seemed to notice nothing unusual in that.

She loved being alone in the flat but nowadays Seb came home at lunch time to have a snack with her. 'And to make sure you're all right,' he said.

'Silly,' she'd scoffed. 'Nothing is going to happen for ages yet.'

But the fear niggled that perhaps it would. She was getting near her time but could come up with no plan to cover what she'd done.

At the end of January, they went together to see their solicitor and sign for their house. They would have vacant possession on 5 March.

'Just in time to get it all fixed up before the baby comes,' Sebastian gloated.

February the first came, a day Isobel wanted to be like all the others. When Sebastian went to school and she'd tidied up, she could feel a slight backache which was unusual, but understandable, surely? With so much weight sticking out in front she found it almost impossible to stand up straight.

She and Seb usually went together to do a week's shopping at a supermarket on Saturdays. On weekdays she often walked down to the nearest shops to buy a few indulgences. Today she didn't feel like it; she had no energy. She lay down on the settee instead and tried to read her library book. She couldn't settle to it; the mild backache persisted. She even felt a twinge or two that could be contractions but she ignored them. They surely couldn't mean anything significant? It was too soon; it would be the foulest of bad luck to give birth early. It would make things too obvious.

She tried to settle to her book but found it hard, which was strange because last night she'd thought it gripping, She must have dozed off because she only had time to put a bit of salad on two plates before Seb came home. She felt hung over and a bit out of sorts. After he'd gone back to school, she went back to the settee with the newspaper he'd brought home.

When she got up to make herself a cup of tea about three o'clock she felt a sudden tightening inside her that made her gasp. Within moments it melted away and she felt perfectly all right again. She told herself it was wind.

She'd drunk her tea when she felt it again, and this time she found herself wondering if this could be how things started. Oh, God! It couldn't be!

She felt hot. Her forehead was damp with sweat, but the sun was shining directly on to the settee. She stood up to open the window and felt suddenly dizzy. There was so much glass and the ground was so far below that she was afraid of falling. She grabbed the floor-length velvet curtain and hung on as her heart began to pound. By now she was really scared and was struggling to get her breath. What was happening to her? Isobel groped her way back to the settee to lie down. She felt overwhelmed with dread. Terror was crawling up her back, bringing her out in goose pimples.

The discomfort was over in a few minutes but left her feeling quite shaken. She dragged herself to the bathroom to splash cold water on her face and pull herself together. She'd panicked at the thought of giving birth but was afraid, very much afraid, it was imminent and earlier than she'd expected. The tightening she'd felt to start with was becoming a hard grip that was growing progressively stronger. By the time Sebastian came home from school, she was certain. She felt trapped, defeated and terrified.

'You're having pains?' He was shocked. 'It's too early, isn't it? Are you sure?'

Isobel was only too sure, and it was far, far too early. She had hoped it wouldn't happen for another month.

'I'd better ring the hospital.' He was back within moments. 'They told me to bring you in. Have you packed the case to go with you?'

'Not yet,' Isobel panted. She could feel herself falling apart.

CHAPTER EIGHT

As Seb drove her to the hospital, Isobel huddled in the seat until another pain came, then she had to stretch herself out. It took all her will not to cry out but she knew she moaned.

Sebastian was nervous. He kept shooting glances in her direction. 'Hold on. We're nearly there now.'

At the hospital, she was examined by a midwife and transferred straight away to the labour ward. The pains were terrible. It felt as though the baby was splitting her in two. Isobel was grabbing for

Seb's hand every time she felt another pain coming.

'Hang on to me,' he said and she squeezed him so hard she heard his gasp of pain.

'Nothing to what I'm feeling,' she said grimly, pushing aside the gas and air mask. It was making her head spin but doing nothing for the pain. She could feel sweat running down her face. Labour seemed to have been going on for hours.

'I want you to push with the next pain,' the midwife said firmly. She was a formidable middle-aged woman wearing a badge with the name Sister Reeve pinned to her uniform.

'It's coming, it's coming,' Isobel screamed, her hand flailing round in search of the mask.

'Right, a good hard push this time. Take a deep breath. Come on now, push.'

Isobel let out a wail caused as much by irritation at the midwife as by the pain. Nothing would induce her to go through this again. It was absolutely dreadful.

'It'll soon be over now,' Sebastian said in soothing tones but it was going on and on and on. Tears were running down her face.

'You're doing well, Mrs Broadbent, nearly there now.' The smelly mask was clamped over her nose and mouth again. 'Take another deep breath through this.'

Isobel wanted to scream at her. She was talking down to her, treating her like a child, but another pain was coming. She couldn't stand much more. She clenched her teeth and pushed.

'The head's coming.' Isobel could sense the change in the midwife's manner. She was more

135

alert; it was all going to happen now. She felt her flesh being ripped apart. It was the most dreadful sensation.

'The head's out.' Sebastian sounded excited.

'It'll all be here with the next pain – we're just waiting for the shoulders. Here it comes.'

Isobel felt it slide out and lay back feeling totally spent.

'It's a girl.' Isobel heard her first cry as the midwife wrapped her in a bath towel and lifted her up.

Seb said, 'Is she all right?'

'Yes, she's lovely, a perfect specimen.'

He'd come forward to see more and leaned over to kiss Isobel. 'To see my daughter born,' he sounded choked, 'was the most moving thing ever.' She could see his face working and tears on his cheeks. The baby was crying lustily. She saw Seb swallow and try to pull himself together. He said to the midwife, 'I thought, being so premature, the baby would have problems. Don't they usually have to be put in an incubator?'

She laughed. 'Not this one, Dad. She may be two weeks early on dates but two weeks makes little difference. She looks a healthy weight, about seven pounds, I'd say. I'll put her on the scales in a minute. Here you are, Mum.' The baby landed in Isobel's arms. 'You can say hello to her now.'

Isobel cringed. She'd been afraid of Sebastian's hearing all this from the moment she knew he'd be with her. She studied the red and crumpled face as the little mouth opened in another roar of protest.

Sebastian said, 'Are you sure? About the dates?'

His voice sounded strangled.

'Yes.' Sister Reeve was consulting a file. 'Expected date of arrival was the tenth of February. She's here on the first. It's not unusual. A relief to you, Mum, isn't it, to have it all over?'

Isobel was appalled to hear her spell out the dates and buried her face in the pillow. This could ruin everything for her. She had to change the subject before there were more revelations. She managed, 'She looks like Winston Churchill.'

'They all do at this stage.' The midwife was filling in forms. 'Time of birth eighteen twenty-nine. What are you going to call her?'

There was a deathly pause. Isobel's mouth had completely dried out. She couldn't speak.

'Sophie Jane,' Sebastian answered dully.

'That's nice.' Name tabs were being written out. One was snapped on Sophie's ankle and the other on her wrist. 'Now let's have her on the scales.'

The baby was lifted away. Sebastian was sitting back white-faced and silent. His chin seemed to have fallen. Isobel felt as though the bottom had dropped out of her world. Sister Reeve had informed him very clearly that she'd lied to him.

'Not a bad guess, she's seven pounds nine ounces. A lovely strong healthy baby.' She was back in Isobel's arms. 'Right, Mum, I'll get you a cup of tea now. I bet you've never wanted one more.'

Sister Reeve was gone and Seb remained silent as the minutes ticked away. Isobel felt hot tears roll down her cheeks.

Husbands and partners were allowed to visit the maternity wards for an hour every evening but Isobel didn't see Sebastian again for forty-eight hours after the birth. It confirmed her worst fears and told her things would never be the same between them again. She lived in dread that he'd want no more to do with her.

She couldn't rest, couldn't think straight and had no idea what she was going to do. She had difficulty getting to sleep at night and when she did was plagued by half-remembered nightmares. She looked at Sophie and thought of Rupes. How he'd have welcomed her birth, how different everything would have been. Isobel was acquainted with some of the other new mothers; they'd met at the antenatal classes. She knew they were sorry for her because she spent the visiting hour alone. She told them her husband was a travelling salesman to explain it.

They all admired Sophie. She had rounded limbs and the prettiest of faces, but she cried more than most. Isobel felt more and more stressed as time went on. When finally she saw Sebastian coming up the ward he looked as though he hadn't slept in all that time. He made no attempt to kiss her and hardly glanced at the baby now swinging in a plastic cradle at the end of her bed. He'd always been very generous with gifts of flowers and chocolate but he had brought her nothing.

'Are you all right?' she asked when he pulled out a chair by her bed.

'No, Izzy, don't pretend you don't know what's bothering me.' She could feel his anger, tightly controlled, battened down inside him. 'This isn't

138

my baby, is it? You tried to foist her on me.'

It was the question Isobel was expecting. This scene had been going round and round in her head since Sophie had been born, and she'd come up with no logical explanation to smooth it over. Impossible to tell him the truth because if he knew it would surely make things worse. She was thankful she and Rupert had kept their relationship quiet. She couldn't admit to any of it.

'It's yours,' she said. 'Please don't turn against us. We need you.'

Sebastian's mouth twisted with impatience. He looked round and deliberately lowered his voice.

'Don't keep saying that. Mathematics was never my strong point, but I can add up the number of weeks since we first slept together and it isn't possible.'

'It is, it has to be. Some people have shorter pregnancies...'

'I'm not a fool. In the last two days I've consulted half a dozen books in the library and I know that medically it isn't. It's not quite thirty weeks since you took me to your flat for the first time. If she were my child, Sophie would be a much lighter and less mature baby. She might even be struggling to survive, but, as Sister Reeve pointed out, she's a healthy full-term baby.'

Isobel felt sick with horror. What was he planning to do? She made herself ask, 'We'll be able to come home tomorrow, all being well. Will you come and fetch us?'

He stared down at her, his cheeks flushing crimson. 'What do you think I'll do? Say no, tell you to take a taxi? Put you out of house and home with a newborn baby?'

'It's my apartment.'

'Izzy, I'm not that sort of an ogre. Of course I'll come for you.'

Isobel found the first few days at home traumatic. For the first time, Sebastian moved out of the bed they'd shared and went to the spare bedroom. He spoke to Isobel only when he had to.

She didn't know how to cope with the baby or Sebastian's stony withdrawal from her. Sophie cried a lot and kept her awake at night. Her milk went and she put the baby on the bottle hoping that would solve the problem. It gave her more work to do and she resented it. She was near despair and found herself looking into the tiny face trying to see some resemblance to Rupert. It was only the thought that Sophie was his daughter that kept her feeding her and changing her napkins.

She lay awake in the nights blaming the baby for causing Rupert's death and ruining her relationship with Sebastian.

The move to the new house was on her before she felt ready. She half expected Sebastian to say he wanted her to stay here and that he planned to move away by himself. When she tried to discuss it, he said impatiently, 'There won't be much for you to do. All our furniture will be delivered from the shop; it's just a matter of putting your books and ornaments out.'

Isobel was relieved. It seemed he expected her and Sophie to move too. She packed her clothes and personal possessions into tea chests and bundled together the baby's things. She'd looked forward to setting up a new home but with the baby she had neither the time nor the energy to do much to it and felt she spent ages living amongst packing cases and cardboard boxes.

When Sebastian came home he sat in his new armchair either correcting school books or reading the newspaper. He hardly seemed to notice Isobel and totally ignored the baby. He never offered help of any sort.

Isobel blamed herself for this and apologised. She was feeling fraught and upset, but did her best to stay calm, to straighten out the house and put a hot meal on the table every evening. She'd thought Sebastian an easygoing person, not one to harbour a grudge; she hoped he'd eventually recover. He'd forgiven Rose, his first wife, and she hoped he'd forgive her. Sophie was two months old when he came home one evening with a bottle of wine.

'We can't go on like this,' he said. 'I've never felt so miserable in all my life. There's no point in tormenting ourselves. Why don't we agree to make the best of it?'

Isobel sighed with relief. She felt she'd been sent to Coventry. 'I'm more than ready to do that.'

She saw him smile rather shamefacedly. 'I do love you, Izzy.'

She made herself answer, 'And I love you.' But she was no longer sure that that was the truth. With such a long stand-off, she'd felt resentment for Sebastian building up. She couldn't take any more of his moodiness.

He said, 'Why don't we start afresh, see if we can make a go of it?'

He moved back into her bed, but things were never the same again.

Isobel wasn't happy. Time and time again Sebastian asked the same question. 'Who was Sophie's father?'

'You are,' she kept telling him. 'She takes after you, for heaven's sake. Just look at her eyes, they're dark green like yours.' Rupes had had green eyes too. 'All my family have blue eyes. Sophie didn't get those from me.' In every other way, the baby did resemble her.

One day she took Sophie into the staffroom to show her off. Naomi told her Seb had been asking round if Isobel had had a previous boyfriend.

'I told him you were positively nunlike until you took up with him. We all thought you'd end up like Miss Molyneaux. You didn't even seem interested in men.'

The house they'd bought was proving expensive. It was bigger than they needed and although Sebastian had planned to work on it himself, he had neither the interest nor the skill. They had to pay contractors to come in to paint it and keep the basic systems working. The new bathrooms and kitchen Isobel had planned were never fitted. They'd spent too much on furniture and carpets and it had been a big mistake to take out any mortgage.

Isobel was comforted to know her name was on the deeds and that she owned half of it. But money troubles continued to bog them down. Seb's salary couldn't be stretched to cover all their needs.

Isobel's growing difficulties with Seb made her cling to her baby. It took weeks for her to feel the first tug of mother love, but once she had she wanted to stay at home and look after her. Sophie was Rupes's child. He'd have welcomed her into the world, and she felt she'd let him down because she hadn't wanted her.

Sebastian tried to ignore the baby, but Sophie wouldn't let him. She woke him up several times each night by yelling, making him hump over in bed and take all the bedclothes off Isobel. She wasn't good at soothing babies and they both lost a lot of sleep, which made them grumpy in the mornings.

He kept telling Isobel that the only way to halt their growing overdraft was for her to return to work and they'd not have a decent life unless she did. Isobel gave up fighting him on that, and when Sophie was four months old she put her in a day nursery. It made her feel guilty, because she was afraid her baby was receiving the minimum of care and affection.

To return to the classroom made her feel more normal, but they couldn't go back to their old life. No longer could Sebastian take her out for meals and jaunts up to the West End. Isobel had to stay in to look after the baby. Sophie had to be bathed and fed and there were nappies to wash.

Hilary didn't go back to work until her twins were nearly eighteen months old. That pleased her, but she'd promised Ben that eventually she would. Her mother had retired, sold her house and moved into the flat above Ben's aunts. All three had become good friends. It was Prudence who announced it would be a threesome taking over the care of the twins and that they were now ready to start.

Hilary had no difficulty finding herself a job with the Cavendish Scott organisation that ran nursing and care homes for the elderly. They had a chain of fifteen in the Merseyside region. It wasn't the most exciting of nursing jobs, but mostly she worked at a home that was only two miles away from the cottage. It was much less demanding than working in a hospital operating theatre, but with the twins and the need to help in the garden centre she felt it would suit her better.

On the first few mornings, she had to tear herself away from her sons. To wave goodbye to Primmy and Prue, each nursing one of her boys, cut her to the quick.

She adored her babies. They were no more alike than normal brothers, but both had inherited Ben's curly hair. Andy's was just one shade darker than flaxen and he was a fraction taller and heavier than Charlie. They were both sturdily built and had cherubic faces. Ben was totally besotted with them.

She had to tell herself they'd be well cared for and she'd have to get used to it if she wanted to help Ben get their life plan back on track.

Isobel received regular letters from her mother urging her to bring her family up for a few days, so Flora might meet her new granddaughter and get to know her son-in-law better. Isobel put it off as long as she could, pleading all sorts of difficulties: Sophie was teething, she wasn't well, Isobel was trying to get her into a routine, or she lacked time and energy. She finally agreed to drive up to Merseyside during the Christmas holidays when Sophie was nearly a year old. All along, Sebastian had refused to go.

It had been a very difficult year. Isobel felt exhausted but thought a break from Seb might do both of them good. Mum fixed her up with a makeshift cot in the rooms she rented from the twin aunts. Everybody billed and cooed over Sophie, who was a very pretty child and could already walk and say a few words. They asked interminable questions about Sebastian and regretted that he hadn't come too.

Hilary took a day off work and invited Isobel and Mum to spend it at her cottage. She seemed very happy with her lot in life, her children, her husband, and the business they were building. Isobel saw that as her own circumstances had worsened, her sister's had improved. Hilary was very keen to see Sophie and compare her to the twins. At eighteen months they were a delightful pair of bright-eyed scallywags who were rarely still.

In the soporific atmosphere after a large lunch, all the children fell into a light doze. Hilary sat nursing her twins, one in each arm. She'd become adept at managing both at once.

'Do you ever wonder how your baby will turn out?' she asked. 'I hold my pair and wonder if they'll grow up to be surgeons or pilots or barristers or what.'

'You're a surprisingly ambitious mother,' Isobel said.

'Of course I am. I want them to be high achievers who make their mark on the world. Don't you have hopes for Sophie like that?'

Isobel looked down on the face of her sleeping daughter and thought of what she herself most wanted. 'I hope she'll find a husband who loves her and have a happy and contented life,' she said.

Hilary was delighted with the progress Ben was making with his business. She enjoyed driving down the road past it to see the entrance gate with its brightly painted sign and the name Oak Tree Garden Centre. She'd count the cars in the car park: they represented customers. Occasionally she drove in to see what improvements he'd made.

Ben had grouped his business buildings together. Potting shed, compost mixing area, cold frames and the huge glasshouses in which he was growing indoor and tropical plants were linked on an internal road system. They were both very pleased with the specially designed shop. The nursery beds stretched away on one side and the container beds on the other. He found it economical to plant directly into containers. He now had twelve of his acres growing different varieties of temperate plants.

'It's taken me a few years, but it's all here now,' Ben gloated. He was bursting with plans for the future and couldn't stop talking about them to Hilary or anybody else who'd listen. 'I need to expand as quickly as possible and increase the variety of what I have on offer.'

Ben had started planting up attractive bowls

with flowering bulbs and perennials. 'I want to tap into the gift market. Cut flowers die so soon,' he explained. 'My bowls will be wrapped in cellophane and tied with ribbons and look equally luxurious but they'll flower for weeks and months and many will come again the following year.'

Hilary knew he'd planted out several large beds of tree seedlings: dwarf varieties of fruit trees and decorative flowering trees, such as magnolia and flowering cherry. He was specialising in roses and was growing a wide variety of them, but he also had shrubs of many sorts.

When he'd first started he'd had to buy established trees of two or three years, some of which he'd planted in attractive tubs. Now he was able to plant up his own stock. He had bedding plants of all descriptions, vegetables as well as flowers, and in addition he sold seeds.

Ben's only full-time employee was a lad from the village who was reputed to be not very bright. As a schoolboy, Rory Grant had hung about the garden centre watching Ben work. One day, when Ben was forking over a piece of land that had previously been rotovated, he said he'd felt Rory's gaze on him and he'd offered him a smaller fork and invited him to help. Ben was the sort of person who enjoyed chatting to everybody, so he'd told Rory what he hoped to grow there.

The lad had come back the next day wanting to do more, and soon he was spending most of his school holidays with Ben, who began to pay him for what he did. The year Rory left school, it was very difficult for any school leaver to get a job.

His mother came into the shop and pleaded with Ben to give him work.

'He's a good lad and he's taken to you,' she'd said, 'though mostly he's too shy to talk to people.'

Rory had been working in the garden centre for the last three years. Ben always had to explain exactly what he wanted him to do, and show him if he hadn't done it before, but once he'd grasped what was needed he worked hard and well. He was nineteen now, a broad-shouldered, well-built lad, but he was still shy and rarely spoke to Hilary. He was no good in the shop – he couldn't deal with customers and adding up bills scared him – but he was devoted to Ben and did a lot of the heavy work. Ben counted Rory a big asset.

To run the shop, Ben relied on several women he employed part time. For them, it was a means of earning pin money. Flora worked there at weekends and in busy periods, but Hilary had not. Ben said she had enough to do with her full-time job, the house and the children, and she needed to spend her off-duty time with them.

Hilary had paced over the site where their new house would be built many times. That was to be Ben's next big project. She was excited at the thought and was seeking out books of house designs with something rather grand in mind.

She knew Ben was trying to be sensible. 'It would be best to build a modest home to start with,' he said. 'Something we can extend later.'

Hilary longed for a big house. They were quite cramped in their cottage. 'Why not build exactly what we want now?' she breathed, jabbing her finger at her book of house plans. 'It'll be cheaper

148

in the long run and we'll have our dream home.'

Ben was pulling a face. 'It would mean a big mortgage on top of what we already have on the business. Together they'd be enormous. A smaller house now...'

'Ben, the mortgage would still be big. I am working,' Hilary protested. 'To have a really nice house would make it all seem worth while.'

'I can't hold out against you,' he said reluctantly. 'Perhaps if we stay in our present cottage for another year... We must ask your mother if she minds waiting a bit longer for it.'

'We need to organise lives of our own,' Prudence kept telling Flora. 'The twins will grow up and go to school and we'll not be needed any more. We don't want to be left sitting at home twiddling our thumbs, do we?'

Flora knew that like herself they'd left behind their old routines and their acquaintances. Their friends were invited to see their new house and they enjoyed entertaining. Flora was always welcome at these teas and suppers.

They joined in village life, took Flora to church and threw themselves into fundraising ideas, baking cakes and stitching aprons for bazaars. It was Primrose who discovered there was a bridge club in the village. She and Prue had been playing for years.

'I wish I could play,' Flora said.

'We'll teach you. You'll soon pick it up.'

Flora wasn't so sure she would, but they loaned her a book setting out the rules and sat down with her and played a few trial rubbers. When they counted her good enough, they took her with them.

It took place in the church hall on Tuesday afternoons, which conveniently was one of the two afternoons when the twins attended a nursery class held in some converted stables nearby to get used to being with other children.

The bridge club usually attracted enough players to make up three or four tables. There were one or two men but they were vastly outnumbered. As Primmy pointed out, it reflected the fact that women usually outlive their menfolk.

Flora was nervous about her ability at first but after a month or so she found she could play as well as any of them. It was all very relaxed and friendly. If anybody made a mistake it was overlooked, and there were no recriminations.

'It's just a game,' Primmy said, and Flora enjoyed it. She felt they were opening new windows for her.

For the whole family, the late nineteen sixties were years of consolidation. Once Flora had been suspicious of Ben. No, that wasn't quite the right word. She'd been wary of him because he'd suddenly changed his mind about Isobel and she was a little afraid he might do the same with Hilary. But in seven years of marriage, he'd proved himself a good husband and father. Flora spent a lot of time with the family and knew they treated each other with great affection. She'd seen Ben look at Hilly with love in his eyes, and she didn't doubt they were both happy.

Also, she admired the way Ben ran his business. He weighed up and discussed every move he made with Hilly, and was still full of enthusiasm. It was taking off and they were all pleased with its progress.

The twins were thriving. They walked and talked at an early age. Flora and the aunts took them out and about, played with them, read to them and taught them nursery rhymes. They had acres of field to kick their balls about and were very healthy.

'They're very bright.' Hilary was proud of them. 'They pick up on everything. We should count ourselves and them lucky, that they'll be going into full-time school when they're only just turned four. It'll give them a good start.'

Flora was pleased with her flat. The kitchen and bathroom were newly fitted. The rooms were large and the ceilings high, and she had plenty of space for all her furniture. She still invited Mavis for dinner on Sundays. Hilary and Ben regularly asked them and the twin aunts for afternoon tea. Today, they walked up through the village together.

'Very good of you to ask us all,' Prudence told Hilary. 'Quite a squash to get us all inside your little cottage. I expect you'll be pleased to get a bigger house?'

Ben said, 'We wanted to talk to you all about that.'

Hilary said, 'We were wondering, Mum, if you'd mind waiting longer for vacant possession of this place.' She explained why.

'We love having you in our house,' Prue told Flora.

'Stay as long as you like, the longer the better,' Primmy said.

'Of course I'll wait,' Flora told Hilary and Ben. 'I'm happy where I am.'

Flora was content with her new circumstances and was grateful to Primmy and Prue. They'd always had full lives and meant to carry on doing so now they'd retired. They all loved looking after the babies. Being a team of three meant that none of them felt overworked and they had time and energy for other things.

When the time came to go home, they walked Mavis to the bus and then Flora strolled home with Primrose and Prue. It was a lovely summer evening, the last rays of the setting sun lighting up the heavy foliage on the trees.

Primmy was unlocking her front door when they heard the telephone beginning to ring. Prue scudded inside to answer it.

'It's for you,' she said, handing it to Flora.

'Hello, Mum.' Isobel sounded falsely bright. 'I was thinking of coming up to see you next week. Is that all right?'

'That would be lovely, dear. I'll look forward to it.'

'It'll be all right to bring Sophie? You can fix up a bed for her?'

'Of course, do bring her. It'll be a makeshift cot, but we'll manage.'

Flora put the phone down and called to Prue, who was in the kitchen, that her daughter would be coming up for a couple of nights.

Prue came to the door. 'That'll be nice for you. The little one's coming too?'

'You don't mind?' Sophie had had a rather noisy temper tantrum on her last visit.

'No, dear. We hardly heard her. This house is very solidly built. She's such a pretty little girl.'

Flora went up to her own rooms thinking of Isobel. Her visits never seemed satisfactory; they were no longer at ease with each other, and they had little in common any more. Isobel brought Sophie but never her husband. Flora didn't think she was happy with him and wondered if she still hankered after Ben.

She was fond of Ben and Hilary was happy with him, he was an attentive husband and a good father to the boys, but Isobel had split herself off and gone her own way and Flora blamed him for that. All the same, she couldn't see Isobel being as supportive to his business as Hilary was.

She was always glad to hear of a proposed visit and threw herself wholeheartedly into preparations for it. There was shopping to do, cakes to bake and beds to arrange.

When the day of Isobel's arrival came, she went to Liverpool to meet her off the train, hoping she'd find her more content with her lot. She knew the moment she saw her coming along the platform towards her that she was not.

Isobel looked stressed and tired. She was carrying a suitcase in one hand and towing her toddler impatiently and almost pulling her off her feet with the other.

When she looked up, Flora waved and saw her smile and relax. She felt sorry for her. 'Lovely to see you,' she said warmly and kissed her. 'You too, Sophie,' she added and bent to kiss her too.

The child turned her face away.

Flora's spirits sank. She ought to try to talk to Isobel, gain her confidence. See if there was anything she could do to help.

'How are you both?' she asked brightly, knowing this was how she usually reacted. It wasn't the best way.

Isobel kept up a steady chatter on the train going under the river to Birkenhead and while they waited for the bus. The school where she worked, Sophie's progress, Hilary's children. She didn't mention Ben or her husband, and it was all rather superficial.

The gloss Isobel had acquired when she'd first gone to London had faded. Her hair, which she used to have cut into the latest style by a good hairdresser and coloured golden blonde, had now reverted to nature. In the summer holidays it could be corn-coloured and in winter a pale dun shade. She'd let it grow and now wore it tied back in a severe ponytail. She wasn't taking the old interest in clothes, either. She looked dispirited and unhappy.

CHAPTER NINE

In the early seventies, Hilary was thrilled to see the foundations for their new home being put in. Ben had asked an architect to design it. He'd turned it sideways to the main road and placed the double garage between the road and the house to cut out the noise. It was also set some way away from the business premises to give privacy. It was to be a spacious five-bedroomed house, detached on a large plot and built of rosy pink bricks. The whole family watched the building take shape with avid interest.

Hilary had arranged that the twins should attend the village primary school which was within easy walking distance. To make the journey safer for them, Ben had had a gate put in the back fence of his premises, so they wouldn't have to go near the main road. Hilary knew that for the first few years she'd need help from her mother and Ben's aunts to take the twins to school and meet them coming out, but having them in full-time school would make it easier for them all.

On the first day of term, Hilary took a day off work to take them. She set off holding one with each hand; they were skipping with excitement and could hardly wait to get there. Some of the other children starting that day had been to the same nursery class and they greeted each other with glee. Hilary knew some of the other mothers. One, Jane Johnson, was a nurse working in the same care home.

'Isn't it nice to see them all so keen to go to school?' Jane smiled. 'Paul can't wait.'

Hilary was hopeful that she'd have more time for writing now. All that had lapsed while the twins were small.

For Isobel, the seventies proved difficult too. She and Sebastian had never been able to get back to the friendly relationship they'd had when he first moved into her apartment, though there were times when she thought they might.

Sophie had grown into a very pretty little girl. Seb liked children and was used to dealing with them. At ten months of age, she'd begun crawling across the room to pull herself to her feet on his trouser legs. She would laugh up into his face and try to play peekaboo with him. The first word with meaning she spoke was Dadda, and from that moment she'd captivated Sebastian.

By two years of age she had a wide vocabulary and he was Daddy. She'd climb on to his knee and throw her arms round him. Sometimes she'd rub noses with him and sometimes pull his hair. Now he was giving her all his attention. He discovered how quickly she could grasp everything he told her, and started teaching her numbers and letters.

'She's a delight to teach,' he chortled to Isobel. Before Sophie was four she could read the first primers and do simple arithmetic.

Sebastian said, 'She makes me realise how much harder the children in my class have to work to get anywhere. For Sophie it's all fun and she romps through it.'

Because she wasn't getting on well with Seb, Isobel knew she turned to Sophie for comfort and realised he was doing the same. It bothered her that they both made so much of the child and were granting her every whim. Was she being spoiled? There were certainly times when it was impossible to do what she wanted. Last night after her bath, for instance, she'd wanted Daddy to take her out to buy crayons instead of going to bed, and when he'd insisted on opening a book to read her a bedtime story, she'd thrown a raging tantrum.

But Sophie had won Seb over; he was showing her fatherly affection while between him and Isobel there was an uneasy truce that could break down to bitter recriminations without any warning. He no longer trusted her, and Isobel couldn't blame him. She knew it was her own fault. It became habit to argue out every point and it seemed they couldn't change. Isobel told him forcibly that it coloured everything, and discontent was souring them.

They both made an effort not to let their deteriorating relationship show at school but it did, and it soon became common knowledge in the staffroom. She sensed the other teachers sided with Sebastian rather than with her, and wanted to get away from them.

She put up with it for another year and then decided it might help if she moved to a different school. She found herself another job and, though moving was stressful, eventually settled in and found it a help to be away from Sebastian for a large part of the day. When Sophie was due to start school, Seb wanted her to enrol at the one where he worked. Isobel insisted she attend hers so she would take Sophie with her every day. That resulted in three days of noisy quarrels and a stand-off lasting weeks.

On top of that, the row about who had fathered Sophie resurfaced time and time again. Isobel had steeled herself never to admit anything, but she could sense Seb's mounting frustration that she wouldn't. She was swearing black was white when they both knew it wasn't.

'Every day,' Ben said, 'there's bad news about the country's economic difficulties. Inflation is taking off and house prices are rising with it. I'm worried this will affect us.'

There was trouble with the trade unions as wages and prices leapfrogged each other at a pace hitherto unknown.

'It's the interest rate rises that bother me,' Hilary groaned. It wasn't long before they rose to a phenomenal height which made their mortgage cripplingly expensive. In addition to this, Hilary could see Ben's profit was being squeezed by the high price of oil, which he used to heat his glass-houses.

In the following months conditions worsened as Britain nosedived into recession. There were regular electricity cuts and a petrol shortage, with little oil available for heating. Ben's flowers and plants were late blooming and therefore late coming on the market, but so were those of other nurseries. Another problem they shared was that customers were few and far between. Flowers and plants had become a luxury people couldn't afford. Ben responded by changing to more temperate plants.

House prices doubled in a year and estate agents had nothing to sell. The miners came out on strike for more money and so did almost every other trade, as well as the nurses and teachers. Industry was shedding labour as recession gripped tighter. Every day companies were going into liquidation and mortgages were being foreclosed.

Ben laid off the part-time ladies who worked in his shop. Flora and his twin aunts volunteered to work for nothing.

'I'd like to stop the work on our new house,' he said, 'but the contracts were all drawn up and work started before we realised the economy was in such a bad state.' There would be penalties if they stopped now. Both he and Hilary feared for their business.

'At least I'm still working,' Hilary said. With her salary they thought they could survive, just.

It was during this time it gradually dawned on her that she was pregnant again. It came as a shock, and to make matters worse she knew it was her own fault. She'd had a bout of cystitis and should have remembered that some antibiotics could reduce the efficacy of the pill.

'Not to worry,' Ben said. She knew he wasn't pleased about it either, but was making light of it so as not to upset her. 'I quite fancy a daughter. It would balance out the family.'

At one time Hilary had quite fancied a daughter too, but not now, not at this moment when her salary was essential to support the mortgage.

'It could be twins again,' she groaned, coming out in a sweat at the very thought. 'We can't afford this.' It was a pregnancy she didn't want. At the very best, it meant another four or five years with a baby needing full-time care.

Having had a Caesarean section with the twins, Hilary knew it was standard practice to advise another as normal labour could bring more problems. She wasn't too happy about that either but there was nothing she could do about it.

Hilary had to grit her teeth and carry on. One of the things she enjoyed most in her day was bathing her twins and putting them to bed. She read them bedtime stories and always they wanted more. Occasionally, she had to work an evening shift, but she did her best to be home with them in the evenings.

Their school reports in their first year were not brilliant. Hilary was disappointed that they didn't do better.

Ben said, 'They're like me, not academic. They prefer to kick a ball about. Don't worry, they'll probably turn out all right.'

She smiled. 'If they turn out like you, then yes, they will.'

Then the birth of the new baby was on her. Ben took her to Clatterbridge Hospital. When she woke from the anaesthetic he was beside her.

'Definitely only one baby this time,' he told her. 'Another boy.'

Hilary felt a pang of disappointment.

'I've given his name as James. That's what we agreed, isn't it?'

'Jamie,' Hilary said.

'He weighed eight pounds; this one's big and strong.'

'I want to see him.'

'I'll go and tell the nurse.'

When the nurse put the child in her arms, round blue eyes stared up at Hilary. She murmured, 'He's absolutely beautiful.'

As soon as she took Jamie home, Primmy and Prue came round, wanting to cuddle him, change him, bath him or help in any way they could. They even bickered between themselves as to which of them should lift him from his crib.

'My turn first,' Prue insisted, parting his shawl to see his rounded limbs better. Hilary thought Primmy the more assertive of the twins; usually she led and Prue followed, but this time she stood back. Prue's face seemed to lose years of her age as she beamed down love on her great-nephew.

'You'd have made a marvellous mother,' Hilary told her. Prue lifted agonised eyes to meet hers. Hilary was alarmed to see them fill with tears.

'You'd better tell her,' Primrose said softly.

Prue snuffled. 'I did have a baby boy,' she choked. 'But he didn't live. He'd have been forty-one this year. Older than you.'

To Hilary it seemed the atmosphere was suddenly charged with emotion.

Primrose said, 'Prue was married, you see.'

'But it didn't work out.' Prue sounded sad.

Hilary asked softly, 'Was he killed in the war like my father and Ben's?'

'No, I left him. He was a good man but he was coming between me and Primmy.'

Primmy said, 'She couldn't forsake all others and keep only unto him. Twins are like that.'

'Bound together hand and foot,' Prue agreed. 'There's no way we can be parted.'

'It's as though we're more one person than two.'

'I couldn't manage without Primmy, not even

for a husband and children.'

Hilary sat in silent thought for a moment. 'What about my twins? Will they be like that?'

Primrose spread open her hands. 'We don't know.'

Hilary knew her boys were close and seldom apart, but that Charlie called Roger Stott his friend, while Andy had Paul and Polly Johnson. Hilary counted a spouse and children a major blessing in life, and hoped they'd feel the same when they grew up.

'They aren't twins like us, from the same egg,' Prudence said. Her tone implied she didn't consider them to be real twins. 'In many ways it's wonderful to be a twin and always have a companion, but I've never learned to stand on my own feet.'

'We really need each other,' Primmy said. 'Sometimes I wonder if we aren't too close.'

Before Hilary's maternity leave was over, her new house was finished and ready to move into. She was delighted with it and had a lovely time choosing new furniture. She tried not to let the mammoth mortgage repayments take any of the shine away.

Ben was thrilled too and said, 'We must have a housewarming party for the family.'

When they took Aunt Mavis round it, her mouth opened with surprise. 'You've been very extravagant,' she told them. 'A house half this size would be more than adequate. Easier for you to clean, too.'

Flora was keen to move into their cottage but

she had it repainted inside and out first. She paid Hilary and Ben with the cash from the sale of her house in Birkenhead, which gave their finances a boost.

Hilary found Jamie was very little trouble. He was easy to feed and settle and slept solidly through the night almost from the beginning. She was able to put his carrycot in the back of her car and get out and about. She helped her mother move into the cottage and could see she was very proud of her new home. She was even finding time to write and had sold two articles of friendly advice to the elderly, one on diet and one on exercise and keeping warm in winter.

When the time came for her to return to work, the older members of the family rallied round to look after Jamie. Hilary felt she was able to go back with very little fuss.

It was several years before the country pulled out of recession, but by 1976 things were back on course for Ben; he was making a profit from his business and they were managing to pay the mortgage.

Hilary was now more worried about the twins. Their school reports had not improved. Since their third year in school, their teachers had been asking her to hear them read every day, and were lending her books of the right standard.

Even worse, the boys were upset about it too. They tried and tried and tried; they wanted above everything to keep up with their classmates. When they'd started school they'd been happy outgoing children, keen to experience anything. Now they were anxious and losing confidence. Charlie in particular had bitten his fingernails down to the quick and had a too-rapid blink rate. Even Flora described him as nervous.

When they were tots, Hilary had taught them nursery rhymes and read them bedtime stories, and once they'd started at the nursery class she tried to teach them the alphabet and help them with their reading. She found it frustrating that they were so slow to learn and couldn't understand why, because they were bright in other ways. And they worked so hard at it.

Hilary had thought at first it was because they were twins. She'd read that twins had a more difficult start in life than a singleton. They'd been squashed in the womb and had had to share the available nourishment. They'd been precipitated into the world five weeks early, though they'd had good birth weights for twins.

Hilary felt her efforts had not helped them much and knew now it would be a difficult problem to overcome. She usually heard them read when she was putting them to bed, before she read the bedtime story to them. They were all tired by then and it wasn't the best time to do it, but she could see no other time in the day when it could be fitted in. Flora took over on the evenings Hilary worked late and heard them read as soon as they'd had their tea.

'You and Isobel picked it up in no time,' she'd said once when they were alone. 'I don't know what's the matter with these two.'

Flora stayed with the boys for the end of term parents' night, so both Hilary and Ben could speak to their teacher, Miss Spooner.

'They're both good at sums and interested and eager to do most things.' She was young and pretty and peered at them through outsize heavily rimmed spectacles. 'But they're having real difficulty learning to read and even more trouble with writing and spelling. Their low marks in tests reflect this.'

'There doesn't seem to be any reason for it,' Hilary said, blinking hard. 'If they're good at sums, surely they can learn to read?'

'They will if you keep them at it.' Miss Spooner handed Hilary new reading books, saying, 'They've made progress during this term. Don't let them slide back during the summer holidays.'

All their teachers had said regular reading practice would help, and every night Hilary insisted they do it. They stumbled and stuttered, and words which they knew one night they seemed not to know the next. It was a daily battle they were not winning and it was making them say they didn't like school.

When they brought home their end of term reports, Hilary sat over them for a long time. Andy's read, *He works hard at things that interest him, but gives up on things that don't.* Charlie's was worse. *Doesn't try hard enough, needs to work harder especially at reading and writing.*

She'd expected big things from them when they were babies. Hadn't she said to Isobel that she hoped to see them earn their livings as surgeons, pilots or barristers? She could see now that she'd been wildly over-ambitious. They were never going to pass their school exams with enough marks in basic subjects to be able to train for careers like that. In another year or so, they'd be taking their eleven-plus exam, and only those who passed would go on to grammar school and the possibility of academic careers.

For the first time she faced the fact that her boys were unlikely to be among them. She knew how important literacy was, and that anybody who didn't achieve a reasonable standard would find it difficult to find employment when they grew up.

Hilary now saw this as their biggest problem and she was afraid that what she was doing wasn't enough.

As the years went on, Isobel thought Sebastian was growing more aggressive towards her. They were always more quarrelsome towards the end of term when they were in need of a rest, but they'd never been quite this bad before. Neither of them could manage money and they had deepening debt problems which didn't help. She was afraid their relationship was worsening. They had row after row.

One evening, after she'd put Sophie to bed, Isobel remembered she had another task before she could watch television. Each year her class of children changed, but she took them through the same curriculum. When she'd first started teaching, she'd prepared a series of notes on each subject and now all she had to do was read them through to refresh her mind at the right moment. Tomorrow, she was going to start a series of lessons on the Romans.

She went downstairs to the room they called the study, though it was more an informal sitting room where they could get away from the television. Sebastian was fond of a red leather armchair they had with a matching footstool. He often settled there to read his newspapers.

Isobel kept her notes filed on cards in an old shoe box that she kept on the bottom shelf of the bookcase. She found the lid had a covering of dust and took it to the kitchen to wipe off with a damp cloth. They had one desk under the study window that they shared. She settled down at it to prepare her lessons for the next day. Sebastian's newspaper crackled as he folded it and tossed it on the table beside him.

'What's that box?' he asked.

Isobel had become engrossed in how the Roman Republic had been set up. 'Just an old shoe box.' The cardboard was beginning to split on one corner. 'I must look for a new one.'

Sebastian stood up to study the lid. 'Where did you get it?'

Something in his voice made her take a second, more searching look. Suddenly the room was spinning round her. She was back in a sunny Saturday long ago when Rupes had taken her out in his boat for a spin along the river. On the way home, he'd stopped his car to collect a pair of shoes from a shop.

Seb read aloud, 'Charles Trevelyan. Bespoke cobbler. Handmade shoes of quality.' He pulled her round to face him, his eyes burning into hers. 'My father used to have his shoes made there. They kept a cast of his feet. All he had to do was choose the style he wanted and they made shoes for him that fitted like gloves.'

Isobel was cringing. She closed her eyes. How had she managed to overlook that?

'How did you get this box?'

She opened her mouth, about to claim that she'd had a pair of shoes made there, but bit back the words in time. It was obvious from the size of the box that it had contained shoes made for a man. She said, 'It must have been yours.'

'No.' Seb was frowning. 'No. I've never been able to afford shoes like that. I wish I could.'

Suddenly his face was twisting with fury. He swung the box over and tipped all her cards out on the desk. Some slid on to the floor.

'Seb,' she shouted. 'They were all filed in order. What's the matter with you?' But she knew and was frightened.

He was studying the inside of the box. Would it show the name of the customer? She didn't know.

'You knew my father, didn't you?'

'No,' she gasped.

'It gives the last number as 146092. I bet that'll be Dad's.'

'I wouldn't know.' She was trying to stack her cards in neat piles. He flung out his arm and swept the rest of them on to the floor.

'Seb!'

'I can find out, can't I? They've probably still got that last on their shelves waiting for Dad to order another pair. If not, they'll have records.'

'It's only an old box.' Isobel was fighting to stay calm. 'What are you getting het up about? What if it did belong to your father? It's years old. You probably used it yourself to store something, and it came round with all your other things. Didn't we pitch everything into the back of my car on that first afternoon?'

He was studying the box. 'It looks old enough.'

'You must have kept something else inside.' Isobel looked again at the lid and her heart missed a beat. Why hadn't she noticed the label before now? It pictured polished Oxfords and shoe trees. The wonder was that Sebastian hadn't noticed before either.

His lip curled in a snarl. 'The game's up. Even you must recognise that, Izzy. I loved you but you've lied and deceived me all these years.'

'No.' Isobel was trying hard. She had to get Seb back on an even keel. 'I loved you too, I still do.'

'How can I believe that? You've been lying through your teeth for years. God knows I've tried hard, but not any more. It was him, wasn't it? He was your lover? My own father?'

She stared up at him. He'd put it into words. The next moment his hand lashed against her cheek. The force of it made her stagger back and bang her head against the wall. It really hurt: the room was spinning round her. Seb had never hit her before, not even in his wildest temper. Never hit anybody, as far as she knew. His was a gentle personality. Tears of pain and anger were rolling down her cheeks.

'You bitch.' He ground the words out. 'It makes me sick to think of it, you and him. That's why you wanted me when he died. You used me. You thought I was the next best thing, didn't you?'

For years, Isobel had forced an innocent look on her face and denied everything, but now something snapped, and she lost control. With her hand on her smarting cheek she screamed, 'Yes, you're right. I loved your father. He was twice the man you are.'

'He was a dirty old man,' he said scornfully. 'He kept you as his mistress. It all adds up now, how you came to have that apartment.' He stopped and she saw his mouth fall open. 'Sophie?'

'Yes,' she shrieked, 'you're right about that too. I was pregnant with her when I first rented the room to you. Sophie's your half sister. Your father was also hers.'

Isobel rushed upstairs to throw herself across their bed in paroxysms of angry tears. After that, divorce seemed her only option.

CHAPTER TEN

1976

Flora put on her mac, picked up her umbrella and shopping bag and stepped out into the summer drizzle. She was going to play bridge and had started deliberately early so she could pop into the village store, which was also the post office and newsagents, to pay her paper bill. She'd noticed they had a good stock of small toys and had told Hilary she'd buy a selection to give away as prizes at the twins' tenth birthday party.

The rain grew heavier so she was glad to reach the shop and sniff the scent of fresh newsprint. As there were other customers, she went round choosing a couple of jigsaw puzzles and some books. Ten was not an easy age to buy for. The Matchbox cars caught her eye. Yes, all little boys liked them; she added several to her heap. Of course, there was Jamie; she knew he'd be asking a few friends too. She added a couple of colouring books to her pile.

Mrs Grant, the village postmistress, was Rory's mother. She passed the time of day with all who had connections to the garden centre, treating them as old friends.

'What other toys d'you have that would suit ten-year-olds?' Flora asked her.

'We have a good selection of Airfix models, some suitable for that age group. They're popular.'

Flora examined them. Mrs Grant had everything marked with its price and they were a bit above that suggested by Hilary for prizes, but Flora also needed to buy birthday gifts for the twins. She chose two aeroplane models and hoped they'd enjoy making them. Hilary had asked her to buy books for them, but she knew the boys were not too keen on books so she wanted to give them something else as well.

'Rory says there's going to be a big do for their birthday. He's been invited too.'

'We'll need his help with the games,' Flora told her. 'Ben's going to get them running races and Rory's going to stand on the finishing line to see who comes in first. He knows the names of all the village children, you see.'

His mother beamed at her. At her suggestion, Flora bought a stock of lollipops, finger-sized bars of milk chocolate and sherbet licks to give away to all who came. She was half aware that behind her the shop was filling up with other customers.

When the bags were finally packed and she turned to leave she felt herself step on something. It made her cannon into another customer and her elbow sent his two paperbacks skidding across the damp floor.

'I'm so sorry...' She was embarrassed at her clumsiness.

'It's all right, don't worry.' The man was picking up his books and putting them on the counter together with his other purchases: a pork pie, a small loaf and a few tomatoes. It looked as though he was providing himself with a lonely meal. Mrs Grant found a duster to dry off his books.

'I trod on your foot, too. I'm sorry.' Then Flora recognised him. 'Haven't I seen you at the bridge club?'

'Yes, I'm on my way there now. I wanted to get some reading matter for tonight.'

She'd heard the other bridge ladies say he looked a real gentleman. He had a pencil moustache and dark wiry hair with tiny flecks of grey through it and tight curls where it was longer on top of his head. He wore very traditional clothes, including a Harris tweed sports jacket of impeccable cut, but no longer new. He had a Jermyn Street shirt, bespoke leather brogues and a silk tie, all wearing well as befitted their quality.

He said, as she was trying to manage her bags at the shop door, 'Can I carry one of those bags for you?'

'There's not much weight in them really. It's just bulky stuff.'

'You can leave your shopping here behind the counter,' Mrs Grant called. 'Collect it when you come out. Yours too, Mr...'

'Waite. Tom Waite.'

'Thank you,' Flora said. 'That'll be best, then I'll be able to put up my umbrella.' She'd left it in a stand at the door. The rain was now a steady downpour.

Tom Waite took it from her to open and hold over her. 'I put my car in the car park before I realised I'd be too early,' he said. 'It was a mistake, although it's only a hundred yards or so.'

'Do shelter yourself too,' Flora urged, 'or you'll look like a drowned rat when you get there.' She moved closer and took his arm. It was the only way an average-sized ladies' umbrella would shelter two. 'Last week was the first time you've been to our club, wasn't it?' she asked.

'Yes, I play in other places. I enjoy bridge and wanted to play more often.'

'A good way of passing a wet afternoon.'

'Any afternoon.' He smiled. 'The occasional evening too.'

Flora said, 'It's a good way to meet people and make friends.'

'I know Mrs Dalrymple. She plays in Eastham too.'

'She runs our club.'

'Yes, she persuaded me to come. Then there's Mrs Morland who makes the tea and Betty who helps her.'

'The ladies were flocking round you last week.'

'Mrs Dalrymple knew I wouldn't know anybody, so I think she put them up to it. She introduced me to almost everybody. I'm sorry, I've forgotten your name.'

'Flora Wilcox.'

'I'm pleased to meet you now, Mrs Wilcox.'

'Flora, please.'

'May I? Thank you. Here we are then.' He collapsed her umbrella. 'All I need to do now is to find a partner to play with. Do you have a regular partner?'

'I often play with Betty, but she deserted me last week to play with you.'

He laughed. 'Would you do me the honour of partnering me then?' He seemed diffident and rather shy.

She smiled. 'I'd like to.'

When it was his turn to shuffle or deal, he seemed to have the skills of a card sharp, but he was slower during play and stopped to think occasionally. He was very good at adding up the scores. They won the first rubber and then the first game.

'You play well,' he told her.

'I had good cards.'

When play resumed, he said, 'Let's see if we can do it again.'

They didn't win either of the other two games played that afternoon, but Flora had never enjoyed a session of bridge so much.

Before she left, Ben's twin aunts came to have a word with her. She said to Tom Waite, 'It's hard to remember names when you meet a lot of people at once. These are the Misses Foster, Primrose and Prudence.' They shook his hand.

'We're off to Canada,' Primmy told her. 'Booked it at last. We've been promising ourselves this trip for years. If we don't do it soon we'll be too old.'

'We're staying for three months.' Prue chortled. 'We're going to spend the rest of the summer and the fall in the Rockies.'

'We're going to miss the boys' birthday party, though. Leaving you all the work, I'm afraid.'

'We'll make the birthday cakes before we go but Hilary will have to find somebody else to provide the music for musical bumps and pass the parcel.'

'They both play the mandolin,' Flora told Tom. 'It sounds marvellous when they play together. The children love it.'

Tom said, 'I'm hearing about this birthday party from all sides. I can't play the mandolin, but if it's music you want, I could run an extension line out from the house for my record player.'

'Would you?' Flora was delighted. 'It's a week on Tuesday. My daughter will be pleased. It's one thing less for her to organise.'

They went back to the village store to collect their shopping. Coming out, he asked, 'Have you come far? Can I offer you a lift?' As the rain had not cleared, Flora accepted gratefully.

He had a big expensive car, a Mercedes, but like everything else he owned it was getting old. It seemed to match him exactly, as though when it was new he'd earned the sort of income that went with belongings like this.

As he drove, he told her about the bridge club he went to on Thursday evenings and asked her if she'd like a second weekly session. 'They're always looking for more players,' he said.

'Yes.' She smiled. 'I would.'

'Good. I'll pick you up on Thursday evening then. Seven fifteen.'

When he pulled up outside her cottage, he got out and helped her carry her bags to the front door. Flora would have liked to ask him in for a cup of tea, but was afraid he might think her too forward. She liked him and was glad she'd be seeing him again.

Hilary had been happy to help Ben achieve his ambition because it brought what she wanted too, but she'd had to put her own ambition to write on hold for years. She was now managing to sell a few articles with a medical slant. There'd been one on Caesarean section and another on self-help for those with high blood pressure. But that was a far cry from writing fiction, which was what she really wanted to do.

With the job and three children it was hard to find time and energy during the day to write. It was sheer determination that made her start getting up at four in the morning to do it before she went to work. In the summer months she found it possible, but in winter the temptation to snuggle down under the eiderdown could defeat her.

Over the last few summers, she'd got up before dawn to work at her typewriter. When a story or article was finished she posted it off to a magazine and when it was returned to her she posted it off to another. She began to keep a register of where she was sending her work so that she'd know where it had been.

She was thrilled when one of her stories was accepted by a women's magazine. It made her try harder but they were not easy to sell and she could only suppose they weren't good enough. She soon had a cupboard full of manuscripts, some finished and some not, some she'd given up on and others that had been rejected by editors.

She didn't talk about what she was doing except to her family. Certainly not at work: her colleagues would tell her she was reaching for the sky. In her saner moments she knew she was, but she was not the only person in the world who wanted to be a writer. She knew the competition to get published was ferocious.

She'd been trying for so long that she thought Ben had given up hope she'd ever make much of a success of it. He no longer seemed to expect her to, but he encouraged her to write because he saw it as her hobby. That was not how Hilary saw it. She wanted to earn her living from writing, but she was beginning to feel she was knocking her head against rock. Neither did it pay. The amount of time and effort she put into her short stories in no way reflected the amount of cash they would bring, even if they sold.

She knew she had to learn fictional techniques and practise them, but their enormous mortgage made her look at the economics of what she was doing. She told herself she could make better use of her time, but she couldn't stop writing. Some inner need drove her on.

What Hilary really wanted to do was write a full-length novel but until now she hadn't tried because it would take such a daunting amount of time. Her increasing success with short stories and articles made her think it might just be possible to do it, and she felt that if she didn't get down to it now, she never would. All last winter she'd worked on the plot in whatever moments she could find. At the beginning of this year she'd started to write, and now the manuscript was almost complete.

The summer sales had started and Flora meant to indulge herself. She'd come to the big Liverpool shops to buy herself a really smart outfit, maybe more than one. She'd been tempted by the pastel-coloured suits swinging on their rails in John Lewis and had bought one as well as a coat.

She was in the changing rooms at George Henry Lees, trying on a navy and white cotton dress. She half turned in front of the mirror to admire it. She was looking for good quality, good cut and classic styling. This dress had all that.

She wanted her wardrobe to say something different about her. Up till now it had said that she'd scrimped and saved all her life and, with only basic skills, often made her own clothes. She twisted the price tag round; even with 50 per cent off, she'd still be paying more than she'd ever spent on a dress before. But she was going to buy it because it suited her, even perhaps flattered her, and not many things did at her age. With a pension from teaching and the girls no longer dependent on her, she was better off than she'd ever been.

Under the harsh lighting her wrinkles showed up more than they did in the mirror at home, but she didn't look too decrepit for a grandmother of sixty-five. She'd been to a good hairdresser to have her hair cut and she'd had a blonde tint put in to cover the grey. It made her look much younger. In future, she was going to have her hair cut every six weeks and tinted regularly.

She wanted to turn over a new leaf. After a humdrum life filled with work and duty, she now had a new interest. Every time she thought of Tom Waite she felt a little frisson of excitement run down her spine.

He'd partnered her at three bridge sessions now. She really liked him and they were getting on well. She was looking forward to the twins' party because he'd promised to come and give them a hand. She needed something smart to wear then, and this navy and white cotton dress would be exactly right.

She wanted to smarten herself up. She wanted to look like the sort of woman Tom Waite would be interested in.

Hilary and Ben counted 20 July a day for family celebrations. Now, in 1976, it was not only the twins' tenth birthday but their own fourteenth wedding anniversary.

Ben hadn't yet taken all of his twenty acres into production. There was a small copse that protected one side of their house, and beyond that the best part of three acres remained as grassland. For the twins' birthday present, Ben had asked the local carpenter to make two sets of goal posts scaled down in size, and Hilary had bought a leather football instead of the plastic ones which

179

never seemed to last long. This morning Ben had set up the goal posts to make a football pitch on the rough grassland.

'It isn't very level,' he said to Hilary, 'but perhaps they won't notice.'

It was the ideal place to hold a summer party. Rory helped him carry the trestle table and set that up in the shade at the edge of the copse.

Hilary thought they had a great deal to be thankful for. She loved the house they'd built. It was three years since it had been finished and though modernistic in design it now looked as though it had been there for ages. It had a small garden round it: Ben had laid the lawns and flowers had bloomed in the borders for the last two years. They were both very proud of their house.

Of course, it meant Hilary had to carry on working full time to pay the huge mortgage, but she told herself it wasn't going to be for ever. The economic climate had improved and their business was showing a profit once more. When it was earning enough to pay the mortgage as well as the household bills she would be able to give up her job.

Since early spring she'd been getting up before dawn to write. She'd finished off a romance called *The Night Star*. She'd been through the manuscript half a dozen times in an effort to get everything in the story right, in the hope that a publisher would like it.

She'd discovered that few publishers would consider unsolicited full-length manuscripts and knew she'd have to have an agent to help her find one. She'd sent off the first three chapters and an outline of the plot to an agent called Fern Granville she'd picked out from a list.

Amongst the twins' birthday cards this morning she'd received a note from Fern. Hilary couldn't believe her luck: it was asking her to send the remainder of the manuscript. She'd been absolutely thrilled. At last it seemed she was in with a chance.

Every time she thought of her novel, finished and about to land on an agent's desk, she buzzed with hope. She'd taken a day's holiday from work today, but she had to prepare for the party now. Tomorrow morning, she'd get up early and parcel up the rest of the manuscript. Writing was one area in her life where she really wanted more but she was grateful Ben's business was coming right at last. Her mother arrived and had to be shown the agent's note.

'I'm delighted,' she said. 'Wouldn't it be wonderful if you could earn a living from writing?' She began unpacking the party goodies she'd brought.

'Mum, did you remember to bring your old scarves for the three-legged race?'

'I could only find five. I don't want my best ones spoiled.'

'That'll be fine. I've looked some out too.'

The kitchen was fragrant with the smell of baking. They spent an hour adding dabs of different coloured icing to cup cakes and making sandwiches.

Jamie stood watching them, his eyes only just above the level of the table. 'I wish it was my birthday.'

'You had yours in February,' Hilary told him. 'But Aunt Primmy has made you a cake. Just a little one because you're midway between birthdays. You can say you're four and a half.'

'I want to see it.'

She took him to the larder and lifted him so he could. 'Look, it's got your name on in blue icing.'

She dropped a kiss on top of his head as she set him down. He had a mop of flaxen curls which earlier this year he'd demanded to have cut short because strangers were mistaking him for a girl. She loved Jamie so much now she couldn't imagine not wanting him, or having a girl in his place.

'Lovely.' He clapped his hands. 'And Charlie and Andy have a cake each.'

'Auntie Prue thought they should.'

It took another hour to collect enough sacks for a sack race, and count out spoons and small potatoes to use instead of eggs for an egg and spoon race.

Hilary laughed. 'It's going to be more like a sports day than a party.'

'No.' Flora disagreed. 'I've drawn a donkey with a loose tail for them to pin on, and there'll be other games too. Are we going to wrap up all these small toys we've got as prizes?'

Hilary surveyed them. 'Let's just put them out on trays and let the winners choose what they want. It'll be one job less.'

It had been a clear sunny morning but by lunch time the sky had turned white and the atmosphere was sultry. The trees hung dusty and motionless in the still air. Tom arrived and began

182

running out his extension cable and soon Hilary could hear distant strains of jolly sea shanties.

Jane Johnson, Hilary's friend at work, put her ginger head round the back door. 'Can I hear dance music? The party can't have started?' She had come early to help, and brought her two children.

'No, it's musical bumps music. The twins are up on the field,' Flora told Paul and Polly. 'Why don't you go and find them?'

'It'll be wonderful to have no mess in the house,' Hilary smiled, 'and it means we've been able to ask almost every child they know.'

She'd been surprised to find the twins had quite a circle of friends. As this was the sort of party that needed a crowd, she told them she'd issue invitations to all the children whose mothers she knew.

At two o'clock the party guests began to arrive and Ben started them running races. Twenty-six small boys and four little girls turned up. They made the field sound like a school playground with their whoops and shouts. Hilary enjoyed it immensely. It was lovely to be outside with the luxury of having time to play with the children. For her, leisure time was very scarce.

It was a hot and sticky afternoon. Flora was kept busy handing out paper cupfuls of homemade lemonade from the six-gallon urn they'd borrowed. Her eyes were never far from Tom, who was wearing cricket flannels and a Panama hat. He'd not only provided music for games like pass the parcel and musical chairs but had provided jolly background music all afternoon.

At four o'clock Flora got him and the twins to help carry out the picnic tea. There were trays of sandwiches, crisps, sausage rolls, fairy cakes and jellies in paper cases. Tom was also helping in any other way he could, and looked as though he was enjoying it.

He made Flora feel like a twenty-year-old again. She couldn't believe this was happening to her. He was opening windows for her that had remained barred and bolted for the last thirty years. She found him stimulating.

When the feast had been demolished, there was ice cream to follow. Then Ben carried out the three birthday cakes, all iced in blue and white. He lit the candles and got them all to sing happy birthday first to Andy, who was the eldest, and then to Charlie. He was cutting the cakes into slices when Jamie said, 'Polly wants a piece of my cake, not Charlie's. She's my friend.'

Ben laughed. 'It's as well we have three, or there wouldn't be enough to go round.'

The games started again. By six, all the children were hot and tired. Parents began to arrive to take them home.

Later that evening, Hilary was lifting Jamie out of the bath. His blue eyes were round and imploring. 'Please, Mummy, the twins said I must ask you. They want just one more treat for their birthday.'

She laughed. 'That depends on what it is. We've all had a lovely day today, haven't we?'

Ben was passing the bathroom on his way to get

184

changed and overheard her. 'It's been a marvellous day. I enjoy this time of the year better than Christmas.'

'Yes, better than Christmas,' Jamie nodded, while she was trying to towel his hair dry, 'but I've got to ask. Charlie made me promise to.'

Hilary felt she hadn't stopped smiling all day. She couldn't remember when she'd last felt as happy as this. The boys had been showered with small gifts and treats but she was quite prepared to grant one more.

'What is it they want?'

Jamie pulled her down to whisper in her ear. 'Don't make them read tonight, Mummy, please. They hate it and say it'll spoil the whole day if you make them.'

'Oh!' Hilary jerked upright. That her twins should feel like that dismayed her, shocked her even. She couldn't understand now why it had taken her so long to realise that they had an almost insurmountable problem and that it was really bothering them.

'All right, love. Nana was going to hear them read, but I'll tell her they're to be let off tonight.'

CHAPTER ELEVEN

Hilary heard her mother calling as she came upstairs.

'I'm here, Hilly. Shall I take over? You'll want to get changed.'

'Thanks, Mum. I could do with a quick shower after all that racing round this afternoon.'

'It was a smashing party wasn't it, boys?'

Hilary went to her bedroom and took her best blue dress out of her wardrobe. It was two years old but she'd always liked it. Ben had gone downstairs again, leaving all his cupboard doors open.

After her shower she sat down in front of her dressing table. One thing she was dissatisfied with was her own looks. Her mouse-brown hair was inclined to frizz and though she'd asked her hairdresser to liven it up with blonde highlights, he never seemed to put in enough. She'd kept asking for more until now she was mostly blonde. It made her feel better but she thought nature had let her down. It was hardly justice to give her a naturally blond husband and children while she had to work so hard at it. Also, she was afraid her skin was a little sallow and didn't really tone in with blonde hair, but the effect did improve in the summer when she sat out in the sun. Unfortunately, these days she couldn't find the time for much of that.

Ben said she had nice blue eyes but she knew they must be hardly visible behind the rimless specs she had to wear because she was short-sighted. A couple of years ago she'd decided to have contact lenses, but she'd never got used to putting them in and she couldn't find time in her day to fiddle with them. Certainly not in the mornings: it could be manic then as she tried to get breakfast on the table, herself ready for work and the children dressed for school. Having decided to keep her contact lenses for high days and holidays, she was struggling to put them in now.

Ben had booked a table for two at a restaurant in Hamilton Square in Birkenhead where they went every year for their wedding anniversary. It had romantic memories for Hilary: it was here that Ben had asked her to marry him. They planned to share a celebratory bottle of wine and get a taxi home.

Ben usually drove the van, with the garden centre's logo in red and green on the sides. They also had a small Ford which was known as Hilary's car because she used it daily to get to work. Tonight, Ben drove the whole family to Hamilton Square in the car. Flora was going to babysit and had volunteered to drive it back home. The children giggled all the way, excited at being out of doors in daylight wearing their pyjamas and slippers.

Hamilton Square was very grand. It boasted granite terraces of fine five-storey houses built for rich merchants in about 1830. Without servants, the houses were found to be too big for residential occupation and many were being used as offices by solicitors, dentists and insurance companies.

The restaurant was on the first floor of one of the houses, and they were shown to a table in the window. Hilary could see lots of young couples walking about in jeans and T-shirts on the street outside. It was getting dark early on this sultry evening, and thunder threatened, but there were quite a few more sitting and lying on the grass in the central garden.

Ben persuaded her to order lobster thermidor. 'Let's be extravagant for once. It looks as though you're getting the hang of this writing business, so we ought to push the boat out.' He asked for a bottle of champagne, but the restaurant couldn't run to that and they settled for a bottle of Chablis instead.

They had a great deal to celebrate, Hilary mused. She wanted what every woman wanted: a loving husband and children, as well as a fair share of the world's material goods for her family. Tonight, she felt fortunate that she had them all.

'It was a great party,' she said. 'The kids loved it. Primmy and Prue made marvellous birthday cakes, didn't they? The icing looked very professional.'

Ben was suddenly serious. 'We wouldn't be able to do all this without their help. And Flora's too, of course.'

'I wouldn't be able to work if they weren't willing to look after the boys for such a lot of the time. It wouldn't be worth it if we had to pay someone else.'

'Primmy apologised for going to Canada and leaving your mum to do everything while they were not in school.'

'I'll be taking two weeks' holiday myself, and Jane's offered to help. Mum said she'd manage the rest of the time.'

'I've tried to pay them,' Ben said, 'but they won't take anything. I have to insist on paying Flora the usual rate when she comes to help in the garden shop over busy weekends.'

Hilary smiled. 'She says she enjoys it, that she'd be bored if she didn't have the shop and the boys to look after.'

'We've got a family in a million and I'm very grateful for what they do. The business had a good day too. I looked across in the middle of the afternoon and the customers' car park had two rows of cars in it.'

Hilary said, 'And there was a steady stream of people in and out of the sheds and glasshouses viewing what you have for sale.'

'I watched a man wheel four rose trees in tubs back to his car,' Ben gloated. He'd worked there most of the morning and this afternoon the shop had been run by two part-time girls.

It was suddenly quite dark, the only light coming from the flickering candles on the tables. He raised his wine glass. 'Let's hope things will continue to go our way.'

She'd seen other women look at Ben and knew they considered him attractive. They were both thirty-four, Hilary being eight months younger. She found Ben's eyes playing with hers across the small table and knew he loved her. After all these years of marriage they were very lucky that they both still felt like this.

He was excited about the letter she'd had from the agent this morning and suddenly even more hopeful than she was. He leaned across the table to refill her glass.

'I haven't played fair with you,' he said. 'I've kept you very short of time to do anything for yourself. You've worked a full shift on five days a week, while I've spent all my time following my own ambitions.'

'You work hard too,' Hilary told him.

'Not as hard as you. Look, love, if you manage

189

to sell this book, I think you should give in your notice at the nursing home.'

Hilary felt all of a flutter. That would be marvellous. 'It's what I want, of course, but... Can we afford it?' The mortgage was not something she could push to the back of her mind.

'You'll be earning something, won't you?'

'I don't suppose it'll be much to start with.'

'This could turn out to be your big chance.'

Hilary could feel herself glowing. She hardly dared believe he might be right.

'You've got to have time to think, Hilly. Nobody can give of their best if they have as much to do as you have. It must make it twice as hard if you're holding down a job as well. After all, you've still got the shopping and the cleaning and the boys to look after.'

'I'd love to have daylight hours to write in. I could do so much while they're at school.' Hilary sipped her wine and felt on top of the world.

'Everything we want in life is falling into place now,' Ben said.

'Except that the boys...'

'We'll still have to work hard to bring the boys' reading up to standard, and you'll have to work at your writing, but everything else is coming right.'

When their dessert was being brought to the table, there was a sudden flash of lightning followed almost immediately by an earsplitting clap of thunder.

'Almost overhead,' Ben said. 'It's been threatening for ages. It'll clear the air.' The rain was drumming down within moments, and the wind was lashing it against the windows. The waiter was hurriedly closing those that had been open. Hilary saw people running from the garden in search of shelter and then within moments she could no longer see anything outside.

'We're lucky it held off this afternoon,' she said. 'Lucky with most things.'

They sat over their coffee until the downpour was moderating. When Ben paid the bill, he asked the cashier to call a taxi for them. A few minutes later they saw a cab pull in to the kerb outside.

'Come on,' Ben said. 'That'll be for us.'

The storm had moved on. Lightning was still flashing over the river but the thunder was now a distant rumble and the air was cool and fresh. It had virtually stopped raining though the pavements glistened wet and water was still rushing in the gutters. Those who'd taken shelter from the storm were beginning to move on.

The town was full of other noises now. A small crowd was collecting in the corner of the square, and as one was looking down Hamilton Street towards the town centre where police sirens could be heard wailing. The taxi driver was taking an interest too. He'd got out of his cab and was walking back the few yards to see.

He said as they approached, 'There's something going on down in town.'

Hilary paused to listen. The night was being broken by a cacophony of sounds: not only were the sirens getting louder, but a car was racing towards them with its engine labouring. Ben went to the edge of the pavement behind the taxi, intent

191

on missing none of the excitement. Hilary followed the taxi driver to the corner of the square.

An instant later, she saw the small crowd flatten themselves back against the railings as a white Jaguar came shooting along Hamilton Street at speed. Ahead of it on the opposite corner of the square two police cars drove into position to block the road. With squealing brakes, the Jaguar took a left turn very wide to drive down the side of the square in front of the restaurant, narrowly missing a cyclist. Hilary glimpsed the driver of the Jaguar struggling to turn the steering wheel and knew he was losing control. The car was followed closely by a police vehicle with its sirens blaring.

There was the grind of tearing metal as the Jaguar scraped along the side of the taxi while the driver roared with rage. For Hilary, it was like watching a film. For an instant before the crash she could see that Ben might be standing in the way. She tried to shout a warning but what came out was a shriek of panic. The Jaguar mounted the pavement and shot across it to crash into the railings, uprooting a few and coming to halt overhanging the basement yard.

As she watched, the driver opened the door and shot out to run like a hare towards Argyle Street, dodging pedestrians as he went. Hilary felt paralysed; gripped by raw terror. She couldn't see Ben any more. Where was he?

'Ben,' she screamed. 'Ben? Are you all right?'

The police car had pulled up in front of the taxi and stopped its siren. Three figures in blue leaped out. People were already crowding round. Hilary was trembling as she tried to push closer.

One of the policemen caught her arm and pulled her back.

'My husband,' she screamed. 'I think he's been hurt!' She could smell petrol, see it leaking out of the crashed car.

She struggled, trying to free herself from the policeman's grasp. Could she see Ben underneath it? It looked like a bundle of rags but there was blue like his shirt and there was certainly blood on the pavement. He must be badly hurt. She had to help him.

'No,' the policeman insisted. 'Leave it to us. Come with me.' All the onlookers were being moved back.

Hilary was raining blows on his chest, tears of shock streaming down her face. 'No, I'm a nurse, he needs help. I've got to get to him.'

'He's trapped under the car. We can't reach him just yet.'

Feeling suddenly sick, she stared at the policeman in disbelief. Horror was washing through her. He was holding both her wrists to prevent her pummelling him more. She tore herself free to vomit in the gutter. Her celebration dinner tasted like bitter aloes on her tongue.

'I'm sorry.' She was frightened and embarrassed and letting the tears roll down her cheeks unchecked.

'Don't worry about it,' he said. 'It's shock. There's an ambulance on its way.' Hilary was being led back inside the restaurant, made to sit down in the reception area. A glass of water was put on the table beside her.

'No,' she protested and tried to stand up. She

wanted to be with Ben. She wanted him to have the help, he needed it, but everybody was fussing round her. The policeman was asking questions: her name and address. Ben's name...

'Is there anyone we can phone for you? You need somebody with you at a time like this.'

She told him about her mother and that she was babysitting in their house. But it was Ben's arms Hilary wanted to feel round her. If he said he was all right everything would be fine. She couldn't stop shaking, couldn't sit still. She stood up again. She had to get to the door to see what was happening outside. In the flashing lights she saw an ambulance had come. She could hear the bell of a fire engine clanging, and a moment later that had arrived too.

'Oh, God!' Hilary could feel her head swimming and her legs buckling under her. Everything was going black. She felt an arm catch her and lower her to the floor. A man's voice said, 'She's fainted.'

When she came round, Hilary found herself lying on the floor in a room she hadn't seen before. It looked like an office and a police-woman was with her now. She tried to sit up.

'How is Ben?' she asked. 'Is he badly hurt?' She was afraid he was dead. Why else would everybody keep her away from him like this?

'I'm Sarah,' the girl said. 'We don't know the extent of your husband's injuries yet. The ambulance has taken him to the General Hospital.'

'I want to be with him.'

'I've telephoned your mother. She can't leave the house because it would mean leaving your children alone. I'll take you home to her.'

'I want to see Ben first.' Hilary did not mean to be put off this time.

'He's in good hands. They'll be doing their best for him.'

'I want to go to the hospital.'

'All right, I'll take you there. We'll find out how he is. Get an up to the minute report from the doctors. Then I'll take you home to your mother. Bed is the best place for you, not waiting about in the hospital.'

Hilary succumbed. She had no fight left in her. It had all happened so quickly. She and Ben had been toasting their achievements at one minute and hoping she had an exciting future opening up before her. They'd been so happy and pleased with their lot, and now this. Without Ben, she didn't know how she'd cope. What if he were to die? The thought made cold terror crawl up her back.

At the hospital, Hilary found the policewoman did most of the talking for her. They were asked to wait. Hilary felt in a different world. It ought to feel familiar but it didn't. The smell of disinfectant reminded her that she'd done her nurse training here; she'd worked in this hospital for some years, but that was a long time ago and it seemed very much changed. She didn't think she'd be much use in a busy casualty department like this any more.

At last a doctor came to see her. She blurted out, 'How is he?'

He looked grave. 'Not good news I'm afraid, Mrs Snow. The car that ran him down caused multiple injuries – his right leg is broken in several places and his pelvis is fractured too. We think he's bleeding internally and we need to stop that as soon as we can.'

Hilary gulped. 'That's bad.' But if everything went well now, he could still recover from those injuries and be all right.

'Yes, it's bad. We aren't sure about his spine yet. He could have a crush injury there.'

Hilary stiffened with horror. She knew that was a very different matter. 'I want to see him.'

'Yes, of course. Come with me.' Her police escort followed. 'I'm afraid you'll only have a minute with him because we've just heard from theatre that they're ready for him now.'

'Is he conscious?'

'Yes. Talk to him – he's very drowsy but he'll know you're there. The medication, you know, painkillers and pre-op.'

Ben was lying on a trolley, his neck and head held rigid in a splint and drips and drains inserted in his body. His face was ashen and devoid of all expression, and his eyes were closed. Hilary was shocked at the change in him. It seemed only minutes since his eyes had been flirting with hers.

'Ben?' She tried to make her voice sound normal. 'How d'you feel now?'

His eyelids flickered but failed to open. His lips were forming words. 'Hello, Hilly.' There was a long pause and she thought that was all he was going to say. Then, 'I'm all right. Don't you worry.'

He seemed so brave, it made her heart turn over. His trolley was being wheeled away when the doctor said, 'They'll be able to examine him properly under anaesthetic so we'll know more about his injuries later.'

In the police car going home, Hilary closed her eyes and prayed. Please don't let Ben have a spinal injury She hadn't even asked why it was suspected, or at what part of the spine. Please let them be wrong.

When they drew up outside her house the only light showing was chinks between the heavy sitting-room curtains. It was the policewoman who led the way to the front door, but Hilary had her key out ready to open it. The sudden light as it was switched on made her blink, but her mother was coming towards her with arms outstretched. She threw herself at the familiar figure and felt wrapped in a sympathetic hug.

'Oh, Hilly, how is he? Is he badly hurt?'

'I don't know.'

'He's in the operating theatre at the moment, Mrs...'

'Wilcox, Flora Wilcox.'

The policewoman was leaving. Hilary tried to thank her. 'You've been very kind.'

She found herself on her own red Dralon sofa, with her mother sitting close and patting her arm. She couldn't stop the tears rolling down her cheeks as she explained what had happened. She felt stunned, unable to think clearly.

Her mother made a hot drink. 'I'd better stay the night, hadn't I?' Her face was agonised. 'You'll need help with the boys in the morning.'

'Yes please, Mum, if you would.' She felt devastated. 'I think the spare bed's made up.'

'Come on then, it's late. Let's go to bed. I'll need to borrow a nightie.'

Hilary sighed. 'I want to ring the hospital first to see if there's any more news about Ben.'

She got through quickly but it took some time for the nurse to find out. Hilary shivered in the hall as she waited for her to come back on the line. At last she came. 'His operation went satisfactorily. The internal bleeding was stopped and he's had two plates put in his right leg. He's shortly going to be transferred to Clatterbridge Hospital.'

'To Clatterbridge?'

'Yes. He'll need special care over the next few days and we can't provide that here. His condition has stabilised; we're just waiting for the ambulance to take him.'

'Thank you.' Hilary had hoped for news of his suspected spinal injury, but was too slow to ask before the nurse had put the phone down. Living where they did, Clatterbridge Hospital was nearer and was in fact their district hospital. At least the news was good as far as it went. All the same she was worried stiff as she climbed into the double bed. That Ben's side remained empty drove home to her how dependent the family was on him. How was she going to manage?

CHAPTER TWELVE

Hilary didn't think she'd be able to sleep but after tossing and turning for what seemed hours, trying to work out what she must do tomorrow, she fell into a deep sleep.

She was woken by Jamie getting in beside her. His hands and feet were cold, showing he'd been out of his bed for some time. It was daylight and her bedside clock told her it was half past seven, later than they usually got up. She felt heavy and sleep-sodden.

'Where's Daddy?' Jamie was trying to shake her. 'He isn't here!'

Hilary pulled the child close against her and said, 'He had an accident last night. Daddy's hurt, and he's in hospital where they can make him better.'

Jamie was shocked and blinking back his tears. 'How is he hurt? What sort of h'accident? When will he be better?' His questions seemed never-ending. They brought the horror flooding to the forefront of Hilary's mind again.

She said, 'Shall I ring the hospital again to find out how he is this morning?' Jamie nodded, his face tense. 'Right. You stay here.'

She ran down to the hall in her nightdress. The house had been built with the latest system to plug in telephones but they hadn't yet bought one for the bedroom. Nobody rang them at night. When she was put through to the intensive care ward at Clatterbridge, she asked about Ben. 'I'm his wife.'

A man's voice said, 'His condition is satis-factory. He's stable but deeply sedated at present.'

'When will you wake him up?'

'He's to be kept like this for at least another twenty-four hours, possibly longer.'

'Oh! Can you tell me whether his spine was damaged or not?'

There was a pause, then, 'There doesn't seem to be anything in his notes about that.'

'I was hoping to speak to him today.' There were a hundred questions she needed to ask about running his business.

'Why don't you come in and see him and we'll ask the doctor to have a word with you?'

'I will,' Hilary said. 'Thank you.'

Her mother came from the kitchen, already dressed. 'I'm making tea. I was about to bring a tray up to your room.'

'I don't want a lie-in, Mum. I've got too much to do.'

'Get your clothes on then, and come and have it here with me. I'm useless until I've had a cup of tea.'

Hilary ran back to her bedroom and sent Jamie to get dressed too. He was upset about his father and needed a lot of comforting. She went to see the twins, who were out of bed and conducting a war between their Action Men. Jamie was telling them about Daddy. They needed hugs too before she could persuade them to start dressing.

Hilary decided she wouldn't be able to go to the care home today. She couldn't leave her mother here to cope with the children as well as the garden centre. If she did go, she knew she'd be useless; her mind would be on Ben. Besides, she wanted to go and see him this morning. She felt on edge, at sixes and sevens with herself, flustered.

She had no appetite for breakfast though she boiled eggs for her mother and the children. As soon as they were all eating, she poured herself another cup of tea and faced her mother across the table.

'I'm worried stiff. How am I going to cope?' She felt she was sagging under the weight of her responsibilities. 'I'll have to get somebody to mind the shop.'

'I could do that. Luckily, I've worked in it.'

Hilary tried to think.

'I want to help all I can,' Flora said.

'I know, Mum, but there's the children to look after too.' It all seemed too much. 'It would happen in the school holidays and when Primmy and Prue are away, wouldn't it?' she wailed. 'It couldn't have come at a worse time.'

'Hilary, we'll manage between us. You mustn't worry about that. Do you want me to move in here with you while Ben's in hospital?'

'Yes please, Mum. I'm afraid it could be for weeks. What would I do without you?'

Her mother had stayed overnight so many times that she and Ben had talked it over and some time ago they'd invited her to move in with them permanently, but Mum had said she preferred to be independent in their old cottage.

'It's my place of refuge,' she'd said, 'when I want a bit of peace from the children.'

Hilary knew that however much Flora loved the boys she found their noise and bustle tiring. She had settled into village life and was loving it. Ben had said it was a good thing she'd moved closer because they could keep an eye on her as she was getting older. But it seemed to Hilary they called on help from her more often than the other way round.

'I'll pop home later and collect some clothes,'

Flora said. The gate Ben had put in the back fence so the children could go to school without having to go near the main road was also a short cut to her cottage.

Shortly after nine o'clock Hilary telephoned Miss Procter, the administrator in charge of the Cavendish Scott group of homes where she worked, to tell her about Ben's accident.

'I'm so sorry.' Miss Procter had a cool and distant manner. 'Is he badly hurt?'

Hilary told her about his fractured leg and pelvis and the doctor's suspicion that he might also have damaged his spinal cord. She made her understand how serious that could turn out to be.

The administrator said, 'I'll put you down for three days' compassionate leave, Mrs Snow. To start immediately.'

'Thank you, that'll be a big help. I was wondering... I've booked two weeks' summer holiday to start on the twenty-eighth of July and that will leave only three more working days in between. I have extra holidays in hand. Would you mind if I took them then?'

Miss Procter gave a weary sigh. 'It won't be easy to get somebody to stand in for you at short notice. Half the staff are away on holiday at this time of year.' Hilary heard another gusty sigh, then a grudging, 'All right then.'

She breathed a sigh of relief. That would give her over three weeks at home. It should be long enough to sort things out as long as Ben had no spinal injury.

Ben didn't like being away from his business for long and this year they'd planned to take the boys camping in the Lake District for a few days. They'd bought a tent last year. Hilary was glad they'd made no bookings.

She went back to the kitchen. Her mother had done the washing up. 'There's a pie in your freezer. Shall I take that out for lunch?'

'Yes please, Mum. My head's in a whirl; I haven't given a thought to meals. To be honest, Ben usually did that. He said he liked cooking and as he was always on hand it was easier for him to do it than me.'

'You get off to the hospital,' her mother said, then thought of something else. 'Oh, Hilly, you wouldn't have a postcard, would you? Aunt Mavis doesn't have a phone and I need to drop her a line.'

'Yes, I think so.'

'You know she always comes to me for her Sunday dinner. I'll have to stop her this week.'

Hilary knew her aunt didn't bother to cook for herself and Sunday was the big day of the week for her.

'She can have her dinner with us,' she said. 'We'll have to cook anyway; one more won't make much difference.'

'Are you sure? Sunday will be a busy day.'

'Would she be able to help?'

'I wouldn't count on it. She's never had anything to do with children.'

'I was thinking of the shop.'

'No. She's never done shop work and she's too set in her ways to learn now. You know what she's like.'

Hilary did. She'd always thought of her aunt as

very old and perhaps a little odd.

Her mother said, 'Right, I'll go over and open the shop. Then I'll ring round the part-timers to see if one will come in today. The boys can come with me. There won't be much doing this early in the morning.'

Flora walked across to the Oak Tree Garden Centre followed by her three grandsons on their bikes. The internal road system was a marvellous place for them to ride up and down. Rory drove the tractor and trailer about and the occasional lorry came in to deliver a load of potting compost or manure, but it was much safer than the road outside.

Last night's storm had freshened things up and it was another clear summer morning. Good weather for business. She unlocked the double gates to the centre and locked them both open, then went to the shop. Everything was neat and tidy. There were banks of pot plants ready for sale. The begonias, petunias, geraniums and fuchsias were a lovely array of colour, and the hanging baskets were a sight to behold. She sniffed at their sharp fresh scent.

Poor Ben. Flora had felt panic-stricken since she'd heard of the accident. It was a disaster, not only for him but for the whole family. She'd never seen such a change in anyone as there was in Hilary. Her face was ghost white this morning and she was tearing round doing three things at once one minute and dithering in a state of indecision the next. Flora felt very close to her elder daughter and wished she could be more help to her in this crisis. She hoped they were both going to have the stamina for what lay ahead. She'd expected, now her daughters were grown up, that she'd have more time to herself.

With an effort, Flora pushed Ben's accident to the back of her mind. It was too upsetting. Now that Tom Waite had befriended her, she felt she might have a life of her own. She'd thought hard about how she might further their friendship and yesterday she'd invited him to her house for supper.

'On Saturday,' she'd said, and knew by his wide smile that he was delighted.

Of course, that had been before Ben's accident and before she'd moved into Hilary's house to help her. She could still manage it; she could go home when the shop closed for the night and put together a light supper. She'd think carefully about the menu and choose food that could be prepared beforehand. She didn't want to concentrate on cooking while Tom was with her.

Flora sighed and looked round at the plants waiting to be sold. She told herself she'd day-dreamed long enough. It seemed strange to be in the shop on her own. What should she be doing? She checked the till: there was a float of small change, all in order there. Before the customers started coming in, she'd better see what Rory was doing and let him know what had happened to Ben.

Hilary drove to Clatterbridge Hospital, which was a hospital of many buildings spread out over a huge site. When at last she found the intensive care unit she thought it a scary place.

The notice on the door warned, *Nothing may be brought into this ward without permission. Please don't bring flowers. Strictly no smoking.* Hilary hardly recognised the inert figure on the bed as her Ben. He was deeply sedated and surrounded with monitors and machines none of which she understood. When she'd trained all those years ago, intensive care had not existed. She'd never worked in a world like this. There were only twelve beds here but each one held a figure that looked as though it was hanging on to life by a thread. How much worse it must be for relatives who had had no previous dealings with hospitals. She sat down on a chair beside him.

'Hello, Ben.' He gave no sign that he'd heard, though she'd been taught that sometimes unconscious patients could hear. 'How d'you feel? I've been so worried about you.' She touched his arm. It was being invaded by numerous tubes. A doctor came in to do something to one of the other patients. In passing, he asked, 'Mrs Snow?'

'Yes.'

'I'd like to have a word with you. In a few minutes.'

Hilary dreaded being told that Ben was failing and wasn't expected to live. It looked as though that was quite possible. A few minutes later, the doctor led her off to an office.

'How is he?' she asked as she sank down on the chair he indicated. He went to the other side of the desk.

'His leg has been satisfactorily plated and his pelvis should heal...'

Hilary burst out, 'It's his spine that's worrying me. At the General last night, they thought it might have been crushed.'

'Yes, he has lacerations in the dorso-lumbar region and we believe his spine has been crushed. On first examination last night, he couldn't move his legs.'

'Oh my God!' Hilary stopped breathing. She felt her heart plummet. Poor Ben – this could change his life for ever. Change her life too.

'But it's not all bad news. He has no vertebral fractures and no dislocation.'

She gasped, 'Does that mean he'll be able to walk?'

'We don't yet know the extent of the damage,' the doctor was going on. 'His spine was crushed in the accident but we don't think severely and we hope for some return of sensation. We've decided to keep him sedated. Keep him at rest for now. We'll know better in a few days.'

Hilary could get no more out of him. She went back to sit by Ben feeling somewhat comforted because the doctor had been quite upbeat. She told herself she mustn't lose hope yet. She watched Ben for the best part of an hour, running her fingers across what she could of the bare flesh of his arm and thinking about their situation. If only they'd left that restaurant five minutes earlier or stayed five minutes longer, this wouldn't have happened to him. He'd very definitely been in the wrong place at the wrong moment.

When the nurses asked her to go to the waiting room while they treated Ben's pressure areas and checked his monitors, Hilary decided to go home.

As she drove past the entrance to the garden centre and slowed to turn into the narrower drive to her house, Hilary saw the great bunch of multi-coloured balloons that Ben had fastened to the gatepost yesterday to mark the house for parents bringing children to their party. Today, they hung shrivelled and deflated and were a miserable sight. She put her car in the garage and fetched a pair of scissors to cut them down. They seemed to mirror what had happened to her and Ben. Yesterday they'd been exultant and self-congratulatory, today she felt overwhelmed with problems. Ben's accident was going to change everything. Worry was building up, a weight in her stomach.

She went to the garden shop. There were no customers at that moment and her mother was on the phone. She knew that whether Ben was here to run it or not, his garden centre had to make a profit; their living depended on it. He'd invested so much in it: all his dreams and a great deal of money.

There was a sudden flurry of activity as several customers came in together. Flora was serving one and Hilary went hesitatingly forward to do likewise. Serving customers was new to her and brought home how little she really knew about the business. She'd have to learn to take it in her stride. As the customers went out, Mum asked, 'How's Ben?' And as soon as she'd related the news, her mother went on, 'Oh, and Isobel rang up here, because she'd failed to get me at home. She and Sophie were coming up to spend a couple of nights with me next week. I told her about Ben's accident and that I was staying here with you. I've put her off until I'm back home again. She said she'd ring you later.'

'Right,' Hilary said. 'Did you manage to get someone to work extra hours today?'

'No. Jenny has her father staying with her and they were just about to set off to spend the day in Chester, but she's down to work on both Saturday and Sunday afternoons. Amy's away in the Isle of Wight and I couldn't get any reply from Stella's number, but she's on the rota to work tomorrow afternoon.'

'Well, we'll have to manage today.'

Her mother nodded. 'Amy and Stella are fine, but I'm not as quick as them. You and I will both be needed here and it'll be too busy this afternoon to have the boys playing at our feet.'

Hilary said, 'I could ask a friend to look after them. Jane would like a shot, but I've a feeling she's on duty today.' She screwed up her forehead in thought. 'Where are the boys now?'

'They got tired of riding their bikes. Rory's keeping an eye on them. Jamie's helping him and the twins went to play football.' Flora smiled. 'At least that's what I hope they're doing. It's a godsend they have all that spare ground to play on.'

'That's what Ben kept saying.'

'And if it's wet there's all these buildings.'

'Ben doesn't like them playing in the greenhouses.'

'I told Rory to bring them here to the shop if they got too much for him. It isn't busy this morning. Ben used to have them here with him, didn't he?'

'Only in an emergency when you and the twin aunts were not about. He said he needed eyes in the back of his head to watch all three – they were into everything.'

At that moment, Hilary could hear Jamie crying. The twins came in from the hothouse pulling their toy trucks, each loaded with a few plants. They were followed by Rory pushing a loaded cart with one hand and towing Jamie with the other. He'd grazed his knee and it was bleeding.

'I'm sorry, missus.' Rory seemed quite upset.

Charlie sang out, 'Jamie fell over Rory's spade.'

'I couldn't help it.' Rory's face was working with anxiety.

'It's not your fault, Rory,' Hilary hastened to say. 'Jamie's always falling over. You mustn't blame yourself.'

Flora said, 'Looking after children is a full-time job and you have your own work to do.'

Hilary tried to stay calm. 'Please do all the daily jobs you did for Ben, just as though he were here. You know more about it than the rest of us. I mean the watering...'

'Yes, the watering.' Rory nodded gravely.

'That's the important thing.'

He asked, 'When will Ben be better?'

'We don't know, I wish we did. It could be a long time.' She put her arms round Jamie. 'Don't cry, love. Let's go and wash your sore knee and make it better. Come on, twinnies, you'd better come too. Say thank you to Rory for looking after you.'

She could see Rory was glad to see them go. Ben had told her they were inclined to tease him and play him up.

Hilary led the way home and straight to the bathroom. She ordered the twins to wash; they always had dirty hands after playing in the garden centre. As she cleaned Jamie's knee she talked to them about seeing Daddy. They were full of questions she couldn't answer and there wasn't much she could say about his condition to children as young as them. She certainly wasn't going to mention that he could be paralysed from the waist down and never walk again. She couldn't bear to think about that herself.

'Right, twinnies, get your reading books. We'll do that next. Take them down in the playroom.'

'Not now, Mummy,' Charlie sighed.

'Yes, now. Better we do it in the morning when you aren't tired.'

They ran off and she stuck a plaster on Jamie's knee, then took him to join the others in the playroom.

'Twins, why haven't you brought your books? Are they still up in your bedroom?'

'Ah, Mummy, not now,' Andy wheedled. 'We want to play with our trains.'

Hilary expected them to obey her. 'Yes, now. You too, Charlie, get your book. This minute.'

'Don't want to read,' Charlie said cheekily. 'I hate reading.'

'Now, please.' Hilary insisted. 'Do as you're told.'

'I'll read for you, Mummy,' Jamie piped up. 'Let me.'

'In a minute, love,' Hilary said. At least Jamie wanted to show off his reading skills. 'Let Charlie

211

go first.'

At last Charlie was sitting down and ready to start. He was the most difficult to deal with. He guessed at words and got them wrong and stumbled over others that he should have found within his grasp. At Miss Spooner's suggestion, Hilary encouraged him to sound out the letters but he seemed unable to manage that. Charlie soon lost all patience and didn't want to go on. Yet more practice seemed the only answer.

Hilary persevered and tried to keep him calm. Miss Spooner had told her that some of the other children in the class were inclined to belittle the twins' efforts and call them dunces. The effect of that was all too obvious: it sapped their confidence and doubled the problem. She thought a schoolteacher must need the patience of a saint.

'You'll enjoy reading,' she told Charlie, 'once you're better at it.'

'We'll never be any good at it,' Andy retorted, but he'd fetched his book with better grace than his brother. She went through the same performance with him. He was less volatile than Charlie and would try harder and concentrate for longer. But even so, Andy didn't improve much, and she was as tense and frustrated as he was by the time he'd come to the end of his daily stint.

'Me now,' Jamie clamoured with his book open. Hilary pulled him on her knee, knowing she had to give him the same amount of attention. The twins often didn't want him to join in their games and he felt left out of the fun. He asked now, 'Why don't I have a twin, Mummy? I want somebody to play with.'

That wasn't easy to explain. She was settling down to hear him read with all the patience she could muster when the telephone rang. Her first thought was that Ben had taken a turn for the worse and they wanted her to come to the hospital. She picked it up with her heart in her mouth.

'Hello, Hilly. It's Isobel.'

Hilary recognised her sister's voice immediately, although these days she seemed almost a stranger. She still felt shaky but told herself not to be silly. Mum had told her to expect this call.

'Mum told me about Ben. How is he?'

Hilary mouthed at Jamie, 'Get your crayons out and play for a bit.' It took a long time to tell her sister what had happened and the consequences. It sounded a tale of woe.

Isobel said, 'Can I be of any help? D'you want me to come up? I could look after the kids for you, couldn't I?'

Hilary was much relieved, though a little surprised. 'That would be a help, a great help. Then Mum and I can both work in the shop.' Mum was always trying to persuade Isobel to come up for a few nights, but she'd fully expected her to postpone her proposed visit until they had more time to spend with her. 'Can you come tomorrow?'

'Tomorrow? I was thinking of next week.'

'I need help now. We'll be busy over the weekend – we always are at this time of year. I feel desperate, Izzy.'

'All right, but I'll have to bring Sophie with me.'

'That's fine. She'll play with the boys, help to keep them amused. What time will you get here?'

'I'll drive up. In the afternoon, say half five or thereabouts. Hard to be exact when I'm coming this distance.'

As her mother was using the spare bedroom, Hilary wondered as she put the phone down which room to put her sister in. She decided she'd move into the smallest bedroom, which they'd furnished as a study, and sleep on the bed settee there. Sophie and Izzy could use her room; the en suite would please them. She went to change the sheets. It would make things easier if Izzy was here to look after the boys. It meant she needn't ask favours from her friends.

CHAPTER THIRTEEN

Hilary went over to help in the shop that afternoon and found it quite difficult. She had to ask her mother to show her how the till worked and where things were kept. Fortunately, Ben insisted that all their wares were priced up for the customers, so she knew how much to charge. All the same, she had to keep asking questions and it made her feel she wasn't on top of the job.

She knew that the work Ben did behind the scenes would be even more difficult for her to master. He planted in the glasshouses and nursery beds to a strict timetable. It was important to know exactly when plants would be in flower so there would always be stock ready for sale. Hilary didn't think it would be much use

214

asking Rory about that sort of thing, or about what basis Ben used for pricing plants. She had so much to learn and right now she couldn't ask Ben for help.

When the time came to close the shop she felt exhausted and emotionally drained, having been on the go all day. But she was somewhat reassured, too. They'd got through the day and the takings were about average.

Her mother looked all in as well, but insisted on helping her get a hot meal together. Nowadays Hilary thought of their relationship as being more like that of sisters or friends than mother and daughter. This was one of the times when Mum seemed to have more energy than Hilary had herself.

Nowadays she was dressing smartly and more fashionably than Hilary, and had a way with scarves and neckties that gave her a touch of elegance. She'd stayed slim and looked a decade younger than her actual years. She was generous with her time and couldn't do enough to help, but she could switch into strict disciplinary mode in an instant and be stronger than Hilary was in dealing with the boys. They all loved her and she let them see how much she loved them.

Hilary said, 'I've been greedy. I expected to get so much from life.' Now Ben had had his awful accident she knew what was really important to her. She wanted Ben, whole and healthy, above everything else. 'How am I going to cope, Mum?' Tears were prickling her eyes. 'What if...?'

'He'll be all right,' her mother said briskly. 'You wait and see, he'll get better.'

Hilary shook her head. 'The doctor said...' He'd given her no such assurance. 'At the very least, Ben will be in hospital for ages.'

While she got the boys ready for bed, her mother went home to get some clean clothes. Hilary read a bedtime story to her boys, listening all the time for Flora's return. She wanted to go back to the hospital to sit with Ben for a while. She needed to reassure herself that he was all right.

When she got there, he didn't seem to have moved in any way since she'd left him this morning.

Ever since Isobel's outburst, when she'd admitted to Sebastian that she'd been his father's mistress and Rupert was Sophie's father, he'd hardly spoken to her. When he did, they were sudden vicious flare-ups. When they were calming down, Sebastian's face would screw up in agony.

'We can't go on like this. You're making my life a misery.'

'I couldn't agree more.'

'I want you to pack your things and go,' Seb told her several times. 'You and I are finished. I want a divorce.'

Isobel stood her ground. 'You'll have to leave, not me. I own half this house.'

He was indignant. 'It was bought with money left to me by my father.'

'Sophie's father too,' she reminded him. 'The house will go with the child and the parent who's given custody.'

'Isn't that always the mother?'

216

'Usually, so that means the law will be on my side.'

'But that isn't justice. Not in our case.'

Isobel recognised that as true. She'd never been all that fond of the house but it represented capital and she had no other.

Neither of them went to a solicitor to get the divorce started. They had to work, so they carried on as they always had. Isobel decided to stick it out for the month that remained until the end of term. They'd have time then to see about the divorce.

Earlier in the term, before the big row, they'd talked of taking Sophie on a trip to Tuscany in the summer holidays. By mutual consent that trip was off now. However, Sebastian was leaving a trail of exotic brochures about the house. He didn't talk about it but it seemed he'd decided to go to the Himalayas alone. Isobel was relieved that he intended to go away: it meant she'd have the house to herself. It would give her peace for a few weeks. School was breaking up when he told her he'd decided not to go after all.

'My mother's ill,' he said. 'She's in hospital. Charlotte's in Hong Kong and wants me to stay near to keep an eye on her.'

'What's the matter with your mother?'

'Heart trouble.'

'She's had heart trouble for years.' Isobel wasn't sympathetic. It meant Sebastian would be here with her all through the holidays and she couldn't stand any more of him. She had to get away.

When she told him she was going up to Merseyside to stay with her family the next day, he was cross because she hadn't told him sooner.

'I couldn't – I've only just made the arrangements,' she snapped. She'd been packing since speaking to Hilary on the phone and was tired.

'How long are you going to stay?' he asked.

'For as long as possible. Hopefully for good.'

'If that's how you really feel, don't come back,' he said, his face white with fury. 'You and I have had just about as much as we can take of each other.'

'Perhaps I'll do that,' she replied through clenched teeth.

The exchange escalated into another row that went on all afternoon, until Sophie threw a tantrum and said she didn't want to go to Auntie Hilary's, she wanted to go to the seaside.

When Isobel was finally ready to leave the next day, Sebastian came out on the doorstep to say, tight-lipped, 'Let's make this the end, Izzy. I'm going to see a solicitor and start divorce proceedings.'

Flora was surprised to hear that Isobel still intended to come up, especially since she couldn't come without her nine-year-old daughter.

'To help?' she asked. When Isobel came up for her rare visits, she felt she waited on her hand and foot, rather as she did Mavis. 'How long will she stay?'

'She didn't say. I rather gathered for as long as she could be of help. You're all being very kind,' Hilary said.

Flora didn't think it was a good idea, but she couldn't say so. Surely Isobel realised she'd make more work for Hilary?

That afternoon the shop was busier than usual and when closing time approached Hilary went back to the house to put a large chicken in the oven to roast. She said, 'If Isobel still isn't here when I've got the supper on, I'll start my daily stint of reading with the boys.'

Flora locked up the shop and cashed up. Then she helped Rory tidy up. When she reached the house, it had gone six, the table was set and there was a heavenly scent of roasting chicken that made her mouth water.

Hilary said, 'I thought Isobel would be here by now.'

'She's often later than she says. Shall I take over and read with Jamie?'

'If you wouldn't mind. I'll bath the twins. They're filthy – they've been digging ramparts in the copse this afternoon. Then I might have time to slip down to see Ben after supper.'

The boys were bathed and in their pyjamas. Flora had washed her face to make herself feel better and was sitting down with a glass of sherry, but she couldn't relax. She was cross with Isobel. What could possibly make her this late? It was turning seven o'clock and there was still no sign of her. If she'd told them seven in the first place...

'I'm hungry,' Jamie said. 'Mummy, when will supper be ready?'

'It is ready, love.' Hilary had had to take the chicken out; it had been in danger of being over-cooked. 'We're just waiting for Auntie Isobel. She won't be long now.'

The twins were in the sitting-room window watching the gate.

'Shall we eat, do you think?' Hilary was asking. 'No point in letting it spoil.'

But at that moment Andy started leaping about and calling, 'Here she is. Sophie's here.' Charlie led the stampede to the front door.

'Thank goodness,' Flora said. 'I was beginning to think she might have had an accident.'

Isobel was getting out of an old and rather battered scarlet Mini. She was stretching when she saw Flora. 'Hello, Mum. How are you?'

Flora hugged her. 'Lovely to see you again.' She watched her daughters exchange cool kisses. Once Isobel had been the polished beauty and Hilary the one who took little interest in her appearance, but now, if anything, that order was reversed.

Hilary's hair had been touched up to maximum effect, though Ben's accident made her looked stressed. Isobel looked equally stressed, her clothes were unkempt and her hair had been carelessly scraped back into a ponytail. It was held in place with an elastic band, of all things. Flora found it hard to equate elastic bands with Isobel's style.

Hilary said, 'Thank you for coming to help.'

Flora asked, 'How is Sebastian? Well, I hope?'

'Yes, he's fine,' Isobel was dismissive of him and turned back to her car. Suitcases, coats, shoes and toys filled the back seat; Sophie, still inert, was curled up in the front.

Isobel opened the car door and said loudly, 'We're here. Come on, Sophie, wake up.' The child sat up blinking, her cheeks flushed with sleep.

220

'What a journey we've had,' Isobel complained. 'I've never seen such traffic. Dead slow and stop all round Birmingham.'

Flora couldn't resist saying, 'If you'd started earlier, you would have got through before the rush hour.'

Slowly, Sophie clambered out, rubbing her eyes and staring at the twins. She was as tall as they though more slender, a very pretty child who had inherited her mother's heart-shaped face. Hilary's three now stood aloofly apart, staring back.

Flora took Sophie's hand and said, 'Twinnies, come and say hello to Sophie. This is little Jamie, their brother.'

'I know that,' Sophie said disdainfully, pulling her hand away to follow her mother into the house. In the kitchen, Hilary gave her a mug of orange squash and offered Isobel a glass of sherry.

'I'd rather have a cup of tea,' she said sweetly.

Flora was brisk. 'Now you're here, dear, I'm going to dish up the dinner. Can you wait until afterwards for the tea?'

She could see Isobel hadn't changed. She'd never thought of anyone but herself. It was now so late that poor Hilary wouldn't have time to go to see Ben again tonight.

Isobel struggled up the stairs with two heavy suitcases. Her mother was leading the way with another case and a collection of dresses over her arm. She said, 'You've brought a lot of luggage with you.'

'Sophie wouldn't let me leave any of her toys behind,' she replied, thinking of all the other things she'd managed to squeeze into the boot of her car. She wished it was bigger, but it was locked and the stuff could stay there for the time being.

She'd been late setting out because she'd had another blazing row with Sebastian and then packed as many of her possessions as possible. She didn't want to go back, not ever.

'Hilary's given up her own bedroom for you and Sophie.' Flora threw open the door.

'It's a big house. I thought she had five bedrooms and plenty of space?'

'Yes, but only one guest room and I'm in that. The twins share one room and little Jamie has another, then she has one room furnished as a study.'

'We could easily bed down somewhere else. Where's Hilary to sleep?'

'In her study. She's got a put-you-up there. She thought you'd be more comfortable here, and after all, there's Sophie to think of.'

When her mother left her, Isobel looked round Hilary's bedroom and felt a flash of envy. She'd been shown over this house both while it was being constructed and after Hilary had moved in, but her eyes were used to her own house which was thirties built, old-fashioned and shabby because Seb did little to maintain it. This house was bigger, thoroughly modern and up to the minute. Hilary had large fitted wardrobes and a gorgeous en suite bathroom with a separate shower! Hilary had gone up in the world.

Isobel opened one suitcase on the bed and started to throw out their nightclothes. It would be time to put Sophie to bed as soon as they'd had supper.

On the journey up she'd been unable to get Sebastian's angry farewell out of her mind. She still felt shocked. He'd actually said he was going to put the divorce in hand. Despite all their rows, Isobel hadn't thought they'd quite reached that point.

In order to get some respite from Sebastian, Isobel had intended to stretch her customary two-night visit to her mother to a couple of weeks if she could. When Hilary had rung her and told her of Ben's accident, she'd offered her help straight away, but she was beginning to regret doing so. Mum was already here to do what was needed and she was in a bad mood. They were all so busy and stressed out, it hardly looked like being a comfortable visit.

Isobel felt low. It had been the spectre of the long summer break stretching ahead that had pushed her to leave. The holiday would throw her and Seb together, give him plenty of time to bait her and have even more ferocious arguments. If divorce was what he intended, she should have stuck it out at home and tried to push Seb out instead.

Now she'd walked out and taken Sophie, Isobel was unable to make up her mind about what she should do. It had been her intention to go back at the end of the holidays at the latest. She'd be expected to start work then and Sophie would have to go back to school. She found it hard to believe that Seb had delivered such an ultimatum, and didn't want them back.

Perhaps she should try to find a job in some

pleasant seaside town, where at the end of the summer season it would be possible to find a flat at a reasonable rent.

It was lack of money that would hold up that move. She hadn't been able to bring anything she couldn't throw in the back of her car. What she hoped to gain now by coming to Birkenhead was time to think and perhaps to save a few pounds. It was anybody's guess as to how long it would take her to find another teaching job, and she'd be expected to work for a month until she was paid. She might need to put up in a boarding house for a while until she found a flat, and they'd surely want a month's rent in advance for that.

Isobel sighed. Really, she'd had more than enough of young children. She wasn't cut out for teaching any more than she was for motherhood. Perhaps, after all, she should have followed Hilly into nursing. Hilly always seemed content with her lot, but she'd had a much more stable life. Things had been easier for her.

The next morning, Flora got up early to help Hilary get breakfast but there was no sign of Isobel.

'Don't take her a cup of tea in bed,' she warned, 'or she'll expect it every morning.'

But Hilary did anyway and Isobel and Sophie came down to breakfast in their dressing gowns. They were all round the big table in the kitchen when they heard the daily paper being pushed through the letter box.

The twins were starting to bicker. Flora hoped to break it up by saying, 'Who's going to fetch the newspaper?'

Sophie scampered off as though it was a race. She came back more slowly, her attention caught by an article on the front page.

'Just listen to this, Mummy.' She started reading. 'It's headed, *Clapham South. Yesterday evening the naked body of Paula Musgrove, age eight, was found hidden under bushes on the common. She is thought to have been...*'

Isobel leaped to her feet and snatched the newspaper from her. 'That's for grown-ups. It'll give you nightmares. Here.' She saw a book of Charlie's on the dresser and pushed it into her daughter's hands. 'Read this.'

'Mummy,' Sophie screamed, hurling the copy of *Thomas the Tank Engine* across the room. 'What did you do that for? I know all about that girl. She's been missing for two weeks. I want to read the rest.'

'Do you know her?' Jamie asked.

'No,' she wailed. 'Yesterday they found her vest and knickers...'

'Go upstairs to the bedroom,' Isobel ordered. 'Don't come back until you can behave.' Sophie went with very bad grace, slamming the door hard enough to make the teaspoons rattle on the saucers.

Flora was transfixed, not by the article or Sophie's bad behaviour but by the ease with which she'd read the *Daily Telegraph* – at the speed of normal speech and with all the right inflexions. One glance at Hilary's face told her she too was shocked at the difference between Sophie's reading ability and that of the twins.

When the boys went off to play, Flora couldn't

help but say, 'Sophie reads very well. She's quite advanced for her age, isn't she?' She knew her voice sounded strained.

Isobel was buttering her toast. 'She's quite bright. She could read reasonably well before she started school.'

'Did you teach her?'

'No, she wanted to learn. If anybody did, it was Sebastian.'

Hilary sounded choked. 'I thought my brood were bright but they can't read like that. I'm worried about them, Izzy. Their teacher asks me to hear them read every day and I do, but it doesn't seem to make any difference. Would you do that for me while you're here? Being a teacher, you'll have the knack. It would be wonderful if you could bring them on a bit.'

'All right,' Isobel said. 'I want to help all I can.'

Flora was surprised. It was almost as though Izzy wanted to be made welcome here.

Flora and Hilary were kept on the go in the shop all the following afternoon. They were glad to have Jenny, the part-timer, with them. She was a housewife in her twenties and regularly worked the weekends here. She knew the routine and was quick and efficient. Ben spoke highly of her.

Flora had invited Tom Waite to have supper with her tonight. She was sorry she'd had to come and stay with Hilary: it meant she couldn't give the occasion quite as much thought and attention as she would otherwise have done.

She wanted to know him better. In particular she wanted to know more about his life, his family and his friends. She'd tried to draw him out by talking about her own family. He seemed interested in them all, but particularly in Hilary and Ben's garden centre. Just about all she could get out of him was that he was a widower of fifty-five, had been made redundant by a building firm and was delighted with his new freedom.

When she related this to Hilary, she said, 'There's lots of building work starting up again. He could surely get another job if he wanted one.'

'Perhaps he doesn't need to,' Flora said.

She hadn't told him she was ten years older; she didn't want to put him off. She told herself that to ask him to supper was her way of repaying the little kindnesses he'd shown her, but really she wanted to deepen their friendship and bring him closer. She wasn't quite sure how much she wanted from him but he quickened her heart and no man had done that for years.

She'd nipped home early this morning, dusted round a bit and made a list of the food she'd have to buy, all chosen to need the least amount of preparation time. Flora always enjoyed Tom's company, but today, as the afternoon wore on, she felt tired out. The hectic routine of the last few days was taking its toll.

It was about four o'clock when he came into the shop. Flora had phoned him to cancel her bridge on Thursday evening so he knew all about the accident. He asked, 'How is Ben?'

Flora related the latest news about him and told him of the extra work she'd taken on to help Hilary.

He said, 'I was wondering about tonight,

227

whether you still wanted me to come. You look exhausted.'

Hilary's difficulties were making her feel low. 'I was so looking forward to it.' But Flora didn't feel up to doing anything more than flopping in front of the television when the shop closed. 'Would you mind if I put it off to another night?' she asked. 'I'm staying here with Hilary at the moment. I did think I could pop home and rustle up a meal there for us, but I'll have to go shopping first and I feel jiggered.'

'Flora,' he said, 'why don't I take you to the Dog and Gun instead? They do a good steak and kidney pie and it'll do you good to sit down and have a rest.'

'That would be wonderful,' she said, brightening up. 'Just what I need.'

'Then I'll pick you up from Hilary's house at seven, all right?'

Flora was pleased. It would be relaxing to sit and chat with Tom over a meal and a bottle of wine. She'd enjoy an evening out away from her family and feel better for it.

They were quite late closing the shop and Flora felt she needed a bath to perk herself up. She was almost ready when she heard the front doorbell ring.

Isobel had heard her mother telling Hilly that she wouldn't be in for supper tonight because she was being taken out for a meal.

As soon as Flora had disappeared upstairs to get ready, Isobel asked, 'Does this mean Mum's got a man friend?' She found it hard to believe. Her

228

mother's friends were generally widows of her own age. She was curious about him. 'What's he like?'

'Very nice. I like him.' They were in the kitchen and Hilary was cooking supper for the rest of the family. 'It does Mum good to go out.'

'She's looking well; he must suit her.' This would be why Mum had smartened herself up.

When the front doorbell rang, Isobel rushed to answer it and gasped aloud when she saw Tom Waite standing on the doorstep. She'd expected an old man, but Tom was in his prime, with a full head of crinkly dark hair. His eyes looked straight into hers and with a wide smile he said, 'You must be Izzy. Your mother's told me all about you.'

'Not the bad things, I hope?' she teased.

'No, she said you were beautiful. What could be better than that?' He offered his hand. 'I'm Tom Waite, by the way.'

'I know who you are,' she said, 'though Mum's kept pretty quiet about you.'

He laughed and his brown eyes creased up at the corners. 'Perhaps you don't see enough of her.'

'Come in. She must be nearly ready by now.' Isobel led him towards the kitchen and Hilly. On the way, he stopped to pat Charlie's head and scoop Jamie up on to his shoulder.

'Higher, higher,' Jamie shouted excitedly.

'Your head's nearly touching the ceiling.' Tom laughed.

'It isn't, the ceiling's way up there.'

'It is, isn't it, Mummy? You'd better duck.' Tom had taken a book from the dresser, and, reaching up behind Jamie, he touched his head with it.

Jamie screamed with delight. 'My head touched

the ceiling.' Tom set him down on his feet. 'More, more,' he clamoured.

Isobel was surprised at how well he got on with the family, and even more amazed that her mother was being taken out by a man like this.

'Would you like a drink while you wait?' she asked him. But already they could hear Mum running downstairs as eagerly as a girl.

When the front door closed behind them, Isobel sank down on a chair. 'By Jove,' she said to her sister. 'If Mum can get a man like that at her age, there's hope for me yet.'

'Why would you want another man?' Hilly asked. 'You've already got a husband.'

That shut Isobel up. She couldn't talk about Seb yet; it was all too raw. Anyway, the family had been airing Hilary's trials and tribulations ever since she'd got here. They'd all sink into depression if she added hers.

CHAPTER FOURTEEN

Flora felt she'd recovered from working all day in the shop. Being with Tom made her feel alive and she was wearing the new navy and white dress and knew she was looking her best, but she was aware of trepidation too. This was the first time Tom had taken her out like this. To play bridge was different; there were so many others there. The Dog and Gun was busy when they arrived and the restaurant tables were all occupied.

'Would you like to wait for a table?' one of the waiters asked. 'Should be one by eight thirty, or if you prefer you can order a bar meal to be served there.'

'Sorry,' Tom said to Flora. 'I telephoned, but they said they didn't take table bookings. I'd forgotten they'd be busy on Saturday nights.'

'It doesn't matter. A bar meal will be fine.'

It was a warm summer evening and many customers were sitting outside in the garden. They found a vacant table there.

'I was going to make an occasion of this,' he said sadly. 'It's our first outing together and you need cheering up with all this bad news about Ben.' He found a bar menu, and after Flora had chosen fish and chips he went in to place their order and returned with a large glass of white wine for her.

'It's very pleasant out here.' Flora could feel the evening sun on her face. 'Peaceful, no customers to serve and not a child in sight.'

'I envy you your grandchildren. I never had any.'

'I love my grandchildren dearly but they can be wearing. I'm no longer used to the hurly-burly of family life. Sitting out in this garden with a drink suits me better.' She talked about how brave Hilary was being and how hard she was finding it to cope with the garden centre.

'Would it help if I came in to give her a hand?' he offered.

'Hilary's a bit anxious about taking on more staff. The added expense...'

'She wouldn't need to pay me,' he said quickly.

231

'I'd be happy just to make myself useful. It can't be easy for her, being suddenly catapulted into running her husband's business.'

'Why don't you come into the shop and talk to her? The trouble with a garden centre is that there's lots of work behind the scenes to get the stock ready for sale.'

Tom was very nice and his manner made her think he might want more than friendship from her. She couldn't help but warm to him.

Night had fallen and a sliver of moon was climbing into the sky by the time they were drinking their coffee. He spoke of his dead wife Grace with great affection and said he still missed her even though it was six years since she'd gone. He seemed a romantic. Flora wondered whether he'd kiss her tonight. So far, he'd made no attempt to do so.

He drove her back to Hilary's house. When he pulled up outside, the only light was that over the front door, left on so she could see her way in.

'Sorry I can't ask you in for a nightcap,' she said. If they'd been outside her own home she would have done. 'Thank you for a lovely evening. I've enjoyed it all, but specially the company.'

'So have I,' he said. 'Thank you for coming.' He pecked her cheek before she got out, and waited until the front door closed behind her.

Hilary had been pushing her worries about Ben to the back of her mind. The doctors and nurses had been reassuring. Yes, his spine had been injured, but they thought not severely. They'd told her they planned to wake him up on Sunday morning, and she was so looking forward to talking to him that she got to the ward too soon.

Ben was only half awake and there were still tubes stuffed into him everywhere, but he recognised her as she came close to his bed and tried to smile. When she pulled out a chair and sat beside him, his hand came out to feel for hers.

Hilary found the intensive care ward an intimidating place. Of the twelve beds here, three were empty this morning. The silence was made heavy by the electronic pulses of the hi-tech machinery with which each bed was surrounded. Each patient had a collection of tubes and drains and monitors attached. She'd never seen anything like this before except perhaps on television and the reality seemed more scary.

The nurses didn't wear the usual uniform. They were dressed in loose green trousers and smocks, more like theatre staff. She sat with Ben for twenty minutes or so and he seemed to be going in and out of consciousness. From time to time he opened his eyes and they searched her face. She talked to him in a whisper about the garden centre but she didn't know whether he was taking it in. Two nurses were working on another patient and eventually they came over.

'Hello, Ben,' one said in a loud voice. 'It's time to wake up.'

The other said, 'Would you mind going to the waiting room for a short time, Mrs Snow? We're going to wake Ben up thoroughly now and take out some of these tubes. He'll be able to talk to you when you come back.'

As Hilary stood up to comply, Ben's hand

snatched at hers and tried to keep her there. He was shaking his head and making guttural sounds. Despite the tube going up his nose and down his throat he managed to convey that he wanted her to stay.

Hilary's eyes were suddenly hot with tears. Ben could give no clearer demonstration that he loved her and wanted her with him.

'It's all right, Ben,' the nurse reassured him. 'Your wife isn't leaving, she's just going to the waiting room while we take your tubes out and make you comfortable.'

Hilary saw the doctor coming over. 'Your wife will want to know how you're getting on, Ben. I'll take her to the office to have a little chat about you. She'll be back soon.'

Hilary followed him out and once more faced him across the desk. One question above all others burned in her mind. 'Will he be able to walk, doctor?'

He put his head on one side. 'It's too early to say one way or the other. His reflexes are returning to his good leg, so we are hopeful.' Really, he had nothing new to tell her. It was still a matter of waiting to see how Ben progressed.

He escorted her to the waiting room when he'd finished. She wanted time to think, but there were other relatives waiting. A young woman was asleep on an armchair. Beside her a young man put down his newspaper.

'The waiting's awful, isn't it?' he said. Hilary decided he must be the girl's husband. 'We've been here all night – my mother...'

Hilary agreed and swallowed hard. Perhaps she

was lucky to live nearby. Not that she'd slept much since the accident, but she was more comfortable there with the rest of her family. Her mind was going round in the same circle. What if Ben could never walk again? She couldn't imagine him in a wheelchair for the rest of his life. How would he cope with his business? It didn't bear thinking about. The last few days had been a nightmare.

At last a nurse came to fetch her. 'Your husband's had a wash, he's wide awake and feeling more himself. He'll be able to talk to you now.'

Hilary slid back on to the chair by his bed and felt for his hand. Ben was trying to smile. She kissed him. 'Ben, how are you?'

His smile wavered. 'All right.'

'You're not all right, love. Not yet.'

'No. I can't move my legs. Oh, Hilly, I'm paralysed! It frightens me.'

She could hardly get her breath. It frightened her too. Her fingers tightened on Ben's. This was dreadful. She did for him what the doctors and nurses had been doing for her over recent days: she tried to soothe his fears.

'The doctor says there's no fractures in your vertebrae and no dislocation. Your spine was crushed but not severely.' She looked up and found the doctor watching them from the nurses' station. He smiled. 'He says you could still recover and be able to walk, but it'll take more time before they can be sure. You must be patient.'

On she went in the same vein. She didn't know whether she comforted him or not. He seemed to be withdrawing into himself and that wasn't like Ben. Hilary knew how difficult it must be for him

235

to accept his changed circumstances. Please let him get better, she prayed as she walked across to the car park later.

As soon as she closed the front door behind her, she could smell the Sunday dinner cooking and knew it must be almost ready. She could hear voices in the sitting room but headed towards the kitchen where she knew she'd find her mother.

Earlier that morning Flora had started cooking Sunday dinner for four adults and four children in Hilary's house. She was used to working in this enormous kitchen; she'd done plenty of it, but rarely for so many people. And the twins had big appetites and could eat almost as much as the grown-ups. It was making her feel flustered.

As she fried off the meat to make a casserole, she wished Isobel would come and give her a hand to peel the potatoes. But perhaps she was being selfish. Isobel was looking after the children. Hilary had asked her to help the twins with their reading, and as she was a schoolteacher she must be good at that. It was a task that would save either her or Hilary an hour or so this evening. The door opened and Sophie came in.

'Nana, can I have a biscuit?' She was so dainty and had such delicate fair skin she'd surely grow up to be a real beauty.

'Sweetheart,' Flora said, 'biscuits will spoil your appetite. Another hour or so and we'll be eating our dinner.'

'I'm hungry now,' she retorted. 'Mummy lets me have biscuits.'

Flora knew she shouldn't try to bribe her, but

236

said, 'I'll give you a slice of this apple I've cut up if you help me shell these peas.'

Sophie's sharp green eyes assessed the apple. 'If you give me two slices I will,' she bargained.

'All right.' Flora held out the dish for her to help herself. 'I'm going to make a tart with them.'

She pulled out a chair at the table, and lifted the child on to it. 'Now you can get to work. Put the peas in this pan and drop the pods here.' She put a bin beside her.

Flora saw Sophie pop a slice of apple in her mouth then pull a face. The next moment, she let out a howl and spat it out on the table. 'I don't like it. It's horrible. It's sour.'

Flora took a deep breath. 'Sophie, clear that half-chewed apple off the table. Put it in the bin if you don't like it.'

'Won't,' she pouted. 'I want some proper apple.'

'Do as you're told, please.'

'Won't.' Her angelic face hardened with rebellion. Flora had to take a firm hold on her temper. Sophie wasn't nearly as sweet as she looked; in fact she was quite a handful. Even Isobel had never been quite this difficult.

'Are you going to help me shell the peas?'

'No, I don't like doing that. I'll do what you're doing, roll out the pastry.'

'Sophie dear, you're being naughty, so I don't want you here with me. I need to get this tart in the oven. You go back to your mother and ask Jamie to come and shell the peas.'

'Why should I?'

Flora told herself to stay calm. She tried to re-

237

member how Isobel dealt with her. 'Go and play with the twins.'

Sophie pulled a face. 'I don't want to. I don't like them. They're stupid, they can't even read. Mummy's trying to teach them.' But she went, slamming the kitchen door behind her, and Flora was left hoping the boys wouldn't hear her say that. Their confidence was being sapped away as it was.

The front doorbell rang. Flora waited for Isobel to answer it because her hands were covered in flour, but when it rang again she picked up a tea towel and wiped them as she hurried up the hall. She guessed it would be her sister Mavis. She was standing on the step looking tired and uncertain.

'Hello. Come on in.'

'I am supposed to come here?'

'Yes, Hilary suggested it. She's gone to the hospital to see Ben.'

Mavis's wrinkled cheeks grimaced. 'Such a terrible thing. How did it happen?'

'Come to the kitchen and I'll tell you all about it. You can shell the peas for me, if you would.' Flora took her sister's shabby black coat and hat and hung them in the cloakroom. 'We're all worried about Ben.'

She'd been listening for Hilary coming home and was at the stove when she heard her open the front door and come running down the hall. Flora was afraid she'd had bad news. She turned to ask, 'How is he, dear?'

'Paralysed,' Hilary gasped and burst into tears. Flora immediately pulled the pan of custard off the light and gave her a hug. She knew she was

238

repeating all the comforting things they'd been saying to each other ever since it happened.

Even Mavis tried. 'Your mother says his spine wasn't too badly crushed, and that it might improve with time. You must have patience, dear.'

The door was pushed open and Jamie came in. 'What are you crying for, Mummy? Is Daddy worse?' His face was working with anxiety.

'No, love,' Flora said. 'Daddy's woken up and been talking to Mummy. We're all going to have a glass of sherry.' She got out the bottle. 'You go and ask Auntie Izzy to come and have one with us.'

Hilary gulped at hers while Flora started to dish up the meal. She told herself it was Ben she'd cried for.

Mavis said, 'The prognosis must be very hard for Ben to face.'

'I must pull myself together,' Hilary said, getting up to carry the dishes of vegetables into the dining room and calling the children to come to the table.

Isobel couldn't drag her eyes away from her Aunt Mavis. She was wolfing her dinner down and looked totally unkempt. Her iron-grey hair was coarse and straight and held back from her eyes with a kirby grip. She made no pretence of having a hairstyle, that was just the way it was when it was cut, which Mum said was not often enough. Her black dress was turning brown with age and there was visible dandruff across the shoulders and bits of fluff all over it.

Yet Mum and Hilary treated Mavis with affection and were always inviting her to meals. She knew from Mum's letters that she was always included in family gatherings at Christmas. On Mavis's birthday, Mum cooked a special dinner for her which was held here in Hilary's house because there was more space.

Her mother asked, 'Will you have a little more of the casserole, Mavis?'

'Yes, just a little – if nobody else wants it.' Her eyes looked damp and sore behind their black-framed spectacles as she looked round the table.

'There's plenty for everybody.' Nobody else had yet cleared their plate.

'It's very good, Flora. You're a good cook.'

'She is,' Hilary agreed. 'Have a little more potato to mop up that gravy?'

Isobel couldn't understand how Mavis could be stick-thin when she was eating like a horse. Not that it gave her a smart figure; she drooped and sagged in all the wrong places and her flesh, where it showed at her neck and wrists, was scrawny.

'Are you feeling better?' Mum asked. 'Didn't you say you had a sore throat last week?'

'I still have and it's gone down to my chest. I'm coughing too now.'

'I meant to pop in and see you,' Flora said, 'but we've all had a busy time here. You should go to the doctor.'

'A waste of time. I could catch worse by sitting around in his waiting room.'

'Suit yourself,' Isobel said, 'but all the same...'

'That's what I am doing. I'll get better anyway. How are you, Isobel? You look a little peaky yourself.'

Isobel didn't like being told she looked peaky.

At the very least it meant she was looking older, but it could be that her troubles were showing on her face.

'We've not seen much of you up here recently,' Mavis went on. 'How's your husband? Sebastian, isn't it?'

To Isobel, it felt as though her aunt had put a finger on a sore spot.

'Daddy's always shouting,' Sophie said. 'Always cross with us.'

All the adults stopped eating and were looking at her. Isobel wanted to shake her daughter. 'He's been working very hard,' she choked. 'He's been feeling stressed recently.'

'I thought he was a primary school teacher like you?' Mavis said, as though no teacher could possibly feel stressed. 'He doesn't have to cope with adolescents?'

'Is everything all right?' Mum's eyes seemed to be boring into hers. Isobel knew Mum would have to know sooner or later, but there'd be no need to tell her everything.

'We probably need a holiday,' she said lamely.

'You always take lovely long holidays at this time of year.' Mavis put down her knife and fork with a satisfied sigh. 'Such a boon for teachers. Where are you planning to go this year?'

'I wanted to go to the seaside,' Sophie said. 'But we've come here.'

Isobel pretended to focus her attention on her dinner. Perhaps it was as well to have it out in the open. Mum would start digging after this. She'd be asking a thousand searching questions.

The garden shop had been hectically busy all Sunday afternoon. It was supposed to close at five but it was half past before the last of the customers had gone. Hilary was relieved to close the doors for the night. Rory was wheeling in more stock for tomorrow and would sweep through the shop before going.

Her mother was cashing up. She said, 'I'm a bit worried about Isobel. Do you think her marriage is breaking up?'

'Could be. She didn't want to talk about it over dinner.'

'She hasn't changed. She's like an ostrich – always hides her head in the sand if she's in trouble. Never wants to face it.'

Hilary said, 'Not in front of Aunt Mavis perhaps?'

'Not in front of us either.'

Hilary hadn't given much thought to her sister's problems. Now she said, 'Poor Izzy. Something is bothering her – she's anything but relaxed. If it's marriage difficulties, I don't know what we can do to help.'

'I hope she took Mavis for a walk this afternoon and that she's got a pot of tea made.'

Usually, on a Sunday, Mum took Mavis for a walk after their dinner, then brought her over to have afternoon tea with Hilary before Ben drove her home. Mavis always came by bus, but buses were few and far between on Sundays.

'I'll run Aunt Mavis home today,' Hilary said, 'and I'll call in at the hospital on the way back to see how Ben's getting on.'

'You have your tea before going,' Mum

ordered. 'It'll be some time before you get any supper.'

Despite the distractions of a busy afternoon, Hilary had thought a lot about Ben. She knew how hard she'd find it to accept life in a wheelchair. Ben might yet recover but the prospect of his not doing so was enough to terrify anyone. She knew he must be going through hell. When she reached his bedside she found he'd slid down from his pillows, his eyes were closed and his face the picture of misery

'Hello, Ben.' She kissed his cheek and sat down. She didn't need to ask how he was; it was all too obvious. Nevertheless, he brightened up when he saw her.

'What a surprise! I didn't expect you to come again, not twice in one day.'

'How are you doing?' She knew she shouldn't have asked as soon as the words were out of her mouth.

'Terrible. What a fool I was. I put myself right in front of that car, didn't I?'

'If it's any consolation, the driver's been caught. It was in last night's newspaper. It said he'd escaped from Walton jail where he was serving a six-year sentence for larceny and grievous bodily harm.'

'Grievous bodily harm? That's what he's done to me,' Ben said quietly.

'Your luck was out.'

'I was on top of the world on Tuesday. Spent all evening crowing that everything was going our way, didn't I? And now this.'

'Just bad luck.'

Ben was becoming agitated. 'Look what I've done to you. Landed you in a right mess, haven't I? How are you going to cope with everything? It's an impossible work load.'

Hilary told him again that she had three weeks' leave from work and that Isobel and her mother were staying with her and doing all they could. 'We've survived this afternoon and it's been busy in the shop.'

'I wish I could be there to help, but I can't. It makes me feel awful lying here when I know you're trying to do my work.' Ben was crying. 'It all looks so hopeless.' Hilary wanted to cry with him, but felt he needed her to remain strong.

A nurse came over. 'You mustn't upset yourself, Ben.' She led Hilary over to their work station. 'We'll give him something to calm him down. He needs to rest. You say good night to him and we'll settle him down and make him comfortable. He'll probably feel better in the morning.'

Hilary found it hard to believe she was glad to leave Ben's bedside, but she was. She felt exhausted and at the end of her tether.

CHAPTER FIFTEEN

While Hilary was driving home she suddenly remembered the letter she'd received from Fern Granville the literary agent, amongst the twins' birthday cards on Tuesday. She'd asked to see the remaining chapters of her book. Hilary couldn't believe she'd forgotten about that. She had thought the letter momentous when she'd received it and had been really excited, and so had Ben. It had seemed the icing on their cake, but that was five whole days ago.

As soon as Hilary returned home she went up to the study where she was now sleeping and looked out the rest of the manuscript. She wrote a covering note by hand. She couldn't be bothered typing it; that would have to do.

She let her pen hover, unsure whether to apologise for the delay, but decided against it. She hadn't a large padded envelope, and to wait until she could buy one would mean further delay. She tipped her typing paper out of the box it had come in, put her manuscript inside and was about to wrap it in brown paper when she heard her mother call, 'Hilary, is that you? Supper's on the table, dear.'

The last thing Hilary wanted was food, but she called, 'I'll be right down, Mum.'

She'd finish wrapping the parcel later and take it out to her car tomorrow. She'd be able to post it in the morning when she went to see Ben. If only her book could find a publisher, she'd be able to give up her job in the care home.

She ran downstairs to have supper. Isobel looked as though she'd been crying. No doubt now that she had problems of her own.

'Izzy,' she said. 'What's the matter? I didn't ask in front of Aunt Mavis and Sophie; I knew you couldn't talk about it then.'

Isobel sniffed. Her eyes felt hot and her handkerchief was a damp ball in her pocket. She hadn't meant to dissolve in tears but Mum had been sympathetic and very kind. She said to her sister, 'It's Sebastian, as you've probably guessed. We aren't getting on very well. In fact, that's the understatement of the year. We aren't getting on at all. It's gone so far that divorce is...'

'Izzy!' Hilary put an arm round her shoulders. 'How awful. And you've kept it to yourself all this time.'

'You have your own worries.' Isobel couldn't hold back another snuffle. 'They seem even worse than mine.'

'It doesn't help to bottle it up,' her mother said gently. 'A trouble shared and all that. Shouldn't you go to Marriage Guidance and try to...?'

'No, it's gone too far for that, Mum.'

'What happened?' Hilary asked.

That was the last thing Isobel wanted to explain. 'We grew apart. Arguments all the time.'

Mum said, 'About money, you said earlier?'

'Yes, money troubles mostly.'

'I'd have thought you were the last couple to have money worries,' Hilary said.

Isobel blew her nose. 'It's been going on for a long time. We had the mother and father of a row before I came here and I don't want to go back. Sebastian is talking of divorce. I think it's the only way now, but everything costs money these days, even that.'

Isobel found it a difficult meal. Even with the children there, Mum kept on handing out advice, particularly about having counselling.

'I've told you, Mum,' she said impatiently. 'Sebastian wants a divorce. I just don't know how

246

we'll be able to afford it.'

'Well, if you've made up your mind.' Mum was frowning. 'Can't you get a divorce on the green card? You know, legal aid?'

Isobel brightened for a moment. Could she? But probably not. 'Wouldn't my salary put me beyond help of that sort?'

'I don't know, but you could ask,' Mum said. 'If you're set on it.'

Isobel hadn't thought of that for herself. It might be worth a try.

Then there were the children to be bathed and put to bed. Isobel returned to the sitting room afterwards but Mum kept asking questions. She went up to bed early because she couldn't stand any more, though there was a good programme on television. Sophie was fast asleep slap in the middle of the bed. Isobel heaved her over to one side without waking her but she couldn't sleep when she put the light out.

She was glad she'd told the family she and Sebastian were about to divorce. Perhaps she should never have married him in the first place; certainly she should never have tried to trick him into it. It seemed unbelievable now that she had. She hadn't been thinking straight. Rupert's death must have unhinged her. At the time, it had seemed the one way out of her predicament, but she hadn't thought about the long term consequences and she should have done.

Isobel tossed and turned and tried to decide on her best course now. She ought to start looking for another job here. She was lucky that teachers were always needed and could work anywhere.

It looked as though Mum meant to stay here with Hilary while Ben was in hospital. She wondered if her mother would allow her to live in her cottage. She'd be able to pay her rent, once she got a job. Finding somewhere for her and Sophie to live was going to be the difficult part. At the very least, Mum might let her stay in her spare room, or perhaps Hilary would let them stay here.

It always boiled down to money, or rather the shortage of it. Isobel looked at her bedside clock. It was eleven but she felt more thoroughly awake than she had when she'd come up at nine. She got up and put on her dressing gown. She'd go down and make herself a cup of tea and see if that would help.

At first, Isobel thought all the lights in the house had been switched off, but once downstairs she could see the kitchen door had been left ajar and a shaft of light was lighting up the hall. She pushed the door open, half expecting to find the room empty, but Hilary sat hunched with her elbows on the kitchen table and her hands wrapped round a mug.

'Hilly! I thought you'd be in bed by now.'

'I'm just about to go.' When her sister turned, her face was so bereft of hope that Isobel was reminded she wasn't the only one in difficulties. 'I'm so worried about Ben.'

Until now, Isobel had felt dissatisfied with her own husband and home while everything in her sister's life seemed to be near perfect. Hilary had a husband who loved her, who was better-looking and richer than her own. He got up and did things, had plenty of energy. She'd been envious

248

of the business Ben was building up and the fine house he'd built. When she'd heard he had been injured and might never walk again, Isobel had been sympathetic but not unhappy about Hilary's changed position. It evened things up a bit.

Now, she was stricken with remorse. Only a jealous monster would think like that. She wished she was more like her sister; kinder and more hard-working. Hilly would never try to use anybody as she'd used Sebastian. Hilary tried to help others.

Isobel said, 'I couldn't sleep. I thought a hot drink might help.'

'There's tea in the pot. I've only just made it.'

'Good.' She filled a mug and sat down next to her sister.

'Mum reckons we're both in trouble now. She says she doesn't know which one of us to help first.'

Isobel sighed. 'You. All this trouble with Ben came out of the blue. None of it is your fault. Besides, there's not much anyone can do for me.'

'She says you were always the hardest to help. You're independent. You've been away and managed by yourself for so long.'

'Managed? I don't think that's the right word. Seb and I have been at loggerheads for years.'

'Was it my fault, Izzy? That you went off by yourself so suddenly and turned your back on us?' Hilary's eyes were troubled. 'Was it because of me and Ben? Mum thinks it was.'

'No. You mustn't blame yourself.'

'But Ben was your boyfriend first.'

'He was until he deserted me for you.'

249

'He said you were getting bored with him and you were getting ready to give him the push.' Hilary sighed. 'But Mum reckons you were upset and that's why you turned away from us.'

Isobel felt guilt-ridden. She knew she'd deliberately given that impression, but even after all these years she couldn't tell Hilly the whole truth. 'My pride was hurt, Hilly, that's all.'

Hilary said, 'I'd never been in love before, you see. Not like I was with Ben. No hard feelings, Izzy?'

'No,' she said, 'of course not.'

Ben was right. They had been beginning to bore each other. She'd even noticed one night when he'd taken her to a dance in the church hall that his eyes were straying to other girls. That had hurt because he'd said he loved her, and she'd really believed she'd found her soulmate and they'd be together for life. She'd given all she had and they'd had some marvellous times on the back seat of his car.

Isobel could remember only too clearly when she'd begun to think she'd made a mistake. Ben had an iron self-discipline and expected her to have the same control. He could put off all pleasure in life for what he hoped would be greater pleasure years later. He liked to squirrel money into savings. He'd told her she was a spendthrift, and was shocked at what she spent on clothes and make-up.

Isobel wanted fun. When she persuaded him to take her to the theatre she wanted to be spoiled with good seats and chocolates, not taken up in the gods with a tube of peppermints. She liked a drink in the interval, not just a boring wait for the curtain to rise again, and it was always straight home afterwards. It was no good suggesting they go for a drink or a bite to eat then. His time-keeping was strict; he liked to go to bed early and get up early.

He was never keen on having a meal out. If she insisted, he'd choose the cheapest thing on the menu and seemed less than pleased if she chose something more expensive. If they had a birthday or something to celebrate, he could be generous, but otherwise she'd begun to think him mercenary.

But he hadn't put off the pleasures of sex, nor had he any intention of doing so. Isobel reckoned he didn't get it from Hilary and that was why he'd been so quick to propose marriage. She wished she'd done the same and not let him near her. The feeling of rejection would surely be less.

It was the fact that he'd taken up with her sister that had upset her. Perhaps they were more suited to each other, though. Hilly didn't seem to want fun either, just peace to scribble in her notebooks.

Once they were married, Isobel had never felt comfortable in Ben's presence. When she'd come up in the school holidays to stay with her mother, Hilary always had them for supper on one night and the only words Ben said directly to her were, 'Hello, how are you keeping?' and 'Goodbye, see you next time you come up.'

There should be no secrets between husband and wife, but there were things she'd prefer him not to have told Hilly. Isobel felt that not knowing what had been said and what had not had made her wary of him.

She could only suppose he felt as awkward with her as she did with him, and perhaps a little guilty too. She was afraid he might not like the idea of an ex-lover occupying his spare room on a more or less permanent basis. Neither did she know how much he'd told Hilary about her. There was certainly no way she could say to her sister, *I lost my virginity with Ben.*

Hilary said, 'It's always bothered me that I spoiled things for you. Mum thinks you were never content after that, and it was the reason you shot away to London as soon as you possibly could.'

She looked so miserable that Isobel felt sorry for her, and said, 'Everything changed for me at that time. It had nothing to do with you and Ben. Anyway, it's all a very long time ago.'

'Fourteen years since Ben and I were married.'

'But another year before you moved out.'

'Yes, and after that you had the big back bedroom to yourself.'

But it hadn't made Isobel any happier at home. She'd had to stay until she'd finished her teacher training course, though she dreamed of getting right away from Birkenhead as soon as she could.

'There was just you and Mum at home then. I thought you'd grow closer.'

Isobel had thought that too; it was what she wanted. She shook her head sadly.

Hilary said, 'Mum wanted you to bring your friends home. It would have broadened her life too, but you never did.'

Isobel tried to smile. 'You were always Mum's

252

favourite. She was still very involved with you.'

'No, that's not true. When you were a baby she was always fussing over you. Being four years older I can remember that. I was quite jealous.'

'Were you?'

'You were the pretty one. When Mum took us out, everybody's eyes went straight to you. I felt almost invisible.'

'Hilly!'

'It's true. I always felt in the background and I couldn't believe my luck when Ben...'

Isobel wondered why she and Hilly hadn't discussed Ben at the time. Instead she'd taken the huff and let it rankle.

'You always had lots of boyfriends when I didn't. He was my first. I want you to know that we've been very happy together. It's been a good marriage up to now.' Isobel saw her sister's lip quiver. 'I don't know what I'll do, Izzy, if he's paralysed and can't walk. I love him so much, but...'

'Don't give up hope yet.' Isobel put an arm round Hilly's shoulders, pulled her closer and tried to find words of comfort. Yes, she might have fancied Ben once but she knew she wouldn't want to be chained to him now, not if he was going to be an invalid for the rest of his life. Even if they were chains of love, she didn't think she'd have it in her. But Hilary said she loved him and she wouldn't think of leaving him. They'd been so careful and so sensible up to now, but look where it had landed her. Everything depended on Hilary now.

What was the good of a beautiful house if she had no time to enjoy it and was scared stiff the

253

mortgage would be foreclosed on it? Isobel had been in that position; she understood how helpless it made you feel.

Hilary looked mournful. 'You always managed to find a boyfriend to take you out, but after Ben there never seemed to be anyone special.'

'No.' Isobel couldn't talk about Rupes and what she'd done to his son. It was all too raw and she didn't want Hilly to know just how selfish she'd been. Looking back, she'd treated Sebastian shamefully. She sighed. If she were to be honest, she deserved all she'd got.

Hilary let out a gusty sigh. 'It's all getting on top of me tonight. I'm worried about the twins, too. What d'you think of their reading? Are they being left far behind?'

Isobel felt ashamed. That was yet another instance of how selfish she could be. She'd promised Hilary she'd hear the boys read and make them practise, but she'd just been going through the motions. She'd been letting them off after they'd read a couple of lines each. She'd hardly listened, her mind on her own problems. Now when Hilary was asking her opinion of the standard they'd reached, she hadn't got one. She hadn't even bothered to think about it.

She straightened her lips. Even worse, she knew immediately how to hide her lapse. 'We're both shattered, Hilly. I promise we'll have a good talk about the twins tomorrow. It's getting late now; we ought to go to bed.'

'You're right.' Hilary put their mugs in the sink and they crept upstairs together.

Isobel crawled into bed beside Sophie feeling

sorry for her sister. Life had dealt her a blow she didn't deserve. Unlike Isobel, she'd been a good wife and a good mother. To lead Hilly to believe her twins were being helped to read when they were not was a terrible thing to do. Really wicked. She'd turned into an evil woman whom nobody would like. She felt ashamed of herself.

Isobel made up her mind to turn over a new leaf and be more like her sister. She had to be more patient with the twins, help them to read. She was going to be a more upright person from now on.

Isobel was dreaming she was safe with Rupert again when something woke her and made her put both hands up to her face. She was still half asleep when she heard Sophie giggle and found she'd been tickling her nose with a feather pulled from a pillow. Sleepily, Isobel took it from her, but Sophie was using her fingers to tickle her ribs. 'Laugh, Mummy,' she urged.

Isobel didn't feel like laughing. She wanted to be left to drowse in peace, but she knew there was no hope of that. The sun was streaming through the curtains already. She lifted Sophie away from her and sat up. The noise from the twins' bedroom told her it was high time to get up. When she took Sophie down to the kitchen the rest of the family were there and her mother had breakfast laid out on the table.

Flora looked from her to Hilly and said, 'You girls stayed up very late last night. That does you no good when you've got a busy day ahead. What were you doing?'

Isobel saw the small intimate smile Hilary gave her before saying, 'We were just chatting over a cup of tea.'

Isobel was glad they'd done it. It had helped her understand her sister better. Perhaps understand herself better too.

Mum and Hilary seemed to shoot off to open the shop with indecent haste, leaving her with the breakfast washing up as well as four kids to look after.

'Can we go to play football?' Charlie asked. 'Up on our own pitch? We won't get on your nerves there and Daddy says it's safe for us.'

'No.' Isobel remembered her promise to Hilary. 'We'll read together first.' Sophie had disappeared. Isobel hadn't seen her for a while, which made her wonder what she could be up to. 'Get your books out. I'll be back in a minute.'

She ran up to the bedroom to see if her daughter was there. As she opened the door, Sophie looked up from Hilary's dressing table. She had one of the drawers open and was sorting through her aunt's possessions.

'What are you doing?' Isobel scolded. Hilary would be cross if she saw this.

'Auntie Hilly's got some lovely scarves, and just look at these beads.' The child smiled up at her and Isobel could see she'd been trying on her aunt's lipstick.

She said irritably, 'Put those things back and shut the drawer. You've no business to be going through her things.'

'You do it, Mummy. I saw you going through her frocks in the wardrobe the other night when you thought I was asleep.'

'I was trying to find space to hang our clothes,' Isobel lied, then pulled herself up. This wasn't turning over a new leaf. Sophie was right: she was nosy. She'd been surprised to find Hilary had no decent clothes. Of course, she wasn't interested in clothes, but she was interested in houses and this one was an absolute cracker.

'Wash your face and come downstairs. Bring a book or something to keep you occupied while I hear your cousins read.'

Isobel didn't feel like doing it. She'd had her fair share of children with reading difficulties in her class and found teaching them hard work.

She'd thought about the twins last night, and had decided Hilly was probably over-concerned about their reading. She was too ambitious for them. They were probably average for their age but not academic. They were the sort of boys who preferred to race round kicking balls about.

But she'd promised to give her opinion, and after fifteen minutes listening to Charlie stumble through a few short paragraphs, his face screwing with effort, she changed her mind. This was a side of Charlie she hadn't seen before. Just to ask him to read aloud caused him to tense up and he really lacked confidence. Andy was a little better but they were both backward. At ten years of age, she'd put their reading age below that of an eight-year-old.

Jamie was lying on the kitchen floor daubing at a picture in a paint book. He had a green smudge down one cheek.

'Do you have a reading book?' she asked. Jamie

257

didn't have to be persuaded to show what he could do. He was easier to cope with than the twins, and rather sweet.

'Yes. Mummy got one for me.' He brought it to her.

'I'd like to hear you read now.'

Jamie opened it at the first page and set off with confidence. It took her only a moment to realise he wasn't looking at the printed words at all but using the large coloured pictures to make up the story.

'Jamie, have you read this book before?'

'Yes. Mummy reads it to me. It's all about this red hen.' His small finger tapped at the picture. 'I like it, it's nice.'

'What's this word? Sound out the letters for me. H...' But she had to help him. 'H ... e ... n.' Isobel knew that many children couldn't read at his age, but most would make a better stab at it than Jamie.

'How long have you been going to school?'

'A long time.' His eyes were innocent and round. She felt sorry for him. On the spur of the moment, she put four pieces of writing paper on the playroom table and found a pencil for each child. Then she read very slowly from Jamie's story, which was told mainly in words of three letters, and asked them to write down what she said. She could guess what was going to happen. Only Sophie would be able to do it.

Isobel found she was right. She gave the boys a few lines to copy from the book itself. Jamie found it almost impossible – he couldn't name the letters of the alphabet – and the twins made many mistakes.

Things were worse than she'd supposed and the twins were looking very down in the mouth. To cheer them up, Isobel set up a game of numbers for them to play that always went down well in her classes. Soon they were their laughing boisterous selves, and wanting to go out to the field to play football.

Isobel made herself a cup of coffee and pondered on their difficulties. She'd heard the teachers she worked with talking about dyslexia in the staffroom. Some didn't believe there was such a thing. It was just a word middle-class parents had latched on to when their children were slow to learn to read, and they couldn't accept that their offspring were backward or lazy.

Sebastian had believed it existed, though, and had taken a good deal of interest in it. He'd left books on dyslexia lying about the house but she'd never read them herself. Isobel had always preferred to teach the brightest pupils, those who asked questions and were interested in everything; those who could get good marks in tests.

Sebastian taught the remedial class and had said he regularly had the odd child who was as bright as a load of monkeys in some ways, but still couldn't learn to read and write. Her nephews certainly seemed to have that difficulty. It was plain to see that it was going to give them big problems in the future.

Isobel had been teaching long enough to envisage the outcome. Sophie would sail through her education and be able to train for a career she'd find interesting which would earn her a reasonable income. Isobel knew what it was to be ambitious for a child. Sophie had it in her to do better than teaching at primary school level. It saddened her to think of what her nephews were likely to achieve.

CHAPTER SIXTEEN

It was half-past five yet again, before Hilary and Mum closed the shop and came back to the house. To Isobel it had seemed a long drawn out and boring afternoon. For her, being in charge of children equalled work. Although her attitude to Sophie had changed once she held her in her arms, she'd never envied Hilary having three.

She'd made cottage pie for them all, because she felt she had to justify her presence here, though at home she rarely cooked. She hated the monotony of housework, and while she had a job she'd paid somebody else to clean her house.

Her mother collapsed on a chair and Hilary said, 'I'm shattered.'

Isobel got out three glasses and went to pour them each a glass of sherry. The bottle was almost empty: it filled just one glass. 'Have you got another bottle, Hilly?'

Her sister was pulling a face. 'No. You'd better have it, Mum. Oh dear.' She got up to put the two small glasses back in the cupboard. 'I'll get some more tomorrow.'

'I'll go shopping for you,' Isobel offered. She

couldn't stand another whole day here alone with the kids.

'Sorry about that, Izzy. An orange squash?'

'Don't you have anything stronger? A bottle of wine or some gin or something?'

'Yes, but we usually keep that for visitors or Christmas or...'

'Count me a visitor, Hilly. We could really do with a restorative now.'

'You're right, we could. I'll get it. Wine, yes? Red or white?'

'Red.'

Flora clutched her sherry; she was leaning back in her chair with her eyes closed. 'It'll do you good, Hilary.'

'I can't have much. I'm going to drive to the hospital later. Where are the boys?'

'Up on the field. A couple of their friends came round this afternoon.' Isobel gulped at the wine. It was good and heavy, just what she needed. 'Sophie, set the table for me please.' The child had been curled up on the window seat reading, and now she got up obediently. Isobel had given her a good talking-to about her behaviour. She started sliding knives and forks along the big kitchen table because they were all sitting round it.

'We'll need pickles and tomato sauce,' Hilary prompted. 'They're in the fridge.' Sophie obliged.

'Now, please go up to the field and tell the boys to come in for their supper,' Isobel said. She was pleased to be able to show them what a nice child Sophie could be.

'I usually go to the back door and blow a whistle.' Hilary indicated the school whistle on an orange band hanging on the dresser but Sophie had already skipped off. 'The boys know what it means.'

'No need to save Sophie's legs,' Isobel said. 'Besides, I want to talk to you and I'd rather she was out of the way. I got the boys to read to me this afternoon.'

'Thanks, Izzy. It'll save me doing it later. What d'you think? Will you be able to give them a bit of extra tuition to bring them on while you're here?'

It would take a miracle to do that, Isobel thought, but it wouldn't help Hilly to hear that now. She said cautiously, 'It's going to take quite a lot of extra tuition, I'm afraid.'

'Are they that bad?'

'It's not just their reading,' she said, topping up her wine glass. 'Their writing is poor too. Jamie doesn't know his letters yet, though he says he's going to school. How long has he been going?'

'He's had two terms in a pre-school group where they begin teaching them to read. He'll be starting primary school in September. He's backward too?'

'Not backward. He's at the very beginning of his schooling. But some children start school better prepared than others. You've always read to him and he has older brothers who generally would bring him on. I'm not sure yet about Jamie. He might or might not have the same problem.'

Hilary sighed heavily. 'How I wish they could read as well as Sophie.'

Isobel felt proud to be able to say, 'For her age, Sophie's reading is better than average. Don't judge their standard against hers. She's bright.'

'I thought my boys were too.' It was a cry from the heart. Hilary took off her glasses and polished them on a kitchen towel. Tears glistened in her eyes.

Isobel went on, 'And don't forget that in early life, little girls are always ahead of little boys. At Jamie's age, the girls in the same class are on average a year in advance.'

'Are you saying that the boys catch up later?'

'Yes, in their teens. The twins aren't dim, don't think that,' Isobel said quickly. She needed to praise the boys to lift Hilary's spirits. 'I also tried them on mental arithmetic – well, I passed it off as a game and persuaded them to play. The twins did as well as Sophie at that; if anything Andy was better. I told him he'd won.'

'Thank goodness they're good at something.' Hilary was wearing her glasses again. 'Miss Spooner says they're good at sums.'

'Yes, and that shows it isn't lack of intelligence that's holding back their reading. It's what makes me think they could be dyslexic.'

'I've heard the word,' Hilary said. 'Ben and I wondered... What exactly does it mean?'

'Word blindness. Nobody seems to know why, but some children just can't take in the alphabet and put letters together to make words.'

Hilary was looking very serious. 'I've been worried. Ben has too. You're a teacher, you've had a different sort of life from me, you know about this sort of thing.'

'Well, I've certainly had children with reading difficulties in my class. Dyslexia is a new word to us teachers – it's not something we heard about in our training. It's more Seb's line. He's very interested. We used to pass all those with reading difficulties over to him in the first school I taught in. He told me about a little girl he had in his class last year with much the same problem; quick enough in some ways but as far as reading and writing went, he said she was virtually unteachable.'

'What?' Her sister's jaw dropped open.

'I don't mean your children are,' Isobel hastened to add, though it must be only too obvious that was what she had meant. 'There are different degrees of dyslexia.' She felt contrite. She must keep a closer watch on her tongue in future.

Hilary was almost in tears again. 'Help them, please, Izzy,' she implored. 'You can do it better than I can. You must be able to.'

'I'll do my best.'

'Thank you. Is there anything else that would help?'

'When the new term starts, you could go and see their headmistress...'

'It's a headmaster.'

Isobel shrugged. 'Whatever. Tell him about your worries, ask to have the boys assessed by the educational psychologist, every education department has one. Hopefully they'll be given special coaching.'

'I'll do that,' Hilary said. 'Anything else?'

'More of what you're already doing. Daily reading and writing practice, and teach Jamie his letters.'

'I must say you know a lot more than I ever did,' Flora put in. 'Things have moved on since my day.'

Isobel smiled. It was a pleasant change to hear Mum admit that. Usually she was pointing out her lack of skill, lack of thought and lack of common sense.

Hilary looked serious. 'And they will learn eventually?'

'Yes, but it'll be hard for them. It'll take time and effort. I'm afraid it'll be a long hard slog.'

'Literacy is absolutely essential in the modern world, isn't it?' Hilary looked defeated.

Isobel said nothing. She knew the worst thing was that the boys probably weren't keeping up with their other class work.

There was a commotion at the back door and the four children almost fell into the kitchen.

'Go and wash your hands. We're ready to eat now,' Hilary told them.

Isobel went to the oven to get out the two big cottage pies she'd made.

Hilary had no appetite. She found it difficult to get the cottage pie down, though Mum was telling Isobel how good it was. In the past she'd worried about the twins' reading difficulties, but she'd thought a little extra practice and they'd catch up. Now it seemed their problem was bigger than she and Ben had supposed. She hadn't thought it through. It had taken Isobel, who had the right experience, to point out the long term consequences.

She had a hundred more questions about dyslexia but it was only when the children were all tucked up in bed that she felt she could bring up the subject again. She couldn't answer questions from the twins until she knew more about it herself. Isobel's prognosis had depressed her. She made some coffee and took it into the sitting room for her mother and sister.

'Are you saying the boys ought to be in the remedial class?' she asked Isobel. Rory's mother had told her he'd been in the remedial class all his school life. She was sure Rory was very different. The twins were already more fluent in speech than he was.

'I think there's a special sort of coaching for dyslexics that's said to bring them on. Seb was always going on about the need for it. But there's been nothing but remedial classes at the schools where I've worked.'

'I wish he'd come up with you, so we could ask him,' Flora put in.

'Are you saying that's all they're likely to have at their school here?' Hilary was frowning.

'More than likely. I honestly don't know all that much about it. I'll go to the library tomorrow and see if I can find a book on it.'

'Thank you. I've always hoped the boys would enter the professions when they grew up. Be accountants or something like that and earn good salaries – but will they be able to? It seems an impossible dream now.'

'Who's to say? But they will find exams difficult.'

'Now you're trying to let me down gently.'

'They'll probably have to be very determined to get through them.'

'There are other ways of earning a good living,' her mother put in. 'Think of Ben running his own business. They can do that too. They don't have to be academic.'

Isobel was frowning. 'Speaking of Ben, I understand dyslexia is hereditary.'

'What d'you mean?'

'Well, we're all right, aren't we? It doesn't seem to have come from our side of the family. Does Ben have problems that way?'

Hilary said slowly, 'He reads quite a lot, we both do. We get books from the library and he loves the newspapers.'

Isobel asked, 'What about his writing and spelling?'

Hilary gave it some thought. 'The words don't come to him as easily as they do to me.'

'But you want to be a writer.'

'Yes.' Writing smooth sentences was her one talent. 'He's not as fluent on paper as when he talks.' Hilary felt suddenly cold. He usually left his business letters for her to write.

Isobel persisted. 'Can he spell, Hilly?'

Ben did ask her how to spell words, some of which were easy, and he kept a well-thumbed dictionary on his desk. She didn't want to believe anything bad could come from Ben. She shrugged. 'My spelling isn't perfect.'

Then a vision of his mother rose up before her eyes and tore at her heart. How could she have forgotten Ethel Snow? She'd adored Ben, her only son, yet wouldn't write to him when he was away on National Service; she was so ashamed of her writing and spelling she couldn't bring herself to put pen to paper. She'd relied on Prue and Primmy to do everything for her, including that.

She'd even pretended to read though Ben said she'd never really managed it.

Hilary felt her heart begin to thump. She'd felt so sorry for her. Ethel had been an unhappy woman who'd lived an empty life without friends, yet something in her personality had made her find fault with everything her family did and adopt a guise of being superior to everybody else. Hilary hoped her children would have better lives than that.

She looked up and met Isobel's penetrating gaze. She had to get away from her. She went up to her bedroom, taking off her glasses and wiping her eyes. If dyslexia had been Ethel's problem and it was hereditary, as Isobel suggested, it meant her beautiful twin boys might end up like her: bitter, frustrated and lacking confidence to face the normal challenges of life. Hilary threw herself down on the hard springs of the put-you-up and wept, her hope of their being high achievers dashed for ever.

After ten minutes, she pulled herself together and went downstairs for the rest of the evening, but anxiety seemed to fill the house. Nothing was as she'd supposed.

That night she tossed and turned in bed, almost sure now that Ben had the same problems. In a way she found that comforting. He was coping with it and was happy building up his own business. He'd been successful – well, up to now he had. The twins could do the same, couldn't they? Perhaps the garden centre would support them all by the time they left school.

She thought more about Ben. There were things

he could do that she couldn't. He could fix problems in engines and plumbing intuitively; he had a good grasp of business matters and a marvellous sense of direction. He had green fingers, too. Every plant he touched blossomed, and he never gave up on anything. He'd keep trying until he did succeed. Perhaps being dyslexic had advantages as well as drawbacks. Hilary was determined her children wouldn't become like Ethel Snow, but all the same it left her feeling depressed.

The next morning, Hilary got up early. She'd go and see Ben first thing this morning, before things got busy in the shop. She wouldn't mention dyslexia to him; he had enough to worry him at the moment.

She was pleased to find he'd been moved from intensive care to a high dependency ward. Hilary met the ward sister at the door and was told that Ben was much more cheerful. As she walked up the ward, he smiled at her and seemed quite excited.

'I'm getting better. They've taken the catheter out of my bladder. They're going to see if I can pee to order. I've done it once, and you wouldn't believe how good that makes me feel. I was afraid I'd be incontinent for the rest of my life.'

Hilary was awash with relief. She bent to kiss him. 'I'm delighted to hear that. How are the legs?'

'They're getting better too. My broken one hurts; who would have thought I'd be glad to feel pain? I'm so relieved, Hilly. I can feel prickling and a sort of pins and needles in the good one too. I'm to start physiotherapy, which means a bit of slap and tickle to start with, but hopefully it will get me going.'

The doctor saw her get up to leave and joined her in the corridor where Ben couldn't see them. He told her that although Ben was having some return of sensation and power, it didn't automatically follow that he'd make a complete recovery. He was hopeful that he would, but he might be left with some residual disability.

Hilary walked back to her car aware that some of the relief she'd felt had been taken away, but it was still excellent news. She hurried home feeling more hopeful about the future.

That same Tuesday morning, Isobel was up early too. She was looking forward to going shopping. 'Have you made a list?' she asked her sister.

Hilary said, 'It's on the dresser.'

Isobel picked it up. 'Gosh, there's pages of it.'

'There's a lot of us to feed. You don't mind, do you?'

'I'll be glad to get out and see something different.'

'I've suggested we start a housekeeping purse,' Flora called from the utility room where she was stacking the dishwasher. 'We can't expect Hilary to foot the bill for feeding us all. I suggest ten pounds each and half the amount per child and we can see how long it lasts.'

Isobel said, 'Good idea,' and opened her purse. With her family's thrifty ways, she ought to be able to save while she was here.

'How long will you be able to stay, Izzy?' Hilary

wanted to know. 'Till the end of the holidays?'

'Yes, if you want me to,' she said cautiously. She felt she was in limbo with no decisions made about her future. She really ought to be job hunting and house hunting if she planned to stay here.

'Yes please,' Hilary said. 'Primmy and Prue will be back soon after that. Just my rotten luck that they were away when Ben had his accident.'

Isobel remembered the rooms her mother had rented in the twin aunts' house. She'd stayed there when she'd come up for a couple of nights. It had been a pleasant first floor flat surrounded by trees, just the place for her and Sophie. She asked, 'Have they got anybody else living in those rooms Mum used to rent?'

'Yes, a policeman and his wife. Primmy says it makes them feel the house is safe from burglars.'

'I was thinking it might do for me,' Isobel said ruefully.

'You stay here. I don't know what I'd do without you to look after the kids. And you do a lot about the house, Izzy.'

'Of course I'll stay.' But it wasn't that easy, and the new school term didn't seem all that far off. Sophie would have to go to school. Seb had said he intended to start divorce proceedings and she assumed he'd already put them in hand, but as yet she'd heard nothing either from him or from a solicitor.

Neither had she made any plans for herself and Sophie. She hadn't told the headmistress at the London school that she wouldn't be coming back, so if she didn't get a job here she'd have to go home when the new term started.

She was ready to set out shopping when Hilary said, 'You won't forget about going to the library? See if you can get a book on dyslexia. Here's my library ticket and a couple of books to return.'

'Right.' Isobel decided she would look through the professional journals in the library and see if any suitable jobs were being advertised. She'd already left it very late to get a position starting in September. 'Look, I can't cope with four kids, the shopping and the library.'

'I want to come with you, Mummy.' Sophie was beginning to jump up and down, not wanting to be left behind.

'Fine, you can.'

'The twins will be all right out on the field,' Flora said. 'I'll keep an eye out for them.'

Hilary said, 'Jamie wants to go with you. Could you manage him as well?'

Jamie's eyes, round and innocent, sought out Isobel's, begging to be taken too. She tried hard not to sound too reluctant. 'All right. Go and put your sandals on, Jamie.' He whooped all the way up to his bedroom.

Isobel had intended to drive in to the central library in Birkenhead, where she knew exactly where everything was, but Hilary's books and ticket were from the Eastham branch, which was virtually on the doorstep. Mum had told her where to find a nearby supermarket too.

At the library, the assistant helped her find a book on dyslexia, but by the time she had the teaching journals open in front of her the children were restless and wouldn't let her concentrate.

272

There seemed to be plenty of advertisements for primary school posts but she couldn't see any for Birkenhead, or the South Wirral village schools nearby. She decided she'd ring the education office when she got back to Hilary's house.

Isobel liked being out and about amongst people; it gave her a lift. Even shopping for food was better than being stuck in Hilary's house with four kids. She sat Jamie up on the trolley where he couldn't get into mischief and set off down the aisles.

Her trolley was loaded up when she heard a voice say, 'Hello. How's Jamie this morning?'

Isobel lifted her gaze from the detergents to see Tom Waite, her mother's friend. The silver threads in his dark wiry hair shone under the shop lights, and he had crinkles round his eyes when he smiled. She liked older men.

'Hello,' she said. 'Fancy seeing you here.'

'Why? I have to eat too.' He had half a dozen eggs in his basket and a small packet of sausages.

'I thought Mum said you lived in lodgings?'

'I have a bedsit, with use of kitchen and bath.'

'Oh.' Isobel's mind was on her own problems. 'Is it easy to get accommodation like that?'

'Not really. I was lucky to find it.'

'Though with Sophie, I could do with more space.'

'I'd like Mummy and me to have a house,' Sophie said, putting out her chest. 'That's what she'd really like.'

'So would I,' he told her drily.

'Why don't you get one then?'

Jamie was holding his arms up to Tom. 'I want

273

to go high,' he trilled. 'Want to touch the ceiling.'

'It's much too high here, young man. I couldn't possibly. I'd have to be a giant.'

'You're good with children,' Isobel said. 'Have you had much practice?'

'I have a son and a daughter but they're grown up now, probably older than you.'

'How old's that?' she asked.

'Twenty-six and twenty-eight.'

'I can beat that,' she said, 'I'm thirty-four. Where did you find those eggs? I can't find anything in this shop.'

'Round this way.'

'Hang on. I need flour too.'

Sophie was tugging at her skirt. 'I want some of those biscuits with icing on,' she whined.

'No.' Isobel hauled her past them, and tossed a packet of Marie biscuits on top of her trolley.

'I don't like those.'

'I do,' Jamie said, reaching for them.

'Don't open them here.' Isobel snatched the biscuits from him and pushed them lower into the mass of groceries where he couldn't reach them.

'Shopping's no picnic with this pair,' she said to Tom.

It was going to be another hot day. Already her forehead felt damp. She swept her hair back from her face. She'd often thought she was in the wrong job. To be in charge of children day in and day out didn't suit her, though everybody assumed it did.

Tom took over her trolley and pushed it for her. She found room in it for two dozen eggs and wondered why he'd attached himself to her instead of

274

going his own way. When they arrived at the check out, Tom went first and bought a tube of sweets for each of the children. They started on them right away, which meant they wouldn't eat the next meal, but it seemed churlish to snatch them back. At least it kept them quiet.

He wheeled her trolley across the car park with his small bag balanced on top.

'Your family hasn't lived in these parts for long?'

'No, but Birkenhead isn't far. Ben moved them out here because it was a good place to start a garden centre.'

'Yes, so I heard. He's built up a good business.'

'Not that good. Could be touch and go right now. Hilary's worried.'

'Really? How is he?'

'Making progress.' Isobel gave him the latest report. 'Unfortunately, he won't be back running things for some time.'

'How's your mother?'

'Fine.'

'She looks tired. I'm afraid she could be doing too much.'

'We all are,' Isobel said sharply. 'There's no other way. We have to keep Ben's business going or his family will starve.'

Tom smiled disarmingly. 'I'm sure it can't be quite that bad. Ben seems well organised. He'll have made plenty of provision, insurance and such like.'

'No. Ben was running it like a one man band and he'd never given a thought as to what would happen if he couldn't work.'

'It must have good potential to earn.' He

275

looked thoughtful. 'Can I help? Perhaps talk to Hilary about it? A bank would probably lend...'

'No, don't mention that to her. They've already borrowed to the hilt.'

'But the car in the accident, the Jaguar?'

'Stolen.'

'Couldn't your mother help? Buy a share of the business?'

'No.' That turned Isobel off. Was he trying to find out whether Mum was as well heeled as she looked? She might as well let him know Mum had no money, so if that was what he was after he'd know he was wasting his time.

She put the children in her car. Sophie opened the door and tried to get out, and Isobel shooed her back.

'Auntie Izzy, I want to go home. It's too hot in here.' Jamie put his head out of the window. His face was scarlet in the heat.

'We're just going, sweetheart.'

'Your mother seems to understand business matters, and so does Hilary. Your father had his own business, didn't he?'

'No. He worked for a carpet company in Liverpool.'

Isobel thought he was probing too hard. She laid it on heavily. 'When he was killed, Mum faced real financial hardship. She had to slave to bring up me and Hilly. I'll have to go. My butter will be melting.'

As they drove away, Sophie said crossly, 'I don't like that man. He talks to you and to Jamie, but he's never nice to me.'

Isobel wasn't sure whether she liked him or not.

He'd seemed a bit nosy and that made her suspicious. Did he think her family was rich? Apparently it cost a good deal to set up a business like Ben's.

Mum looked as though she was going up in the world. She'd always been interested in clothes but she'd never dressed as smartly as she did now. Indecently smart for a woman in her sixties. Isobel knew she was very interested in Tom, but was he looking to line his own pockets?

She decided he was a bit strange, bombarding her with questions like that.

CHAPTER SEVENTEEN

Over the next week, Hilary could see Ben improving. She didn't mention to him what the doctor had told her. They both had to hope that his recovery would be complete. Within days he was telling her he could move his good leg and twiddle the toes on his broken one.

Hilary knew Ben would be in hospital for some time, possibly months. He was asking questions now about his business, wanting to know exactly what they were doing from day to day and what the takings were.

He said, 'I know how hard you and Flora must be working. I hate having to leave everything to you.'

'We're coping. We'll keep it going until you're better, don't you worry.'

'I wish I could do more to help...'

'You can, Ben. I've brought a pen and a note-book. I want you to list all the jobs that Rory must do over this next week. I want to know exactly what seeds and bulbs have to be planted to keep up the supply to the shop. What has to be potted up and what supplies do I need to order? If we're to have the poinsettias and the spring bulbs in flower at Christmas we have to prepare now, don't we?'

Ben pulled the notebook closer. She thought he'd brightened up at the thought of having something to do.

'The order book is in the desk drawer. If you look back to see what we ordered last year at this time, you'll need much the same. Bring it in with you next time you come, so I can check through it.'

'I will. I've also been thinking about the open-ing hours of the shop. You had plenty of time to work there and to start with you didn't want to miss a sale, but I don't have that luxury. I've got other things I need to do.'

'You could find somebody to help you.'

'I don't want to put the running costs up if I can help it. We're busy at this time of year, but when winter closes in wouldn't it be better if the shop remained closed on Mondays? We're open Saturdays and Sundays, and that's when we're busiest. And there's not much point in opening up at nine every morning for the same reason. If we don't open until ten, we wouldn't lose much trade. Better really to stay open an hour later in the evenings, especially in the summer.'

278

'You have been thinking about it.'

'I'm so glad you've recovered enough for this,' she told him as she kissed him goodbye. 'It's so much easier now I can talk to you.'

One rainy evening, she and Mum had locked up the shop and were in the kitchen helping Isobel dish up their supper when the telephone rang in the hall. Hilary rushed to answer it.

'Hello.' A woman's voice with a cut-glass accent asked, 'Is that Hilary Snow?'

'Yes.'

'I'm Fern Granville, literary agent.' Hilary let out an audible gasp of surprise. She was expecting a letter, not a phone call. 'You sent me your novel, *The Night Star...*'

Hilary's knees had turned to water. She had to support herself on the back of the hall chair. 'Do you think it's good?' Surely she must, or she'd have returned it by post.

'I like your writing style.'

Hilary could feel joy coursing through her. 'Will you take it on, try to find a publisher for it?'

'Well, I think it needs a bit of rewriting first. The beginning is a bit slow, and in fact it quite confused me.'

'Oh!'

'What I'd like you to do is to knock off most of the first chapter and possibly some of the second. It needs more action. You ought to get the reader into the story more quickly. You've waffled on too much at the start.'

'Oh! Ye-es.' It wasn't all good news then. She pulled the chair round and sank down on it.

'I do like the rest of the story though, and the end is good. Do you think you'll be able to do that?'

'Yes.' Hilary's voice had sunk to a whisper.

'Sorry? I didn't hear you.'

'Yes,' she said firmly. 'Yes, I could.'

'If you can do it to the standard of the rest of the book, then I'll take you on and try to find a publisher for it.'

'Oh!' Hilary felt overwhelmed. 'Thank you. Yes, of course I'll do it.'

'Then I'll send the manuscript back to you.'

'Thank you, yes. I'll send you the revised version as soon as I can.'

'Right. Goodbye then.'

'Thank you.' Hilary felt quite fluttery as she put the phone down. Up until now nobody in the trade had shown the slightest interest in any of her books, but now an agent had said she liked it! Hilary was afraid she'd sounded like a tongue-tied idiot. This was the chance she'd craved. She felt swept up on a tide of euphoria.

She rushed back to the kitchen and beamed round at her family. 'Guess what? Good news this time. Super news. Gosh, I'm thrilled.'

'Ben?' Mum asked.

'No, not about Ben. I told you, didn't I, I'd finished a book and sent it to an agent? That was her and she says she likes my writing style. This is my big chance.'

'That's excellent!' Mum was radiant at the news. 'What you've always wanted. I'm delighted for you, Hilly. You need something nice to happen for a change.'

'It's going to be published?' Isobel asked, amazed.

'Well, I hope so. Nothing's certain at this stage.'

Isobel sounded excited. 'Wouldn't it be marvellous if it turned out to be a bestseller? It would solve your worries about mortgages once and for all.'

'There's just one thing,' Hilary said. 'The agent wants me to rewrite some of it before she does anything.' Her feelings of triumph were fading fast. Rewrite the first couple of chapters? When was she going to get time to do that? Every hour of every day seemed crammed full of things she must do, and when her leave was over she'd have to work eight hours a day in the care home too.

There was a moment's stunned silence, then Isobel hooted with derision.

'You'll never find time to do that now.'

Hilary could tell from her mother's face that she thought the same.

'I know how it must look to you,' she faltered. 'You've both come to help and you're working long hours for me and Ben, and now it looks as though I'll be asking you to do more while I sit and write. But I won't let it make any difference to you. I'll get up at four in the morning...'

'Hilly, you can't,' her mother said. 'You'll exhaust yourself. You're doing too much now, trying to run the shop and rushing back and forth to the hospital.'

'I can't pass this chance up. I might never get another. I'm going to revise my book if I have to stay up all night.'

'You feel worn out now, don't you?' Flora

asked. 'I know I do and you're doing more. You won't be able to do good work when you're tired out. You've got to get your sleep.'

Isobel asked, 'Is there any guarantee it'll be published? I mean, even if you do rewrite the beginning?'

Hilary shook her head.

'You're chasing after rainbows,' Isobel told her. 'You'd be better off spending the time reading with your kids.'

Hilary felt as if she'd been slapped in the face. But as soon as supper was cleared away, she went up to her study and got out the carbon copy of her book to see what the agent had meant. She started marking the bits she needed to keep with a pencil, but flicking through the pages made her feel disorientated. She was too tired now to do this.

She went to bed reeling with indecision. They were right, of course, her chance had not come at the most opportune moment, but there was one other thing she could do to give herself more time. She could jack in her job at the care home. The problem then would be the mortgages. Most of her salary went on paying them. It was a risk. She could hardly expect any payment for the book in the short term, and most writers were thought to earn very little. What would happen if she didn't make enough money from the garden centre to pay their outgoings?

On the spur of the moment she switched on the light and got out of bed. There was an advantage in sleeping in the study where all the files were kept. She selected the one containing the documents relating to the mortgages and got back into bed to read it. They had two, one on the house and an even bigger one on the business. Each month they paid interest on the money they'd borrowed as well as repaying a small portion of the capital. If they couldn't pay, their house and business would be repossessed and sold off to cover their debt.

She shivered at the thought, but it now looked as though Ben would eventually recover and be able to run the garden centre again. If she gave up her job, they might find themselves in financial difficulties over this year, but in the long term they ought to be able to pull back up.

Hilary decided to go in to their building society and talk to somebody about it. If they would extend the period of the mortgages, the risk would be less. It was a difficult decision to make and could have the most awful consequences if she got it wrong.

She got out the business ledgers and tried to anticipate the profit they would make this year. It was very late indeed when she went to sleep.

The next morning, Hilary went to their building society and then on to the hospital to see Ben. She found he'd been moved again, to an orthopaedic ward this time. He was cheerful and quite sure now he'd make a good recovery.

'The physiotherapist has had me out of bed,' he said, 'and she's given me those crutches.' They were propped against the wall. 'I didn't manage to move about much, it was more her explaining what she wanted me to do, but she said I didn't do badly for a first go. She'll be back for more tomorrow.'

283

Hilary could see Ben was encouraged. He talked about the business as though their future would still be what they'd planned; as though it was just a matter of time and treatment before he'd be able to dig and plant and serve in his shop. She felt as though a burden had been lifted from her back.

She told him about the phone call she'd had from the agent, and what Fern had said about her book.

'You've been hoping for a chance like this for years,' he said grimly, 'and now it's come, my accident has ruined it for you. How are you going to find time to write now?'

'I'm going to try,' she said firmly. 'I can't let a chance like this slip away.'

'But how will you find the time?'

'The only way will be to give up my job.' She saw the look of horror on his face and went on hurriedly. 'You did say the time for that was coming; that the business was making almost enough.'

'Yes, I did.' He was shaking his head. 'But then I expected to be there and be able to work. I know how to wring the maximum profit from it, but it won't be so easy for you. You've never spent much time...'

'I'm there now and I'm learning fast,' she said. 'If I didn't have to go to work I'd have more time to spend in the garden centre too. I'm learning to cope with the shop and it'll get easier when I'm into the routine of it and the children are back at school.'

He seemed taken aback. She usually fell in with his wishes. 'But there's still the mortgages,' he protested. 'It scares me when I think of them.'

'Well, it scares me too. I thought the best thing to do was go in to the building society and ask. I've just come from there,' she said. 'I told them about your accident. It alters things.'

'What did they say?'

'They were sympathetic. They'll consider giving us a break from the monthly payments. It will extend the period of the loan and give us more time to pay. We may not need it, but if we do, it would be possible to organise.'

'Hilly, you're very clever to think of that, but...'

'So you see, it'll be all right.' Hilary had known from the moment she'd seen Ben in intensive care that she'd have to be the strong one. Lying in bed, in pain as he was, would be bound to rob him of his confidence.

'All the same,' he said, 'I wish it hadn't come now. I don't like to think of you giving up work. That's our guarantee that we can keep up the monthly payments.'

'I know, but I've waited for this chance for years; worked for it, dreamed of it, hoped for it. Now it's come I'm going to grab it. We don't get many chances in this life.'

'Hilly!' Lines of tension were showing round his eyes again. She had to harden her heart.

'I've got to give up my job. It's the only way. I'll regret it for the rest of my life if I don't do it now.' To take Ben's mind off it, she started to tell him what Isobel had said about the twins' reading. 'Did you have any trouble learning?'

'Yes,' he said.

It was the first time she'd come to the hospital

to find him cheerful and left him looking worried. It made her feel terrible, but this was a chance she was determined not to miss.

She went home, and before she could change her mind she rang up the administrator of the Cavendish Scott Care Homes.

'Miss Procter,' she said firmly, 'I'm sorry, but I won't be able to come back to work. I'm having to run the family business. I want to give in my notice.'

'Are you sure?'

'I know I'm making it difficult for you, but I've so much on my mind, I don't think I could give the old people the care and attention they need. I'd like to leave as soon as possible.'

'Mrs Snow, your contract states you must give a month's notice. We have to have time to find a replacement for you.'

Hilary had expected that. 'I'm not due back for another three days. If I date my letter today, will I be allowed to count those days as part of my notice?'

'I'd prefer you to take holiday money in lieu.'

'All right,' Hilary said. She might well be glad of a few days' extra pay, so she wouldn't quibble about working a few days more.

'I'm sorry to see you leave,' Miss Procter said stiffly. 'You've been reliable up to now. If, when your husband is better, you want to return to work, I would be happy to consider your application.'

'Thank you.' Hilary felt better. If they were desperate for money, she could always go back. She hadn't burned any boats there.

'Even part time, Mrs Snow. I hope your husband gets better soon.'

Hilary sat down for a moment. It had been a big decision to take, but she was sure it was the right one.

Flora felt cross and out of sorts because Hilary had given up her job at the care home. How many times had she pointed out the economics of that to her? It would pay her to carry on working and bring in the part-time girls for the busy periods. They were very obliging and seemed more than willing to help out. Flora had spent every day in the shop since Isobel had come and was ready to go on doing so.

The shop was empty for the first time this morning, and she was glad to sit down for a minute. Her feet ached. Although it was not far off time to close for lunch, Hilary had gone to make them a cup of tea in the little office at the back. They'd missed their elevenses because they'd been busy and were both desperate for a drink now.

Flora looked up when the doorbell clanged again, expecting it to be another customer. It was Tom Waite.

'Hello. I'm glad I've caught you at a quiet moment. I was wondering if you'd be coming to play bridge this afternoon? You weren't sure when I spoke to you last time.'

Flora was glad Hilary was returning with their tea. It would do her good to hear this.

'I'd love to, Tom. Nothing I'd like better than a relaxing afternoon playing bridge, but you know how it is. I'm needed here.'

Hilary put a mug of tea on the counter in front of her. 'Hello, Tom. Can I interest you in a cup of tea?'

'No, no thanks. I just wanted to see if Flora...'

'I can come to the evening session on Thursday,' she said. 'But I'm afraid afternoons are off for the time being.'

He smiled at Hilary. 'Your mother's very good to you.'

'Don't I know it?'

'I could give you a hand too, if you want, Hilary.'

'Thanks. Everybody is being very helpful to me.'

'Take me up on it if you get stuck,' he said. 'Any time. I don't know all that much about plants but I'm willing to learn. I'll pick you up on Thursday evening then, Flora.'

The doorbell clanged behind him and there was a moment's uncomfortable silence.

Then Hilary said, 'You could go this afternoon, Mum, if you want to. I'm getting better at serving – I'm nearly as good as you now.'

Flora thought longingly of Tom and the pleasant afternoons she'd had playing bridge. 'I want to help you, dear. If I can make myself useful here, that's more important.'

A customer came in and they both leaped up to serve her. Flora won.

Hilary said, 'It's gone suddenly slack, hasn't it? I'll pop and see what Rory's doing.'

Flora had always thought of Hilary as being reliable and dutiful, but she was showing a lack of responsibility by giving up a job that would pay the mortgages. After all, Ben could do nothing about it just now and she'd encouraged him to spend extravagantly on the house. Her novel was already written, for heaven's sake. Why did she have to give up her job just to rewrite two chapters? Surely she could put that off until Ben was home and able to work again?

Flora felt she was giving up a lot to help Hilary and now it looked as though she wouldn't help herself. At the same time, Flora was surprised to find Isobel so sympathetic and helpful; she was putting herself out to help the boys read, and doing a lot about the house as well as cooking a hot meal every evening.

She'd always thought of Isobel as the selfish one who went out to satisfy her own needs and had little sympathy for others. Perhaps she'd done Isobel an injustice, or the girls were more alike than she'd realised.

During a lull in the afternoon, Hilary said, 'I've been thinking, Mum, about what Tom said this morning. Rory's fine on routine stuff but Ben's writing down reams of instructions. He wants plants moved from the garden to the hothouse and seedlings transplanted and there's a long list of plants that need propagating.'

'There's a lot to think about.'

'Too much for me and Rory. If Tom came in on two or three mornings a week until Ben comes home, it would make all the difference.'

'Tell him, then. He said he'd be glad to help.'

'Let me have his phone number and I'll give him a ring.'

Flora did, and watched Hilary disappear into the back room. She returned a few minutes later.

'He's coming round to see me,' she said. 'To find out what exactly I want him to do.'

The customers were coming in steadily and Flora was kept busy but she saw Tom smile at her as Hilary led him through to the office at the back.

Business had slackened off when Hilary came out. 'Tom's happy to come in two mornings a week. He'll help Rory follow Ben's written instructions about planting and sowing. He's very kind; he offered to do it for nothing, but I told him we all have to live. I've made some tea, so you go and have a cup with him. I'll stay here.'

Flora was pleased. It meant she'd see more of Tom.

'I hope this will keep us out of trouble in the glasshouses,' Hilary said.

Later, when Tom had gone to talk to Rory, Hilary told Flora of some other changes she wanted to make.

'We're going to open at ten and close at six,' she said, pinning a notice to the door and another to the counter. 'And in the winter the shop will stay closed on Mondays. Rory has always had Sundays and Mondays off but Ben just worked on.'

Flora said, 'I've always thought it wrong for him to work seven days a week.'

'I quite agree. We can't go on like this. I want us both to take a day off every week from now on.'

'I feel I could do with a break. Which day?'

'Tuesdays or Wednesdays are our less busy days. You choose.'

'Tuesday, I think. Then I can play bridge in the afternoon.'

'Right, then I'll have Wednesday, if you can

manage in the shop on your own. Anyway, I'll only be over in the house if things get desperate.'

Flora thought Hilary was being very sensible and decided that on Tuesday she'd ask Tom to her house for that supper she'd postponed.

Isobel was preparing fish pie for lunch when she decided she'd phone the education department while she was alone in the house. She'd washed her hands and was walking towards the phone when it rang.

She picked it up and almost dropped it again when she heard Sebastian's voice.

'Are you all right?' he asked.

'Yes,' she said firmly, though she felt anything but all right.

'And Sophie?'

'She's fine.'

'I was wondering, Izzy ... when are you coming home?'

'What? You told me not to come back, not ever.'

'I know. I was angry. We both were.'

'Well, yes we were.'

'We said some terrible things.'

'You said you were going to start divorce proceedings.'

'Yes, I know...'

'That was weeks ago and as I've heard nothing since I assumed you meant it and were going ahead. Have you seen a solicitor about it?'

'No.' There was a pause. 'Have you?'

'No. I've no money to spend on solicitor's fees, as you know, and as I'll never want to get married again after this, it'll be just the same if I stay here and you stay down there.'

He said in a more placatory tone, 'Were we too hasty? Too worked up with all the arguments to think straight?'

'It's certainly been more peaceful away from you.'

'Izzy, don't let's start rowing again. I was wondering if we should give it another go?'

'I thought you wanted...'

'Is divorce what you want, Izzy?'

'I don't know what I want. I'm so mixed up I don't know whether I'm coming or going.'

'It's lonely without you.' His change of heart, so sudden and unexpected, floored her. 'I'd like you and Sophie to come home so we can discuss calmly what we do want.'

'And have a few more blistering rows while we're about it?'

'No, of course not.' She could hear the anger in his voice.

'I don't know, Seb. I'm not up to this.' She put the phone down with a little crash.

Speaking to Seb had stirred up all the emotion she'd felt before she'd come up here. The fact was, she'd have to go home if she couldn't find a job up here to support herself and Sophie. She'd been about to ring the education department to find out if there were any jobs going. She lifted the phone again; she'd do that now.

'We have no local vacancies at present,' she was told, 'but we are seeking to recruit supply teachers.'

Isobel felt very put out.

'You'll need to bring in your certificates and be

interviewed by Mr Morris. Do you want me to make an appointment for that now?'

Isobel said yes but she couldn't make plans on the strength of that. She put the phone down feeling insecure and disappointed. Perhaps she should try Chester? From here, it was within reasonable reach. On the spur of the moment, she looked up the number of their education department and dialled it. Chester had no posts vacant for primary school teachers either. She was shocked. She hadn't foreseen this.

She was undecided then about what she should do. Supply teaching meant she could rely on nothing, that she'd only work if a regular teacher was off sick. If she was lucky, she'd get work, but it was likely to be a fortnight on and a fortnight off, and then a week at this school and a week at that. She wouldn't know the pupils and by the time she did she'd be moved somewhere else. Or, even worse, she'd be sitting at home waiting for another vacancy to come up.

Damn Sebastian. He didn't know what he wanted either. She'd be better off staying on Merseyside near her family, who would provide a roof over her head, but without a reliable income she'd never be able to get a home of her own. Ben wouldn't be in hospital for ever, and he'd need his bed when he came out. She felt unsettled and uneasy.

CHAPTER EIGHTEEN

Hilary was full of trepidation when she thought of the future.

Mum had been very much against her jacking in her job and so had Ben, but she'd had to. This was the first hint of a chance that had ever come her way and she couldn't throw it away.

Knowing she had to work out the month's notice she'd contracted to give the care home, Hilary had gone back this week. Mum and Izzy had found their work load almost impossible to get through as a result.

On the way home, she'd called at the hospital to see Ben. Now he was in an orthopaedic ward she was supposed to respect ordinary visiting hours, but the ward sister was a half-remembered acquaintance. They'd trained together at the General years before, so Hilary was allowed in as long as the ward was quiet.

Because of her own busy schedule she was able to spend only a few minutes each evening with Ben. Tonight he'd said, 'You are making sure the greenhouse skylights are open all day in this heat and closed at night, aren't you?'

Hilary had never given them a thought and was immediately afraid it wasn't being done.

'If it gets cold at night it could ruin the whole crop.' Ben frowned. 'I've asked Rory to see to it, but I usually check that he's doing it.'

'I'll make sure,' she choked. No point in worrying Ben yet, but she was certainly concerned. On her return she went straight to the greenhouses and found the skylights closed, the plants thriving and the atmosphere damp and cosy. The soil and its moisture level seemed right: Rory was doing what was needed. She breathed a sigh of relief.

Mum said she'd checked that he was watering routinely but hadn't known about opening and closing the skylights.

As she would be at work, Hilary said, 'Tomorrow, you must tell Rory how pleased we are with what he's doing. He's saved our bacon there.'

They all felt exhausted. Hilary herself had been up till midnight on the last few nights making sure all was well with the nursery plants and working on the books. There was absolutely no way they could carry on permanently in this way, and even to keep it up for three more weeks was going to be hard.

On the Friday morning, Miss Procter told her that two of the part-time nurses had asked if they might work full time, which would replace Hilary's hours. 'No hand-over will be needed, so if you want to leave immediately that will be all right.' Hilary was more than glad to do so.

Saturday was usually a busy day, but the next morning Hilary felt more relaxed. From now on, she'd be able to give all her attention to the business in the daytime. She was eager to start rewriting her book, and decided she would begin tomorrow morning.

She took a Thermos full of instant coffee up to

295

bed with her so she wouldn't have to go down to the kitchen when she got up, which might wake the rest of the family. Then she set her alarm clock for four o'clock and settled down to sleep. It seemed only minutes later it was going off with the clangour of a fire engine. She pulled it under the bedclothes and groped for the switch to put it off. It felt like the middle of the night.

She told herself it was a matter of self-discipline and heaved herself out of bed to dress quickly. The coffee was very welcome; she hoped it would wake her up, but her mind still felt fuddled when she opened up her manuscript. What had the literary agent told her to do? Hilary's fingers were stiff and clumsy when she started to type.

What was the matter with her? She'd done this for weeks in the spring and early summer in order to finish *The Night Star*. But once she got used to making an early start, she'd be all right.

Lunch was over. Andy watched the rain washing down the kitchen window. It looked as though it would never end.

'Can we go out to play?' he asked, though he knew it wouldn't be allowed.

'Out where?' his mother wanted to know. The grown-ups were sitting over their endless cups of tea.

'Only to the field, for football.'

'No. You'll get soaked.'

'Can we come to the shop and help then?' Charlie suggested. 'We're bored.' They'd been indoors all morning.

'No,' Hilary said. 'We'll be closing early. There

hasn't been much doing today and I want to work on the accounts to keep the books up to date.'

'Ah, Mum, please.' Andy saw the look his mother gave Auntie Izzy, who gave him a tired smile.

'We'll have a game of Snap.'

'We played that this morning.'

'Happy Families then.'

'No. We're tired of cards.' The twins always spoke for each other.

Hilary said, 'What about those jigsaw puzzles you were given for your birthdays?'

'We've done them,' Charlie said. 'They're finished, both of them, on trays in the playroom.'

'I wondered where those trays had gone.' Hilary smiled. 'But there's no need for you to feel at a loose end. You were given all sorts of games and things. You can't be tired of them yet.'

Flora said, 'What about building those model aeroplanes I gave you?'

'Yes, Nana.' Charlie was quite keen. 'Let's do that, it'll be good. Mine's a Spitfire.'

'Mine's a Hurricane,' Andy shouted as he ran for the stairs after Charlie to fetch it from their bedroom.

'Bring them down here,' his mother called after them. 'I don't want glue on your bedroom carpet.'

Andy found his box. The picture on the front was exciting. He'd opened it up on his birthday but had been unable to see how all those plastic pieces fitted together. It looked like being a long job and he'd had so many other things to do then. Now, he took it down to show it to the grown-ups in the kitchen.

'When I've built it, I'm going to paint it and keep it on my chest of drawers.'

Nana pushed her teacup away from her. 'A good idea. It'll make a nice ornament.'

'On the playroom table,' Mum ordered as she and Nana went back to work in the shop. 'You'll be out of everybody's way there.' She handed him some old newspapers. 'Put these on the table first,' she told him. Mum could be fussy about that sort of thing.

Charlie led the way and helped him spread the paper out. Jamie climbed on the chair at the end of the table and rested his chin on his arms. Andy could see his gaze was riveted on the box containing his model aeroplane. He opened it carefully so as not to lose any of the small pieces.

Sophie was frowning. Pushing closer, she said, 'It's not fair. I want a model to build.'

'Me too,' Jamie added.

Auntie Izzy sounded exasperated. 'If you haven't got models of your own, you'll have to help the twins or play with something else. Settle down nicely now.'

'It's easy to see the body of the plane and the wings,' Andy said as he lifted them out and lined them up in front of him. From the heap of small pieces, he picked out the wheels and the propellers.

'This is going to be great.' Charlie was excited as he did the same with his.

'Where do we start?' Andy opened up the printed instruction leaflet. There was a diagram showing where the parts fitted. 'It looks quite difficult.'

'Does this piece go on to this one?' Charlie wanted to know.

'You must work out what it tells you to do,' Isobel said. 'Have you got glue?'

'Yes. There's a tube in the box.'

Andy liked her to leave them alone when she looked after them. He knew she was going to the sitting room to put her feet up. Daddy said that must be a no-toy area, a refuge for adults.

'The wings have to be stuck into those holes,' Sophie said. 'Why don't you get on with it?'

'I want it to be right. Make a good job of it.' Andy was studying the printed instructions.

'What does it say?' Sophie demanded.

He didn't know. He tried to sound out the letters to himself as Miss Spooner had taught him. There was one big word he didn't understand. He wanted to know what it meant but he wasn't going to ask Sophie. She'd crow if he did. He took the instruction sheet to ask Auntie Izzy.

'Fuselage,' she said.

'What's that?'

'It's just another name for the body of the plane.'

'Then why not call it the body? It just makes things harder.'

'I know.' She seemed to understand and be willing to help. 'What's this word then?'

Andy tried, 'W... I ... n – wings.'

'That's right. And this word is glue.' Her finger moved along the line of print. 'You put a dab of glue on to these tabs on the wings and fit them into the holes on the body.'

'Oh! That's what Sophie said.' He didn't like

299

that, but he could do it now.

'You need the glue to keep the pieces firmly in place, all right?' Auntie was returning to her book.

He nodded. 'I can't wait to see it all finished. Will it fly, Auntie?'

'No. It isn't meant to fly, it's a model.'

Andy went back to the playroom to build it. With both wings on, his model was taking shape. The wheels next ... but there must be other pieces between them and the body. He consulted the instructions, but the words were hard to make out. He shook the box of bits looking for the right pieces and studied the coloured picture on the lid. It was tantalizing. He wanted to build it.

He could feel Sophie's breath on the back of his neck. She took the instruction sheet from him.

'Here,' she said. 'It says the struts fit into these little holes. These are the struts.' She picked them out of his box. 'Piece number nine. There's two of them.'

Sophie made him cross. 'You go and play some-where else,' he said. 'I'm doing this. I don't want your help.' She flounced round to the other side of the table and sat next to Charlie.

Andy followed her suggestions and glued on the struts. He had the wheels but there was something else that went on first.

'Those mudguard things,' Sophie said from the other side of the table. She was picking them out from Charlie's box.

'Go away,' he shouted. 'They're our models. We're going to build them. Girls don't do this sort of thing.'

'All right, if you don't want me.'

'We don't,' Charlie assured her.

Andy could hear her talking to her mother as he glued his wheels on. His Hurricane was looking better and better, and on the diagram he could see a sort of nose-shaped piece that fitted at the front ... yes, and the propellers went on to that. He didn't need the instructions. They were rubbish.

Charlie was frowning and looking at Andy's plane so he could copy what he'd done. He said, 'They're quite hard to do.'

Andy wanted to do the tail part next. The diagram was no help. There seemed to be a lot of pieces and it wasn't clear where they would fit.

'That's a door,' Charlie said. 'Should we have put the doors on first?'

'And the RAF rondells.' Andy stuck his on.

'You've got to paint it before we stick those on,' Charlie said, so Andy peeled them off and went back to the instructions for the tail.

He felt thwarted. 'How d'you spell tail, Charlie? If I could pick out that word I might get a clue from what comes next to it.'

Charlie was no help. 'It's hopeless.'

'No,' Andy insisted. 'I think it's spelt t ... a ... l ... e, but there's nothing exactly like that.' He studied Charlie's instructions in case they were easier, but found they were much the same. 'I think this piece must go here on the top.' He glued it on.

'That doesn't look right,' Charlie told him.

Andy could feel a ball of frustration growing in his stomach. He thumped the table with his fists before taking it off again. 'It's got to go some-where near...' He was blinking back tears of disappointment. He'd never be able to manage it. He looked at his twin.

Charlie was agitated and screamed, 'These models are rubbish. They're no good.'

Defeated, he swiped at the Spitfire with the back of his hand and knocked it across the table. One of the wings fell off, but Jamie bounded after it and, holding it aloft, zoomed it round the room.

'You can't do it.' Sophie was back and crowing in the doorway. 'You're a dunce, Charlie.'

He turned round and thumped her as hard as he could. Sophie was slight but as tall as he was, and prepared to give as good as she got. She launched herself at him, and moments later they were locked together and rolling on the carpet. Charlie's shouts and Sophie's screams pierced Andy's ears and brought Auntie Izzy rushing in. She parted them and pulled them to their feet.

'Charlie hit me,' Sophie said accusingly, straightening her cardigan. 'He started it. He hurt me.'

'She was saying horrible things,' Charlie blustered. There were scratch marks on his cheeks. 'And she bit me.'

'Why can't you all play nicely together?' Auntie Izzy sounded cross. 'Why don't you finish your models?'

'They're too hard,' Charlie screamed at her. 'Much too hard.'

Sophie recovered immediately. 'Look, it says for ages nine to eleven on the lid. I can do them all right and I'm only nine.' She was triumphant. 'They're easy. They can't do them because they can't read.'

Andy curled up with embarrassment. He felt

humiliated, but he knew Sophie was right. He hadn't been able to make sense of the instructions.

Isobel said, 'Come to the sitting room all of you and I'll read you a story. I want you to calm down and sit quietly. Charlie, fetch the story books. Do you want *Robin Hood* or... What about *Swallows and Amazons?*'

'No. We don't want stories. We've had both those read to us until we're sick of them,' he screamed. 'I'm going out.' He grabbed his football and went racing out through the back door without stopping to put on his coat. The rain was still coming down in sheets.

'Silly child,' Auntie Izzy said through clenched teeth. 'He's going to get drenched.'

Isobel knew tension had reached flashpoint in the playroom. Experience had taught her that she must take control. She said to Sophie, 'You can choose the book for me to read. Go and get one.'

Sophie's shoulders were rigid, her eyes hostile and defiant. 'I don't need you to read to me. I can do it myself, thank you very much.' With a show of great dignity she stalked upstairs.

Isobel knew she mustn't lose her temper; it would make matters worse. Andy and Jamie were still sitting at the table, anxious and wary. She sat down with them and pulled one of the instruction sheets towards her. With great effort, she hid her irritation and assumed a gentle voice. 'Shall we read this together and find out what has to be done?'

'No, I don't want to. I'm sick of trying.' For once Andy was belligerent too. 'I can't do models.'

303

Isobel prickled with guilt. She should have done more to help them. Instead she'd settled down to read a book she'd found in the library. She'd lapsed back into her old selfish ways, instead of being more like Hilary. She needed to try harder.

'Your reading is improving, Andy. You're making progress now. You could do these models if you learned to read just a little better. There's so much you can do when you can read.'

'I want to learn,' Jamie said, trying to climb on to her knee. Isobel's arms tightened round him and pulled him closer. Jamie was more lovable than most children and Andy did try hard. She moved her chair nearer to him.

'Yours is the Hurricane, yes? OK, let's start at the top of the leaflet and go through the instructions step by step.'

She pulled his model in front of them so they could identify each piece as it was mentioned. When she'd finished, she said, 'You try to put it together now.'

With his tongue clamped between his teeth, Andy was concentrating hard.

'I want to make the other,' Jamie whispered.

'The Spitfire might be a bit hard for you.'

'No, I want to try.'

Isobel pointed out the bits to him and showed him where they fitted on the half-finished model. Then she left them to it and went to make herself a cup of tea. Charlie came back, his thin summer clothes soaked through and sticking to his skin. He looked so miserable, she wasn't sure whether the moisture running down his face was tears or rain. He shivered.

She felt sorry for him, and put an arm round his shoulders. 'Off with those sandals,' she said, trying to sound kind and cheerful. 'You'll spoil your mummy's carpets if you go upstairs in them. And those wet socks too. I'm going to run a hot bath for you, then we'll look for some dry clothes. You could catch your death of cold going out in a downpour like that.'

When she got him down to the playroom again, Andy had finished his model and was helping Jamie, who had almost finished the Spitfire.

'That was mine,' Charlie roared at his small brother. 'I wanted to make it.'

'You should have stayed here and done it then,' Isobel told him sharply, 'instead of stamping off in a rage. And you mustn't fight, especially not fight girls.'

Andy supported his twin. 'Sophie can stand up for herself,' he said.

Isobel had noticed that. She'd had to dab antiseptic on the scratches she'd inflicted on Charlie.

He said, 'She's a real tiger.'

'All the more reason not to fight. If you behave yourselves, I'll try to get three more models next time I go shopping.' The boys could do with more practice.

Andy said with enthusiasm, 'They have models for ships in the paper shop.'

'And cars,' Charlie added. He looked subdued now.

'We'll see.' Isobel sighed. She'd have to make sure they were meant for the right age group. She'd buy four models: she mustn't forget Sophie.

That reminded her that she hadn't seen her daughter for some time. She took the steps up to the bedroom they shared two at a time. As soon as she opened the door she realised the room smelled heavily of Chanel No. 5.

'Sophie!' she scolded. 'How many times do I have to tell you to leave my things alone?' All the irritation she'd choked down earlier came rushing back. 'You must not waste my perfume. It costs a lot of money.' It was her favourite, and she was angry.

Sophie looked up guiltily. She had the contents of Hilary's drawers spread over the bed and the floor, and her face was daubed with lipstick again. At that moment Isobel's foot kicked against her perfume bottle and sent it crashing against the skirting board.

'What made you leave it on the floor?' she demanded.

'I put it there to be safe.'

Isobel felt a rush of anger when she saw that the stopper had come out. She rushed to pick it up but the whole room was heavy with scent. The neck of the bottle was chipped; the stopper wouldn't fit properly in future.

'What a terrible waste!'

'Sorry, Mummy.' Sophie was the picture of guilt.

Isobel wanted to scream. She was not cut out for this. Yes, she loved her daughter, but there were times when she tried her patience beyond endurance.

That night, Andy and Charlie were put into their identical twin beds by Nana.

'I'll leave the light on,' she said. 'You can read to yourselves for a few minutes. Mummy will be up soon to kiss you good night.'

When they were alone, Andy, feeling bewildered, said, 'What's the matter with us, Charlie? I don't understand why we can't read when everybody else finds it so easy.'

'They expect us to do it, but we can't. They keep making us try, though I say I'd rather do extra sums.'

'It's our fault, isn't it? Miss Spooner told me I was lazy.'

'I hate reading.' Charlie flung his book across the bedroom.

'So do I,' Andy agreed, but he put his book down without the same show of temper.

'It makes everybody cross with us, but they keep on making us do it. Reading is very hard.'

'But only for us,' Andy wailed. 'The rest of our class finds it easy.'

'Not Emily Brooks.'

'She's a dunce. Everybody says so.'

'They say we are too. They think we're bumbling idiots, as thick as two short planks.'

'That's how I feel. A complete fool.'

'Me too.'

'Miss Spooner says we must try harder.'

'I've tried and tried and tried, and I still can't do it.'

'I did it this afternoon. I read those 'structions, I was able to make this aeroplane.' It was in pride of place on his chest of drawers.

Charlie gave a grunt of distress.

Flora moved back to her own house on Monday evening, delighted at the prospect of having the whole of Tuesday to herself. Being back in her own home and sleeping in her own bed was bliss. She got up late, had a lazy breakfast, and felt so much more relaxed without the hectic rush and the noisy grandchildren.

Tom had said he'd pick her up and take her to the bridge session in the afternoon. He'd agreed to run her home and stay on for supper. Flora was very much looking forward to this evening, and as Isobel had already done the shopping for her she spent most of the day preparing for it.

It was a wet day and quite chilly. Flora decided she would light a log fire this evening and pull her sofa up in front of it. When they'd eaten she wanted them to talk; it would be easier here where there'd be no interruptions and no distractions. She wanted to get to know Tom better.

In this tiny house, her table was in her one living room. She set it carefully with her best china and cutlery. She'd always been interested in food and cooking came easily to her. She'd chosen rump steak for the main course because most men liked that.

She had everything prepared before Tom came to pick her up for bridge. He partnered her and they were lucky with the cards. The other ladies asked after Ben and said they were pleased to see her back with them. Flora enjoyed herself.

As soon as she got home, she put a match to her fire. She straightened up to find that Tom was offering her a bottle of wine as well as a fancy package.

'I hope you like chocolates,' he said. 'I didn't think you'd want flowers, not when you're surrounded by them every day in the shop.'

She smiled. 'Thank you. Chocolates are more of a treat to me.'

She took him to the kitchen, because she needed to be there. 'Come and have a drink and watch me cook. What would you like? I have most things.'

He chose whisky and water, and she poured herself a glass of sherry. She had put a rocking chair in her kitchen for him; it was better than leaving him every few minutes to see to things. He looked very relaxed as he talked of the propagating and thinning out he was doing in the garden centre.

Flora thought the meal was a great success and he congratulated her on it several times. He had an excellent appetite so she was glad she'd produced four courses. They ate by the flickering light of the fire and for the first time she noticed the days were beginning to draw in. Only when she brought in the coffee did she move him to the sofa.

Tom was a good conversationalist. He had an opinion on everything from politics to sport, but Flora wanted him to talk about his own life. They were both getting on in years; a good deal had happened to her and the same must apply to him, but somehow he shied away from anything touching on his own history.

Flora talked about her own affairs and her own family history in the hope that he'd do likewise. She even asked a few questions and hinted that she'd like to know more, but she learned little that was new. It was getting late when she gave up.

'I need to go back to Hilary's,' she said. 'To be on hand for the morning rush and to open the shop tomorrow.'

'I'll run you back,' he said, but before they went he put his arms round her and kissed her. Flora felt something ignite between them. She was tingling down to her fingertips. For her this was love. She thought Tom felt the same but he didn't say so.

He thanked her for a lovely evening. 'I do appreciate being invited to your home. So much nicer than a pub or a restaurant.'

When she reached Hilary's guest room, Flora felt a little disappointed. She felt a hunger to know more about Tom than he was telling her. He seemed to like her but he wasn't opening up about his past.

She felt she'd had to prise out of him the basic facts she knew. He'd been happily married for twenty-six years, but Grace had died suddenly.

Flora had asked what had caused her death and he'd seemed reluctant to tell her even that. 'Pneumonia,' he'd said at last.

He gave out as common knowledge that he'd always worked in the building trade and had been made redundant in the early seventies, when many businesses had been in trouble. He was drawing a curtain over all those years, almost as though he wanted to hide something from her. Isobel was right: there was something odd about Tom. Something strange.

CHAPTER NINETEEN

On Friday, Hilary had made arrangements with her friend Jane to have the children, so Isobel could go shopping without them. She was going to drop them off on the way.

The house was quiet. Mum had already gone to open the shop. Hilary was stuffing the washing machine with clothes and generally tidying up when the phone rang. A man's voice asked for Isobel.

'Sebastian? Seb?' Hilary was more than surprised. She'd met him only once, on the day he'd married her sister, and had had no contact with him since. She didn't think Isobel had recently.

'She is there with you?' He sounded as though he wasn't sure where she was.

'Oh, yes, but I'm afraid she's out at the moment. Gone to do a big weekend shop for us.'

'Oh. How is your husband? I believe he had a bad accident.'

'He's getting better but still in hospital. Izzy's been a great help.'

She was even more surprised to hear him say, 'I was wondering when she planned to come home. The holidays are nearly over and the schools will be opening their gates next week.'

It shocked her to find he didn't know Isobel was planning not to return at all. Did he even know she was talking of a divorce? She said lamely, 'I don't know.'

He asked after Sophie and seemed a pleasant sort of person. Isobel had said it was money troubles that caused their rows, but they'd seemed to have so much. And why argue? Surely it was better to pool their resources and work out a budget as she and Ben did.

She remembered then that Sebastian was a remedial teacher and knew about dyslexia. She told him about the difficulties her boys were having. He tried to be helpful and made some suggestions. She decided she'd like to meet him and be able to talk things through with him.

'Ask Isobel to ring me, will you?' he said before he put the phone down. 'Sophie will have to come home to go to school. Well, Izzy will too, of course, to work.'

When Hilary went over to the shop she told her mother. Between customers they discussed Isobel's marriage and how very little they knew about her husband.

'I liked him. He treated us very well when we went down for their wedding,' Flora said.

It was only when the shop closed at lunch time that Hilary was able to tell Isobel that Seb had rung.

Isobel had quite enjoyed another morning out at the shops. Hilly's friend Jane had offered her a cup of coffee when she'd returned to collect the children. For a few hours she'd been able to put her problems out of her mind. She'd had to rush round madly to make scrambled eggs on toast for seven of them for lunch, but the break had been

312

worth it. She'd done the children's meal first and had them all sitting up when the adults came in.

Hilly said, 'Seb rang this morning. He wants you to ring him back.'

'Oh!' Isobel was none too pleased. She'd called in to a solicitor's office a few days ago. His clerk had given her a leaflet about legal aid and confirmed what she'd suspected, that her salary as a teacher was too high for her to qualify. But if the only work she could get was supply teaching, that might be a different matter. Except that then she wouldn't be earning enough to support herself and Sophie. The question of whether it would be possible for her to stay here had been going round in her head ever since.

Though Isobel had had time to think about what she wanted, she'd not been able to come to any decision. It was too complicated; there were too many details to consider.

Should she go back to the job she had in London and live with Seb until they could get a divorce and their property was divided? It would mean the same sort of existence they'd had over the last nine years. There had been days when they'd rubbed along together but they were always followed by noisy quarrels and running battles. She didn't want any more of that.

She'd prefer to make a clean break now, but to stay here without a proper job? She could hardly throw herself on Hilary, who was struggling with two mortgages and trying to run a business. If anything she was in a worse position than Isobel.

Mum had been noncommittal when Isobel had asked if she and Sophie might use the spare bedroom in her cottage for a few months while she looked for a place of her own. Isobel felt that now she was a grown woman in her thirties, it was wrong of her to expect Mum to open her house to them. It was boiling down to money again: for Isobel it always did. She was glad her name was on the deeds of Seb's house; at a very minimum, she'd have half the value of that and Seb might possibly help to maintain Sophie. Isobel decided she'd settle for that. It would be worth it not to have to live with him.

Hilary said, 'Seb seems to be expecting you to go home next week.'

Isobel was annoyed. She could see two sets of questioning eyes focusing on her.

'Are you going to go?' her mother pressed.

'Are we going home?' Sophie was jumping up and down, her eyes shining. 'When are we going, Mummy?' She was excited at the prospect.

'We'll have to see,' she said guardedly. Sophie never missed a thing. Isobel felt cross and out of sorts; she knew she'd have to make up her mind soon. Time was not on her side any more.

Her mother said, 'If you children have finished eating you can get down and play.'

The boys whooped off to the playroom with Sophie in pursuit.

Flora straightened up on her chair. 'You really should think through what you're doing, Isobel. You're making a decision that will change your whole life. Sophie's too.'

'D'you think I don't know that?' Isobel flared up. 'I do nothing else but think about it, but it's difficult.'

314

'But Seb doesn't seem to know where he stands.'

'That makes two of us.' Isobel hadn't told the family she'd spoken to Seb on the phone. 'He rang me.'

'So what did you decide?'

'Nothing!' Isobel hadn't told them she was looking for a job here, but anyway it didn't look as though that plan was going to work out.

Hilary said haltingly, 'Are you really thinking of a divorce?'

'I can't afford to pay a solicitor's bill; that's out of the question. But as I don't think I'll ever want to get married again, it doesn't matter, does it? I might just not go back to him.'

'Isobel dear.' Her mother lost her patience. 'I think you should talk this over with Sebastian. Shall we invite him here for the weekend so you can? You wouldn't mind if he came for a day or two, Hilly?'

'No,' Isobel screamed vehemently. 'Don't you do any such thing.'

'I'm sure it's the most sensible...'

'No!'

Isobel jumped to her feet and ran upstairs to her room. She didn't intend to phone Seb and she couldn't stand any more of her mother's urging her to do so. She was still lying on the bed when she heard her mother call upstairs, 'Isobel, we're going back to reopen the shop.'

Mum would be thinking of the children and the need for someone to keep an eye on them. Isobel raised herself on her elbow and called back, 'Right, Mum, I'll be down in a minute.'

She flopped back on the pillows. If only she still had Rupes, all this mess would never have blown up. He'd taken all the hard decisions with her well-being at heart. He'd looked after her. She'd never get used to being alone.

Sophie came in and wheedled, 'Mummy, I want to go home. When can we go?'

Isobel swung her feet to the floor. There'd be no peace now. It was a breezy but sunny afternoon. The kids were less trouble out of doors and the house stayed tidy. The boys were always ready for a game of football and, with their own private pitch, what could be better? She collected cricket bats and tennis balls in case football palled, and took them with her. Sophie had brought her doll but soon forgot about it and joined in with the boys.

Isobel sat on her coat with her back against a tree watching them. If only, if only, Rupes was still here. They'd been so much in love; the fact that she was his mistress and not his wife hadn't mattered in the least. And perhaps, if he hadn't died, she'd have been his wife not Seb's for the last nine years. She would have been truly happy with Rupes, she was sure. She closed her eyes to daydream about what might have been.

The football bouncing against a nearby tree brought her back to reality. The summer holidays were coming to an end, and any arrangement now would be very last minute. She couldn't afford to drag her feet any longer.

She felt she was being forced to make an impossible decision yet again, but her only other option was to get herself a job somewhere else. She'd paid another visit to the library while she was out this morning and found jobs advertised in Weston-super-Mare, Brighton and Ramsgate. Although it seemed an act of desperation, she'd apply for them all this evening. Soon it would be autumn and in a seaside town there would be holiday accommodation available to rent cheaply over the winter months. That would give her time to sort herself out.

By the following morning, it had occurred to Isobel that if she wasn't going back to Sebastian, she'd have to fetch the rest of her belongings. Both she and Sophie would need their winter clothes before long. She decided she'd have to ring him and arrange to go down, but it was almost time for the shop to close and she needed to prepare lunch. Mum and Hilary came over before she had the salad made and the children rounded up. She told them what was on her mind.

Hilary said, as she helped chop up tomatoes, 'There's no sign of Ben coming home yet, so there's no hurry for you to leave. It's been lovely having you here.'

Flora opened the back door and blew several blasts on the whistle to call in the children. 'There's Sophie to think of too, you know,' she said. 'She'll have to go to school next week.'

'I know, and it's adding to the pressure.'

'I'd like you to stay,' Hilary said. 'You've been such a help. You want her to stay, don't you, Mum?'

'Isobel must make up her own mind. I don't think we should try to persuade her one way or the other. To end a marriage is a big decision.'

Hilary said, 'I feel we've just got to know each other again, Izzy. We were close as children but then somehow we drifted apart.'

'We lived apart,' Isobel said. 'We didn't see much of each other.' That was her fault too. Mum would have come down on her like a ton of bricks if she'd known about Rupes. But she was comforted by her family's support now.

While she did the washing up, Isobel was psyching herself up to ring Seb, but before she'd finished the phone rang and it was he.

She said, 'I was just about to ring you.'

'Have you decided to come back, Izzy?'

'I thought I'd come down on Monday to pick up some more clothes.'

'You're not going to stay?' His tone was belligerent.

'I don't know what to do.' She could feel tears prickling her eyes.

He said, 'What about your job? The new term starts next Tuesday. The head will be expecting you back.'

For Isobel, the decision had been going round in her head for weeks. She was beginning to feel it was beyond her. 'I'll have to think about it.'

'Haven't you had all the holiday to think about it?'

'Look, I'll come down on Monday.'

'Couldn't you come tomorrow? There isn't much time left.'

'No, Saturdays and Sundays are the busy days for Hilary. She needs someone to look after the children. It'll have to be Monday now.'

'Right. I'll get us some steak for lunch.'

'I'll need breakfast first. I'll start early, maybe four in the morning, if I can get up. That way I'll miss the traffic.'

She didn't want to spend the night with him, but even with an early start she probably wouldn't be able to get there and back in one day. She'd probably drop with exhaustion if she tried it.

'Egg and bacon first then.'

Isobel collapsed with her head in her hands at the kitchen table, half deciding she might go back to Seb, depending on what sort of reception she got from him on Monday. She wouldn't take Sophie with her, so she'd have to come back to Birkenhead. She was afraid he'd persuade her into bed and they'd be right back where they had been, arguing. On the other hand she couldn't stay here without regular work.

It left Isobel feeling even more fraught, but in mid-afternoon she had a telephone call from the man who'd interviewed her in the education office.

'Mrs Broadbent,' he said. 'I've just written to you to say one of our teachers was involved in a road accident in Spain. She's now back in this country but in hospital and she'll be off sick for some time, so they'll need a supply teacher in Neston Primary from the beginning of term.'

Isobel's spirits rose. Neston was conveniently close.

'And I've just been handed a resignation letter from another teacher, who is to be married shortly and will be moving to London with her husband. So we have an unexpected permanent vacancy in Hooton too. I'm ringing to find out if you would be interested in one or the other?'

Isobel didn't need to think about it. 'I'd like to have the permanent vacancy in Hooton, please.'

'I'll tell the headmistress ... let me see, yes, Mrs Symmonds to expect you. The new term starts next Tuesday.'

'Would you also let her know I have a daughter I'd like to enter in the school?' Isobel said, giving Sophie's name and date of birth. 'It's easier if we're both at the same school.'

She put the phone down slowly, feeling this made her choice easier. She was about to ring the Wandsworth education office but decided to leave it until she'd seen Seb. She could do it while she was in London. Now she had a real choice, he'd have to make more effort to keep her there.

The next day she received a letter from Weston-super-Mare inviting her for an interview for the job she'd applied for. She wrote to say she'd already accepted another post. She felt in a much stronger position than she had yesterday. She could now stay here with Hilary. When she'd worked for a month or so and had her salary coming in, she could find a flat for herself and Sophie.

Isobel was feeling wary as she drove into London on Monday. Sebastian must have seen her turn into the drive because he came out of the house to meet her. Everything looked achingly familiar, including Seb. His hair was neatly combed back and still damp from the shower.

'Hello.' He bent to kiss her cheek. 'You look well.'

That couldn't be true. She'd had a traumatic time recently – she probably looked haggard. 'So do you,' she responded. 'You look suntanned and rested.'

'That's holidays for you. Come on in, it won't take me long to cook breakfast. Are you hungry?'

They were both on their best behaviour. She sat down and watched him cook. It had been a long drive and she was tired.

'How's Sophie?' He went on to ask after Ben and Hilary and her mother and she kept the social chitchat going about things that didn't matter. It was only when they'd finished eating breakfast that he said, 'I've missed you. I rattle round this house when I'm alone here.'

Isobel noticed it was not as clean as it had been when she'd left.

'I'd like us to try again. If we sorted out a budget and did some work on the house, turned over a new leaf...'

She looked out of the window. 'You've been doing more in the garden.'

'That wasn't what I meant, but I have had a good go out there this last week, cut everything back. I bet you've never seen it so tidy.'

'It looks good.' He was smiling at her, his teeth sparkling white against his glowing skin. 'Is that where you got your suntan, in the garden?'

'No, in the Himalayas. You knew I was going trekking? It was a marvellous holiday.'

That pulled Isobel up with a jolt. 'I thought you were going to cancel that? You said you wouldn't go, that you couldn't leave your mother while she was ill.'

'She was quite poorly. She had a small stroke and was taken into hospital.'

'Well then?'

'Charlotte decided to come home to see her and said she'd stay while I took my holiday. I was desperate to get away on my own, after...' His green eyes, so like Rupert's, met hers tentatively.

Isobel felt the blood run up her cheeks. 'Yes. The last few weeks of term were terrible for me too.'

'I'm sorry. I want us to make a pact not to argue.'

'Why didn't you tell me?' she demanded irritably. 'If I'd known you were going away I'd have stayed here.' Not that she was sorry she'd gone back to her own family; it had brought them closer.

'Well ... I knew that. To be honest, I didn't want to make things easy for you. We were fighting tooth and nail. I wanted to hurt you.'

'What?'

'That's the truth. I think we should be honest with each other from now on.'

She could feel her anger boiling up. 'It's possible to be too honest, Seb.'

'Let me explain. I really needed to get away. I wanted time to think about you and me. About where we were going.'

'And where has all this thinking got you? You've come up with the same old thing, that we ought to try again.'

'You don't understand, Izzy. It isn't just you and me. I'm no good at relationships, they go wrong and I walk away instead of trying to mend them. I cut people off. First there was Dad, then Rose my first wife, now you and I are heading down the same path. I'm going to end up on my own if I carry on like this.'

'You've always said there's more fish in the sea than came out of it.'

'In the past I might have tried to comfort myself with that, yes. But I don't want to go on like this. I don't want to lose you and Sophie.'

Isobel rubbed her eyes. 'I feel too tired to think.'

'Give yourself time. Stay overnight.'

She didn't want to do that. Once she was in bed with Seb, he could talk her into anything.

He was anxious. 'You haven't found somebody else?'

'No, Seb, it's just us. I know it's my fault. I did a terrible thing and you can't forgive me, but I can't stand the fighting any longer.'

'I'm willing to put it all behind me if you are.'

She could see he meant it and was half tempted. It would be so much easier than coping with a new job and finding a new home.

But no. 'We've tried it, Seb, time and time again. It always breaks down and there'll still be the debts to face.'

'Most people have money problems. I'll have them whether you're here or not. No doubt you will wherever you are.'

'Yes.' She thought of what Hilary was facing.

'I'll make more effort to do the house up a bit. It all needs painting again...'

'No, Seb. I think we should finish it. Make a clean break.'

The colour had faded from his face and his lips

had straightened. 'Is that your answer?'

'Yes. We'd be fighting like a pair of cocks again in no time. Do you want to go on turning over new leaves for ever?'

Isobel had made her decision. She meant to return to Merseyside and make a new life for herself and Sophie. She wanted no more of Sebastian Broadbent.

Hilary was getting up early every morning to work on her manuscript. It wasn't too difficult while the mornings were still light and warm. Her book was coming on well: she'd bounced the reader straight into the story and the action. It wouldn't be such a long job after all. What she needed to do now was retype the first few chapters. It would take only three or four more mornings to have it ready. Once it was back with Fern Granville, she could think of it as out seeking a publisher.

Already she was trying to pull together some ideas for another novel and had no intention of giving up her early morning writing sessions. The thought of what might happen in the future gave her a warm glow.

It was a relief when the autumn term started and the twins were back in school. Jamie was delighted to be going with them.

Hilary was pleased Isobel had decided to stay with them, particularly as she'd come up with a plan to pack more into the daily hour she spent hearing the twins read. In future, she would prepare writing practice for them as well, and while one twin read the other would be at the opposite end of the playroom table getting on with that. Then they would change places.

Isobel thought Jamie wouldn't be able to concentrate for an hour but she was planning to give him a shortened version. She said that if she was working for an hour, she might as well see the boys did too. Being a teacher, she'd have no trouble managing three pupils at once.

Hilary gave up one early morning writing session to drive to Manchester Airport to meet Ben's twin aunts returning from Canada. They both looked very well despite the long journey and the pre-dawn hour.

'We've had such a marvellous time. A holiday of a lifetime.'

She took them straight to their house. Flora was there to welcome them and make them some breakfast. She'd aired their place yesterday, dusted round and bought a few basic groceries for them.

Hilary went home to get the children up for school and afterwards went to visit Ben, who seemed more cheerful. He was being given regular physiotherapy.

'I'm told I'm making good progress,' he said. 'I'm hoping I won't be here for much longer.'

Hilary was afraid his discharge might still be some way off, but she didn't say so. Ben always wanted to know what the takings in the shop had been, and over the last few days, and particularly yesterday, they'd been up.

That cheered him even more. 'Autumn's a good time for selling trees and winter flowering plants.'

'The shoots are pushing through in those bowls

of bulbs you told me to cover.'

'Let them have light now. With luck they'll be in flower for Christmas. I think it's guaranteed I'll be home by then.'

CHAPTER TWENTY

On the first day of term, Hilary took Jamie into school. He was thrilled to be starting. The twins had moved up with their class at the start of the new school year and had a new teacher. Miss Witchell was much older and more experienced than Miss Spooner. Hilary hoped they'd do better with her. She made a point of going into school a day or two later to see her and discuss their reading. She was growing increasingly worried about it.

'I've read the reports on the twins' progress,' Miss Witchell said distantly. 'It'll take me a little while to form my own opinion.'

Hilary returned the books Miss Spooner had loaned them and asked for more. She felt rather in awe of Miss Witchell's bristling efficiency, and soon discovered that the twins hadn't taken to her.

'I wish we could have Miss Spooner back,' Andy told her. 'We liked her better.'

Isobel was sympathetic. 'It could just be that they don't know her,' she said. 'And once they do, they'll like her better. I've bought something that might help Jamie.' She opened a box containing the letters of the alphabet in brightly coloured plastic. 'Seb suggested these. He says some children find it easier to learn if they use the sense of touch as well as sight. Jamie and I will play with them together and I'll be able to have spelling games with the twins. They might prove more popular than books.'

Hilary wanted to get more help for them in school and Isobel was spurring her on to make an appointment to see Mr Leyland, their headmaster. She was priming her with the questions she should put to him and the requests she should make.

Hilary knew him, of course, but had found him unapproachable and had not had a great deal of contact with him up to now. The school secretary wanted to know what she wished to discuss with him, and an appointment was made for a week ahead.

Mr Leyland was an extremely handsome man of about Hilary's own age, but he was full of his own importance and had a rather arrogant and overbearing manner. She told him she was worried that her three boys could be dyslexic.

He said haughtily, 'I've spoken to Miss Witchell about them. She says they're making progress.'

'And Jamie's teacher? I think he could be affected too.'

He waved that off. 'Jamie's only just starting school. It's too soon to know what he can or can't do.'

When Hilary asked, as Isobel had suggested, if they could be assessed by the educational psychologist, he agreed, though with some reluctance. When she asked if she might be present at these assessments, he told her it wouldn't be possible.

'You can come and see me again,' he'd told her, 'when the school psychologist has seen them. I'll let you know when.'

It took several weeks, but yesterday the school secretary had telephoned to say Mr Leyland would see her at two o'clock this afternoon if that was convenient.

'Yes,' she told her. 'Yes.'

Hilary felt uneasy about seeing Mr Leyland again and wished Izzy was able to come with her. Instead, Izzy talked about what he might tell her and told her to be sure to ask what special coaching or extra tuition was recommended. Hilary presented herself to the school secretary at the appointed time. Mr Leyland came to the door of his study to meet her.

'Hello, Mrs Snow Come on in.' Waving her towards the seat on the other side of his broad desk, he asked, 'How is Mr Snow? Better, I hope?'

'Yes, he's improving, thank you, but still in hospital. About the twins...'

'Ah yes. I have the reports from the school psychologist.' He took two pieces of paper from a file cover and laid them side by side in front of him. Each page was two-thirds covered with spidery handwriting.

'Well, there's good news for you. He doesn't think the twins are dyslexic.'

'Oh!' Hilary felt as though the wind had been taken out of her sails. Isobel had been so sure. And the books on the subject she'd borrowed from the library and read so carefully had seemed to support Isobel's opinion.

She said, 'You must know they're having great difficulty learning to read and write? Other teachers before Miss Spooner drew my attention to it. If that isn't due to dyslexia, would you say it was due to low intelligence?'

'No. The psychologist is sure they have sufficient intelligence to learn to read.'

'Then there must be some reason why they're finding it so difficult.'

'Yes. He believes their problem is caused by crossed laterality.'

Hilary sat up straighter on the chair. 'Crossed laterality? What's that?'

'It means they are right-handed, but in both cases the left eye and left foot leads. Have you noticed that?'

Hilary shook her head. 'I hadn't, but their father said they both kicked a football with their left foot.'

'There you are then.'

Hilary tried to think. She was right-handed, but at her last eye test she'd been told her left eye was much stronger than her right, and at school the girls had laughed at her because she always got on and off her bike on the opposite side to everybody else.

'I have crossed laterality,' she said. 'But I learned to read and write normally, so why should it cause the twins such difficulties?'

'I don't know, but seemingly in some cases it does.'

She asked, 'What help will they have to overcome it?'

'In the opinion of our psychologist, if you give them plenty of practice, hear them read on a daily basis, they should be able to catch up without too much trouble.'

Hilary was upset and disappointed. 'But I've been doing that since they started school and it isn't working. They do need more help. I'm afraid they're going to fall further behind the rest of their class if they don't get it.'

Mr Leyland was standing up as a sign of dismissal. Hilary sat firm. 'They have a cousin eight months younger than them and she can read fluently. The difference between her ability and theirs shocked me.'

He told her some of the medical reasons why twins might be expected to be slow.

'I know about those.'

'Girls, too, are always more advanced than boys in the early years; it's an accepted fact. We in education take all that into consideration.'

He was moving towards the door, a stronger hint to her. She said, 'May I read those reports?'

'Well, no, I'm sorry. I'm afraid they're confidential to the school service.'

'What about Jamie? What did the psychologist say about him?'

'I decided it was too soon to be worried about Jamie. He's only started school this term. If we find he's slow to learn we can always refer him to the school psychologist next year.'

Hilary felt an angry flush run up her cheeks. 'He doesn't yet know the letters of the alphabet.'

It was almost as though she'd questioned the quality of teaching in his school. He said stiffly,

'Mrs Snow, I think you are worrying unduly.'

Hilary left, feeling she hadn't helped her boys at all.

At four o'clock, Hilary was working in the shop but watching for Isobel's return. As soon as she saw her car pull in front of the house she ran across to tell her what Mr Leyland had said. By then Izzy was in the kitchen looking hot and tired and setting out a snack for the children.

'I half expected it,' she confessed. 'It's a question of what each education department provides. By law, they have to provide normal education for every child and extra tuition for those falling behind or with learning difficulties. But extra or specialised tuition is expensive, and what funds they have go into the remedial classes. That being the case, they believe it's wiser not to assess children as being in need of it.'

Hilary was shocked. 'Not being in need of it! But that's terrible when they are.'

'Yes, but it's a fact of life, and a general remedial class would not suit them. Your children are not the only ones with this problem. It's thought that ten per cent of the population is dyslexic and many others are backward in their reading. I've heard it said that about sixty per cent of the prison population has failed to learn to read and write.'

Hilary was dumbfounded. 'What? I hope my kids don't go to prison!'

'I didn't mean...'

'The government ought to do something.'

'It would cost money, so they don't.'

'I'll write to the education department.'

'Hilly, it's difficult if not impossible to fight government policy.'

'But what can we do?'

'Look after your own. Carry on as we are. They are making progress, honestly.'

Hilary felt defeated. 'Even Charlie?'

To Hilary, the breakfast stampede seemed more difficult to cope with than usual. 'Come on, Charlie, eat up your egg. Everybody else has finished.'

'I'm not well, Mummy. I don't want it.'

She sat down next to him. 'In what way, not well? What's the matter, love?'

'I've got tummy ache.' His eyes were wide with assumed innocence. 'I'm not well enough to go to school today.'

Hilary sighed. Charlie had been tearing round as full of beans as usual until five minutes ago. He'd said things like this before.

Isobel was at the door, holding Sophie by the hand. 'We're on our way, Hilly.' She lowered her voice to a whisper. 'School phobia? I'll have to leave you to deal with that.'

Hilary put her hand on Charlie's forehead. She didn't want to be wrong about this, but already this morning she'd had evidence that his bowels and appetite were normal. He didn't feel as though he had a temperature.

'Charlie, I'm sorry, but I can't keep you off school unless you're really sick. You have to go, it's the law. Every child has to.'

The tears in his eyes seemed further proof that he was anxious about what was happening at school rather than sick. His fingernails were bitten down to the quick and he looked pale and worried, but what could she do? If she let him stay off school today, there would be a repeat performance tomorrow. It wouldn't get him anywhere.

'Come on,' she said gently. 'Andy and Jamie are ready. It's time to go.'

'Charlie isn't well.' Andy was pushing in close. 'And I've got tummy ache too.'

'Get your coats on, all of you,' she said firmly. 'I'm sorry, but you have to go to school. I'll walk down with you this morning.'

Hilary knew neither of the twins was happy at school and today Charlie was upset. To see her children like this upset her too.

Isobel came home from school and saw the twins playing out on the field as she drove in. She sent Sophie to fetch them, having decided that they were more co-operative if she read with them at this time of day rather than at bedtime.

The phone rang while she was in the hall making sure they all changed their shoes and washed their hands. Hilary rushed out of the kitchen to answer it and instantly Isobel saw a crimson flush run up her cheeks and knew she was excited. She couldn't keep still.

Isobel sent the boys to get their reading books and shamelessly stayed to listen. She gathered Hilary was talking to the literary agent who was taking an interest in her book. She knew her sister had been on edge since she'd posted the revised version to her. The sight of the postman heading to the front door could make her jittery.

She'd said, 'I'm half expecting it to come back with a note saying it still isn't good enough.'

Isobel could see now that Hilary's fears had been unfounded. Her eyes were shining as she put the phone down. 'What did she say?'

'That I did a good job on rewriting the beginning and it's fine now.'

'That's marvellous. Is she...'

'Yes, she's going to try to find a publisher for it.'

'That's wonderful news, Hilly!' she said. 'You're going to get your chance now.'

Isobel was envious. She needed something like that to change her life, but she didn't have Hilly's talent – or was it luck? She was no longer certain she'd done the right thing by staying up on Merseyside. In a way, she missed Sebastian. He'd wanted her to go back... Perhaps she should have given it more thought, but she hadn't had the time.

Her sister looked half dazed. 'I can't believe it!'

Isobel pulled herself together. She had to snap out of these selfish ways. 'Your luck's turned at last, Hilly. Not before time. Now then, which of you boys wants to read first?'

'I do,' Jamie said.

'I can't thank you enough,' Hilary told her. 'You make them stick at it day after day. Jamie's coming on well now, aren't you, love? Those plastic letters you bought are really helping him.'

Isobel had bought two more sets to give them enough to play spelling games with. Even Sophie joined in but they'd had to handicap her. Isobel was trying to devise more games to play with them.

She had asked her sister to buy more model kits to be given out as rewards for hard work and effort. The twins were enjoying them, and they didn't need help to do them now they'd practised a bit. They were proud of their new skill.

Andy was making better progress with his reading than Charlie, because he could concentrate for longer, but it was clear they both found the books provided by the school boring. Because their reading age was low, the stories tended to be aimed at a younger age group. They were mostly about toys or farm animals that spoke.

Isobel thought it would help if she could find books that used language simple enough for them to read, but had subjects they would find more interesting. She asked around her fellow teachers and they'd suggested a series of true stories about other countries. She decided to start with a book about Arctic explorers. It had the effect she'd sought: the twins were spellbound.

'Is it true?' Charlie wanted to know. 'Did Nansen's ship really get caught in the ice and drift right across the Arctic Ocean?'

'It did,' Isobel said. 'Can you tell me what that proved?'

'That there was no land there,' Andy said.

'And what was the name of his ship?'

'The *Fram*,' Jamie chuckled.

'Good. You're both right.'

Charlie said, 'I want to go to the Arctic. I'll be an explorer when I grow up. Can I catch a ship from Liverpool to take me there?'

'You probably could have done in Nansen's day, but he was Norwegian. He'd have sailed from a port near his home.'

'Miss Witchell says Liverpool is one of the biggest ports in the country and ships go all round the world from there.'

'Well, they certainly did, but perhaps not so much nowadays.'

'Daddy took us to the Pier Head in Liverpool last summer. There were lots and lots of ships there. We went on one.'

'That was the ferry. It was only crossing the Mersey.'

'There was another Arctic expedition in 1969,' Sophie said in a superior voice. 'That's not very long ago. They went with dog sleds to find the North Pole.'

Charlie was indignant. 'You said there wasn't any land there.'

Isobel explained, 'The sea freezes over it's so cold.'

They loved the books and were eager to learn all they could about the places they read about. She was pleased because they read more and no longer fought to avoid reading practice. They were also learning a little geography at the same time.

This evening, they brought their books but Charlie had a long face.

'What's the matter?' she asked.

'Nothing.'

'I can see there is, Charlie.'

'I hate reading.'

'No you don't,' Isobel said. 'You're enjoying this book about going to the North Pole.'

Andy said, 'Miss Witchell was cross with Charlie in class.'

'She thinks I'm not trying,' he muttered through the corner of his mouth.

'You're upset,' Isobel said. She could understand why.

'I do try,' he burst out. She could see he was not far from tears.

'I know. Perhaps Miss Witchell doesn't understand how hard it is for you.'

'I'll never do it. It's too hard for me.'

'It isn't. You're improving, Charlie. You're much better than you were, but I'm afraid you have to keep on trying. There's no other way. Come on, let's try now.'

Isobel had schooled herself never to lose patience, but she felt she'd exhausted it by the time Charlie had read the usual amount. He was in no mood to concentrate.

The next morning, after a hectic start, getting herself and Sophie ready for school and helping with the breakfasts, Isobel tried to use the ten-minute drive time to prepare herself to face the day, but today she was thinking of Sebastian again.

She should have allowed herself more time to talk things through with him. She'd been too hasty. But he'd told her he meant to stay home to look after his mother, and then had gone swanning off on a trip to the Himalayas as soon as she'd turned her back. She'd lost her temper with him.

But perhaps it wasn't such a bad decision? She'd found her feet in her new job and had welcomed reports that Sophie had settled down quickly in her new class.

'Mummy,' Sophie said for the second time.

'Why won't you listen to me? I want to tell you something.'

'Tell me what?' The lights changed and the line of cars moved on.

'Charlie's going to run away today instead of going to school.'

'What?' The shock made the car jerk towards the kerb. 'He seemed all right at breakfast.'

'Mummy, he hates it. He hates school.'

'He set off with Andy and Jamie as usual.' She'd seen him, he'd shown no sign... 'Is Andy going to run away too?'

'I don't think so.'

'But they go everywhere together.'

'He gave Charlie seven pence he had left from his pocket money. For bus fares.'

'Oh my goodness! Why?' But she knew why. Charlie had been upset last night. 'Where's he going?'

'He's planning to go to Liverpool and stow away on a ship. He's going to look for one going to the Arctic.'

The car swerved again, as Isobel swore under her breath. 'Are you sure?'

'Yes. The twins got up early to cut sandwiches for Charlie to take with him.'

Isobel drove into the school car park, switched off the engine and put her head down on the steering wheel. She was appalled. She remembered Hilary saying, 'Where did all that bread go?' as she took another loaf from the freezer to make the breakfast toast. Isobel didn't doubt that Sophie believed Charlie meant to run away.

'You did right to tell me,' she said. 'You go into

the playground – the bell will be ringing any minute. I'm going to phone Auntie Hilary. She ought to know about this.'

Isobel almost ran into school. The staffroom was noisy with chatter. When she'd dialled Hilary's number, she could hear the phone ringing in an empty house. As she put it down and dialled the shop number, the school bell rang and the staffroom began to empty. Thank goodness, it was Hilary who picked it up.

'Hilly, Charlie was in trouble at school yesterday.'

'Yes, I know. I spent ages trying to cheer him up.'

'Sophie says he's planning to run away.'

'No, he wouldn't do that. He went off to school quite happily. He's forgotten yesterday's troubles.'

She said more urgently, 'He hasn't, Hilly. I'm sure he means to go.'

'But there's nowhere he can go. He goes to Jane's to play, but her children will be in school. He knows that.'

'Sophie says he's aiming to run off to the Arctic. We've been reading stories about it.'

Hilary was agitated now. 'Oh Lord! What can I do?'

'Ring his school, find out if he's there. If he's going to do a runner, the sooner you know the better.'

'Yes, all right, thanks...'

'If he's not there, ring the police straight away.'

Isobel slid the phone down feeling guilt-stricken. Damn the Arctic. She hurried along to her classroom wishing she'd kept Charlie reading stories about sheep that spoke.

Hilary's hand was shaking as she put the receiver down. She knew she was panicking as she scrabbled through the phone directory looking for the school. She dialled but got a wrong number. She was a bag of nerves.

'What's the matter?' her mother was asking, but she couldn't stop to tell her. The school secretary answered.

'Could I speak to Mr Leyland, please? It's rather urgent.'

'I'm sorry, he's engaged at the moment. He's about to take assembly. Can I help?'

Hilary was pouring out her tale, almost incoherent with anxiety. 'Is Charlie in school now?'

'I'm not sure. The registers will have been taken, but...'

'Can you find out for me, please? I need to know urgently if he isn't there.'

'I'll run along to his classroom to see,' she said. 'I'd better ring you back.'

'No, I'll hold on,' Hilary said, fearing she'd be kept waiting for ages if she didn't.

'Right.'

The line went dead. Hilary turned to tell her mother what had happened, but she had the gist. She said, 'Charlie was a bit fraught last night.'

'He seemed all right this morning,' Hilary said. 'Or was it that I didn't notice?' She could hear the sounds of school, the babble of children's voices, the slither of many feet. It seemed ages before she heard the click of high heels coming back.

'Mrs Snow, both the twins are here, there's no need to worry.'

'You're sure?'

'Yes, I saw them with my own eyes. Miss Witchell's class was filing into the hall for morning assembly.'

Hilary felt her knees go weak with relief. 'Thank you.'

'It was just a game,' her mother said. 'Surprising what children get up to these days.'

Hilary went to the hospital to see Ben. It took her an hour to get over her fright. After that she threw herself into work. She spent a few hours typing her new book, and felt more normal after that. At lunch time, Isobel rang her and seemed relieved to hear Charlie was in school.

In the afternoon Hilary went to help her mother in the shop. She'd told the boys to come there if they found nobody in the house when they returned from school. When she saw Andy come in towing Jamie by the hand, a wave of panic washed over her. She could hardly get the words out.

'Where's Charlie?'

Andy was biting his lip. 'Isn't he here?'

'No! I haven't seen him.'

'I thought he might come home.'

'Andy, where's he gone?'

Her mother was serving a customer. She said, 'I can manage here. You'd better take the children home.'

CHAPTER TWENTY-ONE

That afternoon, Isobel pulled her car on to Hilary's drive in time to see her sister striding blindly towards the house. She knew the worst had happened because only Andy and Jamie were with her.

Hilary saw her. 'He's gone,' she called. 'Charlie's gone.'

Sophie said, 'I told you he would, didn't I?'

'Go and look in the little wood and round the field and in every glasshouse and building on this site,' her mother ordered. 'Andy, you come with me. I want to know where Charlie's gone.'

'To the Arctic,' Sophie said.

'Do what I said,' Isobel thundered. 'Hilly, you make us a cup of tea.'

In the kitchen she sat the children at the table. 'Come on, Andy, we've got to know where Charlie's gone.'

'I promised I wouldn't tell.'

'He went into school with you first thing this morning?'

He nodded. Hilary slid a glass of milk each in front of him and Jamie.

'When did you last see him?' Isobel demanded, looking from one child to the other.

'At morning playtime,' Jamie said.

'Andy, what happened then?'

'He said he was going to the Arctic,' Jamie said.

'He caught the bus.'

'You saw him catch a bus?'

Jamie's eyes were round and anxious. 'Will he be all right?'

'No, he won't. He'll be on his own and a long way from home. He won't know where he is or how to get back. Where was the bus going?'

Andy said, 'A boy in our class said Woodside. It had it on the front.'

Isobel heard her sister's swift intake of breath and was feeling increasingly uneasy herself.

'It stops outside our school every morning playtime,' Andy volunteered. 'Charlie decided that was the best time to go.'

'Oh my God!' Hilly whispered.

'Was he heading for Pier Head? In Liverpool? Hoping to catch a ship from there to the Arctic?'

Andy nodded numbly. Sophie came back. 'Charlie's not here. I didn't think he would be. Can I have some milk, Mummy? I want a biscuit too.'

Hilary automatically saw to her needs. Isobel said, 'Andy, you've got to help us find him. How much money did he have?'

'Ten pence, and I gave him seven more.'

'I gave him two pence,' Jamie said.

Sophie added, 'I gave him six.'

Hilary added them up. 'So he had twenty-five pence. Would that be enough to get him to the Pier Head?'

'He was planning to stow away.' Sophie looked at her as though she were a halfwit. 'He won't need money for that.'

Hilary sighed. 'I've no idea what half fare to

Liverpool would cost. If it got him there, it's hardly likely to be enough to get him back again, even if he could manage to retrace his steps.'

'Ring the police,' Isobel advised. 'The sooner they're involved now, the better.' She drank her tea, which had grown cold. She got up to pour herself another cup. Her sister came back looking worried stiff. 'I feel awful, Hilly. I planted those ideas in his head. I'll go over to the Pier Head. See if he's there.'

'The police said they'd come round to see us.'

'You talk to them. If Charlie isn't at Pier Head, we haven't a clue where he could be, have we?'

'I'll come with you,' Sophie offered.

'No, love.' Isobel was afraid she'd be a distraction, and she needed to concentrate on finding Charlie. 'You stay here and tell the policeman what you know. That's important. OK?' she whispered to Hilary.

Isobel drove down to Woodside. It was a cold bleak afternoon and the wind off the river cut through her coat. She parked her car and went into the terminal building and as far as the ticket booth. It was closed and there was nobody about, certainly not Charlie.

She looked across the mile-wide expanse of choppy brown water and shivered, then walked back to the tourist shop and asked if they'd seen a ten-year-old boy hanging about. A boy on his own. They said they hadn't. When Isobel was young there'd been a ferry service running every fifteen minutes or so. Now it had become a tourist attraction. During the summer there was an hourly service, calling at three terminals on the Mersey, but now it was early November and already dusk.

She asked, 'Has there been a boat over to Pier Head today?'

It seemed there had. 'When is the next one?'

'Tomorrow morning.'

Isobel told herself she couldn't go home without satisfying herself Charlie had not reached Pier Head. He could have gone over on the ferry earlier in the day. If he hadn't, she doubted he'd know any other way of getting to Liverpool from here. Mum used to take her and Hilary over to the shops, but that wouldn't be in Charlie's experience.

She strode rapidly up to Hamilton Square station and caught the underground across. She was going in the opposite direction to the crowd of commuters, which was something. The wind seemed even sharper on the other side of the river.

Pier Head was almost deserted except for the seagulls. The route down to the landing stage where the ferry berthed was closed, as was the gift shop. Isobel walked round, wishing she'd put on a warmer coat. She remembered there was a bar facing the Liver Building. It was open and she looked inside, but she didn't think he'd go in there. There was a café facing the river and she could see that was closed, but there was a small porch at the entrance and in the gathering dusk she could just make out something darker on one side. As she drew nearer, she could see it was a small figure huddled in one corner.

'Charlie!'

It was him! It was such a relief to have found him. She threw her arms round him, but not before she'd glimpsed the answering relief on his face. He was gripping her hard, as though reluctant to release his hold in case she disappeared.

'Are you all right?'

He nodded. 'I'm hungry.' When she got him under a light he looked numb with cold.

'Come on, let's get you home. If we walk fast you'll get warmer. I've been so worried about you. Your mummy's almost out of her mind. Let's see if we can find a phone booth, and we'll let her know you're safe.'

They reached James Street underground station without seeing a phone. Isobel hurried him into the crush to cross the river. The trains were packed with commuters now, and full of warmth. Once out of the station on the Birkenhead side, she saw a phone box. Charlie was still shivering, but he was sheltered from the wind here when they both squeezed inside.

Hilary sounded hysterical with joy and Charlie was in tears as he spoke to her. Hand in hand, they ran down to the ferry car park then, and as she started the drive home she saw a chip shop. She pulled into the next side road and they went back and bought some. The shop was warm and bright and sending out delicious scents. Charlie seem to thaw out at last. They sat in her car and shared the chips.

Isobel and Charlie received a magnificent welcome from the family when they reached home. A policewoman was waiting to ask Charlie a few questions. Hilary took him into the sitting room.

Flora followed Isobel to the kitchen. 'You did

well, Izzy, to find him. Can I make you a cup of tea?'

'I could do with something stronger.'

'Charlie's home safe and sound, so I don't think Hilary will object if we open a bottle of wine. How far did he get?'

'Pier Head. He stowed away on a ferry boat to get there. I think he enjoyed that part. He found the only boats sailing from there these days went to Ireland or the Isle of Man. The Irish boat was due to sail at eleven o'clock tonight and he'd decided to try to stow away on that. The Isle of Man boat was not due to leave until ten o'clock tomorrow morning. Charlie said if he failed to get on the first he meant to try again on the second, but he had no idea where he was going to spend the night. I found him cowering in the doorway of that café on the waterfront. It was cold and dark and he looked very miserable. He was more than glad to be brought home. He had no money at all; he'd spent the coppers left from his bus fare on sweets.'

Her mother said, 'I hope he isn't going to make a habit of this.'

'He's had a fright. I think he might have learned his lesson. Anyway, he promised he'd try harder with his reading.'

Cooking the Sunday dinner was a job Flora enjoyed. It was a change from working in the garden shop. She'd asked Isobel if she'd give Hilary a hand there so that she could.

Rain was splashing against the kitchen window. It was a cold dark morning; winter seemed sud-

347

denly on them. Flora was glad she was inside and close to the stove. It was giving out heat and succulent scents of roasting beef. There was to be Yorkshire pudding and all the trimmings with a jam sponge to follow.

The weekends were still busy. Hilary had arranged with her friend Jane to pick up the children and take them to Sunday school with her own two. She'd said she'd take them home with her to play for an hour or so, then deliver them back here in time for lunch.

Flora needed to have the meal ready to dish up at twelve thirty because the shop closed then for an hour. She looked at the clock and found she was on schedule. It was time to start carving the joint. But where was Mavis? She was usually here long before now, in good time to have a glass of sherry first. There was only an hourly bus service on Sundays.

She was looking out of the window to see if there was any sign of her when Jane's car turned into the drive. Flora went to open the door and the children came scampering in.

'Thank you for looking after them,' she called to Jane. 'Take your coats off, children, and change your shoes.'

It was time to dish up. A few moments later the back door opened letting in a gust of cold air and her daughters were home.

'Smells lovely,' Isobel said. 'I'm starving. Go and wash your hands, Sophie, and you too, boys.'

'Where's Aunt Mavis?' Hilary wanted to know.

'She's late. She must have missed the bus.'

'The next one will be here in ten minutes,'

Hilary said. 'Had we better wait?'

'Yes,' Flora said. 'The dinner won't hurt in that time. This isn't like Mavis; she gets into a routine and keeps to it.'

When ten minutes had passed, Hilary said, 'It doesn't look as though she's on this bus either.'

'Let's have our dinner.' Flora was worried. 'Where is she? She's never failed to turn up before. I wish she'd have a phone put in so we could talk to her.'

'Perhaps she isn't well?'

'If she didn't intend coming, she'd surely have rung to let us know? There's a public phone box near her paper shop.'

'If she was sick,' Sophie said, 'very sick, she wouldn't want to go out.'

'She wouldn't want her dinner either,' Charlie pointed out. That didn't soothe Flora's fears.

Hilary said, 'Mavis wouldn't forget, would she? If we aren't busy, I could go down and find out what's happened to her.'

They were busy and it was almost time to close the shop before she got away. She had to cross the town to reach the North End, which was down near the docks. The street Aunt Mavis lived in consisted of two identical facing terraces of small houses.

Mavis's was very much in need of a coat of paint; threadbare green cotton curtains were stretched across the living-room window. There was no bell, so Hilary hammered on the front door. Nothing seemed to stir inside. She knocked again and shouted through the letter box. While she was wondering what to do, the door of the

349

next house opened and a stout middle-aged woman wearing a soiled pinafore came out. Hilary asked her about Mavis.

'I haven't seen her for a day or two.'

Hilary's stomach turned over. That was bad news.

'Don't see her much.'

'How can I get in?'

'Have you tried the back door?'

'No.' She couldn't remember ever having been round the back. The woman was setting off down the street in her carpet slippers.

'How do I...' Then, hearing something inside, she opened the letter box and peered in.

'All right, all right,' she heard her aunt say irritably. 'Who is it?'

'Hilary.' She was flooding with relief. 'It's all right, thank you, she's coming,' but the next door neighbour had gone.

Every time Hilary had driven her aunt home, she'd dropped her here on the pavement. Never once had she been invited in. Now she could hear the rasp of heavy breathing and the rattle of bolts being withdrawn. The door opened a crack and she caught a glimpse of Mavis in a greying flannelette nightgown with a torn shawl round her shoulders.

'What d'you want?' she demanded brusquely.

Hilary pushed the door and stepped inside as quickly as she could. 'I've come to see if you're all right.'

'I'm sick.' She coughed; it was a racking cough. 'Flu, I think.'

'Go back to bed, Aunt Mavis.' Hilary had never

seen her look so ill. 'I'll follow you up.'

She led Hilary across the front room to the kitchen at the back. Behind a door was a steep staircase with linoleum on the treads. The air was still and very cold. Hilary knew her mother had been brought up in this two up, two down house and had heard her say nothing much had changed in it since.

'You didn't come for your lunch today – we were worried about you. Mum wanted me to call down to find out why.'

'At this time of night?'

'It's only half past five.' Even in the light from a forty-watt bulb in the ceiling, the bedroom looked grimy. 'Have you had any dinner today?'

'No. I didn't want to go out. Didn't want any dinner.'

'But you made yourself something?'

'No. I wasn't hungry.'

'You must eat, Auntie. I could make you something now. What would you like?'

'Tea. I'd like some tea.'

'Right.' Hilary felt her way downstairs to the kitchen. There was an ancient gas stove and a battered kettle. She put some water on to boil. She peeped in the large enamel bread bin to see the heel of a stale loaf, and decided it would toast. She opened the door to a walk-in larder. The shelves were bare, except for two eggs and a cheese dish with a small piece of cheddar inside, growing thick green mould.

She found a tin containing black leaf tea but there was no milk. A milk bottle stood sour and empty on the table. She wondered if she could

351

borrow some, though the woman next door hadn't been helpful. She found a jug, rinsed it at the sink and decided to try the house on the other side.

Letting herself out, she placed an incredibly worn and twisted shoe of Mavis's into the door frame where it would stop the door slamming behind her. The woman she'd spoken to before was ringing her own doorbell. She asked, 'Is she all right?'

'No, my aunt's ill. Flu, I think.' Hilary hesitated a moment and then, as her front door was opening, said, 'I'm making her some tea but she's run out of milk. Could I possibly borrow some for her?'

A burly man in shirt sleeves and braces stood on the step. 'No. We've no milk or anything else to give away. Not to anyone.' The woman went in and the door slammed in Hilary's face.

She stepped back in surprise. Mum said it was a rough area, but she'd expected more neighbourliness than that. She went to the house on the other side to knock. This time, it was a frail elderly woman who answered and she was given half a jug of milk.

'I'll replace it for you tomorrow,' she said.

'It's all right, I've got plenty/ I'm glad you've come to do something for her.' The woman's grey head nodded towards Mavis's house. 'We hardly ever see her but she worries us.'

Hilary went back to make scrambled eggs and set the meal out on a tray. She took it upstairs and helped her aunt to sit up, but there were not enough pillows to make her comfortable. As Hilary placed the tray in front of her, her toe caught against a brimming chamber pot under the bed.

She asked, 'Where is your lavatory?' She'd seen no sign of one.

'Out in the yard. I can't get out there when I'm ill.'

'No, of course not. I'll empty this.'

Hilary found the pot by no means easy to carry down the narrow slippery stairs without spilling. She couldn't believe the conditions her aunt lived in and felt ashamed that she hadn't asked and done something to improve them before now.

Mavis had been spitting into bits of pink newsprint torn from the *Financial Times* which she'd crumpled up and thrown all over her bedroom floor. Hilary collected them into a plastic bag, of which there seemed to be hundreds about the house, and put it out in the dustbin.

When she went back to the bedroom, Mavis had eaten every crumb of the food. 'That was very nice. Thank you. You're a good nurse.'

'Would you like a wash? It'll make you feel better.' Mavis looked as though she needed one so Hilary didn't wait for an answer. She had to boil the kettle again to get warm water. 'A clean nightie too?'

She failed to find a clean one but there were several very grey and stained ones in the kitchen. She brushed Mavis's thin and greasy hair for her and pinned it back. It was going to be a mammoth job to clean this place up; she'd have to get Mum here. Thank goodness the shop was now closed on Mondays. It would give them time to do it.

'I'll come back tomorrow and do some shopping for you. You've no food in the house. I expect Mum will want to come too.'

Before going, she found a Thermos flask which needed scalding before it could be used, and made Mavis a hot drink for later. Then she kissed the soft sagging cheek and went home.

When she arrived she found Isobel had bathed all the children and put them to bed. She and her mother were sitting at the kitchen table having mugs of malted milk. Flora was shocked at what Hilary had to tell her about Mavis. 'Your aunt won't have been to the doctor or taken anything for her flu.'

'She had some cough mixture there and some aspirin. She's dosing herself.'

'I wish she was closer, so we could do more,' Flora said. 'It's nine miles or more, isn't it? And you have to cross the town.'

Hilary was thoughtful. 'Perhaps we should bring her here.'

'She could share my bed. It's a double one, there'd be plenty of room.'

'No, Mum, I don't want you to catch whatever it is she's got. Besides, you won't be getting your rest if she's sharing your bed, and neither will she.'

'We could put her in my house until she's better. It would be so much nearer and we could go down and spring clean her place without her fussing round us.'

'She'd be on her own all day,' Hilary pointed out. 'Better if we brought her here. We can do it with a bit of juggling. Mum, if you allow Isobel and Sophie to move into your house, I'll move back to my own bed and take Jamie in with me.

That means Mavis can have Jamie's room to herself. We can leave the windows open for a few days before he goes back.'

'No.' Flora was adamant. 'I'll go home. Mavis can have your spare room.' It was one thing to have Mavis in her house – she'd want to go home in a day or two. Isobel was a different matter. It was beginning to look as if she'd need a roof over her head for a long time.

Hilary looked as though she was trying to be patient. 'But then you'd have the walk up here and back, morning and evening. Izzy can drive round.'

Isobel was pleading. 'I'll look after your things, Mum, keep everything shipshape.'

Flora was at a loss. To say she wanted her house to herself would sound selfish when Isobel lacked a home of her own, but it was something she didn't intend to give way on. Tom Waite lived in a bed-sitting room and had said, 'I'm afraid it's not the sort of place where I can entertain. Sorry about that. I'd enjoy having you there if it was halfway decent.' Having him to a meal in her house had been lovely but with Isobel and Sophie there they'd have no privacy.

'No, I'd rather go home.' She could see the disappointment on her younger daughter's face and felt guilty. She was afraid Isobel had been banking on it.

'Right,' Hilary said briskly. 'Izzy, you and Sophie can move to the spare room. At least, if I'm back in my own bed, we won't all have to move round again when Ben comes home.'

The next day, Flora helped Hilary strip the

beds and make Jamie's room ready for Mavis. Then they went down together to fetch her.

'Go to Hilary's house? I'm perfectly all right here,' Mavis told them.

Flora stood firm. It was some time since she'd been inside the house and hadn't realised what a state it was in. 'Mavis, you need a bit of help when you're ill. You can't possibly go out to buy your food when you're like this.'

'If you just got a few things in for me I'd manage.'

'You'd still have to cook and you don't feel like that yet. Come up to Hilary's and let us look after you.'

'I'll be such a lot of work for you.'

'Not so much as if we had to keep coming down here,' Flora said sharply. It took some time to persuade her, but eventually she started to collect a few things to take with her.

'You won't need all those notebooks, Mavis.'

'I'd like to take them, and these too.' She pointed to several bulging files filled with business letters, pink newspaper cuttings and bank statements.

'Surely not all of them?' Would Hilary object to such mounds of dusty papers in her nice clean house?

'Yes, all,' Mavis insisted, her eyes going to the sliding piles of glossy company reports as thick as monthly magazines, stacked all along one wall of her bedroom.

'Not those too? They won't all fit in your car, will they, Hilly?'

'I might need them.'

356

Flora decided it was impossible to argue with her. 'Just one or two of the most important then.'

She pulled a suitcase down from the top of the wardrobe. Once it had belonged to their mother and was covered with the dust of ages which, once disturbed, was flying round the room. She started to pack Mavis's papers, and when she lifted one file the bank statements it contained slid out at her feet.

Mavis gave a cry of alarm and bent to bundle them back as quickly as she could.

'What do you want all these for?' Flora asked in amazement.

'I like to keep up with market movements,' she said. 'It keeps my mind active.'

'Your hobby?' Hilary suggested.

At last Flora was able to persuade Mavis to put a bedjacket on under her coat and go downstairs. Hilary stripped her bed while this was going on, and collected a mountain of clothes and bedding that needed washing. 'It'll be easier if I use my own washing machine,' she said.

As soon as they arrived, Flora ran a bath for her sister and helped her shampoo her hair. She presented her with two of her own nightdresses and a dressing gown of Hilary's. 'I wonder whether we should call the doctor?'

'No,' Mavis said. 'I don't want a doctor.'

Hilary whispered, 'We'll see how she is tomorrow. She might be all right if she has plenty of rest and good food.'

'I do feel better,' Mavis said when she'd settled into Jamie's bed. 'It's such a light airy room and so nice and clean.' She was opening her notebooks and packets of dusty cuttings on the white counterpane and leaving dirty marks.

Flora tried not to notice. 'I'd like to arrange for you to have a phone put in your house,' she said. 'Then you could let us know when you weren't well.'

'I'm not paying bills for a telephone.' Mavis was indignant. 'I can't hear all that well on those things and who would I ring but you?'

Flora made her lunch and set a tray with a lace cloth and the last rose from the garden.

'You've got some very posh ways now, Flora,' her sister said. 'It was never like this at home. It's like being in a hotel.'

Hilary brought her some books and magazines and said, 'There won't be any service this afternoon. We're all going out.'

'Don't worry about me. I'm not used to service.'

'I want you to have a nap if you can. Isobel will be back when school's over to keep an eye on the boys. I'll leave a note to say you're here and ask her to make you some tea. We'll be back in time to cook supper.'

Flora was taking a collection of brushes and dustpans, cloths and soap out to Hilary's car. They drove back to Mavis's house to start cleaning. Hilary frowned. 'What a mess. How can she live like this?'

'She's sick.' Flora tried to make excuses for her.

'It didn't get like this in two or three days.'

'It was never like this when I lived here. The whole place needs redecorating.'

'Having only an outside lavatory must make

358

things difficult for Auntie when she's ill. Wouldn't it be possible to have one put inside for her?'

'Where?' Flora asked. 'I suppose the second bedroom could be turned into a bathroom. But that would leave only one bedroom.'

'One is all she uses,' Hilary said firmly. 'It would make all the difference to her.'

'She doesn't own this house, it's rented. She won't want to spend money on it.'

'Rented or not, if she's going to stay here, we should do something. In this day and age, it's ridiculous for an old person not to have an indoor lavatory. Think of Mavis having to go out through the yard in this weather. No wonder she's got flu.'

'Working in that care home has made you an expert on the elderly, has it?'

Hilary said slowly, 'It makes me feel guilty to have three lavatories in my house while she hasn't even one.'

'It would be more sensible for her to move somewhere better, somewhere closer to us. I have suggested that but she won't hear of it.'

'Would it be worth asking Tom to come down and take a look? He used to work for a building firm, didn't he?'

Flora sighed. 'I suppose I could pay for her to have a lavatory put in. Tom would have more idea than we do about what it would cost.'

CHAPTER TWENTY-TWO

Flora was tired with all the cleaning she'd done, but she rang Tom as soon as she returned to Hilary's house and asked for his opinion.

'She needs a proper bathroom, of course, but just an indoor lavatory would be a big help. Have you any idea what that would cost?'

'It's hard to say without seeing the place,' he said. 'Would you like me to drive you down later this evening, and take a look?'

'Yes please,' she said.

For Flora, any outing with Tom was a pleasure. Then, because Isobel had already started to cook their supper and Hilary was helping her, Flora went up to talk to Mavis, taking two glasses and the bottle of sherry with her. She told her what she'd been doing as she put a brimming glass into Mavis's hand.

She said, 'Put in a bathroom? In my old house? Don't be daft.'

'Think of the comfort you'd get. Going outside on cold wintry nights...'

'I've been doing it all my life, Flora, as well you know. I'm used to it. I don't want workmen in my house. Anyway, it isn't as though I own it. It's rented.'

'I know, but you're getting on in years. If you had the use of it for the rest of your life, wouldn't that make it worth while?'

'No. It isn't worth spending money on that house. The whole place is scheduled for demolition.'

'Scheduled for demolition? The whole street?'

'Half a dozen streets at least. A slum clearance scheme.'

Flora was amazed. 'When?'

'Heaven only knows. I got the notice ages ago.'

'Why didn't you tell me?'

'I thought I had.'

'No. I did notice some of the houses were empty...'

Mavis was defensive. 'There's still a lot being lived in.'

'Well, perhaps you should be thinking of a move. Would you like me to ask round the estate agents for something nearer here?'

'No. I don't want to move. I'm not going to. Stop fussing, Flora. Leave me alone.'

'But Mavis, think of...'

'It could last my time out. No point in my moving until I have to. You manage your own affairs and let me manage mine.'

Hilary took Mavis's supper tray up to her. Mum had told her what had happened and said she wasn't going near her again tonight. Mavis was sitting up in Jamie's bed with her ledgers open, surrounded with crumpled pink newspaper cuttings and looking more alert than she had.

Hilary went to move some of her bits and pieces in order to make room for the tray.

'No.' Mavis held up her hands forbidding it. 'You'll mix them up and I won't be able to find them again. Just put the tray on top, Hilary.'

'What are you doing, Auntie? What are all these cuttings for?'

'To help me keep up to date with company news, dear. I should have brought my wireless, but Flora said it was far too heavy and that you'd be able to lend me one.'

'Of course. We have a little trannie in our bedroom. I'll get it.'

She put it on the bedside table. Mavis looked at it suspiciously. 'A trannie?'

'A transistor radio.'

Aunt Mavis shook her head, perplexed. 'I've never heard a wireless called that before. How do I put this thing on?'

'Just here.' Hilary demonstrated and a burst of music throbbed through the room. 'Is this the sort of music you like?'

'I don't want any music. Where will I find the business news?'

Mavis concentrated hard while Hilary tried to show her. Her wrinkled face was set in hard lines.

Flora was cross. When she'd tried to ring Tom before supper to let him know Mavis had refused to have anything done in her house, and that it was pointless for them to go, the phone rang and rang but nobody answered it.

After supper, he was at the door before she'd rung again. With some exasperation, she explained about the proposed demolition order.

'And nobody will ever get Mavis to leave the place,' she said. 'They'll have to carry her out the day they come to pull it down. I knew she wouldn't want to spend money on it, but I thought I'd do it for her if it didn't cost much.'

He was smiling at her. 'Well, if we aren't going to see your sister's house, how about a drink at the Dog and Gun?'

'That would be nice.' Flora's heart leaped in anticipation.

Tonight the pub was very quiet. Over a glass of wine Flora talked about her sister.

Tom said seriously, 'Having her with you must mean more work for you and Hilary. As if you haven't got enough to do.'

'We couldn't leave her alone in that house when she was ill, could we? It was in a terrible state; we've spent all afternoon trying to clean it up. Hilary was talking of giving it a coat of paint.'

He laughed. 'You're gluttons for punishment. If it's not worth putting in a lavatory, is it worth painting?'

'It would make it look cleaner. It looked awful this afternoon, a two-bedroom terrace house built to house a Victorian docker's family. It seems very poky after Hilary's house, but I was brought up there, one of five children.'

'You were brought up there?'

'Yes. I don't know how my mother managed.'

'Only two bedrooms?'

'We had a pink curtain down the middle to separate the boys' half from the girls'. You're surprised to find I come from a place like that?' Flora could see he was. She'd never heard Tom speak of his upbringing and felt she ought to know more about him. She said, 'I don't suppose you were brought up in a house like that?'

'No. I think it could have been bigger.'

Nothing else. It could hardly have been smaller, but why didn't he volunteer some details? Isobel thought he was trying to hide something. Flora could almost feel it there between them. She understood secrets, she had some of her own, but she sensed Tom had one he knew he ought to tell her, but couldn't bring himself to. It must be something he thought would put her off.

He said, 'You could go to the council and ask them if they have a definite date for demolition.'

'What a good idea. I'll do that. Whatever date it is, the best thing for Mavis would be to move somewhere nearer to us. But she won't. She's as obstinate as a mule and she won't have anything done to her house. She never seems to have any money.'

'Do any of us?' he asked.

'Would you have been able to put a bathroom in for her?'

'No, but I know people who could. We'd have had to get a quote.'

Flora smiled. It was as she'd thought. His hands were immaculate: they'd never done any practical building work. He must have been a manager of this firm he'd worked for. It surprised her to hear the call for last orders. The time she spent with Tom seemed to pass at twice the normal speed.

As he opened his car door to usher her into the passenger seat his hand brushed against hers, sending what felt like an electric current up her arm. In the half light of the car park his dark eyes seemed filled with desire. When they were together, she could feel the sexual tension. Tom seemed to give off sparks.

Flora stole glances at him as he concentrated on driving. He was a handsome man. She wondered if he'd thought about having sex with her. She felt he wanted it, even thought a lot about it, but he was a man who was very much in control of himself. His kisses were cool, as though designed not to excite. Possibly they didn't excite him but they certainly did her.

She wondered if he'd ever get round to suggesting it and what she'd say if he did. Not only had she been a faithful wife but she'd had no experience of sex since Harold had died. She'd thought it was something she could live without, that it belonged to youth, but things had changed radically since her day. Since the sixties, a very different view of sex had become the norm. Now it was thought everybody needed it, and, to be fulfilled, should have it. Even people of her age.

The pill had made it safe for them to do so, and had changed the moral climate. She was thankful she wouldn't even need the pill. There were very few reasons to be thankful for the advancing years, but it helped to know that sex couldn't possibly result in pregnancy now.

He drew his car to the kerb outside Hilary's house and kissed her. It was not the lover's kiss she'd hoped for, more a show of gentle affection. Flora thought Tom felt the same way as she did, but perhaps he needed more time to be able to tell her so.

The following night, when Isobel and Hilary were making supper, Flora said, 'Mavis is feeling better. I've persuaded her to come down and eat with us tonight.'

She came wearing Hilary's dressing gown, swaying slightly and feeling for the back of each chair as she passed on her way to the bottom of the table.

'I'm a dreadful nuisance to you,' she told Hilary, 'but I'm well enough to go home again now. Tomorrow...'

'You really aren't well enough,' Flora said. She'd rung the council but hadn't been able to get a definite date for the demolition. However, she was given the impression it wasn't imminent. 'Why don't you stay till next week? Isobel will go down over the weekend to give the place a coat of paint.' It would also give her and Hilary time for another cleaning session.

'It doesn't need painting.' Mavis was indignant. She looked Isobel in the eye. 'Why should you paint my house?'

'Mum asked me to.'

Mavis snorted with frustration. 'It'll be too much for you. I wish you wouldn't...'

Flora said, 'Isobel and Tom have offered to start on Saturday.'

'No. Leave my place alone. I don't want it painted.' Mavis glowered round the table at them all. 'I'm being a nuisance.' She sighed heavily. 'This Tom, is he the one who brings my *FT* in the morning?'

'No, that's Rory. His mother runs the village shop where they sell papers.'

'Well, I've been glad of it, but I'd rather go home now. I feel fine and I'm just in the way here. I'd like to go home tomorrow. I do hope you won't keep me here any longer.'

'If that's how you feel, Auntie,' Hilary said. 'We'll take you home tomorrow evening after we've closed the shop.'

'Why not in the morning, or even now?'

Flora lost patience with her. 'Mavis, you've got to be able to manage on your own when you get there.'

'We'll have to get some food in for you,' Hilary explained. 'You won't feel like going shopping yet, will you?'

Flora calmed down again. 'We'll help you make a list of what you need now, then I'll phone Rory's mother. He can bring it up with him when he comes to work tomorrow.'

Mavis pulled a face. 'I haven't got any money here to pay him.'

'I'll do that,' Hilary said. 'You can pay me back when I take you home.'

The phone rang before they'd finished eating. 'I'll get it.' Hilary put down her knife and fork and went out to the hall.

'Fern Granville here.' Hilary was able to recognise her cut-glass voice now. She hadn't expected to hear it again so soon, and it had the power to make her heart race. When previously she'd tried sending her books to publishers and agents, she'd had to wait months for a reply. She'd learned to be patient. Surely Fern couldn't have sold it already?

She said, 'I've got some good news for you and some bad.'

'Oh!'

'I've found a publisher who is interested in your book. Porterhouse Press.'

'Wow! That's marvellous!'

'But here's the bad news. Elizabeth Jones, their commissioning editor, doesn't like the end of your story, and she wants you to do some more rewriting. If you can do that to her satisfaction, she'll be prepared to publish it.'

Hilary's head swam with confused emotions. Would she be able to manage it? Of course she was thrilled and excited to have this chance, but the first time Fern had telephoned, hadn't she said she liked the end?

'You are prepared to do a bit more rewriting?'

'Yes – yes, of course.'

'You must look at it like this: you're almost there, and Elizabeth will help you hone it into shape. She loves your book.'

Hilary was prepared to do whatever was needed to get published. She felt triumphant, lifted up on a wave of pure happiness as she went back to the kitchen to tell her family the good news.

Flora said, 'I think it's very exciting, a writer in the family. Of course you'll be able to do what she wants, Hilly.'

Isobel rather burst the bubble. 'More work on the book you'd finished?'

'Yes.'

'How much?'

'The editor is going to write to me and send me the manuscript back. I think she wants the last chapter or so cut off and a slightly different ending.'

'That sounds a lot of work.' Flora was frowning. 'Will you be able to do what she wants?'

'I hope so.'

The following morning, Hilary received a closely typed four-page letter from Elizabeth Jones with a full explanation of what she wanted her to do. She could see immediately that the editor's suggestions would pull the story together and tighten the book.

She would work on it for two or three hours after breakfast every morning when she felt fresh and the shop was reasonably quiet. Before going to sleep at night, she would look through what she'd done that morning and polish it up. She wanted it finished as soon as possible so she could send it back.

Mavis had her cases packed at lunch time and was saying she'd like to set out as soon as they'd eaten. Hilary had to explain that they had the shop to run. They took her to see it because she said she never had, but once there amongst the flowers she remembered seeing it on several occasions. Hilary insisted that Mavis stay until after supper.

'Then you can go straight to bed with a hot water bottle. Your house is cold – it hasn't been lived in for a few days. Mum's laid the fire, so you can nip down in the morning and light that and then go back to bed for an hour until the place warms up.'

When Mavis saw how they'd cleaned and tidied up her house she was delighted and full of thanks. She went from the living room to the kitchen and back again. To see her so pleased was sufficient repayment for Flora and Hilary for the effort they'd put into it.

It took several journeys back to the car to carry in the stock of food they'd bought and the mounds of laundry Hilary had done for her. Then together they made up Mavis's bed.

'I shall be very comfortable now.' Mavis beamed at them.

'You really could do with a fridge.' Flora was putting the food in the larder and boiling water for a hot water bottle.

'A fridge... That sort of thing's expensive and I really don't need...'

'You wouldn't have to go shopping every day if you had one,' Flora said. 'Then if you didn't feel like going out, you wouldn't have to.'

'There's no power point,' Hilary whispered. 'Forget it.'

'I'm perfectly happy the way things are,' Mavis burst out at Flora. 'All you want to do is to put me to a lot of expense.'

Hilary said, 'Talking of expense, here's the bill for the food we bought from the village shop for you. You said you'd pay us back.'

'Yes, well...' She turned on her sister and demanded, 'Flora, did you or Hilary go in my wardrobe when you were here cleaning up?'

Hilary had tried when she'd been collecting up dirty clothes to take home and wash. 'No. It's locked.'

Mavis was on her feet and heading upstairs, moving more quickly than she had done for ages.

Flora said softly, 'I should have remembered how mean she is.'

Mavis was back with the exact money she'd

already counted out. 'Who shall I give this to? You or Hilary?'

Flora said, 'Hilary,' and the pile of used notes was pressed into her hand.

'I am grateful,' Mavis told her. 'You've done a lot for me, I know.'

November was bringing misty mornings and afternoons of thin sunshine.

'Good for business,' Flora said to Hilary as they opened up the shop one Saturday morning. And so it proved: customers started coming in straight away. Almost immediately, Hilary was struggling with one of the drawers at the back of the counter.

'Why can't I get this open?'

Flora did her share of tugging at it too, but she couldn't budge it either. It contained ribbons and decorative cords for tying up their bowls of flowers. The counter looked solid from the front, but at the back there was a row of five drawers and below them was a shelf where the wrapping paper and cellophane were kept. One customer who couldn't wait went away with an ornate bowl of dahlias wrapped in cellophane paper held together only with sellotape.

Sophie and Jamie were playing about, smelling the flowers and giggling. Flora found it hard to work with the children underfoot but for once they might be useful. She said, 'Sophie, go and find Tom or Rory. We need a strong hand here.'

'All right, Nana.' She zoomed off with her arms outstretched.

'We are being bees,' Jamie yelled, following in her wake. Tom came in, wheeling in a tub containing an ornamental tree.

'Can you get this drawer open for us?' Flora asked. She was serving another customer by then.

'What's the matter with it?'

'It's stuck and we can't get at the ribbon. The scissors are in there too,' Hilary told him, as she gift-wrapped a pot of chrysanthemums. 'I've had to use whole sheets of paper and bite off the sellotape. We really need it opened.'

Flora said, 'Sophie, take Jamie back to the house. We're too busy for you to play here this morning.'

'It's boring there. There's nothing to do.'

'Your mother will think of something. Why don't you ask her?'

'She's teaching the twins.'

'Go. We can't do with you here,' Flora said forcefully, before turning to the next customer.

With a superhuman wrench, Tom had the drawer open. 'I think the wood's warped a bit. Your cash register must be heavy.' It was positioned right over it. 'Probably it's been pressing down on the drawer.'

The cash register was open because Flora was getting change from it. He lifted it further along the counter.

'Yes, you can see, the top has sunk a bit there. It needs supporting from underneath. I'll come and do it when you close the shop.'

Jamie came tearing back, threading his way through the customers and screaming at the top of his voice. 'Help, Sophie's going to put a horrible insect on me.' He ran into Tom's legs. 'Lift me up or it'll get me.'

372

Flora saw Tom swing him up, while Sophie skidded to a halt in front of him. Tears were rolling down Jamie's face. 'It'll suck my blood out and grow into a big dragon while I shrink.'

Sophie had one fist clasped tight. Tom bent down and held her wrist. 'What have you got there? Come on, open up.' He smiled. 'It's only an earwig, Jamie, look. You must have seen lots of these in the hothouse. It won't hurt you – it's a tiny harmless thing.' He turned back to Sophie. 'Come along, young lady, let's put it outside in the border.' Tom tried to march her out to do it, but she twisted and pulled away. The earwig fell to the floor.

'Look,' Jamie screeched. 'It's got pinchers on its head. That's how it bites into you to get your blood.'

Tom put him down to scoop the insect up and put it outside.

Sophie was stamping with rage. 'I don't like you,' she told Tom, her eyes glistening and her face scarlet.

He bent down to her. 'And I don't like little girls who try to frighten those younger than themselves,' he told her.

Flora was losing patience. 'Go and play somewhere else, Sophie,' she told her as she attended to yet another customer. She knew Sophie had gone to hide behind the door leading to the hothouses. Jamie was clinging to Tom and a customer was offering him a sweet to distract him.

It was some time later that Flora felt Sophie pulling at her skirt. 'I saw that man taking some money from the till,' she told her.

'Sophie, you mustn't tell stories like that. It's naughty.'

Isobel turned up at that moment looking for her daughter. 'Come along,' she said. 'We're all going for a walk. We need another loaf.'

Sophie asked, 'Can we have sweets too?'

'No,' her mother said. 'You know you can't have them before lunch.'

'Jamie's had some already,' she retorted.

Once they'd gone, the shop quietened and the morning seemed more normal. Rory and Tom were in and out bringing in more stock. Hilly made them all a cup of tea.

As she drank hers, Flora found herself alone with Tom in the little office behind the shop. 'Would you like to go out for a meal tonight?' he asked.

'I'd love to,' Flora was saying when Hilary shouted for her help in the shop.

'I'll pick you up at seven tonight,' he said, beaming at her.

CHAPTER TWENTY-THREE

At five thirty that afternoon Flora began cashing up. She felt tired and was thinking of having a long soak in the bath before going out. She wasn't concentrating on what she was doing, but when she had a total she had the feeling that the takings were less than they should be. She remembered changing several ten pound notes.

There ought to be more of them under their clip.

It was a modern till that added up all the amounts that had been rung up during the day. Flora stared at the total in disbelief. She had an empty feeling in her stomach as she started to count the money again more carefully. She'd been right the first time; it was thirty pounds short. Only then did she remember Sophie's words. 'I saw that man taking money from the till.'

The idea made Flora curl up in horror. At the time, she'd thought it another of Sophie's play fantasies. Or that she'd taken a dislike to Tom because he'd ticked her off about frightening Jamie. But what if she really had seen Tom take money? The shop had been hectic at that moment; it would have been possible for him to do it without her or Hilary noticing. No. She pulled herself up short. That would mean Tom was dishonest. She rushed into the hothouses to find Hilary, feeling upset and somehow disappointed in Tom.

'He wouldn't do that, Mum.' Hilary put an arm round her shoulders and gave her a squeeze. 'He didn't want to be paid for the time he works here. He said he'd be happy to do it for nothing, so it makes no sense.'

'No. Tom wants to help you keep the business ticking over until Ben comes out. He's really concerned.'

'Yes. I had to insist on paying him. I mean he lives in that old house that's been divided up into flatlets and bedsits, so he can't have that much cash, can he?'

'He counts the pennies just as I do.' Flora was whispering. Did that make it more likely he might have taken it? 'He said he'd take me out tonight. You don't think he's got the money from...'

'Don't be silly, Mum. He'd never do that. Why don't you ask Sophie what exactly she did see? You'll know if she's telling the truth or not. She's a little tinker, that one.'

Isobel was cooking when they went home. Flora could see Sophie out in the garden picking mint to go with the lamb chops. She went out to ask her.

Sophie tossed her blonde curls defiantly. 'Yes, I did see him. I'm sure Tom took something from the till.'

'What d'you mean "something"? You said he took money this morning.'

'There's nothing else in the till, is there?'

'You're quite sure?'

Her nose went up in the air; she was indignant. 'I wouldn't have told you, Nana, if I wasn't.'

Flora was worried. She had to conclude that Sophie was telling the truth. She went upstairs to have her bath with a heavy heart.

'I decided against the Dog and Gun,' Tom told her as soon as they were in his car. 'They don't take bookings, and it gets packed out on a Saturday night. I've booked a table for us at a restaurant called Sheldrakes. Have you heard of it? It's down near Heswall beach.'

Flora was impressed. 'I've never been, but I've heard it has a reputation for good food.'

'It'll have to be very good to come up to the standard you can produce,' he said. 'I want to take you somewhere nice.'

It was another cold evening. The wind was roaring across the River Dee, but the restaurant was cosy. It couldn't have been a nicer place and the service was swift. Tom ordered drinks and also a bottle of wine. Flora chose whitebait and roast duck from the extensive menu.

She couldn't get the missing money out of her mind. Hilary had suggested she discuss it with Tom, but looking at him now, relaxed and comfortable and trying quite clearly to please her, she was afraid he'd think she was accusing him. He was a lovely person and very generous. To put this poisoning suspicion into words might spoil what she and Tom had.

Yet she was gripped by a fierce need to know one way or the other. Hilary couldn't afford to lose money like that. She had to tell him.

He smiled at her. 'How's your duck?'

'Delicious.'

He paused, watching her. 'You're very quiet tonight.'

Flora knew she wouldn't rest until she'd told him. 'I'm worried,' she faltered. His dark eyes jerked up to meet hers. 'About the takings at the shop.'

'Surely it did well today? You were busy.'

'Somebody has taken money from the till.'

'What!' No mistaking his amazement and, yes, shock. 'What happened?'

'When I came to cash up, there was thirty pounds missing.'

He whistled through his teeth. 'You're sure?'

'Yes. The till adds up the sales we make. That was thirty pounds more than was in it.'

'But who could have taken it? Who apart from your family were there?'

'Stella was in this afternoon. She's one of our part-time ladies and has worked for Ben since the shop opened. There's never been any trouble like this before. It won't be her.'

His dark eyes looked into hers. 'It wasn't me, Flora.'

Her heart seemed to flip over. He'd understood what she was asking. 'I believe you, of course, but Sophie said she saw you take it.'

'Sophie! Oh my God! What must you be thinking? She's telling fibs, Flora. Really she is. I must talk to her tomorrow, have it out.'

'You don't have to, Tom. Hilary said you wouldn't do such a thing.'

But she knew his feelings were hurt and his pride injured. She could feel him withdrawing from her.

She tried to put the whole thing out of her mind. She talked of their bridge sessions and the ladies they played with, but the theft had soured everything. When the bill came, she suggested she pay half, but he waved her offer away imperiously. He drove her home almost in silence. Flora knew she'd spoiled what would otherwise have been a very pleasant evening, and one Tom had meant to be a special treat.

When he pulled up in front of Hilary's house, she thanked him.

'I'll be round tomorrow morning to have it out with Miss Sophie,' he said rather curtly.

Hilary locked the day's takings into the safe Ben

378

had had bolted to the wall and hidden inside a cupboard in their study. She was more than upset; she was blinking back tears. It was money they'd worked hard for and could ill afford to lose. The till didn't lie: thirty pounds had gone. Somebody had taken their money.

She had difficulty eating the lamb chops Isobel had cooked, although she told her they were exceptionally good.

'Is something the matter?' Izzy wanted to know.

She shook her head. She didn't want to say anything in front of Sophie. She waited until supper was over and then sent the children to the playroom, so she could tell her sister what had happened.

Isobel had a face like thunder. 'If the money's gone, perhaps she did see Tom take it.'

'I hope not.' Hilary groaned. 'Mum sees him as a white knight.'

'He is a bit strange, though, Hilly. That time in the supermarket...'

'You know Mum thinks the sun shines out of him.'

'I think even Mum believes he could be hiding something. I'll put Sophie to bed tonight. You see to your lot. Don't worry, I'll get to the bottom of what she saw or didn't see.'

Isobel's face was grim as she went to the playroom to find Sophie. She was half afraid her daughter had taken the money. Not that she'd stolen anything before, but if ever there was trouble Sophie could be relied on to be the cause of it. Isobel needed to nip this in the bud.

The children were using a skipping rope to have a noisy tug of war, Sophie and Charlie against Andy and Jamie. Sophie's cheeks were pink with exercise.

Isobel marched her up to the bathroom and started to run a bath. Now they were sharing the guest bedroom there was no en suite. Isobel missed it.

'Get undressed, please.' She believed that to strip off Sophie's clothes would leave her feeling she had no place to hide. Sophie shed her clothes on to the bedroom floor and ran to the bathroom. She got in and reached for Hilary's bubble bath.

'No.' Isobel took it from her hand and put it out of reach. 'No treats tonight. I don't think you've been a good girl.' She started soaping the slim wiry body. 'Auntie Hilly's upset,' she went on. 'There's a lot of money missing from the shop till.'

Sophie was silently screwing up her face.

'Nana says you knew about it. Is that right?'

She didn't answer.

'Didn't you tell her you saw Uncle Tom taking it this morning?'

'Yes, Mummy,' she whispered.

'And did you?'

'Yes.'

'Are you sure?'

She didn't answer. She was squeezing her eyes tight shut.

'Open your eyes, Sophie.'

'Nasty soap in them.'

Isobel rinsed off any vestige of soap and stood her up in the bath. 'Now, let's see you.'

Reluctantly Sophie opened her green eyes.

They were full of assumed innocence.

'I don't think you saw any such thing. What really happened? Did you take the money?'

Isobel could barely hear the word. 'Yes.'

'Oh, for heaven's sake! It's very naughty to tell lies like that.'

Sophie's chin went up. 'He doesn't like me.'

'I'm not surprised. Would you like somebody who told other people you were a thief? What did you do with the money?'

'I want to be dried.'

'What did you do with the money?'

'It's in my pocket.'

Isobel strode back to the bedroom and searched through the clothes Sophie had thrown on the floor. The pink jeans she had begged Isobel to buy from M&S had deep pockets. Folded at the bottom of one and kept in place with a conker were three ten pound notes.

She rushed back to the bathroom. Sophie had climbed out and was shivering on the bath mat.

'You must not steal and you must not tell lies. I'm going to spank you for that.' Sophie's rounded pink bottom was still wet. Twice Isobel brought the flat of her hand down hard on it. It felt cold. Sophie responded by opening her mouth in a wail of protest.

'And you must not blame other people for the things you do. You've been very naughty, Sophie.'

She wrapped her in a towel and rubbed her dry, marched her into the bedroom and pulled her nightdress over her head. 'Into bed now.'

Still howling, Sophie leaped in and disappeared under the bedclothes. Isobel went back to run the bath water out and tidy up. When she returned, Sophie was still weeping audibly. Isobel went to sit on the bed and pulled the bedclothes away.

'Come on now,' she said more gently. 'Let me kiss you good night.'

Sophie's arms went round her. 'I'm sorry, Mummy.'

'Yes, well tomorrow I want you to say that to Nana and Tom. It was a terrible thing to do.'

'I did it for you.' It was another wail. 'You're always saying you have no money.'

That was true. Isobel felt guilty. 'Yes, but we can't take other people's.' Her arms tightened round Sophie in a hug. 'Come on, love, it's time you were going to sleep. Let's forget about it now.'

Flora was depressed. She let herself into Hilary's house and saw the lights were still on in the kitchen. Isobel and Hilary were sitting at the table having cocoa and biscuits. Flora's eyes were drawn to three ten pound notes tucked under the sugar basin. She swallowed hard. 'What's that money? Is it...'

'Yes.' Isobel sighed. 'Sophie took it.'

'The little witch!' Flora sank down on a chair and covered her face with her hands. 'Oh Lord! I believed her when she said Tom...'

Hilary asked, 'Did you say anything to him about it?'

'Yes, far too much. I told him Sophie said she'd seen him take it. He thought I was accusing him.'

'I suppose it would sound like that, but he is a bit odd. Nobody in the village knows much about him.'

Flora said, 'That doesn't mean he's dishonest.'

'But he's sophisticated, well educated and gives the impression ... well, of having known better times.'

Flora groaned. 'I was just trying to find out what had happened.'

Isobel said, 'The best thing to do would be to give him a ring now. Tell him before he sleeps on it.'

'A good idea. I'll hang on for five minutes to give him time to get indoors.'

'I'm sorry, Mum.' Isobel was downcast. 'Sophie's caused a lot of trouble. She can be a real pain.'

What sickened Flora was that she'd had to force herself to talk about the missing money in the restaurant. She'd thought she owed it to Hilary and now she wished she'd chickened out.

'It cast a real damper on everything. Spoiled our night out.'

It was nearly fifteen minutes later when she went out to the hall and rang his number.

Mrs Phelps, his landlady, answered, and, when she asked to have a word with Tom, said, 'I'm sorry, he's not home yet.'

'Oh!' Flora was surprised; he'd had plenty of time since dropping her. 'Thank you,' she said. 'I'll try again later.'

Mrs Phelps was brusque. 'I'd much prefer you to leave it until morning. My other lodgers have all retired and I would very much like to do so myself. Our phone is in the hall and wakes everybody when it rings.'

'Yes, of course. I'm sorry.' Flora slid the phone

gently on its hook, feeling abashed. She was up early the next morning, but as it was Sunday she didn't like to phone him before nine o'clock. When she did, the phone rang and rang and nobody answered it. It was lunch time before she was able to contact him.

'Where have you been? I've been trying to get hold of you since last night.'

Tom sounded depressed. 'When I left you, I knew I wouldn't be able to sleep. I decided to go to the Dog and Gun, but it was closing time. I just tramped round in the dark.'

'I'm so sorry.' Flora felt a shaft of guilt. 'I knew I'd upset you. I wanted to apologise and let you know Sophie took the money.'

'Really? Sophie took it? I'm glad it's cleared up, but it set me thinking. I need to talk to you.'

'What about?' Flora's heart was sinking. Did he think she should have been more trusting?

'I'll explain later. When would be a good time?'

'Tuesday? I'm having a day off. Come round to my house in the morning and have a cup of coffee.'

There was a pause. 'Tuesday seems a long time off.' He sounded defeated. 'Couldn't you make it sooner?'

'You could come for coffee tonight.'

'Thank you. I'd like to do that.' Tom was stiff and awkward, no longer at ease with her. 'What time?'

'Half six to seven?' Flora decided to go home as soon as she'd cashed up. She needed only to put a match to the fire, but they'd soon be hungry. When she told Hilary she wouldn't be in to supper, Hilary said, 'Take something with you,

Mum. We could fix you an indoor picnic.'

It was quarter to seven when Tom knocked on her door. By then she had the fire lit and the coffee was filling her living room with its scent. Tom looked abashed and as though he hadn't slept.

Flora said, 'I'm terribly sorry. How I've wished I'd never mentioned the missing money. I was just asking you, Tom. I wasn't trying to blame...'

'I know. It shocked me, but thinking it over it could be my own fault, couldn't it?'

'Why?' She drew him to the sofa and sat down in the opposite corner.

'I've been thinking a lot about you and your family, but it never occurred to me until now that you might be thinking about me and my circumstances.'

'I've done my share of that.' She smiled. 'You don't say much about your past life. It puzzles me.'

With a cup of coffee in his hands, he said, 'Something bad happened to me. I can't think about it, even now. I avoid talking about it.'

'Tom! Am I prying?'

'It's not that.'

Flora said sympathetically, 'I can feel something there, some dark secret between us. I want to get to know you better but it's stopping me.'

He nodded. 'It's also stopping me making progress. I have to put it all behind me and move on.'

'What is it?' Flora felt he'd come to tell her, that he needed help to get it out. He certainly looked troubled and, at this moment, older than his years.

'I'm ashamed of something I did. I don't usually tell lies...'

'Of course not.'

385

His lip was puckering. 'But I told you I'd been employed by a building firm. That wasn't true. I owned it and let it go bankrupt.'

'Why would you be ashamed of that?'

'I inherited the business from my father, as he had from his father.' Tom sighed. 'Clogs to clogs in three generations, isn't that what's predicted for family firms? It was certainly true for ours.' He stared silently into the fire.

'What happened?' Flora asked softly.

'I didn't pay enough attention to it. I suppose I didn't show enough interest. All the time I was growing up, it had ticked over quietly in the background, providing a good living for my family. I thought it would do the same when I was running it. I didn't appreciate the effort my father put in. I was more interested in sailing, having a good time. I had a sea-going yacht called *Lucky Lady*. Not so lucky as it turned out but I loved her, and so did my wife Grace. We used to race at Cowes every year.'

Flora sat back, afraid to interrupt in case she made him dry up.

'The early seventies were difficult for business, as you'll no doubt remember: an economic nightmare. The trade unions were militant, wanting ever bigger wage increases, and workers were forever being called out on strike. The country had a balance of payments deficit, a three-day week and soaring oil prices to contend with. It wasn't just my firm – many others went to the wall. I was building houses while house prices were roaring upwards out of control. I failed to notice how far they had risen and was selling too cheaply.'

'But that's not anything to be ashamed of.'

'It is. With a little more effort on my part, it could have been avoided. I neglected my business while seeking my own pleasure. A lot of people lost money because of me.'

'You must have lost money yourself?' Flora felt she was understanding him better.

'Yes, and I lost my home and my boat. But, far, worse, I lost my wife. Grace.'

'She left you, because of that?' Flora thought no wife worth her salt would leave her husband for that reason.

His eyes seemed unnaturally bright. 'You have to live through things like that to realise how much it hurts.' He paused for so long, Flora wondered whether he meant to go on. 'Grace was used to a big comfortable house with a high standard of living. Long weekends spent sailing and a good social life. All that was swept away.'

'Oh!' Flora could see now how painful that might be. 'You said you had children?'

'Yes, a son and a daughter. Eric lost the business he'd expected to inherit one day. He was just nineteen and working in it, until he was thrown on the job market without much in the way of qualifications. It was very difficult for youngsters to find jobs at that time. After a year, he emigrated to Australia. He's doing all right now.'

'And your daughter?'

'Carol came out of it better than any of us. She'd never expected to get much from her dad. She got a degree in modern languages, found a job with a merchant bank in London and went on to marry someone in a similar position. She still has a high standard of living.'

'You must be pleased they're both doing well.'

'Yes, except I see very little of them these days. Carol and her husband both got jobs in New York. My car was once hers. She gave it to me when she was going to America.'

'Oh!' Flora had assumed it had survived from his past life.

'I live on social security now. My mistake cost me dear: I haven't been able to get a job since. I lost everything, my pride, my confidence and my self-respect.'

'Aren't you going a bit over the top?' Flora asked. 'You've still got your health...'

'I haven't told you the worse part yet. Grace couldn't face losing her home and being made penniless. We were offered a council flat in Toxteth. It was too big a fall for her. She committed suicide, gassed herself in her car.'

'Tom! How dreadful for you.'

'I feel very much to blame for that. I've never managed to get over it.' There were tears on his cheek now. Flora felt sorry for him. She put her arms round him and gave him a hug.

That unlocked his emotions, brought his lips down on hers in a passionate kiss. She was seeing a side of Tom she hadn't known existed. His firm grip on self-control was loosened. He was all Flora had hoped for.

Her eagerness diluted with some trepidation, she took him up to her bedroom, knowing she intended to taste fruit that had been considered forbidden for most of her life. But times had changed and she wanted to change with them.

She wanted more from life.

After an evening such as she'd never envisaged, Flora took a bath and ran one for Tom.

'D' you feel hungry?' she asked.

'Starving. Would we be too late to get something at the Dog and Gun?'

'They don't do meals on Sunday nights,' Flora said. 'Hilary packed something for me to bring down. She called it an indoor picnic.'

She unpacked the basket in her kitchen: a bottle of wine, a plastic box of salad, some slices of cold beef left from Sunday lunch, some cheese and a couple of slices of homemade apple pie. While she set it out on her best plates, Tom made up the fire, which had almost gone out. He was relaxed now his secret was out.

Flora felt it was a day for confessions, and told him she was ten years older than he was. She felt she needed to get that said before it became harder to do so.

'You don't look it,' he said in disbelieving tones as his eyes searched her face. 'Sixty-five?'

She nodded.

'You walk with real bounce. You must have had an easier life than me.'

'No. Times were hard when I was young.'

'Then it's because you've been with children all day and every day. Being a teacher kept you young.'

'I wasn't a very good one. I never felt properly trained. At the end of the war, when there was a desperate shortage of teachers, the government brought in a special shortened course. I wasn't as good as the rest. I wasn't good at discipline. No, I wasn't too happy as a teacher.'

'But you stayed?'

'I had to. I was paid the same as the others and I needed the money to look after my daughters. I also needed the short working day and the long holidays to fit in with them. I suppose it wasn't all that bad. I'd worked in a munitions factory during the war and went into an office when it finished. I thought I'd like that, but I was the dogsbody. I did the filing and made the tea. I'd have had to learn shorthand and typing to get anywhere and I hadn't the money for the training. I was given a government grant for my teaching course.'

Flora had intended to walk up to Hilary's house that night, to sleep there and be on hand in the morning, but she didn't want to. She rang Hilary and told her she'd be up in time for breakfast. Tom stayed the night with her. It had been a day that changed everything for them.

CHAPTER TWENTY-FOUR

Hilary was expecting to hear today that Ben would be discharged from hospital. She couldn't wait to get him home, but it didn't stop her thinking about her book.

All her hopes were pinned on the manuscript and the waiting was making her feel twitchy. She'd been hoping to hear from Elizabeth Jones for the last day or two as to whether she was now happy with the last chapters of *The Night Star*. She was filled alternately with wild hope that she'd take her on, and despair that she'd say it wasn't good enough.

She was hoovering in the sitting room to have everything spick and span for when Ben came home. Through the window she saw the red van stop at her gate and the postman get out and come towards her front door. She froze. If he rang the bell he'd be returning the package and it would ruin this day of all days. She only started to breathe again when she heard letters slither through the letter box on to the mat. With her heart in her mouth, she rushed to see what he'd brought. There was a letter from *her*. She tore at the envelope with nervous fingers.

Elizabeth wrote that she was pleased with the changes and felt they now had a very good book; she was sending it out to the copy editor and had scheduled it for publication in ten months' time.

Hilary collapsed on to the settee with a gurgle of joy. It was excellent news and made her feel on top of the world. At last, she was going to achieve what she'd been aiming for all her life. Furthermore, she'd be paid for it.

She needed to have the money as soon as possible; the balance of their joint account was drifting lower. It scared her to see that their nest egg had all but gone.

An hour later Fern Granville phoned to congratulate her. It gave Hilary the opportunity to ask about terms.

'Well, first you'll get a contract. They'll be drawing it up now,' she told her. 'You'll have to sign that and it'll probably be another couple of months before you get your advance.'

'Could you tell me how much that's likely to be?'

'Their contract rate for beginners is I think two hundred pounds, but payment is a royalty on sales. How much you eventually get depends on how many copies they manage to sell.'

'Thank you. That's fine.'

She was afraid the money wouldn't come soon enough, but she mustn't let that spoil today. The boys were looking forward to having Ben with them again. Their hospital visits on Sunday afternoons had been stiff and formal and no fun at all. They had painted welcome home posters days ago, and Hilary began sticking them up round the kitchen. The last one was barely in place when Ben rang to say the specialist had done his ward round and given him the all clear to go home.

'I'll come to fetch you right away.' Hilary was excited at the prospect. Last night, she'd packed a suitcase with clothes for him to come home in. Now she tossed it in the boot of her car and set off. Ben was waiting for her at the ward door with a beaming smile on his face.

The nurses pulled screens round his bed so he could get dressed. Hilary emptied the suitcase on his bed and started repacking it with his hospital kit.

'It'll be marvellous to have you home and get back to normal,' she told him.

He was in high spirits. 'I can't wait.'

But on the way out she noticed he wasn't

walking all that well. He needed to hang on to her arm as well as use a stick on the other side. Hilary found the suitcase was heavy with books and it was hard to manage as well as Ben. She persuaded him to sit in the entrance hall and wait until she brought the car round. She was afraid they wouldn't be getting back to normal just yet.

No sooner did she get him home than Ben wanted to go over to the garden centre.

'I've been thinking about you managing on your own all these months,' he said. 'I want to see things for myself and say hello to everybody.'

Family and staff gathered round to welcome him back and tell him how well he looked, though Hilary didn't think he looked all that good. The boys were delighted to see him when they came home from school and wouldn't leave him alone. Hilary had arranged a special steak supper for his first night back and Isobel had bought a bottle of champagne.

'I meant it to toast your health, Ben,' she said. 'But now Hilly's heard about her book, we can toast that too.' They had a very jolly evening.

In bed that night, Ben said, 'I should have let you get on with your writing long ago instead of expecting you to work full time all these years to further my ambitions.'

She told him the story line of her second book and how she was trying to push on with it.

'No guarantees for this one, but my publisher has asked for first refusal.'

'It's been a smashing day,' Ben said as he settled down to sleep.

Over the following days his bonhomie leaked

away. Hilary could see he wasn't able to do as much as he wanted to. Working in the shop tired him, even though she'd moved a chair in so that he could sit down.

'I feel so damned weak,' he complained.

'You're bound to, to start with,' she comforted him. 'Take it slowly. In time, you'll build your strength up again.'

She knew it bothered Ben that he had to rely so much on other people. It frustrated him that he couldn't do any physical work. Her mother had been running the shop for weeks and had things well under control. Rory and Tom had coped well with bringing the stock on for sale.

Ben said, 'I feel out of touch. I have to keep asking everybody what they're doing.'

Hilary said, 'Give yourself a day or two and you'll be back in your stride. Things have moved on while you've been in hospital.'

She felt their relationship had altered. He'd lost his confidence and was grumpy and unhappy with the changes she'd made to the shop opening hours. He blamed the drop in business on that.

'It seemed the right thing to do at the time,' Hilary said. 'No point in keeping the shop open if the customers aren't coming.' Ben was all for opening on Mondays again.

'It would be sensible to leave things as they are until the spring,' she said. 'You'll be feeling better by then and there'll be more business.'

Worse still, he was spending long hours poring over the accounts and was worried that the business wasn't taking as much money as it had last year. He was also upset about how little there was in their bank accounts.

'How are we going to pay the mortgages?' he demanded. 'I'm worried stiff. Our little cushion of savings has gone. We're going to be in shooks next month. Honestly, Hilly, I think the only way out of this is for you to ask for your nursing job back.'

Hilary stiffened. Now she'd tasted success with her writing, she wanted to carry on. She wanted to grasp this chance with both hands. She was fearful it would slip away. She said stiffly, 'I'm just getting into my new book.'

'Surely that can wait? We can't risk losing our home and business.'

'I'd very much like to get on with it. We could go down and see the building society. They said they'd arrange a break for a few months if we found ourselves in difficulties.'

'But that just puts it off. We'll have to pay eventually.'

'Ben, we'll be all right for another month,' she said. 'Then it's Christmas and we do take more then. By the New Year I might have my advance.'

'It's all might, might, might. What if we aren't all right?'

That upset Hilary. She said crossly, 'I'm sorry if I didn't run your garden centre as well as you expected.'

Flora overheard and said, when Ben had banged out of the room, 'You managed too well when he was in hospital. It's made him feel superfluous.'

Isobel had hoped her mother would let her move to her cottage before Ben came out of hospital, so she could keep out of his way. Mum, who had always bent over backwards to do anything she and Hilly wanted, was being firm on this point. Isobel knew why, of course: Tom Waite was visiting her. She wanted her cottage to herself and Isobel couldn't blame her for that.

Now, every mealtime, Isobel was conscious of Ben's presence on the opposite side of the table. It made her feel uneasy.

According to her mother, Ben was an excellent husband and father. She'd envied Hilly that. Ben had been prepared to go out on a limb to get a house to be proud of and a business that would provide a few luxuries. Before the accident, he'd had more energy and far more get up and go than Sebastian; he hadn't been afraid of hard work. He wasn't like that now, but Hilary expected he would be in a few weeks.

By comparison, Sebastian had always been lazy. He'd come home from school every afternoon feeling he'd done all that was needed. He could ignore things like house maintenance and gardening.

But seeing Ben again after all this time, Isobel knew she wouldn't want him as a husband. She didn't like the way he pressurised Hilly in front of them all. Between Ben and Charlie, poor Hilly was having rather a hard time of it.

Isobel thought Charlie's reading was improving slowly, but he'd fallen behind Andy's standard and was increasingly discouraged. He was developing a school phobia and was full of complaints about his teacher.

Isobel didn't know Miss Witchell personally, but a colleague who did thought she was competent in the classroom. It was just that she was nearing retirement age and her patience had been worn thin by generations of difficult children.

That same afternoon, Charlie sat huddled at his desk with every muscle tensed. For what seemed hours he'd been watching the hands of the classroom clock move round at a snail's pace. Twenty minutes more of this before home time. He'd found it hard to learn to tell the time, but Nana had helped him. She'd brought him a broken alarm clock and they'd twisted the hands round and round and practised until he'd got it. But reading was even harder.

He hated, loathed and detested reading lessons; dreaded having to read a whole paragraph aloud in front of everybody, but his turn was coming. Miss Witchell was going round the class; there'd be no escape. She was horrible to everybody, but seemed to pick him out for special torment.

He was scared of her when she was cross. Scared of her all the time really. She had a stern, bad-tempered face and looked older than Aunt Primmy and Aunt Prue. She had black hair and wore black clothes, and her eyes were sharp and missed nothing. Right now they were glaring at him from behind large spectacles that flashed warlike sparks when she got angry. They all called her the Witch.

It was Paul Stone's turn to read. He was good at it. The words were coming out smoothly and much faster than Charlie could do it.

'Paul, there's a comma there. You should pause,' Miss Witchell cut in from her desk at the front. 'Read that sentence again.'

Commas! Charlie hadn't got round to thinking about commas; it was all he could do to make sense of the letters. He knew he should be following the words in his book as Paul read them, but the whole page danced before his eyes and he couldn't concentrate.

Beside him, Andy whispered, 'This will be your paragraph.' He turned the page and prodded halfway down. 'Practise it now.'

'Twins!' Miss Witchell's ruler rapped down on her desk. 'Stop whispering.'

Charlie's heart began to pound as he turned to the page in his own book to do what Andy had advised.

'Charlie! Stop turning over pages. You must follow the words as they're read. You'll never learn if you play around like this in class.'

Obediently, Charlie turned back and put his finger on the last word that had been read. He could see his hand trembling.

'Carry on, Paul.'

Charlie stole a glance at the clock. Had it stopped?

Miss Witchell said, 'That will do, Paul. Charlie, we'll have you next.'

He let out a little gasp. It wasn't fair. It wasn't his turn. She'd left three people out.

'Stand up,' she ordered.

They were all required to stand when they read. As he did so his book slid to the floor and closed up.

'Stop messing about, Charlie. You're making a nuisance of yourself.' Her tone was severe.

'I'm sorry, miss.' He was scrabbling through the leaves with nervous fingers and couldn't find the page. Andy pushed his own book in front of him and took the other away. Thank goodness, but now he couldn't find the paragraph.

After what seemed an age, he started. 'The bus...' He dried up. The next word was a long one.

'Sound it out, Charlie.' Miss Witchell sounded as though her patience was being severely tried.

'G...a...th...'

'Gathered speed,' Andy prompted under his breath.

'Gathered speed.'

Miss Witchell's voice roared out, 'Andy, go and sit at that desk on the back row by yourself. You'll get your turn to read in a moment.'

Charlie wanted to shout out that without Andy he was no good at anything. He needed him next to him.

'Come on, Charlie.'

He read the sentence haltingly, at a painfully slow pace. The Witch kept barking at him to sound the letters out. She was making him so nervous he couldn't think. He stuttered and stopped again.

'Come on, Charlie, you know this word. P ... r... You've had it before many times.'

Charlie obediently said, 'P ... r...'

'You read it last week without any trouble. Come on, it's easy.'

Charlie repeated, 'P ... r...' He couldn't think with the Witch's tongue goading him, making him feel a complete idiot.

'Now Charlie.' Her tone changed to one of

condemnation. 'We've had enough of this. You're being silly. Stop playing about.'

'No,' he gasped. His heart was thudding, his mouth dry; he was trying. 'P ... r ... a...'

'Not a. Look at that letter again. What is it?'

The letter danced before Charlie's eyes. Surely that was an a? He felt desperate and near panic. He knew Miss Witchell's frown had deepened, her lips settled in a sterner line.

'It's e, isn't it?'

He could feel tears prickling his eyes and knew he mustn't cry in front of the whole class. They'd poke fun at him, never let him forget it.

'Charlie, I won't tell you again.' Miss Witchell's patience was exhausted. 'Get on with it. P ... r ... e ...'

Charlie couldn't do it. He just couldn't. He had a brain that wouldn't work. His mind had gone completely blank; something snapped inside him. With all the force he could muster, he hurled his reading book at his tormentor. He aimed for the cruel eyes behind the flashing glasses but it caught her on the shoulder.

'Oh!' she cried in alarm. The book crashed to the floor and was ignored.

Charlie heard a wave of sound eddying round the room. There was more than one whoop of pleasure, a brief cheer hastily subdued, together with gasps of horror at his daring and half-choked laughter at the Witch's discomfort. The last titter died away, leaving a shocked and lasting silence.

The bell signalling the end of afternoon school clanged into it. Miss Witchell recovered. Her voice, loud and distinct, rose above it.

'Monitors, collect the books. Children, stand up. Charlie, you will stay behind. I'm not having that sort of behaviour in my class.'

To end the school day, the Witch liked her class to sing unaccompanied. They began chanting through the familiar hymn, eager to be gone.

Now the day is over, night is drawing nigh,
Shadows of the evening, steal across the sky.

'Class dismiss. Good afternoon, children.'

'Good afternoon, Miss Witchell,' they chorused.

Amongst the shuffling of feet and the banging of desk seats, Charlie heard Paul Stone behind him say in a superior voice, 'Charlie can't read. He's thick.'

A moment later, he felt Miss Witchell's powerful fingers bite into his shoulder and steer him towards the headmaster's study. His knees felt weak, and he knew he was in big trouble. Children were only taken there for major rule breaking.

In the corridor full of noisy children, his teacher stopped and turned.

'Andy, there's no need for you to come. Go home.'

Charlie saw Andy pause, undecided. 'Don't leave me, Andy,' he implored.

The Witch's hand came down heavily on his shoulder again, driving him forward. They met Mr Leyland coming out of his study.

'I'd like a word,' Miss Witchell barked at him.

The headmaster turned back. 'Come in. Charlie, you wait here with Miss Collins.'

The school secretary got up to close the door to

the corridor but he could see Andy already there, peering in, hot and anxious. 'There's no need for you to wait, Andy,' Miss Collins said.

'I can't go without Charlie,' he gulped.

'Yes you can. This has nothing to do with you. Off you go now.'

The door closed in his face. Charlie felt she'd cut off his lifeline. The next moment, Mr Leyland was beckoning him into his room. He stumbled in holding his breath.

'We insist on good behaviour and good manners in this school.' The headmaster looked fierce. His face was down on a level with Charlie's.

'You've gone too far. Throwing books...'

Charlie closed his eyes, expecting the worst. He was shaking, suddenly afraid he was going to wet himself. He tried to hold it back but couldn't. A trickle of warmth ran down his legs to splash on the floor. He was absolutely horror-stricken. A pool was soaking into the headmaster's carpet and, even worse, he'd sprinkled Miss Witchell's highly polished shoes.

She stepped back. 'You disgusting boy,' she thundered.

Charlie felt gripped by fear, embarrassment and humiliation. He wanted to die.

Hilary aimed to finish her writing day by four o'clock when the children came home from school. She was having a cup of tea in the kitchen with Ben when Jamie came in.

'Have you come home alone?' Ben asked. 'Where are the twins?'

Hilary had impressed upon them that they had

402

to collect Jamie every afternoon and see him safely home, and up until now they had.

'They've been kept in.'

'Why?' Hilary asked as she poured him a glass of milk. 'Have they been naughty?'

'I think so.'

'Oh dear. I wonder what they've been up to?'

As Jamie was safely home, she was not unduly concerned until Andy came rushing in alone, gulping down his distress.

'Where's Charlie?' she demanded. Her first thought was that he'd run away again.

'He's in big trouble. The Witch got him. Took him to the headmaster.' Andy couldn't get the words out quickly enough.

'Why? What did he do?'

'He threw a book at her. She went wild. She was being awful to him. Told him to stop fooling when he was really trying and doing his best.' Andy looked close to tears.

'It's all right, Andy.' Ben pulled him down to sit beside him and put a protective arm round his shoulders. Hilary put a glass of milk in front of him.

'They're keeping him in, but they wouldn't let me stay with him.'

Jamie asked, 'What will the headmaster do to him?'

Hilary was churning inside. She could guess what had happened and was burning with anger. She'd tried hard to explain the difficulties the twins had and she'd asked for understanding.

She said to Ben, 'Should I go down and see Mr Leyland?' She was undecided. Of course, he'd feel he had to maintain discipline and Charlie would have to be punished, but to tell him to stop fooling when he was trying hard...

'Better sit down, love,' Ben said. 'Wait and see what happens. I don't suppose he'll keep Charlie in for long.'

Hilary was edgy. She poured herself another cup of tea, but was too restless to drink more than half.

'I'm going,' she said. 'He'll feel all alone, that Andy's deserted him. You know what he's like.' She meant nervous, but didn't want to say the word in front of the other children.

She cut through the garden centre, past the nursery beds, but before she reached the gate in the back wall she could hear Charlie's sobs. He let himself in. She could see his face screwing with distress and knew he'd had a terrible time. When he saw her, he threw himself at her. She hugged him hard. Great sobs were racking his body.

'It's all right, Charlie. You're safely home. You're all right.'

'I wet myself,' he sobbed. 'I couldn't help it.'

Hilary ached with sympathy for him.

'I can't read,' he wailed. 'It's no good, I can't do it.'

'Auntie Izzy says you're coming on. She's pleased with your progress.'

'I can read better for Aunt Izzy. She never gets cross with me and doesn't wind me up. I hate school.'

Hilary took him straight upstairs to the bathroom and started running a bath for him.

'Miss Witchell said I was a disgusting boy

because I splashed her feet.' The whole story was coming out between sobs. She knew Charlie was deeply ashamed that he'd lost control and wet himself. He hadn't had an accident like that since he was a tot.

'They're all going to make fun of me,' he said. 'They'll never let me forget it.'

'If it happened in the headmaster's room,' Hilary pointed out, 'the other boys won't know about it. Not unless you tell them.'

That seemed to cheer him up a little. But how could she keep making him go to school when they let this sort of thing happen? She dreaded to think what he'd be like at half past eight tomorrow morning.

She took Charlie down to the kitchen dressed in his new track suit.

Sophie admired it, and Andy said, 'Can I wear mine?'

'Yes,' she said. 'Go and change.'

Hilary was stuffing Charlie's clothes into the washing machine when she found a crumpled envelope in the pocket of his trousers. It was addressed to her. She tore it open to find a note from Mr Leyland.

'What does he say?' Charlie asked, helping himself to milk.

'That you are to be kept in at morning playtime for the rest of the week.

'As punishment for what he calls disruptive behaviour in class. You mustn't do that again, Charlie.'

He nodded. 'It's not too bad. To be kept in at playtime.'

'Better leave reading practice until later,' she told Isobel. As she pushed the note in front of her sister, there was a tap at the door. She went to see who it was.

'Hello, Mrs Snow,' Paul Johnson was there with four other little boys.

'Can the twins come out for a game of football? I've brought the team round.'

Andy was pushing past her. 'Yes,' he said. 'Good idea. Charlie, are you coming?' Charlie followed slowly, nibbling a biscuit.

'What a nerve you've got, Charlie.' Paul said. 'Throwing your book at the Witch like that.'

'You didn't let her walk all over you.'

'I'd never be able to stand up for myself like that.'

'I couldn't believe my eyes.'

'Her face! She nearly hit the roof.'

'She deserved it. She was being a right pig.'

Hilary watched them go. She didn't approve of their attitude. Charlie mustn't throw his books at the teacher. But Charlie's back had straightened as they moved off. Perhaps after all he'd be willing to go to school tomorrow.

CHAPTER TWENTY-FIVE

Flora was finding Tom very different. They were instantly more relaxed and at ease with each other. He told her he'd put his past history behind him.

Now Ben was home and wanting to run his business again, Flora was spending less time in the shop. It meant she had more time to spend with Tom and they were taking advantage of it. He was taking her out and about more, and she often brought him home to spend the evening in her cottage.

This evening, it was getting dark when they returned. Flora drew the curtains and turned on two table lamps to give the room a warm glow. While Tom put a match to the fire, she made a cup of tea. Flora went to sit beside him on the settee and together they watched the yellow flames curl up through the wood. She felt Tom's arm come round her shoulders and pull her closer. 'I do love you,' he said. 'I feel very lucky to have you come into my life.'

Flora kissed him. 'You've made a big difference to mine.' She'd been taking him regularly up to her bedroom to make love. She'd never felt so fully alive and energetic. 'When you're not with me I can't stop thinking about you.'

'Me too. I wish I could be with you all the time.'

The fire had caught now. The logs were beginning to crackle, and Flora could feel its warmth on her face. 'What's stopping you? I mean, if we make each other happy, why not?'

Tom turned towards her, his dark eyes full of love. In the soft light she could see him struggling to find the right words.

'How do you see the future?' she asked him. 'With me?'

'That's what I want. I'd like to think we could get together permanently, but...' He was hesitating and she wondered if she'd misread his intentions. 'There are difficulties.'

'What d'you mean?'

'To be honest, I've been thinking about asking you to marry me.'

Flora's heart filled with love for him.

'But what have I got to bring to a marriage? That's held me up for months. It's like asking you to share your home and your pension and the good life you've scrimped and saved for with me. That's a great deal to ask of you and not really right, is it?'

'It might be.' Flora was cautious. Ever since Tom had explained his circumstances, she'd deliberated on that too. She'd thought herself miserly to put financial considerations above love, but that's the way she'd always been. That was why she had security now. But after all these months she'd decided she wanted Tom here with her.

'We could live together,' she suggested. 'We don't have to get married.'

'Flora! What would your children think?'

'Why not? Everybody else is doing it.'

He was smiling. 'You mean that way you'd have no legal commitment to keep me for the rest of my life?'

'It sounds horrible when you put it like that. But surely, what's good for the young should be all right for us?'

'I'm not sure that's true. We're all set in our own time warp. In our heyday, it just wasn't done.'

Flora smiled. 'We've already gone further than would have been acceptable in our day.'

'Yes, and that makes me feel guilty. A woman like you, living with a man she isn't married to?

It would put you in a... Well, it's not something I'd want to do to you. It feels wrong.'

'Well then?'

'I see marriage as a commitment for both of us. We're promising to love and care for each other for the rest of our lives. I like that, but in addition you're legally committing yourself to sharing all your worldly goods with me while I have none to share with you. It isn't a fair bargain, is it?'

'You're too proud, Tom, that's your trouble.'

'Perhaps, but I know what it is to be forced to lower one's standard of living. When poverty comes in at the door, love flies out through the window.'

Flora sighed. He was a good, kind man and she loved him.

'Well, I'm for it,' she said. But it looked as though Tom was hung up on it.

On Sunday morning, Flora asked Isobel to fetch Aunt Mavis for her Sunday lunch. She said, 'She wasn't looking too good again last week. She might not feel well enough to come on the bus.'

Flora was cooking for them as usual, so Hilary and Ben could work in the shop. Isobel took the children with her to keep them out of everybody's way. When she got back she was surprised to find Ben at home, though the shop was still open.

He would usually act as a welcoming host, pouring them all a glass of sherry before they ate, but today he was slumped at the kitchen table looking miserable.

Mum poured the sherry instead, before sending the children to wash their hands. When she took the joint out of the oven, Ben said he didn't want to carve, so she did that too.

Hilary came over and they all trooped into the dining room to eat. Isobel thought there was something of an atmosphere. She was cutting Jamie's portion into small pieces when Ben announced, 'I'm going to stop Tom working. I don't need his services any longer.'

That made them all stare at him. Isobel saw her mother put down her knife and fork in surprise.

It was Hilary who asked, 'Are you sure you can manage without him? Tom does a lot of bending and lifting.'

He was short with her. 'I'll have to. The business can't afford all these extra wages. Trade has fallen off. There's not enough work to justify it.'

'It's not that bad,' Hilary said in a mild voice.

'I'll manage well enough with Rory and a few odd hours from the part-timers. I've done it before and I can do it again.'

Isobel could see neither Hilary nor Mum was pleased. They'd asked Tom to help and Ben was putting him off without consulting anybody.

Ben helped himself to mustard. 'The same applies to you, Flora. I'll have to cut your hours.'

'You already have,' she said. 'I'm only doing a few at the weekend now.'

Hilary said sharply, 'Mum came to cook for us this morning to help. We aren't paying her for it.'

Isobel felt embarrassed. She could see her mother and Aunt Mavis were too.

Sophie asked in a loud voice, 'Is Uncle Ben cross?'

Flora ignored her and said, 'I know you want to

get the business back in shape, but you don't have to go at it like a horse at a fence. Take your time, Ben.'

'Time isn't a luxury we have,' he said, looking round the table. 'It's of the essence. Hilly, the logical thing to do would be to try to get your nursing job back.'

She looked astounded. 'I thought we'd agreed I should have more time for writing?'

'Then you'll have to start getting up early again,' he retorted.

'Ben, you hated me getting up at four in the morning. You said I woke you up and it seemed like the middle of the night.'

'There are times when we all have to do things we'd rather not.' Mavis rarely opened her mouth until spoken to, but she said, 'Now Hilary has a publisher for her first book, she must have time to write the second. Surely that's common sense?'

Ben said coldly, 'She really doesn't have much choice. If we can't pay the mortgage she might not have a roof over her head.'

Hilary gulped and said, 'My advance can go towards the mortgage.' Isobel could see nobody was enjoying their meal now. Ben's hostility was charging the air.

He said, 'It'll only cover one month's payment and heaven knows when you'll get it.'

'More than that,' she answered calmly. 'With all the cutbacks you're making we can to stretch it to two. And there'll be more eventually.'

'Not as much as you'd get from the nursing job. It won't be enough.'

Isobel put down her knife and fork. 'Hilly, do

411

you mean,' she asked, 'that you worked in that care home for years and gave up all you earned to pay the mortgage?' She looked at Ben askance. 'The *joint* mortgage?'

She could see Hilly had. 'And now you aren't earning as much, he's kicking up? Blow that for a lark. You're far too soft with him. No wonder you never seem to have a penny to spend on yourself. You won't find many doing that, Ben Snow. I certainly wouldn't.'

She got up from the table and swept out of the dining room. She knew from Ben's face he thought she'd gone too far. She struggled into her coat. She had to get away from them all. She'd said too much; the last thing she wanted was for Ben to ask her to leave.

Isobel hadn't reached the gate before Sophie came running after her, still pulling on her coat. 'I'm coming too, Mummy.' A small hand pushed into hers.

She squeezed it warmly, seeking support for what she'd done.

'Uncle Ben's naughty, isn't he, Mummy? What's the matter with him?'

'He isn't well.'

'He was being nasty to Aunt Hilly. I thought she was going to cry.'

'No, love.'

Hilary was certainly being put on, but Isobel knew she'd done some stupid things too. If abortion had been legal in 1966, Sophie wouldn't be here now. Isobel had wanted an abortion above everything else. Now she understood that it'd have been her loss. There were times when Sophie tried her patience to the limit, and drove her to despair. But unaccountably she'd developed a fierce love for her. She was proud of Sophie's pretty face and quick mind. Her life'd be emptier without her.

She hadn't chosen the right course when she'd found herself pregnant and alone. With the benefit of hindsight, she should either have found the courage to tell Sebastian the truth, or come straight back here to her family. Then she wouldn't be in the mess she was now.

Hilary was upset with Ben. When it was time to reopen the shop after lunch, they walked over together.

He was fuming. 'Isobel went too far,' he muttered. 'Telling me I'm kicking up, when it's plain common sense. She's a guest in my house for God's sake and should have more manners.'

'Our house, Ben,' Hilary said quietly. 'You're quick to call it that when it's a question of paying the mortgage.'

'I don't know why we have to have her here.'

'She's here because she came to help me in the summer holidays. Without her, I couldn't have looked after the boys and coped with the business.' Hilary unlocked the shop door. 'Why did you have to sound off like that over lunch? Now the whole family will think we're at loggerheads.'

'Your family are always with us. There's no getting away from them.'

'We need them, for heaven's sake.'

Ben followed her in and collapsed on his chair. 'Are we at loggerheads?'

'Well we aren't in agreement. You sounded

totally unreasonable. Telling us you're going to sack Tom and lay Mum off. Why didn't you say something to me first? What were you thinking of?'

'I'm sorry, Hilly.'

'Have you said anything to Tom?'

'Not yet.'

'Then please don't for the time being. He knows he's only helping out in the short term, but you still need him. You upset Mum by turning on us all like that.'

'I'll apologise. She's been very good to you.'

'Yes, to both of us.'

'I'm worried stiff we're going to lose everything. It's knocked the stuffing out of me.'

'You're right about that. It really has.' Hilary sighed and perched herself on the counter. 'You've always been what Mum calls a worry-guts.'

Ben's long stay in hospital had forced her to take over many of his responsibilities. Hilary knew he felt robbed of his status.

'We won't lose anything, Ben. You're not well. You aren't seeing straight; you've got everything out of proportion. Why don't we go down to the building society together tomorrow and have a word? A three-month break from making payments could make all the difference.'

'You think that's what we should do?'

'Yes. I don't want to go back to my old job. It's not just the question of the time it takes but also the energy. I need both for writing my book and coping with the children.'

'The children are all right.'

'They aren't, Ben. I'm more worried about them than anything else. The twins are not learning to read and write as they should. Isobel is doing a lot for them, bringing them on.'

He was pursing his lips. 'When is she going home?'

'I don't know. She has her own problems, but we need her here for the boys.'

'They seem happy enough to me.'

'No they aren't. Charlie's a nervous wreck. Look at his fingernails, they're bitten down like yours. The boys are just as anxious as you. They need help.'

Ben stared silently at the pot-grown chrysanthemums.

'Being an invalid for months has sapped your confidence. Having reading difficulties has done the same for the twins, especially Charlie. You're getting better now. You'll gradually take over the running of the business again and be your old self in a few more weeks. Time will do nothing to help the twins: they're getting further and further behind with their other school work. I feel we've got to do all we can to help them. Employers set huge importance on literacy skills, and I'm afraid our lads aren't going to have them.'

Ben sighed noisily.

'You found that out the hard way, didn't you?'

'Yes, and that's why having my own business is so important to me.'

Hilary was watching him closely. 'This problem is said to be inherited.'

He looked up at her, horrified. 'Are you saying it's my fault?'

'No. We none of us can help what's in our genes. That's the luck of the draw.'

'Or otherwise, as the case may be,' he said quietly.

They were granted a break from paying the mortgage, and Hilary could see Ben improving. He'd given up his walking stick, saying it was high time he managed without it, though he still had a slight limp. He was eating and sleeping better and the colour was back in his cheeks.

He reckoned he was capable of working a full day again. He talked to Tom about it and arranged amicably that Tom should cut down to one day a week. Next month, he'd finish altogether. Hilary knew her mother had offered to work for nothing, and that had shamed him into agreeing she should continue to work full time on Saturdays and Sundays. Now he was gathering strength, Flora was going to work only on the odd busy afternoon.

This weekend, when Isobel went down to collect Mavis for her Sunday dinner, she had to hammer hard several times on the front door. Mavis eventually came shuffling down and opened the door a few inches.

She looked shocked. 'Oh, Isobel! I'd forgotten it was Sunday.'

Isobel pushed the door open and stepped inside. Mavis had come down in a flannelette nightie with a shawl thrown round her shoulders.

'I can wait, Auntie, while you get dressed.'

'I don't know. Perhaps I won't come this week.'

Isobel looked round. The living room was an untidy mess again and the grate full of cold ash. She shivered; it was cold enough to strike down to the bone.

'I think you should. It'll cheer you up to have a bit of company and a hot meal inside you.'

'I'm not hungry. I haven't felt well all week.' She was grey and looked frail.

'I can't tell Mum that, can I? She'll want me to bring her down here straight away.' It was dawning on Isobel that her aunt was ill again. 'Look, if you don't feel like getting dressed why don't I button you into your coat and you get in my car?'

'Well, I don't know...'

'Come on. Shall I pack a few things for you? Your dressing gown?' Hilary had given her that only a few weeks ago. 'You can't stay here alone if you aren't well. You sit down for a moment and I'll put a few things in a case.'

Upstairs, it looked as though nothing had been touched since Flora and Hilary's spring clean. She put her aunt's notebooks and files into her suitcase together with some clothes. She wondered what Ben would say when she arrived with Mavis in this state, but when they got to the house he seemed quite concerned.

It was only when Mavis refused her habitual glass of sherry and was pushing the roast pork round her plate that they realised just how ill she was.

'I think you should stay with us again for a few days,' Hilary said. 'Just until you're better.'

'I'll be all right.'

'No, you stay here so we can look after you.'

'Here?' Ben asked in a hollow voice. 'With Isobel and Sophie here, we really don't have room for more.'

They were all a bit wary of Ben since his last

417

outburst. Hilary said, 'Mum?'

Flora said, 'I'll take you home with me, Mavis. You can't manage by yourself when you're sick.' It was the last thing she wanted to do, but she mustn't let Mavis see she wasn't welcome. She was flooding with disappointment. 'You'll be very comfortable in my little cottage.'

Tom was coming round almost every evening and bringing a bottle of wine with him. She lit her fire and provided a snack and had never enjoyed her evenings so much. She was expecting him round tonight.

She and Tom were beginning to explore their love. It had opened up new windows in her life and his too. They needed space. How could she take Tom up to her bedroom in her small house with Mavis in the next room? She could think of nothing more inhibiting.

She could see Isobel watching her closely. Flora had refused to let Isobel live with her and now she looked upset to hear Mavis being persuaded to come. Yet how could she do otherwise when Mavis was ill? Hilly would be willing to have her, of course, but having Ben home changed everything. They needed space too.

Ben was plainly relieved she was not moving in, though Hilary looked guilty and Isobel had a face like thunder. Even so, Flora had to ask Isobel to drive her and Mavis home, and as Ben was expecting her to work in the shop that afternoon she had to leave Isobel to settle Mavis in. Mavis said she wanted to go straight to bed.

Ben was in a good mood all afternoon, as well he might be since he'd got his way. Hilary brought

418

some cake over to the shop for them to have with their afternoon tea and when they were alone for a moment whispered, 'Thanks, Mum, for taking Auntie. Ben's finding things hard just now.'

Flora couldn't stop herself saying, 'Aren't we all?' and then as soon as Hilary had gone home she felt guilty because she'd laid it on heavily when she knew Mavis would want to go home in a few days.

When the shop closed, she hurried home to see how her sister was and was surprised to see Isobel's car still parked outside. She could feel her heart pounding as she let herself in. Had Mavis taken a turn for the worse? Isobel was in a better mood. She'd lit the fire, and the living room felt cosy.

Flora asked, 'Has something happened?'

'Aunt Mavis looked so ill, Mum, I thought I'd better call the doctor out. He wasn't pleased, seeing it was Sunday afternoon and Auntie isn't his patient, but he sent the on-call locum. She's got a chest infection, and he prescribed antibiotics. I've got them and given her the first dose, so she should feel better soon.'

'Oh, Isobel, I'm so grateful.' Flora was relieved all that had been done for her. 'Thank goodness I can depend on my daughters to do what's needed.'

'Not always,' she said with a rueful smile. 'Mavis has had a cup of tea and was asleep last time I looked. I'd better go now you're back, in case Sophie's playing up.'

Flora went upstairs quietly to look in on Mavis, telling herself it was selfish to want her house to herself all the time. Mavis was asleep with her ledgers and papers spread all over the counter-pane. Flora wondered what she found so fascinating in company reports.

CHAPTER TWENTY-SIX

Christmas was close. Hilary and Flora had decorated both the house and the shop.

Sunday dinner was over and the children had gone off to the playroom leaving the adults sitting over their coffee. These days the twin aunts came over to help Flora cook. Mavis, who had recovered from her chest infection and was back in her own house, much to Flora's slightly guilty relief, was still coming and now Tom was included too, so the family party was growing.

Ben was pleased because trade was picking up. He said, 'The shop looks very festive with the poinsettias and Christmas roses.'

'I'm glad we timed the bowls of hyacinths and crocuses right,' Hilary said. They were just coming into bloom.

'This is always a busy time,' Flora said. 'I'm looking forward to enjoying myself and having a good rest over the holiday.'

Isobel yawned. 'I love Christmas but I feel shattered.'

'Teachers are always exhausted by the end of term,' her mother said. 'It won't have been an easy one for you. Starting at a new school never is.'

Isobel had dark circles round her eyes. Flora

was afraid she was being plagued by doubts about what she was doing. Whatever her daughter said, Flora thought her decision to leave Sebastian had been taken too lightly and that she might now be regretting it.

'Lessons are virtually over now,' Isobel said. 'In school, it's all nativity sketches and carols as we get ready for the Christmas concert. I've got tickets for the whole family. For you, Tom, too. The kids will love it.'

'So will we,' Primmy said. 'Two concerts this year, one at the boys' school and one at Sophie's. We'll certainly know it's Christmas.'

Flora, Hilary and the twin aunts had already made the plum puddings, mince pies and cakes and the turkey had been ordered.

'There's still the tree to decorate,' Ben said. 'The children will want to do most of that.'

'I'll ask Rory to come over to do the top branches, he'll like that. It's one of the trees we grew in a tub.'

'Saturday's the day to do it,' Hilary said. 'It'll keep them occupied.'

'We'll come over to help,' Prue said. 'It'll be fun.'

Hilary had a satisfied smile. 'Apart from a few more cards to send and the presents to wrap, I'm all ready for it.'

'I'm not,' Isobel wailed. 'I haven't bought any presents yet. I would like to do that before school breaks up. What about next Saturday? Can I leave Sophie with you and the boys?'

'Yes, of course. You certainly can't take her with you.'

'I'll get up early and go to Liverpool.'

On the appointed morning, Isobel set off in good time to reach Liverpool as the shops were opening. Flora was working more hours over the busy run-up to Christmas and went with Ben to open the shop. Hilary went up in the loft to find the Christmas tree ornaments and tinsel.

It was mid-morning when Flora discovered the jar of instant coffee in the shop was empty. She went back to the house to get another. The phone rang as she was crossing the hall, so she picked it up.

'Sebastian, hello. I'm afraid Isobel's not here. She's gone Christmas shopping.'

He sounded disappointed. 'I wanted to tell her about the house. Ask her...'

'I'll get her to ring you when she comes back.'

'How are they both?'

'Sophie's fine. Isobel's a bit stressed, but we're all very busy getting ready for Christmas. Will you be doing anything exciting?'

'No. My mother's been taken into hospital again. She's quite poorly. I don't think she'll be coming out in time.'

He sounded depressed and she felt sorry for him. 'Why don't you come up and spend it with us? Can you be spared?'

He seemed quite pleased to be asked.

Flora said, 'I don't think Isobel's given enough thought to this separation. You need time together to talk things through. I don't think she's happy.' She looked up to see Hilary with a horrified expression on her face. She shook her head. It made Flora change tack. 'Sophie's here with us. Would you like to talk to her?'

'Yes – yes please.'

Hilary was already fetching her from the play-room. With Sophie on the phone, Flora felt herself being pulled into the kitchen. 'Did he say he'd come?'

'Yes.'

There was a scream of delight from the hall. 'Daddy! Are you coming up?'

Hilary's voice was low and urgent. 'Isobel won't want him here. She'll go ballistic.'

'She knows what I think. They really do need to sit down calmly and discuss their problems. She's running away from him.'

'You didn't have to talk him into coming.'

'He wants to.'

'Oh Lord!'

'You go and talk to him, Hilly.'

'I can't stop him coming now.'

'Of course not. You said you wanted him to come so you could discuss the twins. He knows all about reading difficulties.'

Hilary went, but hadn't managed to dislodge an excited Sophie from the phone when Flora went past with a new jar of coffee. She left them to it, feeling a little guilty at overriding Isobel's wishes, even though she was sure it was the right thing to do.

Isobel was weary when she returned. She'd left her Mini in the car park at Hooton station and gone into Liverpool on the train, which meant she'd been lugging parcels about all morning. She'd locked the car in the garage now. She'd leave the presents where they were until the children were in bed.

'Daddy's coming up for Christmas, Mummy,' an excited Sophie was shouting before she was inside the door. 'Nana asked him, and he's said yes.'

Isobel felt the heat run up her body. She threw off her coat and swung round on her mother to grind out, 'Mum, you've no business to interfere.'

The shop had closed for lunch. Her family were still at the table but had finished eating. She saw their faces through a haze of fury and knew she was spoiling for a fight with her mother. She managed to hold it back. She'd been at this point with Sebastian many times and what had it achieved but friction and bitterness?

She sank deflated on to a chair. If she didn't keep a firm hold on her tongue she knew she'd spoil the friendly way the family supported each other.

'Do you want something to eat?' Hilary asked. 'There's some broth left.'

'No thanks. I had a sandwich in town. I could do with a cup of tea, though.'

Her mother got up to pour it for her and Isobel managed to say, 'Sorry, Mum.' No doubt she'd thought she was doing the right thing.

Isobel knew she mustn't start any stormy exchanges. That way could lead to resentment and a rift in the family. What she'd gone through with Seb made her value the peace and goodwill she'd found here.

It was Christmas Eve and Isobel felt very much on edge. Sebastian was due to arrive at any moment. Her mother had gone home after lunch because she was expecting Mavis to stay for a couple of nights over the holiday. Ben had elected to close the shop at four o'clock when it began to get dark and customers were no longer coming in.

He was pleased. The shop had done well during the run-up to Christmas. He'd given the last poinsettia to Rory to take home to his mother and brought the last two bowls of hyacinths into the house.

Hilary had tomorrow's big lunch organised. She and Ben seemed at their most relaxed though the children were screaming with excitement. The preparations were made, the fun was about to begin. Isobel saw the headlights of a car sweep in at the gate.

'Sebastian's here,' she said. Swallowing back her nerves she went out to meet him. Sophie barged past her letting out whoops of joy and threw herself at Seb as he was getting out of the car.

'Daddy, Daddy, Daddy, hello!' He swept her up in a great bear hug. Isobel hadn't expected such a show of affection from either of them. It made her feel guilty that she'd presumed to break that bond.

He came towards her. Under the outside lights he looked different. More handsome. He'd had a new smart haircut. His eyes were searching into hers.

'Isobel, how are you?' He pecked at her cheek and slid one arm round her shoulders to pull her closer. Sophie was still swinging on the other.

Hilary and her family were spilling out of the door. Sebastian stepped forward to greet them, and Isobel had to introduce Ben and the boys. They were impressed with his car, a BMW.

'It's my mother's,' he told them, 'but she hasn't

been able to drive it for some time. She thought it would do it good to have a long run up here. I'd better get my case.'

When he opened the boot, Isobel saw two cases. 'This one's full of presents for the kids,' he whispered. She carried it indoors.

'Up here.' Sophie was dragging him up to the bedroom she shared with her mother. 'This is our room.'

Isobel said, 'We've been trying to persuade her to sleep on the put-you-up in the study while you were here, but she says no.'

'I want to stay with you,' Sophie sang out, pulling her parents closer so she could hold a hand of each. 'If I move out, Father Christmas won't be able to find me and I'll get no presents.'

Isobel saw Seb raise his eyebrows at her. 'Couldn't we leave a note to Father Christmas to tell him where you are?'

'I sent him a letter,' Isobel said. 'He'll find you all right, Sophie.'

Sebastian surveyed the bed. 'I don't think there's enough room for us all in that.'

'There is,' Sophie said firmly. 'It's a big bed.'

On the way downstairs, Sebastian whispered, 'I thought she'd stopped believing in Father Christmas when she was five?'

There was a succulent joint of boiled ham for supper, and a real party atmosphere. Isobel thought everybody seemed in high spirits except her. While she and Hilary cleared up after the meal, the men oversaw the children's baths. She knew Seb and Sophie were loving it. When finally all the youngsters were settled into bed, Hilary claimed Sebastian's attention. She'd long wanted to talk to him about her boys' problems with reading. 'I'd like to have your opinion.'

Isobel listened, and saw how interested he was in dyslexia and how much more he knew about it than she did.

Hilary asked, 'Have you taught any dyslexic children?'

'Yes. Nearly all the slow readers in the school come to my remedial class. The cause is not always dyslexia, but those badly affected by it can be the hardest to teach. I have a little Down's Syndrome girl at the moment and she's learning to read and write more easily than my dyslexic boys.'

'Oh dear!'

'It can be overcome, Hilary. I'll help all I can. I'll talk to your boys over the next few days and watch them play. Say nothing to them. It's Christmas and they need to forget their difficulties.'

'What do you suggest we do?' Ben was frowning.

'I think the next step is for you to have them privately assessed. If they're found officially to be dyslexic they'll be given extra time in public exams. Bangor University leads the field in researching the condition and it isn't too far from here. You'll have to pay, but I understand it isn't that expensive. It will tell the twins that there's a specific reason for their problem and that other children have it too. Hopefully, they'll feel better about it.'

'It'll point out that they aren't just stupid?'

'Exactly. Because nothing is done for these children until they are seen to fail at things their peers find easy, they're robbed of any self-confidence. Children can be very cruel to each other and it can cause behavioural problems.'

Hilary knew all about that. She asked, 'Once the teachers have this proof, will they provide extra tuition?'

Sebastian hesitated. 'I wouldn't bank on it.'

'Then it won't help improve their reading and writing,' Ben said. 'Stands to reason.'

'If the university finds they are dyslexic then they'll recommend a teacher who's had special training to help them. One who lives in this area.'

Ben was frowning. 'That's going to take ages – and we'd have to pay for it?'

'Yes.'

Isobel said, 'In the meantime they'll have to put up with me. You'll have to give me some tips, Seb, so I can help them more.'

Hilary smiled at her. 'Thanks, Izzy.'

'They're my nephews too,' she said. 'It's very true, you know, the more you put yourself out for somebody, the more attached to them you become.'

'I thought you said you had more than enough of kids at school?'

'I did,' she smiled, feeling better now, 'but it seems my lot in life to be surrounded with the little angels.'

Isobel had been thinking a lot about sleeping with Sebastian. It was many months since she had. She'd moved out of the bedroom they'd shared on the day he'd found her using his father's shoe box. That had not been the first time she'd moved to their spare room, but usually Seb had persuaded her back fairly quickly. If they were on reasonable terms, he could be rather good in bed.

When it was time to go upstairs, Isobel put on the landing light and the light in the study. 'I've made up the bed there. We can just slot Sophie in.'

Sebastian scooped her up. 'Good job she sleeps like a log.'

'She never wakes up. I need to get her Christmas stocking down from the top of the wardrobe.' She had a lot of other presents down on the floor by the time he came back.

'I seem to remember this is the one morning of the year she'll wake up before dawn.' He was smiling. 'Let's take most of this stuff downstairs and put it under the tree, or we'll be woken by whoops of joy and the sound of tearing paper.'

Back in their bedroom and alone together for the first time, Sebastian put his arms round her in a hug. 'Oh, Izzy, I do love you. What are we doing to each other?'

She put her head down on his shoulder and clung to him. There were times when she needed his support. Coping without him hadn't been easy.

'I came up to talk to you about it, but we haven't had a chance yet, have we? We need to sort ourselves out.' He kissed her and tenderly stroked the back of her neck. Isobel knew within seconds it was too late to shy away from him.

'Let's get into bed,' she said, and he helped her off with her pullover and started unbuttoning her blouse. His touch made her shiver with anticipation. It had always been like this with Seb. Perhaps that's why they'd stayed together all these years.

Christmas had softened her antagonism towards him. Or was it because he'd been kind to Hilary and sweet to Sophie since he'd arrived?

They didn't talk when they got into bed. His lovemaking was urgent, a mutual need that had built up over their months apart. It was afterwards, as they lay spent, that Sebastian said softly, 'This way our marriage has always been good, hasn't it? I want you back. I want us to try again, Izzy I'm no good without you.'

Wrapped in his arms, Isobel whispered, 'I should have stayed with you. It's done no good to put two hundred miles between us. I've made a mess of things, haven't I?'

'We both have.'

'No, it's been my fault. I started us off on the wrong foot with my lies. I can't believe I was that selfish. And stupid to think I could get away with it.'

'You didn't.'

'No.' Isobel took a great pent-up breath. 'I was afraid you'd want nothing more to do with me once that midwife spelled it out to you.'

'You'd just given birth, Izzy. How could I leave you then, when you needed me? I told you I'd forgiven you for that, but I suppose it's always at the back of my mind. As soon as we disagree about anything, it races to the forefront and my hackles go up.'

'I betrayed your trust,' Isobel said sadly. 'I won't do it again, but now it's gone. You've no trust left for me. It's too late.'

'No it isn't. If we're going to get over this, I've got to forgive you, really forgive you, and you've got to forgive yourself too. I've said some terrible things to you. We've had some vicious rows, but we've got to forgive each other and put the fighting behind us, once and for all.'

'If only it hadn't been your father, it would have been easier. We've let it fester, that's the trouble.'

'We both have to accept that it happened and put it behind us for good.'

'I did love him, you know.'

'So did I, though it was a difficult relationship.' He was silent for a long time, and she wondered whether he was going to sleep. Then he asked, 'Have you been happy here with your family?'

'In some ways, but I don't like living permanently in Hilary's house. I don't know what I do want, do I?'

Sebastian whispered, 'Then why not do what I want?'

'I think being here without you has brought me to my senses. Helping the twins has made me see I've a great deal to be thankful for. It's the first time I've ever put myself out for somebody else and really worked at it. You're different, you'll help anybody.'

'Will you come back with me? Start afresh?'

Isobel sighed. 'It isn't all that easy now, is it? I've started Sophie in a new school. Chopping and changing schools won't help her. I've promised to keep tutoring Hilary's boys and I'd have to walk away from that as well as my new job. I've really messed up this time, haven't I? Unless... How about you coming up here to live with us?' Isobel thought that would be brilliant. 'We could sell our house and get another here.'

431

She could stay with her family.

Sebastian sighed heavily. 'In many ways, Izzy, I'd like to. A new house, a new job, a complete change, it might help us both. But my mother... I can't turn my back on her.'

Isobel was disappointed and couldn't help reminding him, 'You have before. You walked out on your family and did your own thing.'

'I've grown up since then, and everything's changed. My mother's ill, Izzy. She's old and alone now. I couldn't.'

'There's no way, then?'

'Not at the moment. If you really don't want to come back to London, I could put our house on the market. I don't think either of us ever really liked it. What d'you think? Half of it is yours, after all.'

'You'd give me half the money?'

'Of course. It's legally yours – I don't think I could avoid giving it to you.'

'But where would you live?'

'I'm already spending a lot of time at Mother's. She's asked me to move in with her.'

'Your old home?'

'Yes. It's a lot more comfortable. She has a woman who comes in daily to clean, Dora who does the cooking, and a gardener.'

Isobel had to smile. It was typical of Sebastian. 'You've fallen on your feet. You've got everything you could possibly want.'

'No. I want you, Izzy. And Sophie. Think about it. One of us will have to give.'

They settled down to sleep but Isobel went on thinking. She was comforted that Seb was keen to try again and seemed willing to join her here, but everything was still very much up in the air as to when that could happen. Or even if it ever could. It was very late when she got to sleep and it seemed only moments before Sophie came bouncing in to snuggle in between them, her feet cold and her arms full of toys that she wanted to show them. Ten minutes later, the twins started a record of children's carols blasting through the house.

CHAPTER TWENTY-SEVEN

For Isobel, Christmas passed very quickly. Sebastian spent a lot of time with Hilary's boys and then discussed their problems and how best to help them with Hilary and Ben. He'd brought up a lot of material that he thought would help, and advised Isobel about tutoring them.

'He's a lovely person,' Hilary told Isobel. 'I can't imagine why you want to divorce him. He can't do enough for the twins.'

Isobel knew he was worried about his mother and felt he had to go back to London the day after Boxing Day. He'd telephoned the hospital every day, and said, 'They tell me there's no change in her condition, and that she's as comfortable as can be expected, but I'm sure she'll be fretting because neither I nor Charlotte is there. Come down with me, Izzy, and bring Sophie. There's no reason why we can't spend the rest of the holiday together.'

433

'It would make a lovely change,' she said. She arranged with Primrose and Prudence to give the boys reading and writing practice while she was away and began to think of other arrangements. 'Will there be any food in the house? Had we better take some with us?'

Sebastian thought for a moment. 'I think I'll ring Dora. Would you mind if we stay there?'

'Won't your mother mind?'

'No. She can't do enough for me now. Dora can have a hot meal ready for us and the beds made up. It'll be getting dark by the time we've driven down and we'll be tired. No sense in going to our own house. It'll be stone cold after standing empty these last weeks.'

Isobel was a little scared of her mother-in-law and was quite glad not to be meeting her that evening. Up to now, she'd seen only the drawing room and dining room of her house, but found there was also a study, a library and a billiards room downstairs. In daylight the next day, she was able to appreciate the two acres of gardens.

'It's a magnificent house,' she told Sebastian.

'Too big,' he said briefly. 'Impossible to run without paid help.' When Isobel had seen the six bedrooms, three bathrooms and two dressing rooms as well as the attic bedrooms, she had to agree.

The next day, Sebastian took her and Sophie to visit his mother. Isobel was worried, convinced she knew of her connection with Rupert.

'It's all in your mind, love,' Sebastian told her. 'You'll see she knows nothing about it.'

All the same, Isobel was apprehensive. Sophie

seemed a little overawed by the hospital surroundings when they got there, but Seb lifted her up. 'Say hello to Grannie,' he said, and she seemed happy to do so.

'What about a kiss?' the old lady asked, and Sophie obliged happily. 'What a good girl you are. A pretty child, too. I see a resemblance to Charlotte about her eyes, but Charlotte had darker colouring.'

Isobel thought she seemed a little distant towards her, but she wasn't going to let that upset her. Sitting up against banked pillows Margaret Broadbent looked a frail old lady, though she talked of going home in a week or so.

Afterwards, when they were alone, Sebastian said, 'I told you it would be all right, Izzy. I don't think Father had time to tell her anything about you before he had his heart attack. Mother seems to accept Sophie as her grandchild.'

Isobel was thoughtful. 'She does. She made quite a fuss of her.'

'There you are then. It's a secret only you and me know, and if I can accept what happened then you must too. To the rest of the world, we are an ordinary family. There is no problem.'

'Yes.' Sebastian had to be right, but all the same Isobel still felt uneasy. She must try to put it out of her mind. There was no way of finding out for certain what Rupert had said or not said.

They visited their old home, where Isobel and Sophie collected up a few of their belongings to take back. It looked neglected and needed a great deal doing to it.

'Let's sell it,' Seb said. 'If you do come back to

live here, we could find a house we like better.'
They went straight to an estate agent and put it
on the market.

When the school holidays were almost over, the
day before old Mrs Broadbent was due out of
hospital, Sebastian drove Isobel and Sophie to
the train. Isobel felt a lot better. Not one cross
word had been spoken and she'd felt they'd
enjoyed being together as a family again. What
was more, with Dora in charge of the housework
Isobel felt she'd had a good rest.

At the station, Sebastian kissed her and whispered, 'You see, we get on fine. I'll be up for a
weekend soon. Take care.'

For the rest of the winter Mavis had repeated
bouts of ill health. When she was ill, Hilary or
Isobel would bring her from her own house to
Flora's, and when she said she felt better they'd
take her back.

'I'll be all right when the weather picks up,'
Mavis said many times. 'I long to see the sun
again.'

But in the spring Isobel went down to collect
her for dinner one Sunday and found she was ill
with yet another chest infection. This time
despite antibiotics she didn't pick up and was
never well enough to return home.

The days had lengthened into summer when
Hilary said, 'She isn't going to get better, Mum.
You do realise? It's only a matter of time.'

Flora didn't need to be told. 'How long, do you
think?'

'I don't know. Not long.'

The doctor said much the same, that she must prepare for the end.

Flora was saddened. She felt closer to Mavis now than she'd done for years, and though she thought she was prepared it still came as a shock.

One Sunday she made them both an early morning cup of tea, put them on a tray and took them upstairs. She'd got into the habit of sitting down with Mavis for ten minutes or so for a little chat. She pushed the bedroom door open.

'Morning, Mavis,' she said cheerily and, thinking she was still asleep, moved closer.

She saw then that she was dead and panic overtook her. One cup of tea slid off the tray before she could put it down. It scalded her foot.

She leaned against the bed until the pain subsided a little. She knew there were things she must do but couldn't think what. She picked up the cup and saucer, which hadn't broken, and set about mopping at the rug with her handkerchief. She straightened up. This wasn't what she should be doing. This wasn't important. She couldn't think.

She made herself sit down and drink the other cup of tea. Her head cleared and she felt a little better. She rang the doctor and left a message for him, then rang Hilary's number. It was Isobel who answered and she came straight away and took charge, though there was little she could do because it was Sunday.

Isobel rang Tom and insisted on taking her mother back to Hilary's house with her. It was a cool wet day of torrential downpour. Tom was supportive and took Flora out for a drive after lunch.

'I should go down and decide what's to be done with her things.' She sighed. 'But I can't face it just yet.'

On Monday, Isobel went to work and Hilly and Ben did what was necessary. Flora felt fraught throughout the ten days she had to wait for the funeral. On the day itself, Hilary had decided that the children should go to school as usual. It was a sad event with only Tom and the adult members of the family there. There were no tears and it drove home just how much of a recluse Mavis had become.

Flora had prepared a cold buffet lunch for them at her house but they were all miserable and didn't stay long. She was left drinking a second cup of tea with Isobel, who had arranged to take the whole day off work.

'I'm glad it's over,' Isobel said. 'I hope we can get back to normal now.'

'There's still a lot to be done.' Flora felt she'd lost all her energy. She'd been sitting about staring into space. 'I must write and tell her landlord what has happened. Until I do, he'll expect the rent to be paid.'

Isobel sighed. 'I've been wondering whether I should try to take over the tenancy of Auntie's house. As a temporary measure.'

Flora was shocked. 'You don't want to live there, do you?'

'It would be a roof over my head, Mum. Seb hasn't had an offer for our London house yet.'

'It's a long way to drive to school every day.'

'Not too far. I could manage it for a few months, until I can find something better. I think

I've imposed on Hilly long enough, and I'd love a place of my own.'

'Not that one, Izzy. Nobody is giving a date for the demolition, but it can't be that far off now. I don't think it's a good idea. I was brought up there and I couldn't wait to get away. You wouldn't like it.'

'Mum, Ben wants me to go. Hilly won't say so because she knows I've nowhere else, but they want their house to themselves. And Seb's coming up more.'

Flora was overcome with guilt. 'You can use my spare room for the short term,' she said. 'Anyway, if Sebastian is going to sell your house, you'll have money from that to buy another up here.'

Isobel said slowly, 'I've been looking round, of course, but it seems like wishful thinking at the moment.' What if Seb changed his mind about coming up? And anyway, his mother was no better. It was difficult to plan when nothing could be definitely settled.

Flora said, 'Look, I've heard the cottage at the end of this row is coming up for sale. Wouldn't you rather have that?'

She saw Isobel's face light up. 'You know I would, but I'm not sure I could afford it. I can't stretch my money as far as you and Hilly. I'm just not that thrifty.'

'You said Sebastian had put a big down payment on your house, and London prices are higher than they are here. They've gone up, too, since you bought that.'

'Renting is one thing, buying another,' Isobel said. 'It's another of those big life-changing deci-

439

sions. Do I stay here or go back to London?'

'I thought you'd already decided to stay here?'

'I told you, if Seb and I are to get back together I might have to go back. I can't make up my mind about that either. Can't make up my mind about anything.'

'I want you to stay, and so does Hilly.'

'I want that too, but Seb doesn't know when he can get away. It could be years. Now I have to make all those decisions over again.'

'And quite right that you should.' Flora made up her mind. 'Let's walk to the end of the terrace – it won't hurt to look at the cottage. If Mrs Morris is in, I'll ask her if we could have a quick look round.'

Isobel was keen. As soon as her mother's front door clicked shut, her eyes went to the last cottage in the row, six houses down. It looked essentially the same from the front, but this one had been newly painted, the brasses on the front door shone and the tiny front garden was as neat as a pin.

Once inside Isobel craned to see every detail. It was cosy like Mum's but here an extension had been built on with a large kitchen on the ground floor and a bathroom above it, so it was bigger than Mum's house. In hers, the third bedroom had been turned into a bathroom and she was using the original kitchen.

'It's very nice,' her mother said. 'It looks so fresh and clean.'

'It's been repainted throughout.' Mrs Morris, the owner, was clearly proud of it.

'I love it.' Isobel was thrilled. If she could have this she'd be set up for life.

'We've had it valued,' Mrs Morris said, naming

a figure. 'It'll be advertised for sale next week.'

Isobel found herself out on the pavement clutching her mother's arm. 'Oh, Mum, it's gorgeous. It's been beautifully done up.'

'It has, but she's asking a lot for it.'

'Too much, d'you think?' Disappointment was already tearing at Isobel. Was she reaching for the moon?

'You'd better ring Sebastian and talk about it.'

'Can I use your phone?' She caught him before afternoon school started.

'If you're really keen, Izzy, go ahead. You need a home for Sophie. But you'd better go to the bank and enquire about bridging loans in case the house here doesn't sell quickly enough. Perhaps you should ask about a mortgage as well, and then we can make up our minds whether it would be better to keep some capital behind us.'

Isobel's spirits soared again. 'I'll go and do that now.'

An hour later, Isobel knew she could have either a bridging loan or a mortgage of two and a half times her salary. She'd always known that building societies considered it safe to lend to teachers. It was time then to collect Sophie from school, and because she wanted to tell her mother the news she went back to see her.

She felt full of energy and was itching to get on with things. 'If I can get this cottage, would I be able to have some of Mavis's furniture? She'll have willed it to you, won't she?'

'Knowing Mavis, I doubt she'll have got round to making a will. But I can't think of anybody else who would want her furniture. Except... There's

441

a little mahogany sewing table that used to be Mother's; Mavis used it as a bedside table. Apart from that there's nothing I want. You take your pick. It's mostly worn and battered.'

'Some of the hard furnishings are all right – her dining table and the bedroom suite. Are you sure you don't want to start sorting through her things now?'

'We could spend a couple of hours down there, couldn't we? What about...?'

She nodded towards Sophie, who was finishing off some of the buffet left over from their lunch. Isobel picked up the last ham roll and a slice of quiche for herself.

'I'll ask Hilly if she can stay with the boys and I'll get out of my glad rags first.'

It was a damp winter evening and the cold in Mavis's house struck down into Isobel's bones.

'Shall I light the fire?' she asked. Her mother had laid it ready for Mavis's return.

'No, we'll feel no benefit upstairs. We'll keep our coats on.'

Isobel eyed the furniture. There was more than enough in the house in London but that was a long way away, and it was stuff that had been fashionable a decade ago.

'I'd like to have that table.' It was very plain and nobody could fault the shape, but it was scratched and battered. It would need french-polishing. 'The dining chairs too, if I may.' They were old-fashioned and would suit the cottage better. 'But definitely not the sideboard, that's ugly.'

'These red curtains were mine. We only put

442

them up last year.' Flora fingered them. 'They would be fine for the cottage.'

'Yes, I'd like them. What d'you want me to do, Mum?'

'Empty her wardrobe and the drawers in her dressing table. We'll need to dump her clothes, nobody will want them. I've brought some plastic sacks.'

Isobel took a couple of sacks upstairs. She opened the top drawer, and a pungent smell of mothballs seared her nostrils. It was crammed with a jumble of underwear, a mix of artificial silk and flannelette, but all greyish and stained. She began to push torn bodices, petticoats and pairs of directoire knickers, some without elastic, into the sack. Nightdresses and blouses without buttons, corsets without hooks and laces, followed.

'Poor old Mavis. She didn't spend much on clothes,' she said as her mother came up.

'She had only a small pension.'

'Plus her old age one. I bet you don't get much more, but you manage better on it.'

'I get a good pension from teaching, and Mavis had been drawing hers for much longer.' Her mother was filling a sack with battered hats and shoes worn almost through.

Isobel opened another drawer. It was full of twisted lisle stockings. She asked, 'Is it worth looking through these to see if there are any without ladders?' The one she lifted up had a large hole in the toe.

'No.' Her mother shuddered. 'It's horrible to see all this rubbish and know it was all Mavis had. What did she get out of life?'

Isobel could see her mother's eyes awash with tears and knew she was upset. 'Leave this to me,' she said, and went to the wardrobe to slide dresses from their hangers: the black wool with bugle beads on the bodice, the black coat with the astrakhan collar. 'These must all be twenty or thirty years old.'

'She's never thrown anything away in her life,' Flora said. 'That blouse is made of parachute silk; it dates from the end of the war.'

From the back of the wardrobe, Isobel pulled out a huge cardboard box which seemed to be filled with papers. She opened it up and looked at those on top.

'Why did she keep all these business letters? There's a lot of documents here too. What are they?'

'Mavis was always pondering on big business, wasn't she? It was some sort of hobby. We'll burn them.'

The forty-watt ceiling bulb gave out little light. Isobel said, 'Perhaps we should take them home and look through them first.'

'I can't stand this. I'm going to make a cup of tea.'

'Hang on. Is that the little sewing table you want to keep?'

'Yes.' It was standing beside the bed.

'I could put that in my car and take it back to your place tonight.' Isobel moved the tumbler in which Mavis had kept her false teeth and lifted the lid. Inside it was fitted out in watered silk with compartments for thread, buttons and needles. 'This turquoise colour hasn't faded at all.'

Almost covering the silk lid to the centre compartment was a brown manila envelope. It had the word *Will* scrawled on it.

'Mum,' Isobel said. 'Look at this.'

'A will? I didn't think Mavis would get round to anything like that. Shall I open it?'

'Of course. She'll have left her valuables to you.'

'She didn't have any valuables, Izzy.'

Flora tore open the envelope and moved directly under the electric light to read it.

'It's been drawn up by a solicitor. It says this is a copy and the original is in his safe keeping.'

'Good Lord! Mavis actually consulted a solicitor!'

'Well, it's quite straightforward. Everything she had is to be divided equally between me and Hilly and she's appointed us both as executors. What does that mean?'

Isobel felt a stab of jealousy, just as she had in the old days when she thought Hilly got all the affection and the treats and she was left out. 'Does that mean I can't have her furniture?'

'Of course it doesn't. Hilly won't want it and I certainly don't – we've nowhere to put it. It's just that you spent years down in London and Mavis didn't see much of you. It was me and Hilary she knew. Anyway, she's leaving very little as far as I can see.'

Isobel told herself she was being silly. It was ridiculous to be jealous of Hilly at her age. She thought of herself as a mature and sensible woman. She said, 'Let's go home. It's freezing here. We'll take your work table with us and all these papers.'

Her mother said, 'I'd better ring up her solicitor tomorrow and tell him she's died.'

Isobel's Mini was filled to capacity and when she drew up outside her mother's cottage they carried everything inside.

'This work table is very pretty, Mum.'

'Yes, it's Victorian rosewood. A pity the rest of her stuff isn't up to this standard.'

'Did she do any sewing?'

'No, it was my mother's. She liked to sew.' Flora opened the lid. 'I bet all these needles and threads were your grandmother's. Gosh yes, these pins are rusting.'

She lifted the turquoise silk lid to the large central compartment. 'Look at this. It's stuffed tight with more papers. What on earth are they?'

Isobel lifted a couple off the top. 'They look important. Are they share certificates?'

'I don't know. There's more of them upstairs. She insisted on bringing ledgers and goodness knows what with her. All she thought of was how much big businesses earned.'

'Are they worth something?' Isobel asked doubtfully. 'This one says Shell Transport and Trading one thousand shares. They look as though they might be.'

'It was all in her mind, Izzy. A game Mavis played with herself. A bit like Monopoly, I suppose. It'll all have to be burned.'

'Look through it all first,' Isobel cautioned her.

'Not tonight. It's been a long hard day, and I'm too tired.'

'Me too. I'd better go. I need a bath after that.'

'There's a lot more to do at Mavis's place.'

'Saturday morning,' Isobel said. 'We'll do it then.'

The next morning, Flora rang up Mavis's solicitor to tell him she'd died and that she'd found the copy of her will.

'Do you wish me to apply for probate on your behalf?' he asked.

'No,' she told him. 'I don't think it'll be worth while going to that trouble. She had nothing much to leave.'

'You won't be able to withdraw the money she has left in her bank accounts unless you do,' he warned. 'And you need to inform her bank manager that she's deceased.'

That made Flora dig into the documents Mavis had collected. There were monthly bank statements, for both deposit and current accounts. She studied them. Deposits of up to ten thousand pounds were shown one month, only to be withdrawn. It certainly seemed like Monopoly money. She didn't believe Mavis could possibly have had sums like that.

Now she knew where Mavis had banked, she rang the manager.

He said, 'Miss Caldwell? Miss Mavis Caldwell? Yes of course I know her, though she's not been in for a while. I'm so sorry to hear of her death. Please accept our sympathy. Yes, a valued customer.'

Flora sank on to a chair feeling stunned. She didn't think her bank manager would say such things about her when she died. The money in

Mavis's bank accounts must be real. She took out her statements again to ponder on and then found she couldn't read the figures for the tears splashing down. Poor Mavis! She felt desperately sorry for her. To have all that money and be unable to spend it seemed so sad.

She had to stop and make herself a cup of tea to get over the pity of it, and only then did she start to take Mavis's documents seriously. She spent the rest of the morning sorting through the papers, totally absorbed. She found long lists of investments drawn up by a Liverpool stock-broker. She rang him. He too, seemed to have known her sister well.

'We'll need to value her portfolio on the day of her death,' she was told. 'For probate purposes. You're her executor? Perhaps you should come in and see me some time next week.' He made an appointment for her.

Flora put the phone down and realised for the first time what Mavis had been worth. It was almost lunch time. She shot up to see Hilary and tell her what she'd discovered.

Isobel came back from school with Sophie and let them in with her key. The phone was ringing, and she found it was Sebastian. He sounded excited. 'I've just heard from Charlotte. I told you she was expecting a baby?'

'Yes, in June.'

'She's decided she'll come home to have it.'

'That's good?'

'It's marvellous! She'll be home at the end of April. She's worried about Mother and thinks she should be here to help.'

'So you'll be able to come up as soon as she gets here?' Isobel was delighted.

'Not to stay permanently straight away, but it will make it easier to come for a few days. The thing is, her husband's contract in Hong Kong finishes in August, and they've decided not to go abroad again.'

'So when will you be able to come for good?'

'If all goes well, I could give in my notice to leave school at the end of the summer term. That means I'll be here until after Charlotte's had her baby and she'll have had time to get back on her feet. She's always lived with Mother and will be at home all day with her. Far more company for her than I am because I'm at work five days a week.'

Isobel felt buoyant with hope. 'That's great news. Brilliant news.' She could see, now, how and when they could have their new start. 'After that, you'll be happy to come and live with us?'

'Yes.' He was enthusiastic. 'It will be a different life. I'll have plenty of time to look round for a job up your end too.'

'Everything's coming right again for us.' Isobel was thrilled at the thought. 'All I have to do now is make sure we have somewhere to live. Hilary and Ben will be pleased to see the back of me.'

Hilary was at the door. 'I heard most of that.' She gave her a hug. 'Sebastian's coming up to join you?'

'Not straight away, but stupendous news all the same.'

'I'm so pleased for you.'

'Even when he does, I'll not turn my back on your boys,' Isobel told her. 'Don't think that for one minute.'

CHAPTER TWENTY-EIGHT

Later that evening, Isobel sat at her mother's table shuffling the documents from one pile to another. 'Nearly two million?'

'One point eight. Well, that's what Hilly and I made it. It's not the official figure.'

'It's an enormous fortune. I can't believe it. I mean Mavis, accumulating that?'

'None of us can,' Flora said. 'It's taking a long time to sink in. If Mavis had left thousands not millions I still wouldn't have thought it possible.'

'You said it was just a game she was playing, that the sums were mythical.'

'I was wrong. The sums on her bank statements are so enormous, I couldn't believe...'

'But didn't she tell you what she was doing?'

'Dabbling on the stock market, she said.'

'Well, then?'

'My fault. I didn't think she had the knowledge or the ability. Or the money, come to that.'

'She had tons of ability; was very clever at it. Look at what she made.'

'I know.' Her mother sounded agonised. 'I'm the one lacking in knowledge. I didn't understand what she was doing. Mavis didn't spell it out in words of two syllables so I would. I have to confess I rather looked down on her capabilities. Never any promotion when she had a job, never wanted to move on to another. Didn't look after herself or her house properly.'

'Mum, Aunt Mavis was obsessed with the stock market. It was all she cared about and we never realised.'

'According to her stockbroker she'd been dealing in stocks and shares for years. All her life she worked in the investment department of that insurance company. She understood how the stock market worked.'

Isobel said slowly, 'Not everybody makes money like that even if they do. You said she never earned much, that she had only a small pension.'

'She was given a lump sum of three thousand pounds when she retired, but she'd started investing before she got that. All her life, she'd been saving from her salary.'

'But how did she make it grow into this fortune?'

'Apparently, she chose blue chip companies and rarely sold what she'd bought.'

'So now we know why she never seemed to have any money.'

'I'm told that over the last few years she was earning huge dividends from her investments but she never spent a penny of it. All she ever bought was more stock. She invested it all back in the market.'

'I don't think she wanted to spend it.'

'No. She was more interested in watching her fortune grow. She got her pleasure from that. It was her hobby.'

'It was miserly. Fancy living in that awful dump when she didn't have to.'

'Without a bathroom.'

'We invited her to Sunday dinner because we were sorry for her; brought her here when she wasn't well, and all the time she could have moved into the best nursing home to be waited on hand and foot. That's unbelievable too.'

Isobel was amazed and sorry she hadn't known. She'd have loved to talk to Mavis about her talent. They'd all undervalued her.

She sat chewing her lip. There was another thing. Mavis had earned a huge fortune and left it all to Hilary and Mum. All she was going to get was her furniture. She wouldn't get so much as a bean of her money though she'd done a bit to help Mavis over these last months. It would look like very sour grapes to remind Mum of that now.

Hilary found it took a great deal to persuade Ben that their money problems were over.

He said, 'I can't see Mavis as capable of making much money.'

'But she did. More than any of us, though we're all so proud of what we've achieved. We're very lucky – it's better than winning the pools. I'll pay off our mortgages.'

'Marvellous not to have those round our necks. It'll be easy to improve the business now. You can spend all the time in the world on your writing. We'll want for nothing.'

Hilary said, 'Money solves a lot but it won't help the boys with their reading.'

'We can pay for the best teachers.'

'I don't think they'll be any better than Izzy.'

'We can have them properly assessed and find out exactly how bad their reading is.'

'Once Sebastian suggested it,' Hilary said, 'Izzy and I were planning to do that anyway.'

She and Ben had talked about Aunt Mavis's fortune late into the night, and afterwards she'd tossed and turned for ages. How had they all managed to underestimate Mavis so greatly? Her fortune was going to change their lives.

Breakfast time was the usual rush to get Isobel and the children off to school and Ben out to the garden centre. Hilary allowed herself ten minutes' recovery time after that. She'd just poured herself another cup of tea when her mother came in.

'You've timed it well,' Hilary said.

'I meant to. I met the boys as I walked up.'

'Tea?'

'I'll get it, Hilly,' Flora said. 'I want a quiet word. I'm worried that Isobel is excluded from all this money.'

'I know. It isn't fair. She makes no secret of being hard up and she needs a place to live.' Hilary knew how generous her mother could be. 'Are you going to give her some?'

'Yes. I thought I'd give her half mine.'

Hilary felt a flush of guilt because she hadn't thought of doing that herself.

'No, that's not fair either. Why don't we re-arrange things so this fortune is split three ways and Isobel has an equal share? She did a lot for Mavis over the last few months. She does a lot for me too.'

'Are you sure?'

'Quite sure. I want to be able to look my sister in the face.'

'I've been talking to Tom about sharing the money with Isobel. He says the best way is to ask a solicitor to draw up a document which we'll have to sign, setting out that we want to pay part of our inheritance over to her. A sort of variation order. Tom thinks we should apply for probate ourselves; we could save a lot of money by doing that. He says he's done it before and he'll help us. Are you happy with that?'

'If you are.'

'Ask Isobel to come and see me when she comes home from school. Come with her, if you like. We could tell her together.'

When Isobel returned home, she was surprised to hear Hilary say, 'You and I are going down to Mum's for a cup of tea.'

'What about the children?' Usually when Isobel reached home, she attended to their needs.

'Aunt Primmy's here setting out snacks for them. Go to the kitchen, Sophie; the boys are already there. We won't be long.'

'What's this about?' Isobel asked as they walked past the glasshouses on their way to Flora's cottage. 'Has something else come up?'

Hilary laughed. 'Wait and see.'

Isobel felt giddy with hope which she didn't dare put into words. If she was barking up the wrong tree she'd look foolish and greedy. Mum had offered her help to buy Mrs Morris's cottage. Without this windfall she would not have been able to do much, but now...

It could be a whacking great down payment, or, as Hilary seemed to be involved too, though she wouldn't let herself dwell on this, perhaps they'd even buy it for her, pay for it outright.

She would have her cottage to live comfortably here, Sebastian could come up for weekends and in the holidays. And when his mother didn't need him in London...

Hilary seemed happy. Isobel could feel excitement seething in her stomach. As they approached the row of cottages, her eyes went to the one at the end. The For Sale notice wasn't up yet.

Mum had baked a Victoria sandwich and set it out on a lace tablecloth, together with her best china tea service. The kettle was singing.

'It looks as though you're making an occasion of this,' Isobel said as Flora kissed her.

'I am.' She laughed. 'Sit down.' She pulled out a chair at the table. 'I'll just make the tea.'

Isobel was beginning to wonder if she was about to make some announcement about Tom. Perhaps this had nothing to do with the cottage.

With three generous slices of cake cut, her mother said, 'I expect you're wondering what this is all about?'

'Yes,' Isobel said eagerly. They were both looking at her. That surely meant this had nothing to do with Tom.

Hilary took a deep breath and said, 'Mum thinks it isn't fair for us to split Aunt Mavis's money between us. We want to split it three ways and give you an equal share.'

Isobel's head whirled. This was even better than she'd hoped. What couldn't she do with a fortune like that? She hardly heard them explain their reasons, and before she could finish stammering out her thanks Mum had changed tack.

'Do you still want that cottage or would you rather have a bigger house? You could afford either and pay cash. It's decision time again, isn't it?'

For Isobel, it wasn't a decision she found hard to make. 'I think I'd like the cottage. It's quite big enough for the three of us if Seb can come up, but still fine for me and Sophie. It'll be a base for us here even if we do go down to live in London again. It's near you and Hilly. Now I'm here, I feel as though I've come home.'

'Then let's go round and tell Mrs Morris we want to proceed, shall we?'

What she and Sebastian had always needed was a comfortable income. Now, thanks to the generosity of her family, they'd have it. Seb'd seemed a different person when she'd seen him in his childhood home. Isobel sighed with pure contentment.

Isobel was looking forward to the Easter holidays and rang Sebastian to discuss how they should spend the time.

He sounded excited. 'I think we might have a buyer for the house.'

'Excellent.' Isobel was thrilled. 'Will we have the money in time to pay for the cottage?'

'Maybe. Depends how fast they move. Don't bank on it – they haven't signed yet.'

'How's your mother?'

'She's not too bad. You know she didn't like the nurse we had coming in and wanted Dora to do it?'

'I thought that was working out well?'

'It was. She's getting Mother up for half the day, and she's a lot better, but it's Dora I'm worried about now. She's tired and badly in need of a rest. She's getting on in years and hasn't had a break since last summer.'

'You could get another nurse.'

'I've been looking round for a good nursing home that would take Mother for a couple of weeks. Somewhere where she could convalesce. If I can get her in over Easter, I'll come up and spend it with you.'

When Isobel told Hilary, she rang him to say he'd be very welcome to stay in her house again. 'I'm looking forward to hearing what you think of the twins,' she said. 'I think their reading is improving slowly.'

Within a week Sebastian rang to say, 'I've managed it, I've got Mother into a nursing home. It's a lovely old manor house near Hampton Court. It's on the river and I think she should be happy there for a short while.'

When he came, he and Isobel spent a lot of time with the boys. Sebastian suggested they each make their own dictionary of spellings. He told her of a course that was being run in Liverpool on how best to help slow readers.

Isobel was keen. 'I'll see if I can go on that.'

To Hilary and Ben he said, 'I really think it would be helpful to have the twins officially assessed. We all need to know what the situation really is. Shall I write to Bangor University and to see if I can make an appointment to have it done?'

'Yes please,' Ben said.

'I'll see if I can fix it for half term, when they're off school.'

A week or two later, it had all been arranged. Before Sebastian returned to London, Isobel had enrolled for the course to help slow readers. Fortunately, it was being run in the evenings, so she had time to take Sophie home and get something to eat before driving into Liverpool. The twin aunts volunteered to take over reading practice on one night a week.

Hilary had long looked forward to seeing *The Night Star* published. Now, in the early summer, publication day was almost on her. A package arrived containing one of the first copies off the press. To actually see and hold the hardback edition sent a thrill running through her from head to toes.

The hardback, she'd been told, would mainly be sold to libraries; there would be a paperback edition later. She loved the cover. The heroine depicted there was just how she'd imagined her: beautiful, with long flowing tresses. Hilary laid it on the kitchen table, where Ben was the first to see it.

'This is it?' He put his arms round Hilary in a congratulatory hug. 'You are clever and I'm so happy for you. You were right to insist on having the time to work on your writing. You must have thought me very selfish to want you to spend eight hours a day earning money for the mortgage.'

'You're forgiven,' she told him. He stood her book up on the table so he could look at it while he ate. After lunch, she ran down to show it to her mother.

'I'm so proud of you,' Flora said. 'A published author in the family.'

When she came home from school and saw it, Sophie squealed with delight and pulled her mother over to look.

'Hilly,' Isobel said, flicking through the pages. 'I'm very impressed. Can I read it first?'

Half term came. Hilary was feeling apprehensive about having the twins assessed at Bangor University. She asked Isobel, 'Would you come with me and Ben?'

'Why not? We could make it a family outing. We're having a spell of fine weather, so why don't we take a picnic? We could take swimming gear too. I understand we'll have time to go to the beach and there's a good one near there.'

Hilary was pleased. 'A good idea. But we'll be too many to fit in one car.'

'Don't worry. I can follow in mine.'

Hilary said ruefully, 'It's more a question of you leading the way.'

She felt comforted. She'd pinned her hopes on this assessment. She wanted the twins to be reassured and she needed to gain more insight into their difficulties. Most of all, she wanted the school to recognise that they had a problem and provide them with special teaching.

Charlie was anxious. 'What are they going to do to us?' Isobel did her best to soothe his fears.

They were a little late starting off. Before long, Hilary was getting anxious that they wouldn't find the place by the appointed time, but on the dot of eleven the whole party presented themselves at the psychology department. They were greeted by a psychologist who introduced himself as Dr Cockroft.

He said, 'The tests take a couple of hours for each child, so my assistant Mr Templeton will help me, but first come into my office and we'll have a little chat.'

They crowded round his desk. Extra chairs had to be brought.

Sophie announced, 'I can read already. I can write too. I'm not a worry to anybody.'

'Shush.' Isobel was firm. 'This isn't for you.'

'It's us,' Charlie said. 'Our brains have been put in back to front and don't work properly.'

'We'll have to see about that and what can be done to help,' Dr Cockroft told him gravely.

Isobel explained that she was their aunt and that she'd been trying to help them for a year. 'I'm a primary school teacher, and I've taken a course on multi-sensory teaching to help slow readers.' She'd enjoyed it and felt she'd learned a lot. 'My husband is a remedial teacher.'

'So we have both parents, an aunt, a younger brother and a cousin, that's right? And the twins have been blessed with plenty of help?'

'No, only during the past year,' Hilary said. 'But I've always read to them and after a year in school their teacher asked me to hear them read daily, which I did.'

'And that helped?'

'They've improved more with Isobel. But I'm still worried,' Hilary went on. 'They are falling behind generally and losing marks in their school

460

work because of writing and spelling difficulties.'

After considerably more in this vein, the psychologist said, 'I'd like you to leave the twins with us for a couple of hours now.'

They went to the beach, where the sun was sparkling on a calm blue sea. It was a perfect early summer's day. Hilary changed into her swimsuit and lay down on her towel. She didn't feel in the mood for the beach; her thoughts were with her twins. Ben spread his towel beside hers and did likewise.

Isobel took Jamie and Sophie into the sea and their squeals of excitement mingled with the call of seabirds and the sound of waves rushing softly up the shore. To Hilary, it was soporific.

When the time came to return, she felt hot, sticky and sandblown, but she was more relaxed. They were told that the twins had been officially assessed as dyslexic.

Dr Cockroft said, 'I'll send you a written report of our findings and our recommendations, together with a certificate which you can show to their school and which will allow them extra time in public examinations.'

The twins needed to let off steam. They headed back to the beach and soon Andy and Charlie were splashing in and out of the waves in high spirits because their ordeal was over. As soon as Hilary opened up their picnic lunch, they came running back to eat.

Jamie took the ham sandwich she offered and sat watching Sophie cavort in the shallows until a seagull swooped down and snatched it from his hand. He screamed with shock and leaped into

Ben's arms for comfort, but the twins thought it funny, and when another sandwich was offered Jamie was soon giggling with them.

Hilary felt she'd done her best for her boys and was prepared to be patient a little longer while they waited for the written report.

On Saturday, Hilary was in the kitchen pouring coffee for Ben and Isobel, who had just happened to drop in. They all heard the large envelope drop on to the doormat.

'That might be the reports from the psychologist,' Hilary said, rushing out to see. She was opening it with some trepidation when Isobel took her arm and led her and Ben to the sitting room where the children wouldn't hear what they said. Hilary closed the door before pulling out Charlie's certificate and reading aloud.

'*I believe him to be dyslexic in the sense intended in the Disabled Persons Act, 1970, and to qualify for special consideration in examinations as recommended in the Tizard Report, 1972.*' She gasped. 'Disabled Persons Act! Oh my goodness. Charlie and Andy are classed as disabled! That's awful.'

Isobel was reading Charlie's report. 'Listen to this on intellectual function. *On the tests, Charlie obtained a score which puts him on the 96 percentile point for eleven-year-olds. What this means is that he does better than about 96 percent of children of his age on these tests of observation and clear thinking.* He's bright, I knew he was. Oh, and listen to this. *I recommend that the individual remedial tuition given by his aunt and uncle be continued since this has obviously been successful.*'

Hilary was breathing heavily. 'I shall certainly

show that to Mr Leyland when school reopens. To think that he and the school psychologist tried to fob me off by saying it was caused by crossed laterality.'

Isobel said, 'It was not just Mr Leyland and that psychologist. Crossed laterality was generally thought to cause these problems at one time.'

'What about Andy?'

'Let me see.' Ben shuffled through the documents. 'He's obtained a score that puts him on the ninetieth percentile point. That means that intellectually he's in the top ten per cent of the population. They're both more than intelligent enough to read and spell normally.'

'But Charlie's rated higher. Does that mean he's more intelligent?'

'Yes, but possibly more affected by dyslexia too.'

'It's outrageous.' Hilary could feel a tide of fury running through her. 'That nothing is done to help a child until it proves it can't cope; that a child has to fail in class before the school will do anything. There's a preschool medical to pick up physical problems with sight or hearing or speech, but dyslexia is ignored.'

Isobel said, 'Some schools don't admit there is a problem. But by ignoring it, they just make the problems worse. It turns happy kids like your twins into nervous wrecks. As they struggle to do what the teacher asks, they see other children doing it with ease. If they fail at reading and writing, they aren't able to keep up with the curriculum in other subjects and so fail to learn anything. Some miss out on education altogether.'

Ben said, 'And it's not just our children.'

Isobel sighed. 'Roughly ten per cent of people are dyslexic; of those, six per cent are mildly to moderately affected, and four per cent severely so. The twins are probably moderately affected.'

'You mean it could be worse?'

'A lot.'

'What about Jamie? Is he worse?'

'No, though to be honest I'm not quite sure where he fits in. He's worked hard and he's keeping up with his classmates. He has no sense of having failed, because he had extra tuition from an early age. His attitude to reading and writing is quite different from that of the twins. They're nervous and scared of failing yet again, but he's interested in reading, and when he gets something right he's triumphant.'

Hilary sighed. 'But he has no sense of time in the daily sense and no idea of months and years. So he's often missing at mealtimes and he's never ready for anything. Aren't those common traits for dyslexics?'

'I'm afraid so.'

'What causes it?'

'It's thought that some small area of the brain doesn't develop normally. It's inherited so there could be a gene problem.'

Hilary straightened her lips. 'And it's been found to have nothing to do with crossed laterality?'

'Yes. When they tested a group of dyslexic children against a group of those learning to read normally they found more of the latter had crossed laterality.'

'Yet I was fobbed off with that as a reason for their problems.'

Isobel said, 'As yet, nobody really knows the cause. The unlucky ones just have to work ten times harder than other children and make the best of it.'

CHAPTER TWENTY-NINE

During that same summer term, Isobel was delighted to hear that their house in Clapham had definitely sold and the money would be received in time to pay for the cottage, which was just as well because as yet Aunt Mavis's money couldn't be touched. It was still subject to probate.

'We'll be able to pay for it outright,' Sebastian told her in satisfied tones. 'Property doesn't cost as much on Merseyside. There'll even be a little bit over, but I think I might need to buy a car to get to work.'

'Yes,' Isobel said contentedly. She knew they'd never be plagued by money troubles once she had her share of Aunt Mavis's inheritance.

She had the furniture she'd kept from Mavis's house french-polished to smarten it up, and spent her Saturday mornings trawling through the shops for other things she'd need.

She received the keys to the cottage on a Wednesday which made it a red letter day. The whole family turned up to inspect it that evening, and her mother and the twin aunts started to hang the curtains. Sebastian had arranged for a van to deliver the pieces of furniture from their old house that Isobel had said she'd need. Her mother stayed on hand with the keys ready to open up. She'd been primed as to where each piece must go.

The following weekend, Rory and Tom were helping her move the furniture out of Hilary's garage and into the cottage when the phone rang.

Sebastian's voice said, 'Two items of good news for you. I'm coming up next Friday. I've got an interview for a job in Chester.'

'That's great. You'll be able to spend the night in the cottage with me and Sophie. It'll still be higgledy-piggledy, but I'm in the process of moving in. What's the other thing?'

'Charlotte's had her baby. It's a boy, eight pounds two ounces.'

'That's what she wanted, wasn't it? I'll send her a card to wish her well. What's she going to call him?'

'Rupert, after Father.' Isobel's heart turned over. Nobody could replace *him*.

Sebastian asked, 'How are things at your end?'

'Going according to plan. Thrilled to be under my own roof at last. I'll have the place settled before the summer holidays start.'

'I'm really looking forward to the hols, but I'll see you on Friday. I'll drive up – it's easier to get about if I have the car.'

Her mother came to help her make up the beds and afterwards Isobel went to the supermarket to start building up a stock of basic foods. She was singing to herself as she unloaded the plastic bags into her kitchen cupboards, and was looking forward to having Sebastian with her. Soon they'd be a real family again.

Flora was giving a great deal of thought to Mavis's money. It would change so much for her family. Isobel never stopped talking about it.

'Seb and I are quite happy to go on working and it's not that we want a life of luxury, but we'll never need to argue about paying basic bills again. It'll be bliss to have enough for holidays and everything else we want.'

Hilary wasn't all that interested in money, but she'd admitted it was a relief to have their big mortgages paid off.

'We're going to leave the rest invested in the shares Aunt Mavis chose. We'll have the interest to spend on the boys now, and, when the time comes, a bit of capital if they want to start businesses of their own.'

Flora felt satisfied that her girls were well provided for. They'd spend what they'd been given and enjoy what it could bring. She felt by not using it Mavis had wasted the opportunity of her lifetime, and she needed to be careful she didn't do the same.

She looked round her cottage and told herself she had everything she wanted. Perhaps she should buy a small car? She'd had one once to drive herself to work, but when she retired she'd sold it. In Birkenhead it had been easy to catch a bus and to have no car had been a big saving, but what should she do now? She'd find a car useful but it would mean she'd see less of Tom because he was driving her wherever she wanted to go.

Tom!

Flora knew suddenly what she really wanted.

She wanted him here with her, all day and every day and all night too. She wanted him in her family. The money she'd inherited from Mavis would ensure a comfortable old age for both of them.

She put on her coat; she needed to go to the village store. It was Tuesday, and she'd be playing bridge with Tom this afternoon. He'd bring her home and she'd already asked him to stay for a meal. She'd put her proposal to him more strongly this time.

All afternoon she felt driven, spurred on, and determined to change his mind. She played bridge on top of her form, bidding on the high side but making her tricks. Even Tom, who was partnering her, was surprised at her success with the cards. When she let them both into her cottage she led him to the kitchen and turned on her oven. 'I like to have you with me while I cook,' she said.

He settled himself on her old rocking chair. 'I like to watch you.'

She put a gin and tonic in his hand. 'Tom, I want you to forget all this nonsense about marriage being a bad bargain for me. It won't be. It's what I want.'

His dark eyes smiled at her over the top of the glass. 'What's brought this up again?'

'I'm trying to change your mind.'

'I can see that. The advantages are all on my side, Flora. You'd be giving me a financial leg up.'

'Forget your pride. Thanks to Mavis, we've all had a financial leg up. Is her money going to be wasted a second time?'

Tom stood up, put his glass down and took her into his arms. 'Flora, you sound vehement.'

'I am. I feel strongly about this. I don't want my girls to feel sorry for me, I don't want them to say, "Mum's really like Mavis. What a pity both of them were so miserly they wouldn't spend their money. They could have got so much more from life."'

'Is that really what you think?'

'Yes.'

'Flora, you know I want to marry you very much...'

'In that case...'

He smiled. 'Will you do me the honour? Will you be my wife?'

She began to giggle like a young girl. 'You can cut out frills like that. You know it's what I want.'

Within moments Flora was switching off her cooker and going upstairs with Tom's arm round her waist.

Isobel had just put Sophie to bed for the first time in her new home when there was a knock at the front door. Her mother and Tom were on the step.

'Come on in,' she said, throwing the door wide. She'd been unpacking crates all evening and was dropping with fatigue, but she wanted to show her house off. 'I've just got it straight. What d'you think?'

Flora was gazing round, taking in every detail of the living room. 'It's lovely.'

'Comfortable,' Tom said. 'It feels like a real home already. I'm sure you'll be very happy here.'

'I can't wait to show it to Seb.' Isobel laughed aloud. 'It's very different from our last house.'

Her mother was waiting. She had a wide smile on her face. Isobel realised admiring her house was a social preliminary and that she was about to say something important.

She saw her mother feel for Tom's hand. 'We've decided to get married.'

'Wow, Mum!' Isobel gave her a hearty hug. 'I'm so pleased. It's the best thing you could do. Congratulations, Tom.' She kissed his cheek. 'I hope you'll both be very happy. When's this to be?'

'September the third. We've been to see the vicar today – it's all arranged.'

'What? You're not wasting any time.'

'At our age, there's no point in waiting.' Tom too had a broad smile. 'Besides, I want to get the knot tied before Flora changes her mind.'

'I'm hardly likely to do that.' Flora was laughing. 'It's a Saturday so all the family can be with us.'

'That's lovely, Mum. What about the reception? There are several posh hotels round here where you could hold that.'

'We've spoken to Hilary and Ben. They've offered to put it on at their house.'

'Mum, we're always up there. Why don't you do something different? Something special? What about the Manor?'

'No. A wedding is a family affair. Ours is to be a quiet one.'

'You always say that.' Isobel remembered Hilary's wedding. 'With all the money you have now, you could splash out.'

'I don't want to splash out. I want it to be like all our family celebrations and be a welcome to Tom now he's joining the circle.'

Tom said, 'We're getting on a bit. It's the second time round for both of us.'

'Besides.' Flora laughed again. 'Hilary's got a wonderful house for entertaining. What could be better?'

Isobel shook her head. 'You're more like Mavis than you realise. You won't be able to spend a fraction of what you've got.'

'What about you then?' Flora chuckled. 'I thought once you had some money you'd donate all this furniture of Mavis's to St Vincent de Paul and buy new. But you haven't.'

'Her stuff is old like the cottage and suits it. I've put loads of beeswax and plenty of elbow grease on her chairs and they've come up a treat.'

'There you are, then. It proves that sometimes the old way can be the best.'

Isobel laughed. 'I've got a bottle of champagne in the fridge. I meant to keep it till Seb came. I planned a private house-warming, but your news calls for a greater celebration.' She went to fetch it. 'Will you open it, Tom?'

On the first day of the summer holidays, Isobel was on tenterhooks as she waited for Sebastian to arrive. He was coming up in the new car he'd bought so that he might drive to work in Chester when he started at his new school there in September.

She'd bought herself a new white Mini to replace the red one Rupert had given her all those years ago. In a way she was sorry to see it go. It had served her well, but now it was wearing out. She felt she'd cut a chain that had bound her

471

to Rupert, and knew she had to think of the future now.

Sebastian arrived in a short-sleeved shirt looking suntanned and relaxed. Sophie had been watching at the window and rushed out to throw herself at him. Isobel followed and put her arms round them both to give them a hug.

'I like your new car,' Sophie said. 'Mummy didn't say it was blue.'

'Nearly new,' Sebastian said to Isobel. 'I think I've learned some sense. We can't cope with debts, so it's a modest Ford.'

'We probably could now,' Isobel told him, thinking of Mavis's money She couldn't wait to get him indoors. He had seen inside the cottage before but it had been in a moving-in muddle. Now she'd furnished it and she wanted him to like it.

Sophie was dragging him from room to room. 'This is my bedroom. Do you like it?'

'It's very pretty.'

'Mummy let me choose the colours.' She had a pink carpet and pink curtains.

'It's a great room for a little girl. What a lot of toys you've got,' Sebastian told her. To Isobel, he said, 'You've done wonders. I'm afraid I left all the work to you.'

'What d'you think of it?'

Sophie was jumping about with excitement. 'It's all nice, isn't it, Daddy?'

'I love it. It looks so homely, and it's got bags of character. I'm sure we'll be very happy here.'

'Just right for our new start.' Isobel smiled. Nothing must spoil this. 'How's your mother?'

'Much better, quite lively in fact. She loves nursing the baby; she's quite besotted with him.'

Isobel meant to enjoy the long summer break. She and Sebastian had decided not to go away for a holiday this year. It was novelty enough to be together in their new home.

She said, 'We'll have days out instead.'

'That suits me because I've seen hardly anything of Merseyside up to now. Where shall we start?'

Isobel took her little family round the big Liverpool museum where they spent several hours, and both Sebastian and Sophie found it fascinating. Coming out, they saw a notice telling them about a special display of Turner's pictures on show at the Walker Art Gallery a few yards down the road.

'I'd like to see that,' Seb said enthusiastically.

Isobel frowned. She'd not intended to take them there. It was where she'd first met Rupert.

'Sorry,' he said, 'I'd forgotten. If you don't want to...'

'It's all right. They often put on something special for children, too. Sophie will like it.'

'I'm hungry, Daddy,' she said.

'Then let's have a bite to eat and a sit down first.'

Later, when they went inside, Isobel trailed through the long galleries of magnificient paintings feeling that Rupert was very close. She sat down on a seat in the centre which she thought was the same one on which Rupert had rested after he'd had his fall.

She had loved him dearly. Sebastian knew and understood, and had forgiven her the lies she'd told to hide it. She'd never spoken of it to either her mother or her sister and couldn't now. She could just see Sophie's rapt face and blonde curls in an anteroom at the far end as she listened to a story about painters of the past. As far as Sophie was concerned, Isobel knew her affair with Rupert was a secret never to be told.

Sebastian had accepted the responsibilities of fatherhood and nothing must upset that now. She hoped she'd never have to tell lies about it again.

Isobel looked round. She was glad she'd come. It was an interesting place and she'd loved her summer job in those long ago days. Now she felt she could visit it again and enjoy it anew.

They all loved the trips on the Mersey ferry and visits to the other museums in the Albert Docks. They took Sophie to dig in the sand and have donkey rides on New Brighton beach, and there were walks through the lovely Wirral countryside on their doorstep.

Isobel expected to have a rest before the new term started, but it was not to be. Preparations for her mother's wedding were going on apace. One morning, Hilary was having a cup of coffee with her and Sebastian when their mother came round.

'I've bought my wedding outfit. I'm thrilled with it. D'you want to come and see?'

She led them straight up to her bedroom and took the hanger from her wardrobe. It was a dress and matching edge to edge coat in pearl grey wool of the lightest quality. She held it against her then laid it across her bed while she took her hat from its box. She put the big confection in lacy grey straw on her head. 'What d'you think?'

Isobel adjusted the angle of the brim. 'It looks smashing. Why don't you put your dress on? Let's have a proper dress rehearsal.'

'I'm very impressed,' Hilary said a few minutes later. 'You look lovely.'

'I'll have flowers in mauve or purple; they'll look good against the grey. Do you think a large spray or a small posy?'

'A small posy,' Isobel said. 'You couldn't have chosen better. It's very smart.'

Hilary said, 'I must have something special to wear too. Izzy, will you come with me and help me choose? You're better at that sort of thing than I am.'

'We'll go together,' Isobel promised. 'What about tomorrow?'

The next day they set out to Liverpool. 'Do we get dresses or suits? It's difficult to know what the weather will be like in September. Could be getting cooler by then.'

'I'd like a really smart dress,' Hilary said. 'Good for parties later.'

'Then the answer is to get a coat as well,' Isobel said. 'Not necessarily matching, like Mum's, but suitable to wear over our dresses if it's a coldish day.'

'Where shall we go?'

'George Henry Lees is the best place,' Isobel said. She'd always bought her smarter outfits there. When an assistant came over to help, Isobel explained what they wanted and the girl began picking dresses from the rails.

'If you'd like to come this way and try them on,' she said when she had her arms full.

Isobel was making her own choice from the rails. She picked out a cream dress in soft wool for her sister. 'Try this too. I think cream will suit you.'

As soon as Hilary tried it on she knew it was exactly right for her. 'You don't think I'll upstage the bride, do you?' she asked. 'I mean cream...'

'You won't. It's slightly darker than Mum's pearl grey. And she'll want us to look smart too.'

'I'll have it,' Hilary decided. The assistant brought her a coat of oatmeal tweed to compliment it.

'Exactly right for you,' Isobel told her.

For herself, she chose a blue wool dress with a reversible coat in blue and fawn to cover it. 'I'm not going to get a hat,' she said. 'Hats don't suit me. Nobody wears them these days.'

'Except for weddings,' Hilary said. 'I think I will.'

The assistant was bringing her several styles in cream and brown tones. She chose the one Isobel said looked the best.

'Shoes and handbags now.' Isobel led the way to the shoe department. 'We might as well have everything to blend in. We'll never have a better excuse to spend on clothes than this.'

'Isn't it marvellous,' Hilary breathed, 'to be able to buy all these clothes without worrying about what they're going to cost?'

The twin aunts had set about making a three-tier wedding cake as soon as they heard Flora and Tom were to be married. They excelled at cake baking but had asked one of the ladies from the bridge club to ice and decorate it. She was an expert and ran a night school course on cake decoration.

During the week before the wedding the pace became hectic. They were all cooking and baking at home. Prudence was organising it and had drawn up a list of what every member of the family should prepare to make it the feast of a lifetime.

Isobel woke up on Flora's wedding day to cloudy overcast skies and a brisk and rather chill breeze.

'What a pity,' she said. Straight after breakfast they all set off to Hilary's house. Sebastian had been roped in to play football with the children and return them to the house in time for them to be washed and changed into their wedding finery.

Ben was decorating the house with flowers while Isobel helped Hilary lay out the buffet lunch on the dining-room table. The wedding cake was set out in the middle, flawlessly iced and decorated. The church ceremony was to be at eleven thirty so the reception would be at lunch time and their guests would be hungry.

At quarter to eleven, Isobel took her family home to change and had them back in the church with five minutes to spare. It was almost full.

Isobel had a lump in her throat as she watched her mother come down the aisle on Ben's arm. Tom half turned to smile at his bride and had such an expression of love on his face that she knew Mum was doing the right thing and that they'd be happy. Sophie had asked to be a bridesmaid and looked really sweet in a kilt of scarlet tartan and a white frilly blouse. She performed faultlessly, holding Nana's posy when the ceremony started.

Isobel was sitting next to Sebastian. She could

feel tears pricking her eyes as she listened to the words of the wedding ceremony.

It was ordained for the mutual society, help, and comfort, that the one ought to have of the other...

Isobel knew Seb hadn't had that of her up to now, but was determined he would in future. She needed it too. She didn't want to carry on without him.

A little later, she heard, *Wilt thou have this woman... Wilt thou love her, comfort her, honour, and keep her in sickness and in health, forsaking all other?*

Sebastian's hand was feeling for hers and she knew he too was moved by those words.

It seemed no time at all before the register had been signed and the bridal couple were heading to the door. The clouds had rolled back and a pale sun had come out as they stood on the stone steps for the photographs.

Although Flora had told Isobel it was to be a quiet wedding, many guests had been invited. Rory, looking smart and handsome in a new suit, came with his mother in tow. There were several ladies from the bridge club, and Jane Johnson and her husband. Primrose and Prudence had brought their mandolins and meant to play.

Everybody was hungry and helped themselves to the feast. Ben announced that there wouldn't be traditional speeches afterwards, but he took glasses of champagne round the guests.

Tom raised his. 'I want you to drink to my bride,' he said. 'And to the many years of contentment we'll share in our old age.'